"You led me into a trap," Jozef said. Accusingly, but not angrily. Being hot-tempered when you're surrounded at a corner table in a dark tavern by eight men at least two of whom were armed with knives would be even more stupid than seducing two waitresses in one week who worked at the same establishment.

Szklenski shrugged, looking a bit embarrassed. Only a bit, though.

"Sorry, but we really do have to make sure," he said. "We've got a good reputation with the USE guys here and we can't afford to let it get damaged."

Jozef looked around. "I take it all of you are in the Committees of Correspondence?"

"We're asking the questions, not you," said one of them. That was Bogumil—no last name provided— whom Jozef had already pegged as the surliest of the lot. He didn't think it was an act, either.

"Give us some names," said the man to Bogumil's left. "Something."

Jozef thought about it, for a moment. Acting as if he were an innocent Pole not involved with politics who just happened to wander into Dresden right now was probably pointless. The question then became, what did he claim to be?

In for a penny, in for a pound, as the up-timers said. "Krzysztof Opalinski."

"What about him?" That came from a third man at the table.

"Nothing about him," said Jozef, sounding bored. "I hope you're not expecting me to provide you with details of what we're doing? How do I know *you're* not spies?"

BAEN BOOKS by ERIC FLINT

The Ring of Fire series:

1636

THE SAXON
UPRISING

ERIC FLINT

1636: The Saxon Uprising

Copyright © 2011 by Eric Flint

A Baen Books Original

Baen Publishing Enterprises
P.O. Box 1403
Riverdale, NY 10471
www.baen.com

ISBN: 978-1-4516-3821-9

Cover art by Tom Kidd
Maps by Gorg Huff

First Baen paperback printing, April 2012

Library of Congress Control Number: 2011002044

Distributed by Simon & Schuster
1230 Avenue of the Americas
New York, NY 10020

Pages by Joy Freeman (www.pagesbyjoy.com)
Printed in the United States of America

To the memory of my sister, Kathy Flint.

Born September 11, 1948.

Died October 11, 2010.

Contents

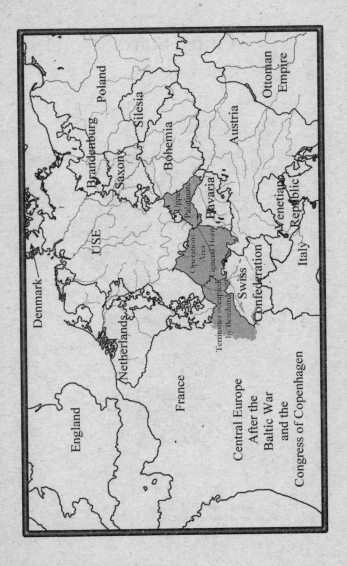

Central Europe
After the
Baltic War
and the
Congress of Copenhagen

United States of Europe

N

Pomerania

Poland

Luebeck

Mecklenburg

Hamburg

Brandenburg

Netherlands

Brunswick

Magdeburg

Saxony

Westphalia

Essen

Hesse-Kassel

Prague

Bohemia

State of Thuringia-Franconia

Province of the Main

Frankfurt

Nuremberg

Oberpfalz (Upper Palatinate)

Upper Rhine

Augsburg

Bavaria

Munich

Swabia

Ulm

Austria

Strassburg

Swiss Confederation

*Swabia is still under direct imperial administration and not yet a self-governing province as of March 1635.

Baltic Sea
Baltic Sea
Rostock
Wismar
Luebeck
Schwerin
Central Europe
USE
Oder
Poland
Brandenburg
Elbe
Berlin
Oder
Poznań
Magdeburg
Elbe
Leipzig
Saxony
Silesia
Dresden
Grantville
Vogtland
Tetschen
Prague
Bohemia
Nuremberg
Regensburg
České Budějovice
Danube
Ingolstadt
Danube
Bavaria
Austria
Vienna
Linz
Munich

Prologue

November 1635

An idle king

Berlin

Colonel Erik Haakansson Hand gazed down at the man who was simultaneously King of Sweden, Emperor of the United States of Europe, and High King of the Union of Kalmar. He was Gustav II Adolf, the preeminent monarch of Europe as the year 1635 came to a close.

The Habsburgs might dispute the claim. And if that powerful dynastic family could by some magic means recombine their splintered realms into the great empire ruled a century earlier by Charles V, they could probably made the claim stick. But the great Holy Roman Emperor was long gone. Today, it would take genuinely magical methods to reunite Spain and Austria—not to mention the newly emerged third branch of the dynasty in the Netherlands.

France was now weak, too. Gustav Adolf's general Lennart Torstensson had crushed the French at the battle of Ahrensbök a year and a half ago. Since then, Cardinal Richelieu's control of France had grown steadily shakier. King Louis XIII's younger brother Gaston, the duke of Orleans—usually called

"Monsieur Gaston"—was and always had been an inveterate schemer who hated Richelieu with a passion. In times past, the cardinal had easily outmaneuvered him. But the disaster to which Richelieu had led France in his ill-fated League of Ostend's war against the United States of Europe had produced widespread dissatisfaction and unrest, especially among the nobility and the urban patrician class.

In short, Gustav Adolf ought to be basking in the most glorious sunlight of a life that had been filled with a great deal of glory since he was a teenage king. Instead, he was lying on a bed in a palace in one of the most wretched cities in the Germanies with his mind apparently gone.

Gustav Adolf's blue eyes stared up at Hand. Did he recognize his cousin? It was hard to say.

You certainly couldn't tell anything from his speech.

"Bandits have knighted almost walrus," said the king of Sweden. "Is there jewel?"

It was very frustrating. Gustav Adolf didn't seem addlepated, exactly. His words made no sense, but they weren't pure gibberish, either. This last sentence, for instance, had clearly been a question, and beneath all of the meaningless sentences you could detect a still intact grammar.

But what was he saying? It was as if his vocabulary was completely jumbled.

Before he left Magdeburg for Berlin, Colonel Hand had spent several hours with the American Moorish doctor, James Nichols. By now, four and a half years after the Ring of Fire that had brought the Moor into this world along with the other Americans in Grantville, it was the generally accepted opinion throughout

Europe that Nichols was the continent's greatest living doctor. Probably even the world's.

One might ask, therefore, why Hand had had to interview Nichols in Magdeburg—instead of here in Berlin, at the bedside of Europe's most powerful ruler and Nichols' own sovereign. Or, perhaps even more to the point, why it was that Gustav Adolf had not been brought to Magdeburg with its superb medical facilities, instead of being kept in primitive Berlin.

He'd posed those questions directly, in fact. The answers had been ... interesting.

"Ask your blessed chancellor," replied Nichols. His tone was blunt, to the point of being almost hostile. "It was Axel Oxenstierna who insisted on keeping Gustav Adolf in Berlin. Just as it was he who insisted—oh, sure, politely, but he had about a dozen goons with him to enforce the matter—that I leave Berlin and come back here, once I eliminated the risk of peritonitis."

"What reasons did he give for his decisions?"

"Bullpucky and hogwash." Hand didn't know those particular Americanisms, but their general meaning was clear enough.

"The bullpucky was that it was too risky to move the king to Magdeburg," Nichols continued. "That's nonsense because General Stearns had *already* transported Gustav Adolf by horse-litter to get him to Berlin in the first place. That took almost a week, in rough conditions—which the king still managed to survive, didn't he? As opposed to spending another two days moving him to Magdeburg in a luxurious river barge."

The black doctor took a deep breath. An angry breath, you could even say.

"As for the hogwash, it's true that I told Oxenstierna that there wasn't *much* that could be done for the king. But 'much' isn't nothing, and however much or little can be done for Gustav Adolf in his present condition, you can be damn sure—to hell with false modesty—that I can do it better than that bunch of quacks he's got up there in Berlin. For Christ's sake, Colonel Hand, one of them is an outright *astrologer*! The jackass seriously thinks you can make diagnoses and prescriptions based on whether Mars is humping Venus or getting buggered by Jupiter while either Sagittarius or Pisces is making a porno movie about it."

Erik burst into laughter. He was not fond of astrologers himself. As one of Gustav Adolf's cousins, he had had close contact with many of Europe's courts. True, he was the son of an illegitimate cousin, but the fact of his royal blood counted for a lot more in such high circles than the picayune matter of his mother's bastardy. Europe's courts were full of bastards, literally as well as figuratively.

Those same royal courts were also full of credulous people, who gave their trust to the advice of astrologers and soothsayers. Not all of them were mere courtiers, either. To name just one instance the colonel was personally familiar with, the new king of Bohemia was positively addicted to astrology. This, despite the fact that in all other respects Wallenstein was an extremely shrewd and intelligent man.

"Can you explain to me what's wrong with my cousin?"

Nichols grimaced. "He suffered a bad head injury in that battle at Lake Bledno, and there was some brain damage done as a result. Whether it's permanent or not, we just don't know yet. And if it is permanent—or some of it, at least—we don't know how much and in what areas."

He shook his head. "Even back up-time, Colonel Hand, brain injuries were often mysterious."

"Can you be more specific?"

"Yes, in at least one respect: whatever other damage may have been done, the emperor clearly suffered damage to his right temporal lobe." Nichols reached up and touched his head just above his right ear; then, moved the finger back and forth an inch or so. "It's located here."

"And this means...?"

"The temporal lobes play a major role in the way our brains process language." Nichols cocked his head slightly. "I take it you haven't seen your cousin yet?"

Hand shook his head. "No. I decided to stop off here on my way to Berlin. I was stationed in the Oberpfalz and Magdeburg was directly on my route."

He hesitated; then, added: "I would appreciate it if you would not mention this visit to anyone, Dr. Nichols. I, ah ... Let us say that my assignment from the king—given to me before his injury, of course—is of a very confidential nature."

Nichols studied him for a moment. The Moor's dark eyes seemed very shrewd, as Hand had feared they might be. He'd been hoping that Europe's greatest medician would be a naïf in all other matters. No great hope, though, given what he knew of the doctor's history.

Suddenly, Nichols smiled. "Do I take it that when you meet Chancellor Oxenstierna you will be equally discreet, Colonel?"

Erik stiffened. "Of course! It is well known among Sweden's highest circles—it is certainly known to Axel—that I serve Gustav Adolf as his personal agent. My business is with the king, and the king alone."

That was true enough, as far as it went. But Hand was fairly certain that Nichols saw through the subterfuge involved. Hand was now operating entirely on his own, a fact that he would try to conceal by referring to his longstanding and close relationship to his cousin.

But the doctor made no further reference to the matter. His smile vanished, and he continued with his medical assessment.

"What you will discover when you come into your cousin's presence is that he speaks—quite easily, in fact—but his speech makes no sense. It's as if the mechanism which translates thoughts into words has been broken. The technical medical term for the condition is 'aphasia.' Beyond that . . ."

He leaned back in the chair in his office. "He's apparently still not recognizing anyone. The temporal lobes are involved in handling visual content, too. He's apparently had no seizures yet, but he might have them in the future. And he's apparently suffering from occasional onsets of blind fury." Sourly, he added, "You'll have to forgive my excessive use of the term 'apparently.' I'm no longer on the scene and the few reports I've gotten since I left are skimpy at best."

"Will he recover?"

"He might, yes. But there's no way to know yet, Colonel—nor, even if he does recover, do we know how long it might take."

"Your best estimate, please."

Nichols shrugged. "Assuming he recovers at all, and given that it's now been several weeks since the injury, I don't see much chance of any major improvement until a few months have gone by. I could easily be proven wrong, you understand."

"Could it take years?"

"Possibly. But..." Nichols made a little face. "Look, here's how it is with brain traumas. Strokes, too. There are some outliers, true enough. There have even been a few cases where people recovered after almost twenty years in a coma. But the general rule of thumb is that once what you might call the normal recovery period has passed, the odds that the patient will recover start dropping pretty quickly. So my gut feeling is that if Gustav Adolf doesn't recover—mostly, anyway—within a year, then he's not going to recover at all."

Hand nodded. "Thank you. That's quite helpful, I think."

Now that he was on the scene in Berlin, Hand could see that the doctor's assessment *had* been quite helpful. It gave him what he most needed as a guide to action: a time frame.

Six months, Hand decided. That would be his framework.

Chancellor Oxenstierna had escorted the colonel into the room in the former elector's palace where Gustav Adolf was kept. He'd been silent since, allowing the king's cousin to interact as best he could without distraction.

Now, finally, he spoke. "As you can see, Erik, he does not have his wits about him any longer."

Hand thought it would be better to say that the

king's wits were wandering somewhere inside his brain, trying to find a way out. But under the circumstances, the less he said to Oxenstierna, the better.

So he simply uttered a noncommittal sound. A hum, you might call it.

Oxenstierna turned to face him. "Will your current assignment . . . ?"

Hand raised his hand a few inches. "Please, Axel. Despite my cousin's current condition, I feel obliged to maintain his confidentiality."

"Yes, of course."

The chancellor seemed on the verge of saying something further, by the expression on his face, but after a few seconds satisfied himself with an equally noncommittal grunt.

He then gave Hand a polite little bow. More in the way of an exaggerated nod, really. "And now I'm afraid I must be off. Urgent affairs of the realm, as you can imagine."

Hand returned the not-quite-a-bow. That was slightly rude, on his part. King's cousin or not, Oxenstierna still ranked him in Sweden's hierarchy. But Hand couldn't afford to give any impression, especially to Oxenstierna, that he was in the least bit intimidated by Gustav Adolf's predicament.

After the chancellor left, Hand glanced at the one other person in the room. That was Gustav Adolf's personal bodyguard Erling Ljungberg, who was perched on a stool in a corner.

Ljungberg was new to the assignment. Silently, Erik cursed the fates on that evil battlefield that had not only struck down the king but slain his bodyguard as well. That had been Anders Jönsson, a man whom

Hand had known very well indeed. Had Anders still been alive...

But, he wasn't. And Erik simply didn't know Ljungberg well enough yet—he'd correct that as soon as possible, of course—to speak freely to him.

He was moving in perilous waters now, which the ancient Roman poet Ovid had described very well indeed. *If treason prospers, none dare call it treason.*

So, he did no more than give Ljungberg the same not-quite-a-bow, and then left the room. As he was passing through the door, he heard Gustav Adolf call out behind him.

"Weather not a wagon! Be drunken blue! Can empty trolls whisper crow?"

A protest? A question?

Probably both, Erik thought. What else would be coming from a king trapped in the chaos of his own mind, while those in power around him plotted treason?

For treason, it surely was. Hand was certain he knew what Oxenstierna and his cohorts were planning—and it was no accident that none of them would have dared propose those same plans to their sovereign while he still had his senses.

Six months. By then, one of them would be publicly given the label of traitor.

That might very well be Erik Haakansson Hand himself, of course, but he'd always enjoyed a challenge. No assignment his cousin had ever given him was as challenging as the one that he hadn't because he could no longer speak.

Six months, then.

Part One

November 1635

The dark, broad seas

Chapter 1

Tetschen, near the border
between Saxony and Bohemia

The view from Freiherr von Thun's castle was magnificent. Set on a rocky knoll right above the quays
of Tetschen, called Děčín by the Czech locals, the
old castle not only dominated the river Elbe, but
provided a fine view to the north. The building had
been designed more as a customs and toll stop,
rather than being a fortification built with combat in
mind. Its old-fashioned curtain walls were ill-suited
to withstand artillery fire of any kind. Still, its few
guns covered the riverfront from bank to bank and
they could be expanded by leaving behind some of
the Third Division's artillery.

For the purpose Mike Stearns had in mind—possible
purpose, he cautioned himself—Tetschen was better
than any other place the Third Division had passed
through since they entered the low range of mountains
that separated the Bohemian and Saxon plains. Those
mountains were called the Erzgebirge in German and
Krušné hory in Czech.

15

Tetschen had three things to recommend it:

First, it was obviously the best bottleneck to thwart an army trying to enter Bohemia from the north or Saxony from the south.

The Erzgebirge were not tall mountains. The two highest peaks, Klínovec and Fichtelberg, were only four thousand feet high. The terrain resembled a scaled-down version of Mike's familiar Appalachia. It was nothing like the Alps or the Carpathians, much less the Rockies. Moreover, Klínovec and Fichtelberg were quite a ways to the west. Here, in the eastern part of the mountain range, the terrain was much lower. The Third Division's engineers had told Mike that the altitude of Tetschen itself was only four hundred and fifty feet above sea level.

Still, as low as they might be, the Erzgebirge were mountains. Not much of an obstacle for a small hiking party, true enough. But for a division of soldiers numbering over ten thousand men, they were well-nigh impassable. By now, the soldiers were hardened and veteran marchers and could probably manage the task as an abstract muscular exercise. But what would they eat and drink? Small mountains streams are fine for half a dozen hikers; for regiments and battalions, they are a laughable water source. While American technology had been able to upgrade many of the weapons used by the USE's army, its logistical methods were still largely those of the seventeenth century. That meant supply wagons drawn by horses and oxen—who needed even more in the way of food and water than soldiers did.

Armies could only pass through even low mountains by following what few natural routes existed. In this eastern portion of the Erzgebirge, that meant following the Elbe, the same river that was dominated by Tetschen here.

Tetschen's second great advantage was that it was a relatively large town. Not a city, certainly. But it was very far from a country village, too. It was large enough to provide a base for a regiment, without requiring constant foraging in the countryside. "Foraging" was military-speak for requisitioning supplies by methods which were often nothing more than legalized plunder. Given that the lands said regiment would be plundering were Czech lands ruled by the very same Wallenstein that Mike and his Third Division had been sent to support, that could get very dicey, very quickly.

But with a town the size of Tetschen, Mike was pretty sure that one of his regiments would be able to get its supplies without overly aggravating the area's residents. That was especially true of the regiment he had in mind for the task.

Finally, Tetschen was very close to Dresden. As the crow flies, probably not more than thirty miles. Mike wasn't sure yet—he wasn't sure at all, actually—but that might turn out to be critical.

As his eyes roamed across the landscape below, yet a fourth advantage to Tetschen came to his mind. There was enough flat land down there to build an airstrip. Nothing fancy, but it would be good enough for one of Jesse Wood's Belles or Gustavs. That might prove quite handy in the future.

"Yes," he murmured to himself. "Here."

He smiled, then, thinking of the reactions he'd get from his staff officers and the newest and youngest colonel in his division.

✧　　　✧　　　✧

In the event, it was the experienced staff officers who raised the objections and the young new colonel who kept his mouth shut.

"But what's the point, sir?" asked Anthony Leebrick. His tone of voice was not quite peevish, but awfully close to it. "There's no chance at all that the Austrians will attack Bohemia from the north."

"I understand that," said Mike. "But Holk and his army are still out there somewhere. They've attacked Bohemia before, you know."

Leebrick almost choked. While he struggled to regain his composure, Colonel Christopher Long spoke up. "The most recent information we have places Holk's forces near Breslau, General Stearns. If he was going to invade Bohemia from there, he'd most likely strike through Trutnov rather than marching all the way back through Saxony to come down the Elbe."

Long used the German name for the city, Breslau, instead of the Polish name Wroclaw. That reflected no particular anti-Polish bias on his part, simply a linguistic preference. He was as fluent in German as he was in his native English, and had only a smattering of Polish.

"Leaving that aside," chimed in the third of Mike's staff officers, Colonel Ulbrecht Duerr, "I think the chance of Holk attacking Bohemia under the current circumstances is about as likely as a lady's lap dog deciding to attack a bear. The time he assaulted Prague was after Wallenstein had taken his army out to meet the Austrians and Holk thought the city was undefended." He barked a sarcastic laugh. "And then look what happened! The sorry bastard was driven off by fucking Jews and university students. Do you really think he's now going to challenge Wallenstein himself—not to mention our division?"

Long's geographical reasoning was impeccable, Duerr's assessment of Holk's state of mind was dead on the money, and Mike had considerable sympathy for Anthony Leebrick's exasperation with his commanding general's lapse into lunacy. But he was still going to stick to his decision, so the only suitable tactic was inscrutable generalissimo-ness.

"Gentlemen, my mind is made up. I appreciate your advice, but the decision stands and there's no point thrashing it over again."

They'd been meeting in one of the rooms on the upper floor of Tetschen's largest tavern. As was *de rigueur* in seventeenth-century warfare, Mike had requisitioned the tavern for his temporary headquarters—which, of course, would now become the more-or-less permanent headquarters of the regiment he was planning to leave behind after the rest of the Third Division resumed its march to Prague.

Up till now, the tavern-keeper had been quite happy with the situation. Mike still had enough USE dollars in the division's coffers to pay in cash. The man would probably be a lot less happy once Mike left and the regiment staying behind explained the new financial arrangements.

Mike swiveled in his chair to look at that regiment's commander. Unlike the three staff officers, who were sitting at the table with Mike, Colonel Jeff Higgins had chosen to perch himself atop a small side table by the door. The arrangement struck Mike as a bit on the chancy side. Higgins was a big man and that side table looked awfully rickety.

"I'm leaving Captain Bartley and his newly formed Exchange Corps here with you, Jeff. I figure this is as good a time and place as any to see if his ideas will really work."

Higgins didn't look particularly thrilled at the news, but he made no protest. He'd barely said a word since the meeting began and Mike announced his decision to leave Higgins and his Hangman Regiment here in Tetschen.

"Any questions, Colonel?" he asked.

Higgins chewed on his lower lip for a few seconds. "I assume Engler and his flying artillery company are still attached to my regiment?"

"Yes. You can figure that's now a pretty permanent situation."

Jeff nodded. "All right. But I'd like some regular artillery as well. Assuming Holk does come ravening up the Elbe"—he said that with a completely straight face; Mike was impressed as well as amused—"having two or three culverins would be handy. Holk will be using flat-bottom barges to haul his supplies, just as we are. Thorsten's volley guns are great against cavalry but they won't do squat to sink a boat." He chewed on his lip for another two or three seconds. "I wouldn't mind some more mortars, either."

Mike looked to Duerr, who served as what an up-time American army would have called the division's G-1 officer, in charge of personnel. "Can we spare anyone, Ulbrecht?"

Unlike the two English staff officers, who were all but rolling their eyes at the absurdity of the whole conversation—culverins to sink nonexistent barges, for the love of God, as if the division couldn't find

better use for the artillery pieces!—Duerr's expression
was placid. He was quite a bit older than Long and
Leebrick, and had seen plenty of idiotic command
decisions in his long career. You just had to be philosophical about it. Generals were like women. Handy
to have around, as a rule, and occasionally delightful;
but also given to peculiar moods and whimsies.

"Not too hard," he said. "We've kept up our recruiting even on the march. Having a reputation helps—
ha!—which we certainly do after Zwenkau and Zielona
Góra. So we're back up to strength and then some.
Still short of cavalry, of course."

That was pretty much a given. Cavalrymen couldn't
be trained quickly, the way infantrymen and artillerymen could. In the nature of things, in the seventeenth
century, most people who already had the horseman-
ship skills to serve in cavalry units came from the
nobility. The lower nobility, as a rule—what Germans
called the *Niederadel* as opposed to the much smaller
Hochadel class comprised mostly of dukes and counts.
But such men still considered themselves part of the
aristocracy and most of them were not friendly to the
Stearns administration that had governed the USE
since its formation.

So, the USE army had always found it difficult to
enlist as many cavalrymen as they would have liked.
The new nation's army made up for it by having
what they considered the continent's best infantry
and artillery.

Duerr liked to suck on a pipe instead of chewing
a lip, when he was pondering something. Mike found
it annoying, not because tobacco smoke irritated him
particularly but because Ulbrecht was *not* smoking.

Very rarely did he actually fill his pipe with tobacco and light it up. Instead, he just sucked—and sucked and sucked and sucked—on an empty pipe.

So be it. Mike had found good staff officers to be a lot like computer geeks. Handy to have around, as a rule, and occasionally indispensable; but also given to gross personal habits.

"I'll strip one of the new artillery companies from the Teutoburg Regiment. That'll give Higgins four guns, which ought to be plenty. And we can strip a couple of the heavy weapons units from them as well, which will provide him with the additional mortars he wants."

Leebrick made a face. "Brigadier von Taupadel is going to raise bloody hell. Not to mention Leoš Hlavacek! That's his regiment you're proposing to skin. It won't help any that he ranks Higgins."

Unlike every other regimental commander in the Third Division, Jeff was a lieutenant colonel instead of a colonel. He was the only lieutenant colonel in the entire USE army, in fact. The title was not officially recognized in the army's table of organization. Mike Stearns had created it as a brevet rank when he set up the Hangman Regiment—which was also not part of the T/O.

Officially, the USE army had a very clear and simple structure:

Each division consisted of nine thousand men commanded by a major general.

Each division had three brigades of three thousand men, commanded by a brigadier.

Each brigade had three regiments of one thousand men, commanded by a colonel.

Each regiment had two infantry battalions of four

hundred men, commanded by a major, and an artillery company of two hundred men usually commanded by a captain.

Finally, the infantry battalions were composed of four companies of one hundred men, commanded by a captain. A company consisted of three platoons of thirty men commanded by a second lieutenant, and a heavy weapons unit of ten men commanded by a sergeant. The company's first lieutenant usually served its captain as his executive officer.

Such was the neat theory reflected in the official table of organization. Mike was pretty sure the ink hadn't dried yet before reality began to diverge from theory.

To begin with, the T/O didn't include cavalry forces at all. Officially, all cavalry forces were under the direct command of the army's commanding officer—that was Lieutenant General Lennart Torstensson—and he assigned the units to whichever divisions he chose in whatever manner he saw fit. Right now, for instance, Mike's Third Division had only one cavalry regiment assigned to it. Torstensson didn't think he needed more than that, since he'd be operating in the fairly constrained terrain of Bohemia and (if open hostilities broke out with Austria) the even more constrained terrain around Linz. Torstensson wanted to keep his cavalry concentrated against the Poles, in the more open terrain of northern Germany and Poland.

Secondly, almost as soon as they were formed the various major units of the army began changing. To give one example, Mike's Third Division had ten regiments instead of nine. The oddball was Jeff Higgins' Hangman Regiment, which Mike had created to maintain discipline in the division after some units ran amok following the capture of the Polish town of Świebodzin.

Jeff's regiment was an oddball in more ways than one. Instead of having the usual artillery company—which the artillerymen themselves invariably and stubbornly insisted on calling a "battery" and to hell with what the T/O said—he'd had Captain Thorsten Engler's flying artillery unit attached instead. Like the cavalry, the flying artillery were not part of the table of organization of the divisions, but were under Torstensson's direct authority.

Now, he'd have most of a regular artillery unit attached to his regiment as well—which would make it grossly oversized according to the T/O. Jeff's sergeants had been assiduously recruiting ever since Zielona Góra had given the Hangman the reputation of being the division's toughest regiment as well as the one that would be disciplining any miscreants. As a result, most of the regiment's companies were oversized also, with an average of one hundred and twenty men instead of the neat one hundred stipulated by the army's powers-that-be. Jeff and all of his officers were firmly of the opinion that the bigger the gun, the better, so most of that added personnel had been assigned to heavy weapons units. Jeff had been able to provide them with the heavy weapons they needed because he now had a close relationship with David Bartley; who, despite being the youngest quartermaster officer in the division, was easily its smartest.

And now, he'd be adding still more heavy weapons units to his regiment, swiped from Hlavacek's Teutoberg Regiment. So what? Jeff saw nothing wrong with hauling coal to Newcastle, and Hlavacek would make up the loss soon enough through recruitment. Unlike most armies in the here and now, the USE army regularly met its payroll. There were always men willing to sign up, even leaving aside the ones—most of them, actually—who joined for ideological reasons.

Jeff didn't have much sympathy for Hlavacek, anyway, since he didn't like the sour Czech mercenary officer. Still, there was no percentage in rubbing salt into the wounds of another regiment.

So all he said was, "Okay."

Chapter 2

"Run that by me again." Jeff Higgins shook his head. "I'm having some trouble with the logic involved."

Captain David Bartley looked a bit lost, as he often did when other people couldn't follow his financial reasoning. "Well..."

He sat up straighter on the stool in a corner of the Hangman Regiment's HQ tent. "Let's try it this way. The key to the whole thing is the new script. What I'm calling the divisional script."

Higgins shook his head again. "Yeah, I got that. But that's also right where my brain goes blank on account of my jaw hits the floor. If I've got this right, you are seriously proposing to issue currency in the name of the Third Division?"

"Exactly. We'll probably need to come up with some sort of clever name for it, though. 'Script' sounds, well, like script."

"Worthless paper, in other words," provided Thorsten Engler. He, like Bartley and Colonel Higgins himself, was also sitting on a stool in the tent. The flying artillery captain was smiling. Unlike Jeff, he found Bartley's unorthodox notions to be quite entertaining.

"Except it won't be—which is why we shouldn't call it 'script.'"

"Why won't it be worthless?" asked Major Reinhold Fruehauf. Unlike the others, he was standing. Slouched against one of the tent poles, more precisely. Fruehauf commanded the regiment's 20th Battalion. Battalions were numbered on a divisional basis, with the 1st and 2nd battalions assigned to the division's "senior" regiment, the Freiheit Regiment commanded by Colonel Albert Zingre. Jeff Higgins' Hangman Regiment being the bastard tenth regiment of the division, its two battalions got the numbers nineteen and twenty.

Bartley squinted a little, as if puzzled by the question. "Why won't it be worthless? Because... Well, because it'll officially be worth something."

The regiment's other battalion commander cocked a skeptical eyebrow. "According to who, Captain? You? Or even the regiment itself?" Major Baldwin Eisenhauer had a truly magnificent sneer. "Ha! Try convincing a farmer of that!"

"He's right, I'm afraid," said Thorsten. His face had a sympathetic expression, though, instead of a sneer. Engler intended to become a psychologist after the war; Major Eisenhauer's ambition was to found a brewery. Their personalities reflected the difference.

"I was once one myself," Engler continued. "There is simply no way that a levelheaded farmer is going to view your script—call it whatever you will—as anything other than the usual 'promissory notes' that foraging troops hand out when they aren't just plundering openly. That is to say, not good for anything except wiping your ass."

Bartley looked more lost than ever. "But—but— *Of*

course it'll be worth something. We'll get it listed as one of the currencies traded on the Grantville and Magdeburg money exchanges. If Mike—uh, General Stearns—calls in some favors, he'll even avoid having it discounted too much." He squared his slender shoulders. "I remind all of you that they don't call him the 'Prince of Germany' for no reason. I can pretty much guarantee that even without any special effort money printed and issued by Mike Stearns will trade at a better value than a lot of European currencies."

Now, it was the turn of the other officers in the tent to look befuddled.

"Can he even *do* that?" asked Captain Theobold Auerbach. He was the commander of the artillery battery that had been transferred to Jeff's unit from the Freiheit Regiment.

Bartley scratched his head. "Well...It's kind of complicated, Theo. First, there's no law on the books that prevents him from doing it."

Auerbach frowned. "I thought the dollar—"

But David was already shaking his head. "No, that's a common misconception. The dollar is issued by the USE and is recognized as its legal tender, sure enough. But no law has ever been passed that makes it the nation's *exclusive* currency."

"Ah! I hadn't realized that," said Thorsten. The slight frown on his face vanished. "There's no problem then, from a legal standpoint, unless the prime minister or General Torstensson tells him he can't do it. But I don't see any reason to even mention it to anyone outside the division yet. Right now, we're just dealing with our own logistical needs."

The expressions on the faces of all the down-timers

in the tent mirrored Engler's. But Jeff Higgins was still frowning.

"I don't get it. You mean to tell me the USE allows any currency to be used within its borders?"

He seemed quite aggrieved. Bartley was grinning, however.

"You're like most up-timers," David said, "especially ones who don't know much history. The situation we have now is no different from what it was for the first seventy-five years or so of the United States—our old one, back in America. There was an official United States currency—the dollar, of course—but the main currency used by most Americans was the Spanish *real*. The name 'dollar' itself comes from the Spanish dollar, a coin that was worth eight *reales*. It wasn't until the Civil War that the U.S. dollar was made the only legal currency."

"I'll be damned," said Jeff. "I didn't know that."

He wasn't in the least bit discomfited. As was true for most Americans, being charged with historical ignorance was like sprinkling water on a duck.

Jeff had been sitting long enough, and the stools weren't particularly comfortable anyway. So he rose and stretched a little. "What you're saying, in other words, is that there's technically no reason—legal reason, I mean—that the Third Division couldn't issue its own currency."

"That's right."

A frown was back on Captain Auerbach's face. "I can't think of any army that's ever done so, though."

David shrugged. "So? We're doing lots of new things."

"Let's take it to the general," said Jeff, heading for

the tent flap. "We haven't got much time, since he's planning to resume the march tomorrow."

Mike was charmed by the idea. "Sure, let's do it. D'you need me to leave one of the printing presses behind?"

Unlike every other general in the known world, Mike Stearns would no more undertake a campaign without his own printing presses than he would without guns and ammunition. In his considered opinion as a former labor organizer, one printing press was as valuable as two or three artillery batteries.

Bartley pursed his lips. "Probably a good idea, sir. I can afford to buy one easily enough. The problem is that I don't know what's available in the area, and we're familiar with the ones the division brought along."

"Done. Anything else you need?"

David and Jeff looked at each other. Then Jeff said: "Well, we need a name for the currency. We don't want to call it script, of course."

Mike scowled. "Company script" was pretty much a profane term among West Virginia coal miners.

"No, we sure as hell don't," he said forcefully. He scratched his chin for a few seconds, and then smiled.

"Let's call it a 'becky,'" he said. "Third Division beckies."

Bartley looked dubious. "Gee, sir, I don't know... Meaning no offense, but isn't that pushing nepotism a bit far?"

Higgins laughed. "In the year sixteen thirty-five? For Christ's sake, David, nepotism is the most favored middle name around. Most rulers in the here and now get their position by inheritance, remember?"

"Well, yeah, but..."

Mike's grin faded a little. "Relax, Captain. The problem with nepotism is that it can lead to incompetence and it's often tied to corruption. But neither of those issues are involved here. It's just a name, that's all."

Bartley thought about it for a moment, and then seemed relieved. "Okay, I can see that."

A moment later, he looked downright pleased. "And now that I think about it, naming the division's unit of currency after your own wife is likely to boost confidence in it. The here and now being the way it is."

The rest of the division resumed the march to Prague early the next morning. Jeff and his officers spent the rest of the day and most of the next three getting the regiment's camp established.

That took some time and effort, because Jeff had decided to billet the regiment's soldiers in or next to the Thun castle on the hill, instead of in the town itself. The castle was vacant since the owner had fled, and Jeff figured he could use the fact of the nobleman's flight as proof positive that he'd been up to no good.

That wouldn't stand up to any kind of serious legal scrutiny, of course. But it didn't have to. All Jeff needed was a fig leaf to cover his sequestering of the castle for the immediate period. Whatever differences there might be between down-time courts and up-time courts, and between down-time legal principles and up-time legal principles, they shared one thing in common. The wheels of justice ground very, very slowly. By the time a court ruled that the Hangman Regiment's seizure of Thun's castle had been illegitimate, the war would be over and the regiment would be long gone anyway.

For that matter, Jeff might have died of old age. He knew of at least one lawsuit in Franconia that was still chugging along—using the term "chugging" very loosely—three-quarters of a century after it was first filed.

Setting up the castle as living quarters for more than a thousand soldiers was not a simple process, however. Fortunately, the kitchens were very large. But there wasn't enough in the way of sleeping quarters and the less said about the castle's toilet facilities the better.

But it wouldn't have made a difference even if the castle had had the most up-to-date and modern plumbing. No edifice except one specifically designed for the purpose of housing large numbers of people will have enough toilets to maintain sanitation for an entire regiment. An oversized regiment, at that. So, proper latrines had to be constructed.

About half the men would have to sleep in their tents anyway. Jeff set up a weekly rotation schedule that would allow every soldier to spend some time in the castle's quarters. Personally, he thought the tents were probably just as comfortable. Or no more uncomfortable, it might be better to say. Winter was almost upon them. But spending a night in a freezing stone castle was not likely to be any more pleasant than spending it in a tent equipped with a portable stove.

However, he knew the men would be happier if they were all rotated through the castle's living quarters. That would seem fair, regardless of whether it actually made any difference in practical terms.

He was tempted to billet some of the soldiers in the town itself. But that would just be asking for trouble. Civilians hated having soldiers billeted into their own homes. That was a given. The American colonists had hated it when the British did it. *Really* hated it—to the point of sharply limiting the practice in the Bill of Rights. It was the third amendment: *No Soldier shall, in time of peace be quartered in any house, without the consent of the Owner, nor in time of war, but in a manner to be prescribed by law.*

Czech civilians wouldn't be any happier in the here and now having mostly German soldiers foisted upon them. The animosities produced would undermine whatever chance there might be to get the new beckies accepted by the local populace. As it was, by keeping the soldiers out of the town's homes, Jeff was generating quite a bit of good will. Billeting troops upon civilians was standard practice in the seventeenth century, and Tetschen's inhabitants had been glumly expecting it.

Very glumly. Even on their best behavior, soldiers crammed into homes that were usually none-too-large to begin with caused difficulties for their "hosts." And billeted troops usually weren't on their best behavior, especially if the home contained anything valuable or had young women present.

When Tetschen's populace learned they would avoid the fate this time, they were immensely relieved. Some of them even went so far as to buy a round of drinks for soldiers in one of the town's taverns. Not often, of course.

All in all, in fact, Tetschen's inhabitants were coming to the conclusion that this might turn out for the best. The taverns were doing a land office business, as was the town's one small brothel—which soon began expanding its work force. And with a regiment apparently stationed permanently in the town, most of the other merchants were looking to increase their business also. Soldiers have needs as well as desires. Uniforms needed to be mended, food needed to be bought and cooked, equipment needed to be repaired—the list went on and on.

Tetschen was becoming quite a cheerful town, in fact. Then the becky made its appearance.

Chapter 3

The miller stared at the piece of paper in Major Fruehauf's hand. It was about twice the size of a U.S. dollar bill. The central portrait was that of a very attractive young woman holding aloft a torch in her right hand and carrying some sort of tablet in the crook of her left arm. The image was patterned after the up-time Statue of Liberty, although neither the major nor the miller was aware of that fact.

Nor were they aware of the one big difference with the statue, since neither of them had ever met Rebecca Abrabanel. And while the major had seen some of the scurrilous pamphlets circulated about her by rabid anti-Semites in previous years, the woodcut images of her contained in them had borne no relationship whatever to reality.

This image, on the other hand, was a pretty fair depiction of Rebecca. The artist who'd designed the woodcut was one of the soldiers attached to the printing press Mike had left behind. The soldier had met the general's wife on two occasions, and had a good memory of her. That wasn't surprising. He was a young man and Rebecca was generally acknowledged as one of the most beautiful women in Europe, even by her enemies. In fact, especially by her enemies. Terms like "temptress" and "succubus" were often connected to her. If you didn't know any better and moved in those circles, you'd be certain that her middle name was Delilah.

Good-looking female image or not, the miller didn't care. He'd never heard the expressions "you can't judge a book by its cover" or "not worth a continental" but it didn't matter. He was no damn fool.

"That's not worth the paper it's printed on," he protested.

Fruehauf shook his head, his expression one of sorrow rather than anger. "How can you claim such a thing? It's even traded on the currency exchanges in Grantville and Magdeburg. By now, probably in Venice and Amsterdam, too."

"Not in Prague," the miller said stoutly.

Fruehauf gave him the sort of look normally reserved for village idiots. "And if it were, would you trust it any more? Correct me if I'm mistaken, but isn't that exchange—and the stock market too, I hear—owned outright by Wallenstein?"

The miller looked even more unhappy. The major was slandering Wallenstein, actually. The king of Bohemia was only one of the partners in Prague's stock exchange and currency exchange. Granted, the majority partner. But he was far too smart not to understand that fiddling with such institutions would, in the long run, simply undermine their value to him. They were run as honestly as the major exchanges in Europe. In fact, the Prague exchange would probably number among them within a year.

"It's still just a piece of paper," the miller complained.

"Are you really that rustic, Johann? Any kind of money is no better than the authority which backs it."

They were speaking in German because the miller, like many of the town's inhabitants, was of German rather than Czech stock.

"Not gold and silver!"

Fruehauf rolled his eyes. "Right. Assuming the king who issues the coin isn't debasing it. And how often is that true?"

Johann said nothing. He really wasn't that rustic. If you searched Europe high and low, you'd certainly find some coins that contained the gold and silver content they were supposed to have. But the big majority wouldn't.

Fruehauf shoved the paper at him. "Look, just try it. General Stearns backs the beckies. He's been accused of a lot of things, but never of being a thief or a swindler."

Mike Stearns had something of a mythic reputation, in central Europe—as much so in Czech lands as German ones, given the critical role played by up-timers in Wallenstein's rebellion against Austria and his subsequent stabilization of an independent Bohemian kingdom. That myth contained many ingredients, that varied widely from person to person. By no means all of them were positive. But the sort of chicanery involved in currency swindles was simply not part of the legendry, any more than it was part of the Arthurian cycles. That was true whether you were speaking of Arthur, Lancelot, Guinevere—or Mordred and Morgan le Fay. Sins and faults aplenty in that crowd, but none of them were petty chiselers.

"Well..."

The major seized Johann's wrist and more-or-less forced the becky into his hand. "Just give it a try," he repeated. "You can either trade it yourself on the exchanges"—from the look on the miller's face there was no chance of that happening—"or, what I personally recommend, is that you trade it back to the regiment to get whatever goods or services we can provide."

"Which would be what?" the miller asked skeptically.

Fruehauf glanced around the mill house. "Don't be stupid, Johann. I was born and raised in a village myself. Any mill house needs repair work—and I'll bet you my good name against that becky in your hand that we've got carpenters and blacksmiths in the regiment that are at least as good as any in Tetschen."

The carpenters and blacksmiths in the town wouldn't be happy to hear that, of course. But that was none of the miller's concern and Fruehauf saw no reason to explain that the regiment would probably wind up trading the miller's flour for the services of the area's carpenters and blacksmiths. Who could say? They might even wind up being used to repair the miller's equipment.

The secret of economics was ultimately simple. Just keep people working. The manner in which that was done didn't really make a big difference. Having a regiment of twelve hundred men living in the area would inevitably stimulate the economy so long as everyone was convinced that peace and stability would be maintained and that the money being circulated was of good value.

The first had already been established. General Stearns had been shrewd in choosing the Hangman to leave behind. The story of the regiment's origins and purpose had spread widely by now. Not least of all because the general's printing presses had seen to it. And Colonel Higgins made sure that his men maintained good behavior in their relations with the townfolk.

Now, if they could just get the becky accepted...

"Well, all right," said the miller. "But just this once! If I'm not satisfied, you won't get any more flour from me."

It was a sign of progress, Fruehauf thought, that the miller obviously wasn't considering the fact that if it chose to do so, the Hangman Regiment could march into his mill house, seize all his flour—and, for that matter, burn it down and kill him and his family in the bargain. Whatever reservations the local inhabitants still had about Higgins and his soldiers, at least they were no longer considered bandits.

Thorsten Engler looked around the room and whistled softly. "Well, it's certainly an improvement over the tent, Colonel. The men might start calling you 'Sultan,' though."

"Very funny." Jeff Higgins waved at one of the unoccupied seats in the salon. He'd appropriated the largest such room in the castle to serve as his headquarters. Conveniently, it had a bedroom attached. But Jeff had the door closed. Truth be told, the bedroom was even more luxurious than the salon. He hadn't chosen these rooms for that reason, but protestations of innocence would be received with the skepticism usually bestowed upon such claims.

The real reason Jeff had selected these quarters was visible in the salon itself. Every single officer of the regiment was present at this meeting, from company level up. That meant fitting into the room one colonel, two majors, ten captains and two first lieutenants. The lieutenants served Jeff as adjutants, which was polite military-speak for gofers.

They all had places to sit, too. Comfortable ones.

"Okay, guys," Jeff began, with his usual lack of formality. He ran the regiment in a manner that bore as much resemblance to his days as the dungeon master of role-playing games as it did to anything a traditional military man would have considered proper behavior for a commanding officer. The reason he got away with it was because his subordinates had complete confidence in him. Jeff would have been surprised, in fact, had he known just how deep that confidence ran. Not much of it was due to his status as Gretchen Richter's husband, either, although that certainly didn't hurt in a regiment as CoC-heavy as the Hangman.

No, it was Jeff himself. Or rather, the Colonel Higgins who had emerged from the battles at Zwenkau and Zielona Góra. Jeff was only vaguely aware of it, but he was one of those people who became calm and unflappable under stress. There was probably no other quality a commanding officer could have that produced more confidence in his soldiers. It was nice, of course, if the commander gave exceedingly intelligent and shrewd orders as well. But all he really needed to do, when a subordinate turned to him for commands, was to be able to give them as naturally and easily as a man orders a meal in a restaurant. Unless the orders were disastrously wrong, their precise nature didn't matter that much.

Battles are not very complicated, when you get right down to it. *Go there. Stay here. Shoot those people over there. Go around that hill and try to shoot them in the back. Blow up this bridge. Burn down this house. Don't burn down this house, you idiot, we need it to sleep in after we win the battle.*

Leaving aside a few euphemisms and technical terms, the vocabulary involved was entirely within reach of a ten-year-old child. The key was that it all had to be done while other people were doing their level best to go around hills and shoot you in the back. That was the stark reality that no child could possibly handle—and not all that many full-grown men could handle well, if they were in a command position.

Jeff Higgins could, and by now his men knew it. So his relaxed, almost collegial style of command helped foster an *esprit de corps* in the regiment instead of undermining his authority with its officers. The truth was, even if they'd been able to see into the bedroom, the officers and men of the regiment wouldn't have done more than make wisecracks about sleeping on a bed so big you needed a map to find your way out of it in the morning. Some of the soldiers would have been tempted to sneak in and swipe the canopy, no doubt. But they probably wouldn't have actually done it. Not the colonel's canopy.

When he had everyone's attention, Jeff used a pointer he'd had made for him by one of the regiment's carpenters to indicate their position on a large map he had hanging on an easel. The map was new, having just been finished by the same artist who'd done the portrait on the beckies.

"You see this stretch of the Elbe, from here north to Königstein?" He waggled the tip of the pointer back and forth across the border. "That's why we're really here, gentlemen. I hope I don't have any officers in this regiment who are so dim-witted that they really think General Stearns left us here to protect Bohemia against that jackass Heinrich Holk."

A little sigh swept the room. They'd wondered, of course.

"The general left you with special orders," ventured Major Eisenhauer.

Jeff shook his head. "No, he didn't say a word to me. He didn't need to." .

He turned to face his officers. "Here's how it is, and if there's anyone here who thinks he'll have trouble with what might be coming, you'd better come talk to me in private after this meeting."

His tone of voice was harsh, which was unusual for Colonel Higgins.

Another little sigh swept the room. They'd wondered about that, too.

"Let me start by making one thing clear. Mike Stearns believes in the rule of law just as much as I do. So if nobody breaks the rules, then you and me and every soldier in this regiment is just going to spend some chilly but probably pleasant enough months twiddling our thumbs here. But if rules do start getting broken..."

He shook his head again. "And being honest, I'm pretty sure they will. The thing is, I know Mike Stearns—but I don't think those other people really do. I don't think they understand just how much they're playing with fire here."

Major Fruehauf spoke up. "So our real task is to make sure that if the Third Division needs to return to the USE—quickly—that there won't be anything in the way."

Jeff nodded. "The key will be the fortress at König-stein." He tapped the map again with the pointer. "I only got a look at it from a distance as we marched past, but it looked plenty tough and by all accounts it is."

One of the infantry captains spoke up. "I have been there, sir. And, yes, it's still quite formidable even if the structure was built four hundred years ago."

"What I figured. We'll maintain some cavalry patrols up and down the Elbe to keep an eye on whatever might be developing at the fortress. But mostly, I figure we'll rely on the air force. The one definite instruction the general gave me was to build an air-field here. By happy coincidence, any plane coming in and out of Tetschen from the USE is just going to naturally overfly the fortress at Königstein."

He turned away from the map and paused for a few seconds. "I will repeat what I said. If any of you have problems with any of this, come talk to me afterward."

The officers glanced around at each other. Then Thorsten Engler said, "I don't think so, Colonel. I think I can speak for every man here. If they play by the rules, we play by the rules. But if they break the rules, then we'll show them why we're called the Hangman."

Chapter 4

Magdeburg, central Germany
Capital of the United States of Europe

"Thank you, Jenny," said Rebecca Abrabanel, as she passed her daughter Kathleen over to the young governess and housekeeper. The child was barely one year old, so the transfer did not disrupt her sleep in the least. She was quite accustomed to the care of Jenny Hayes, anyway, since she spent more time with her than she did with her mother. Rebecca had adopted some of the attitudes of the Americans, but when it came to child-care she was still firmly a woman of the seventeenth century. If you had the money to do so—which she now certainly did—you hired nannies to take care of the tedious portions of child-raising. Which, at Kathleen's age, was most of them.

About the only concession that Rebecca made to up-time custom was that she still breast-fed the girl herself, instead of employing a wet nurse. But she did that mostly because continuing to lactate was the most effective birth control measure available to her, other than keeping track of her monthly cycle or using condoms. Neither she nor her husband Michael wanted to be bothered with that miserable rhythm business. As for the condoms that had been introduced into the market some months earlier, Michael didn't like them and she didn't trust them.

Rebecca enjoyed her children and planned to have at least two more. But she also enjoyed her political career and had no desire to see it crushed flat under the pressure of child-raising.

Being well-to-do helped a great deal in that regard. While Rebecca and Michael were not what anyone would call wealthy, they enjoyed a much larger than average income because of his salary as a major general. And if she finished her book on schedule, the income that derived from its sales might very well double or even triple their income.

Rebecca had been born a Sephardic Jew, and still maintained most of her religion's customs and rituals. When it came to theological matters, though, she tended to share her father's attitudes. Balthazar Abrabanel was not exactly what the up-timers meant by the term "freethinker," but he came awfully close. He still considered himself a Jew even in doctrinal terms, but there were plenty of rabbis who would dispute that claim. The rabbinate of Amsterdam, which was notoriously harsh and reactionary, had even gone so far as to declare him a heretic.

On the other hand, Prague's rabbis—who had considerably more prestige than those of the Dutch city— maintained friendly relations with him. They did so partly, of course, for political reasons. Balthazar's brother Uriel was the spymaster for Morris Roth, who was by far the wealthiest Jew in Prague and was also one of

Wallenstein's closest advisers thanks to his leading role in repelling Holk's attack on Prague two years earlier.

Whatever her doctrinal doubts and questions, however, on one matter Rebecca was a staunch monotheist. Nannies had been sent down to Earth directly by the hand of God.

After Jenny left the vestibule with Kathleen, Rebecca turned and went to the door leading to the room on the second floor of the town house that she used for her political meetings. It was a very large room, in keeping with the town house itself. The three-story building wasn't quite what one could call a "mansion," but it came close.

That was a good thing, too, given that the building also served the Fourth of July Party as its informal national headquarters.

As usual when a meeting was in progress, she could hear Constantin Ableidinger's booming voice before she even opened the door.

"—think we can make such an assumption. As much as I dislike the prime minister's reactionary political views, he's just not the sort of human material out of which ruthless counterrevolutionaries are made."

By the time he finished, Rebecca had passed through the door and closed it behind her. She headed toward her seat at the head of the table. Series of tables, rather.

"No, Wilhelm is not such a man," she said. "As a human being, he's actually quite a decent fellow. But Wilhelm is no longer running the show. Axel Oxenstierna is."

She pulled out her chair and sat down. There had been a time when there had been only four tables in this very large room, arranged in a shallow "U" that allowed everyone to see out the windows. That was no longer true. There were simply too many important leaders of the Fourth of July Party who needed to be present at this meeting. So, there were now eight tables in the room, lined up two abreast and four wide. In effect, a single huge meeting table had been created, measuring about ten feet by thirty feet.

Rebecca's position at one end of the arrangement, facing down the double row of tables, gave her a good view of everyone present. It was also a subtle indication of her position in the party. Officially, she was simply one of the members of the USE Parliament elected from Magdeburg province. Unofficially, especially in the absence of her husband Mike Stearns, she was one of the FoJP's most prominent and influential leaders.

She'd paused for a moment to let the implications of her last statement sink in. Then she added: "And the chancellor of Sweden is most definitely the sort of human material from which ruthless counterrevolutionaries are made. He is and always has been an advocate—I should better say, a true believer—in the principles of aristocratic privilege. It is no secret that he has never been happy with the compromises that Gustav Adolf made with my husband. Neither when they set up the Confederated Principalities of Europe nor—especially!—when they created the United States of Europe."

Again, she paused briefly. "I think it is now clear what has been happening these past few weeks. Ever since the emperor was badly injured at the battle of Lake Bledno and rendered *non compos mentis*,

Oxenstierna has been taking advantage of Gustav Adolf's incapacity to prepare a sweeping counterrevolution. That is why he has insisted on keeping the emperor in Berlin, where he can sequester him and keep him under control. That is why he has been assembling a congress of reactionaries in Berlin. They will declare Berlin the new capital. And that is why, finally—this news has now been confirmed also—he has ordered Princess Kristina to join her father in Berlin. So that she too can be kept under control while the chancellor goes about his bloody business."

One of the members of Parliament from Westphalia province spoke up. "But Oxenstierna is simply the chancellor of Sweden. He has no authority in the United States of Europe."

Ableidinger made a sarcastic snorting sound. "And do you think that little awkwardness is causing him to lose any sleep? Not likely! Not Oxenstierna."

He swiveled in his chair to look at Rebecca. "I don't doubt Oxenstierna's nature is just as you portray it to be. But how can you be so sure that he has reduced the USE's prime minister to a cipher? Giving the devil his due, Wilhelm Wettin is a capable man and not one I would think to be easily intimidated."

"No, he's not—as a man," said Ed Piazza. "But right now he's a prime minister also, and in that capacity I'm afraid he can be quite easily intimidated by Oxenstierna."

Piazza was sitting at the opposite end of the long set of tables from Rebecca, which indicated his own position in the party. Both by virtue of his abilities and his position as the president of the State of Thuringia-Franconia, Piazza wielded as much influence and authority as anyone in the FoJP other than Mike Stearns himself.

But Stearns was hundreds of miles away now, leading his army into Bohemia, and no longer directly part of the political equation.

The man who was probably the third most influential member of the party present at the meeting cocked his head quizzically and said, "I will repeat Constantin's question: How can you be so sure?"

That was Matthias Strigel, the governor of Magdeburg province. That province and the State of Thuringia-Franconia were the two great power centers of the Fourth of July Party. The SoTF was the wealthiest and most populous province of the USE. But Magdeburg province had now surpassed it as an industrial center.

It was also, of course, the province where the capital was located. The city of Magdeburg had an extraordinarily complex political structure. It was simultaneously the national capital of the USE, the capital of the province of Magdeburg, and an imperial city in its own right. Just to make things still more complicated, there was a legal distinction between the "old city" and the metropolitan area. Otto Gericke was the mayor of metropolitan Magdeburg, but within the narrow confines of the original city his authority was legally—if not always in practice—superseded by that of the city council.

"The reason I can be so sure," Ed responded, "is because I agree with Becky's analysis and I've been looking at the situation from a strictly military standpoint lately. The minute you do that, everything gets very clear, very quickly."

He leaned forward to give emphasis to his next words. "The reason the chancellor of Sweden can today intimidate and bully the prime minister of a nation which is many times larger is because Oxenstierna has an army—right there with him, in Berlin—and Wettin hasn't got a damn thing except his own bodyguards. And even those are mercenaries paid for out of the chancellor's purse."

This time it was a member of Parliament from the Province of the Main who protested, Anselm Keller. "But the USE has its own army."

"With a Swedish general in command," said Charlotte Kienitz, one of the leaders of the Fourth of July Party from the province of Mecklenburg.

The mayor of Hamburg shook his head. "Torstensson's authority no longer derives from Sweden. He was appointed by the Reichstag, not the king and emperor."

As he usually did in the middle of an argument, Albert Bugenhagen lapsed into a down-timer's term for the USE's Parliament. Up-timers, speaking English to one another, had a tendency to call it a "Congress," although that wasn't technically correct. Down-timers, speaking to one another, tended to call it a "Reichstag"—that meant "Imperial Diet"—which wasn't technically correct either.

For that matter, the official term "Parliament" wasn't really correct, in the terms that a fussy political scientist might use. When Gustav Adolf and Mike Stearns created the USE in the course of negotiations late in 1633, Mike had deliberately picked a term that was rather foreign to both American up-timers and German down-timers. The USE Parliament was a hybrid two-house creation with elements from up-time America, the down-time Germanies, and both eighteenth-century and twentieth-century Britain.

"I agree with Albert," said Werner von Dalberg. "Lennart Torstensson is a Swede by birth, but when he accepted the position of commanding general of the USE army he swore an oath to uphold the USE's constitution. An oath, I will add pointedly, that Axel Oxenstierna has never sworn. I don't think Torstensson will betray that oath."

Piazza shrugged. "Neither do I. So what, Werner? Torstensson has most of the USE's army besieging the Poles in Poznań. He was ordered to do so, I remind you, by the duly elected prime minister of the United States of Europe, Wilhelm Wettin, who is Lennart's own commander. Torstensson is not going to disobey that order."

"And as the winter comes on, it would become harder and harder to disobey it anyway," said Matthias Strigel. The Magdeburg governor had military experience. "Pulling out of siege lines in winter—certainly against an opponent as aggressive and capable as Grand Hetman Koniecpolski—would be dangerous."

Piazza nodded and then went on. "As for Mike Stearns and the Third Division, Oxenstierna—officially, Wettin, of course—saw to it that he was as far away as possible in Bohemia. That leaves Wettin with only garrison units, logistics units and a small number of mostly specialized troops. Some of them are combat units, but most of them are things like radio operators."

"There is also the navy and the air force," pointed out Helene Gundelfinger. She was the vice president of the State of Thuringia-Franconia.

Ed shrugged. "True, but those forces are the ones that matter the least in a conflict of this nature. Which is—let's finally put the words on the table, shall we?—an outright civil war. There was a time when Wettin could have played an independent role in such a conflict, but that time is past. He has no ground troops worth talking about and Oxenstierna has the entire Swedish army."

Ableidinger grunted. "What's left of it. Koniecpolski hammered them pretty badly at Lake Bledno, from all accounts I've heard."

"'Hammered' is not the right word. He bloodied them, yes. But it was the Poles who quit the field, not the Swedes. That army is still intact and functional and it outnumbers—it certainly outpowers—any other army that will become active in a civil war except the USE army itself. Which Oxenstierna, no fool, has dispersed and sent entirely out of the nation."

There was silence for a moment. Then Strigel leaned back in his chair and said, "There is your own provincial force, Ed. The SoTF's National Guard is probably the most powerful of the provincial armies."

Piazza nodded. "Except for possibly Hesse-Kassel's, in times past. But today, with Wilhelm V dead and many of his troops still with Oxenstierna in Berlin—"

"Not for long, I think," said Liesel Hahn, an MP from Hesse-Kassel. "The landgravine is furious with Wettin and the chancellor. They won't be able to stop her if she orders her soldiers home, which we think she will."

"Why do you think that?" asked Charlotte Kienitz. "I would hardly think Amalie Elizabeth is now taking us into her confidence."

"You might be surprised before much longer, Charlotte," interjected Rebecca. "I've received no fewer than three letters from her over the past two weeks. None of them contain much substance, but the tone is quite friendly. I believe she is determined to keep as many of Hesse-Kassel's bridges intact and unburned as possible."

"Might I speak with you about those letters after the meeting, Rebecca?" asked Hahn. "That's... quite an interesting development."

"Yes, certainly."

Charlotte shook her head, as if to shake off some confusion. "If you didn't already know about the letters, Liesel, why did you think Hesse-Kassel's widow would be recalling her troops?"

Hahn smiled. "I've met her several times, you know. She's actually quite nice in personal encounters. But she's still a Hochadel and has their innate attitudes. It barely registers on her that servants are within hearing range when she discusses her affairs with her counselors and advisers. Several of those servants report to the CoC regularly, and they pass the information on to us."

Piazza had been listening to the exchange with keen interest. Now he spoke up again. "Even if Amalie Elizabeth brings all her troops back, I doubt very much she'll be using them to intervene in any nation-wide civil war."

"I deduce the same thing from her letters," agreed Rebecca. "Not that she speaks of such matters directly, of course. Still, given her well-known attitudes in the past and her current friendliness toward to us—well, that's a bit too strong; call it cordiality, rather—I think we can safely assume that Hesse-Kassel will keep to itself in the event a civil war breaks out."

She looked at Hahn. "And so long as she does, Liesel, I would strongly advise our people there to keep the peace with her."

Hahn nodded several times, very rapidly. That was not so much timidity on her part as a simple recognition of reality. The hold of Hesse-Kassel's traditional rulers was still very strong, in part because they had been careful to make compromises and accommodations whenever necessary. You couldn't call them "absolute monarchs," since the Hesse-Kassel Estates maintained formal and legal—and especially financial—limits on the landgrave's authority in the province. The Estates had deposed Wilhelm V's father, in fact, because of his inveterate spendthrift habits. Still, the power of the landgraves was far greater than anything Americans thought of when they used the term "constitutional monarchy." By that term, up-timers meant British practices of the late nineteenth or twentieth centuries, where Hesse-Kassel had a much greater resemblance to the Britain of the seventeenth century.

In practice, however, while he had been alive Wilhelm V had ruled with a light hand and there was every sign that his widow would continue the practice. Freedom of religion was tacitly accepted and, within limits, so was freedom of speech and freedom of the press. The freedom to assemble was even partially allowed. The landgravine would certainly suppress any large open demonstrations against her, but she made no attempt to prevent political groups and parties like the FoJP from holding regular and publicized meetings.

Of course, those freedoms were enshrined in the USE's constitution, albeit with caveats. But the degree to which they were actually permitted in any given province was primarily determined by the balance of political power there.

Rebecca looked back to Piazza. "I interrupted you. My apologies."

Ed waved his hand in a small gesture, dismissing the matter. There hadn't really been much danger that Hesse-Kassel's party members would go off half-cocked, but it never hurt to make sure.

"The point I was working my way around to was that while I think it's true that the SoTF's provincial military is the most powerful such force in the USE today, I also think it's mostly irrelevant to the equation when it comes to a possible civil war."

The young mayor of Hamburg looked surprised. "Why is that?"

Before Piazza could answer, Werner von Dalberg did it for him. "Bavaria," he said tersely.

Von Dalberg was the FoJP's central leader in the Oberpfalz—or the Upper Palatinate, as it was known in English. His expression was grim. "Gustav Adolf pulled Banér and his army out of the Oberpfalz in order to send him to stabilize Saxony. Well, and good, so long as the emperor himself was still alert and functional. After the beating Banér gave them last year—the man's a swine and a brute, but he's also a very capable general—there wasn't much chance that the Bavarians would start anything again soon. Duke Maximilian has a lot of wounds to lick."

He shook his head. "But with Gustav Adolf incapacitated, and if a civil war breaks out, I think it's quite likely that Maximilian will attack the Oberpfalz again. And all we have to resist them is a single regiment under the command of Colonel Engels, with Major Simpson—he's the admiral's son—in charge of some artillery units." He glanced at Piazza. "If Maximilian does invade, we'll have to call on the State of Thuringia-Franconia to send troops to drive him back."

"Which we'll have to do for a lot of reasons," Piazza chimed in, "and defeating the Bavarian army will require just about everything we've got."

The president of the SoTF looked around the table. "The point being, ladies and gentlemen, that if Oxenstierna does launch a civil war, you're on your own as far as military forces go. I doubt very much if I'll be able to do more than hold my own province solid and defend the Oberpfalz."

Von Dalberg smiled. "On the positive side, the Oberpfalz is already leaning toward us. Rest assured that if the Bavarians attack because the Swedes pulled out their troops and Mr. Piazza comes to the rescue, the prospects for our party thereafter will be splendid. Assuming we've survived the civil war, of course."

A little laugh went around the table. There wasn't much humor in it, though. The implications if the SoTF's army was neutralized by the Bavarians were...

Not good. The Fourth of July Party also controlled Magdeburg province, but its military forces were quite small. The dominance of the Committees of Correspondence in that province, especially in the capital, meant that there was no real need for a powerful provincial military to maintain order. Magdeburg province was quite homogenous, too, both in social as well as geographical terms. In that respect, it was quite unlike the sprawling SoTF, with its variegated terrain and social mosaic.

Given that reality, those CoC activists in the province inclined to join the military volunteered for the USE's national army. On a per capita basis, Magdeburg province provided a larger percentage of the USE army's enlisted ranks than any other province in the nation.

The relationship between the Fourth of July Party and the Committees of Correspondence was complex, and varied some from one region to another. Taken as a whole, the relationship was quite close. Almost unanimously, CoC members voted for the FoJP candidates in any election except in those few places where they ran candidates of their own. In return, once elected to office FoJP politicians were generally supportive of those programs and initiatives desired by the CoCs of their area.

But there were always some frictions, also. As a very rough rule of thumb, CoC activists tended to view their FoJP counterparts as shaky-kneed moderates prone to excessive compromise, and FoJP members looked upon the CoCs as being often impractical and unrealistic firebrands.

Both views were stereotypes, but like many stereotypes they contained some kernels of truth.

"The thing that worries me the most," said Rebecca, "is that the CoC success in crushing the anti-Semites after the Dreeson murder, especially combined with the events in Mecklenburg—"

The populace of that hardscrabble Baltic province had rebelled during the post-Dreeson Incident period, and driven out its aristocracy.

"—has made them overconfident of their own military strength. It is one thing to defeat the sort of disorganized or hastily organized paramilitary forces they encountered during Operation Krystalnacht. It is another thing entirely to confront regular military forces. Even leaving aside the Swedish army under Oxenstierna's direct control, there are a number of significant provincial forces which we can assume will support the chancellor's counterrevolution."

"Can you summarize?" asked Helene Gundelfinger.

"If I may," interjected Ed Piazza, looking at Rebecca. "I've just finished examining the question."

She nodded and leaned back, trying not to smile. She was quite sure that the president and vice president of the SoTF were operating in tandem here and that Helene's question has been prearranged.

Piazza and Gundelfinger got along very well.

Chapter 5

"Here's the way it stands, as best as I can figure." Ed rose from his chair and went over to the wall of the room facing the windows. Where portraits would normally be placed on such a wall in most town houses of this size, hung instead a very large map of the United States of Europe.

There was a wand hanging from a hook next to the map. Ed picked it up and began pointing with it.

"As I said earlier, we have to assume that the SoTF and the Oberpfalz will be preoccupied with Bavaria." He swung the tip of the wand northwest to indicate Hesse-Kassel. "And we figure that, for her own reasons, Amalie Elizabeth will keep her province neutral. That brings us to the heart of the opposition's strength, which today is in Brandenburg."

The wand now pointed to the northeastern province's capital, Berlin. "Oxenstierna has somewhere in the vicinity of twenty thousand Swedish troops here, just about as many men as Torstensson has in his two USE divisions facing Koniecpolski at Poznań. Those are professional soldiers, skilled and experienced, and will do whatever Chancellor Oxenstierna tells them to do."

He swept the wand back and forth across the entire country. "Some provinces with strong and moderate rulers like Hesse-Kassel and Brunswick will try to keep their reactionaries under control. Westphalia too, for somewhat different reasons. But even they won't succeed entirely. In provinces under direct Swedish control like Pomerania, the Main and the Upper Rhine, they won't try at all. In fact, you can be sure and certain that Oxenstierna will be doing all he can to whip them up, especially the Mecklenburg noblemen in exile."

"You're still talking in terms of paramilitary units, though, aren't you?" asked Anselm Keller. "Not much different, really, from the sort of forces the CoCs can put in the field."

"Yes . . . and no. I agree with Becky that the CoCs are overconfident because of their success with Krystalnacht. But there they were fighting only the most extreme anti-Semitic reactionaries. They made it a point not to attack—and the favor was returned in kind—what you might call the more standard sort of reactionaries. Local noblemen, town patricians, guild masters, the like. That meant that they didn't often come up against regular militias with experienced and seasoned leadership. When they do—which they most certainly will in the event of a full civil war—they're going to discover things are a lot tougher for them."

He paused for a moment, studying the map. "Still, if the war was simply fought between the CoCs and the sort of forces that provincial and local reactionaries could put in the field, I'd bet on the CoCs. Hands down, in fact. The CoCs possess a truly national organization with a national program, where the reactionaries are a sack of potatoes. A collection of inveterate squabblers with a thousand petty privileges to defend and twice that number of petty grievances to avenge. If the CoCs in one province get into trouble, CoC columns from elsewhere will come to their aid—as they did in Mecklenburg during Krystalnacht. Rarely will you see provincial reactionaries behaving likewise. There's simply no comparison in terms of leadership, especially on the national level. On the one side, you have people like Gretchen Richter, Spartacus, Achterhof. And on the other?"

He shrugged. "It's hard to even come up with names. Oxenstierna is a titan surrounded by toads. No, the real danger lies elsewhere. With regular armies, not irregular forces."

Piazza moved the tip of the wand all the way across the nation to point to the southernmost province of Swabia. "There are three other large Swedish armies in the USE. The first is here in Swabia, under General Horn."

Bugenhagen started to object but Piazza waved him down with the hand not holding the wand. "Please, Albert. Yes, I know Horn's forces are legally part of the USE army, not the Swedish. In practice, though, Horn's soldiers are mercenaries, not the sort of often-CoC-inspired volunteers that fill the ranks of Torstensson's three divisions. They will do whatever Gustav Horn tells them to do, have no doubt about it."

"And what do you think Horn will tell them to do?" asked Strigel.

"Oh, and isn't that an interesting question." Piazza lowered the wand and tapped it against his leg a few times. "My guess is that Horn will stay out of it. He'll do in Swabia what the landgravine of Hesse-Kassel will do in her province. My reasoning is as follows. First—"

The wand came back up and tapped the area of the map just to the west of Swabia. The only legend there was: *controlled by Saxe-Weimar*. The map had not been updated to reflect the USE's formal recognition of Bernhard's newly formed County of Burgundy as an independent realm, which had happened only recently.

"Horn is specifically assigned in Swabia to keep Bernhard of Saxe-Weimar in check. That assignment came directly from Gustav Adolf himself, which gives Horn a good legal pretext to stay put if he chooses to use it. Second, while he has more troops than Bernhard does, he doesn't have *that* many more. It's a simple fact that if Horn pulled out a large part of his army that Bernhard could probably overrun Swabia."

Rebecca shook her head. "I doubt that he would, Ed."

"I don't think he would either. Bernhard is one of the sharpest pencils in the box. He'll be looking to play both sides against the middle if we fall into civil war and gain whatever advantages he can for that little kingdom-in-all-but-name he's putting together. But he won't take the risk of choosing one side over the other—what if his pick loses?—and he won't try to grab any territory that is clearly under USE jurisdiction. Sooner or later the civil war would end, and whichever side won would come looking for him with blood in their eyes. At which point he'd be a small fox facing an angry bear. No, he'll stay out of it. Besides . . ."

The wand-tip came back to Swabia. "This map doesn't reflect it yet, because it's still not formally established. But the fact is that in the real world the former duchy of Württemberg has seceded from

Swabia and is operating as its own republican province. So far, Horn hasn't used force to squash them. But he can always claim that what few forces he doesn't need to stare down Bernhard will be needed to keep order in Württemberg."

Ed lowered the wand again and went back to thoughtful leg-tapping.

"Horn has plenty of excuses—perfectly legitimate ones, mind you—to keep his army effectively neutral in any civil war. 'Neutral,' at least, so far as the rest of the USE is concerned. I don't doubt he'll rule Swabia with a firm hand and try to keep Württemberg under his thumb. So what it all comes down to is his own temperament and inclinations."

Piazza smiled, quite wickedly. "Happily for us, Axel Oxenstierna was the father of Horn's wife, while she was still alive. By all reports, Horn detested his father-in-law. And still does. So I think it's not likely that he'll be inclined to do as the chancellor says, so long as he can claim a legitimate reason to refuse."

Piazza now pointed farther north on the map, to the adjoining provinces of the Upper Rhine and the Main. "There's another sizeable Swedish army here, under General Nils Brahe. This one's legally as well as practically under the Swedish crown, so there's no ambiguities involved. But my estimate right now is that Brahe will do about the same as Horn. He'll keep the Main and the Upper Rhine stable—that's a genteel way of saying that he'll squash the CoCs there if they get rambunctious—but he won't intervene in any conflicts elsewhere."

"Why wouldn't he?" asked Strigel. The question was not a challenge, simply the product of curiosity.

"I'm guessing, you understand. But, first, Brahe's army isn't as strong as it used to be. I doubt if he even has ten thousand men left. Gustav Adolf figured the French would still be licking their wounds so he could afford to draw down Brahe's forces in order to bolster the ones he was taking into Poland. And while that was probably true then, will it still be true if the USE gets convulsed by a civil war? Cardinal Richelieu is under a lot of political pressure. He might be tempted to relieve it by getting back some of the territory they lost after Ahrensbök."

"Or Monsieur Gaston might go haring off on his own expedition, just to show how it's properly done," chimed in Helene.

"Finally," Ed said, "I think Brahe will stay put along the Rhine because he may have another problem to deal with, which is up here in Westphalia." The wand now moved to indicate the USE's large northwestern province.

"Ah! Of course." That came from Constantin Ableidinger, who suddenly broke into a grin. "I hadn't been thinking of that. If Oxenstierna launches a civil war here in the USE, he will be creating a gigantic Danish headache for himself, won't he?"

"I don't think there's much doubt about it," agreed Ed, nodding. "With Gustav Adolf incapacitated and given the still-fuzzy laws of the Union of Kalmar, you could make a good case that King Christian IV is now Kalmar's regent."

Rebecca smiled. "And I will bet that even as we speak the king of Denmark has every lawyer on his payroll assembling that case."

"Don't anybody take that bet," cautioned Piazza.

"Yes, I'm sure he is. More directly to the point, the governor of Westphalia is none other than Christian's son Frederik. Who, I will remind everyone, is still petitioning to have his title changed to 'Prince of Westphalia.' So what are the chances he will be paying much attention to Oxenstierna?"

"The CoCs are quite strong in Westphalia," said Albert Bugenhagen, "especially in the big cities. They're politically sophisticated, too. If Frederik decides to thwart Oxenstierna, they'll give him tacit support."

"That's what I figure," said Ed, "and it's the final reason I think Brahe won't move far from the Rhineland."

His expression got a lot more grim as he shifted the wand to the east. "We have quite a different situation with the final Swedish force of any size within the USE, Banér's army marching to Saxony from the Oberpfalz. Banér's a brute, pure and simple. A capable one, but still a brute. He doesn't much like Oxenstierna, but then he doesn't much like anyone. He'll still do what Oxenstierna wants him to do, partly because he'll see that as his best route for advancement but mostly for the good and simple reason that he agrees with Oxenstierna."

Ed lowered the wand and took a deep breath. "Things are going to heat up in Saxony before much longer. If there is a civil war, that'll be the cockpit."

Chapter 6

Dresden, capital of Saxony

Gretchen Richter studied the man sitting behind the desk. He was slight of build, with a large-featured face framed by long, light brown hair and decorated with mustachios and a goatee. Two bright blue eyes peered at her above a bony nose. The gaze was composed of equal parts of apprehension, suspicion and curiosity.

He seemed to be using the desk as a shield to protect himself against her—more like a barricade, perhaps. He held an old-fashioned quill pen as if it might serve him as a pike against charging cavalry.

About what she'd expected. The very fact that Duke Ernst of Saxe-Weimar had chosen to meet her in his office with himself seated at his desk told her a great deal about the way the man approached the world. The leaders of the Spanish forces besieging Amsterdam with whom she'd negotiated had been politicians, first and foremost. Despite the vast formal gulf in rank between themselves and a printer's daughter like Gretchen, both Don Fernando—then the cardinal-infante in command of Spain's armies in the Low Countries; now the king in the Netherlands—and his great-aunt Isabella, the Austrian archduchess who was the Netherlands' regent, had always met her sitting down at chairs in an informal setting.

But the duke was not really a politician, no matter that his older brother Wilhelm Wettin was now the prime minister of the USE and his youngest brother Bernhard had carved out an independent principality for himself from the Franche-Comté and parts of Swabia. Instead, Ernst was an administrator—what the Americans called a bureaucrat. His natural and instinctive response when faced with a challenge was to withdraw into his redoubt, his desk. There, armed with pen and ink and paper, he was best equipped to deal with whatever might arise.

A very good administrator, by all accounts. Even a fair-minded one, and no more prone to favoring his own class than was more-or-less inevitable given his origins and upbringing.

Gretchen had spent some time discussing Wettin with Dane Kitt, just a few weeks before coming to Dresden. The SoTF soldier had been in Grantville for the birth of his daughter at the same time Gretchen had been there attending to some personal matters for her husband. Kitt had served in the Oberpfalz during the Bavarian crisis and had given her a hilarious depiction of Wettin's insistence on bombarding the Bavarian defenders of Ingolstadt with Lutheran religious tracts hurled by a catapult. That story meshed with what her grandmother had told her about Mary Simpson's assessment of Wettin: *the slightest whiff of chalk dust acts on that man like perfume.*

She decided that was probably where the chink in his armor could be found.

"Saxony's schools are generally good," she said abruptly. "Especially here in Dresden. But almost none of them are secular. Correcting that problem has to be one of our first priorities."

Fiercely, she added, "We won't be satisfied with purely religious schools, no matter how good they are. They certainly have every right to operate according to the basic principles of the separation of church and state. But those same principles require the creation—or support and expansion, if they already exist—of secular schools established by the government of the province."

Duke Ernst stared at her. Clearly enough, this was not what he'd been expecting to hear from her. Certainly not as her opening remarks in their very first meeting.

"Ah . . ." he said.

"And we won't accept pleas of poverty. Saxony is a rich province. This is not Mecklenburg—and even in Mecklenburg they've begun creating public schools, now that the boot heel of the aristocracy has been thrown off."

That last statement was certainly true, in and of itself, but she'd really added it to allay whatever suspicions the duke might be developing that she was trying to undermine his resolution to oppose her at every point. Which, of course, she was.

One of the negotiating ploys she'd learned from watching Mike Stearns was the value of giving your opposite number a choice between alternatives, one of which was so unsavory that it made the other look tasty by comparison even if it wasn't actually a taste the person would normally enjoy at all. A standard form of that maneuver was to present a choice between persons: *either make a deal with me or*—here a finger would be pointed to a nearby ogre—*you'll have to try coming to terms with that creature.*

As often as not, Gretchen herself had been the ogre to whom Stearns had pointed. The CoCs, at least, if not herself personally.

But there was a variation on the tactic that she'd also learned from watching Stearns. It was a more subtle version in which the opposite party was given a choice between personalities rather than actual persons. In essence: *Either make a deal with me when I'm in a good mood and we're discussing something mutually amenable or we can wrangle over something that puts me in a really foul mood.*

The actual expression she'd heard Stearns use was "or we can talk when I'm on the rag." When she'd asked for a clarification of the expression from Melissa Mailey, she'd been stiffly told that it was quite offensive to women and Melissa would say nothing further on the matter.

That had been enough in itself, of course, to make its meaning clear. Gretchen had found the expression amusing rather than offensive. Who cared what men thought about such things? If men didn't like the inevitable by-products of female anatomy, they could bear their own children and see if they liked being pregnant any better.

So, she was giving Wettin a choice. Shall we spend the afternoon discussing the profoundly foul nature of the aristocracy—to which you belong yourself—or shall we spend it instead talking about the need for educational reform, a subject about which you yourself are enthusiastic?

❖　　　❖　　　❖

By mid-morning, Ernst had half-forgotten that the young woman he was having such a pleasant discussion with was not only the most notorious political radical in the Germanies but someone whom it could even be argued, given the recent change in the USE's government, was an outright enemy of the state. By now, he had discovered that Gretchen Richter was perceptive and astute on the issue under discussion, in addition to being personally quite charming. Neither quality was one he had expected from her reputation.

In retrospect, he could see the errors involved. So far as Richter's understanding of the issue of education was concerned, this was no farm girl or tavern-keeper's daughter. Her formal education might be somewhat limited, but her father had been a printer. Ernst was aware that up-timers viewed the printer's trade as being what they called "blue-collar," signifying work that might require considerable mechanical skills and knowledge but was not in the least bit intellectual. But they came from a world in which the different aspects of most professions had been carved into separate crafts. In the seventeenth century, on the other hand, the distinction between a printer and a publisher and an editor was usually meaningless. A man who owned and ran a print shop did all of those things—and, often enough, served himself as an author as well. Print shops were centers of intellectual discourse and quite often hotbeds of political radicalism. That was the milieu from which Richter came, not milking cows or serving ale.

Then, there was her personality. Allowing for some harshness along the edges, here and there, she was quite pleasant company. Polite and very attentive, among other things.

That should also have been obvious, he now understood. He knew, at least in broad outlines, of the central role she'd played in the siege of Amsterdam. Absurd to think that such a role could have been played by a person who was capable of nothing more than scowling and shouting belligerently!

Eventually, though, he forced himself to remember his duty.

"This has been most pleasant, Frau Richter. Hopefully, productive as well. But now I must return to more immediately pressing matters." He elided over the fact that they'd never actually begun that discussion, since Richter had driven over it right at the beginning. "I am disturbed—let us say 'concerned,' rather—at some of the activities of the Committee of Correspondence here in Dresden."

Richter nodded. "To be precise—if you will forgive me putting words in your mouth, Your Grace—your concerns center on the following." She began counting off her fingers. "First, that the city's militia has largely disintegrated. While a rump of the official force remains, for the most part control of the city in military and police terms has fallen into the hands of the CoC's guard units. Second, those guard units are armed. Third, they are well-armed, many of them with SRG muskets. A few even have breech-loading rifles. Fourth, much of the daily administration of the city has also fallen into the hands of the CoC or one of its affiliated organizations. In particular, the CoC has taken charge of sanitation and medical practices and is enforcing the needed rules vigorously."

Vigorously. Ernst stared at her. He knew of at least one tavern-keeper who'd been brutally beaten by a CoC "sanitation patrol." True, the man had been fouling the streets around his establishment. Quite badly, even by the standards of tavern-keepers. Furthermore, Ernst didn't doubt for a moment that the CoC's "vigorously enforced" sanitation rules were lowering the risk of disease and epidemic—always a major concern, especially in times of war and social unrest.

Still...

Richter pressed on.

"Fifth, you are concerned that we are repairing and strengthening the city's fortifications, as if we are preparing for a siege."

He cleared his throat. You certainly couldn't accuse the woman of evading delicate matters. She brought to mind the image of a very attractive, blond glacier moving toward the sea.

"You are especially concerned because you suspect we are in fact preparing for a siege. Specifically, that we are preparing to defend the city against the approaching Swedish army under the command of Johan Banér."

She paused for an instant, to give him the first look you could really call "cold-eyed" since the meeting began.

"In this suspicion, you are correct. The Swede general Banér is notorious for his brutality and has been specifically known to state that the proper use of a CoC agitator's head is as an adornment for a pike." She tapped the side of her skull. "This is one such head, and I have every intention of keeping it where it is. Under no circumstances will we allow Banér and his army into the city."

Ernst sighed and looked away. He could hardly argue this particular charge. He'd worked with the Swedish general in the Oberpfalz for months. Banér *was* a brute—a thoroughly unpleasant man—and Ernst himself had heard the general make that remark about CoC agitators and pikes.

Before he could say anything, Richter added, "And please spare us both the pointlessness of arguing that we cannot possibly withstand the Swedes. That's nonsense, meaning no offense, and you know it just as well as I do. You have considerable experience with sieges yourself, especially at Ingolstadt. Dresden was well fortified to begin with and we are strengthening the city's defenses still further. The city has a large population, most of whom are highly motivated to keep Banér and his thugs outside the walls.

"That means that any siege will last for some time, which will require Banér to forage supplies from the Saxon countryside—a countryside which was already in rebellion against the elector's depredations and has a large and well-armed military force under the command of the Vogtlander, Georg Kresse. And while the core of that army of irregulars remains Vogtlander, they have recruited a large number of people from the surrounding area since they came down from the mountains. They can't defeat Banér in a pitched battle, of course, but they can bleed his army badly. Given the nature of Banér, that will inevitably produce Swedish atrocities against Saxon villagers, which in turn will ensure that your very worst fear comes to pass."

She paused for just an instant. "That is, you are concerned because in addition to the city's large number of well-trained militiamen—most of whom have now joined the CoC guard contingents—there are also several hundred veterans of the USE's army in the city, recuperating from their wounds. Most of them are from General Stearns' Third Division, and almost all of them are on very good terms with the CoC. You are worried that if a clash of arms develops between Dresden and Banér's army, those USE soldiers will side with Dresden and give the city's defenders a core military force that has already defeated the French, the Saxons and the Poles in open battle."

He looked back at her. A blond glacier indeed— except glaciers didn't move this fast.

"In this worry, Duke Ernst, you are also correct. You may rest assured that I have, am and will do everything I can to ensure that those veterans do the right thing if and when the time comes. And I am quite certain they will do so."

Perhaps he should have stayed on the subject of education, after all.

Chapter 7

Dresden, capital of Saxony

Eric Krenz propped his elbows on the tower's stone railing and gazed out at the Elbe. The river that bisected Dresden was more than a hundred yards wide, and about that far away from his vantage point on the Residenzschloss. The height of the tower provided a magnificent view of the Elbe valley.

He wasn't really studying the scenery at the moment, though. He was just using the appearance of doing so as an excuse to stall giving Tata an answer to her question.

As she well knew. The woman was infernally shrewd.

"How long are you going to procrastinate?" she asked, planting her hands on ample hips. "I'm not pushing you, I just want to know. If it'll be a while, I'll go get some lunch."

Not for the first time, Eric wondered what madness had possessed him to get attracted to this creature.

"Attracted?" Better to say "obsessed," he thought gloomily.

Being fair, when it came to Tata, most of the time his thoughts were quite cheerful. But the woman had an unnerving capacity to seemingly read his mind—and an even more unnerving relentlessness when she wanted Eric to do something.

"I'm not really an expert on this business," he said. "I have no experience with sieges."

"Stop whining. I know that. Gretchen knows that. It doesn't matter right now. Somebody among the soldiers here must have some experience, and you're good at cajoling people into doing things."

"'Things,'" he muttered darkly. "Would that be 'things' as in mutiny and treason?"

She just gave him a level look through dark blue eyes and said nothing.

But he was still just stalling, and he knew it. If that bastard Banér brought his army to Dresden and tried to force his way into the city—and there was every indication he would—then Eric knew perfectly well that a massacre would ensue. It might not be as bad as the sack of Magdeburg at the hands of Tilly's soldiers a few years back, but it would be bad enough.

Eric was far from being the only soldier in Dresden who'd formed attachments with the local folk by now. Even his morose and generally peculiar friend Lieutenant Friedrich Nagel had managed to get the attention of a young woman. A guildmaster's daughter, even, by the name of Hanna Brockhaus.

There was no way the USE soldiers who were in Dresden would stand aside in the event Banér attacked the city. That being the case, it simply made sense to plan and prepare their defenses ahead of time, rather than having to jury-rig something at the last minute.

Eric being Eric, of course, he couldn't resist a last complaint. Even a litany of them.

"Some of the men are still too badly injured to do much of anything. And some of the others have recovered enough that they'll certainly be called back to service soon."

"I said, stop whining. And you really ought to be looking at that last whine from the other end of the telescope."

He frowned. "What does that mean?"

"It's obvious. By now, *most* of you have recovered from your wounds. You certainly have, judging from the way you keep trying to get me in bed."

That ranked among the most cheerful of his thoughts about Tata. He was pretty sure it wouldn't be long before "trying" became "succeeding." Most of Tata's remaining resistance was just the ingrained reflex of a pretty woman who'd been a tavern-keeper's daughter and had been fending off lustful males since she was thirteen.

Tata pressed on. "So what you ought to be asking yourself is why *haven't* you been called back to service by General Stearns?"

That was a good question, actually. Tata was quite right that most of the soldiers from the Third Division who'd been sent to Dresden to recuperate had already done so. Well enough, anyway, to go back to active service. Yet no word had come from the general to join him in Bohemia. To all appearances, he'd forgotten about them.

Yet that was impossible. It was true that small numbers of soldiers got overlooked, from time to time. Eric knew of a volley gun crew that had remained behind in Hamburg after the city was seized during the Ostend War in order to repair badly damaged equipment. Then the commander of their unit had been injured shortly after leaving the city and had forgotten to mention them to the subordinate officer who'd replaced him. The battle of Ahrensbök had taken place a few weeks later and right afterward the subordinate in question had been reassigned. The end result was that the volley gun crew had wound up spending nine months carousing in Hamburg with not a care until someone finally remembered them.

But that was just three men. There were over four hundred soldiers from the Third Division now residing in Dresden. That represented almost five percent of the division's strength and was enough men to form an entire battalion. There was no chance at all that Stearns had simply forgotten about them.

And even if Stearns had forgotten them, Eric was quite certain that Colonel Higgins had not—for the good and simple reason that he got letters from Jeff every week or so. There was a good and reliable courier service between Dresden and Bohemia.

So what was going on?

Tata put his own guess into words. "General Stearns *wants* you to stay here. And he's got a good enough excuse for doing so if anyone asks. 'Recuperating from wounds inflicted in valiant combat with the foe' is the sort of explanation that most people, even shithead Swedes, will hesitate before calling into doubt. And there's only one reason he'd want you to be here."

Eric could figure out the rest for himself. He already knew from filling in fairly obvious blanks in Jeff's letters that the Hangman Regiment had been left behind in Tetschen so that Stearns could bring his whole division back into Saxony in a hurry, if need be. The most likely cause of such a maneuver would be an impending battle in or around Dresden.

A battle with whom?

Eric smiled. General Stearns was nothing if not canny. If anyone ever pressed him on that matter, he'd have a ready-made explanation there also.

After being defeated at Zwenkau in August, the Saxon general von Arnim had withdrawn what was left of his army into Leipzig. There, he'd prepared for a siege while he began negotiating surrender terms with the Swedes. But the negotiations had dragged on for weeks, since Gustav Adolf had been preoccupied with driving forward his offensive into Poland. The elector of Saxony was killed in September, and thereafter Gustav Adolf wasn't particularly concerned with the situation in Leipzig. Von Arnim wasn't a mercenary in the usual sense of the term and his soldiers were mostly Saxons rather than the usual mélange you found in professional armies. Still, with no patron left, von Arnim certainly wasn't going to launch any campaigns, even after Gustav Adolf took almost all of his forces out of Saxony. He'd stay put in Leipzig until the situation got clarified.

And then the king of Sweden had been severely injured at Lake Bledno, in October, and was now out of the political picture altogether—with von Arnim and ten thousand or so of his soldiers still camped in Leipzig. So, if pressed, Stearns could always claim that he was seeing to it that in the event von Arnim resumed hostilities he could bring his Third Division back into Saxony in a hurry.

The CoC had gotten word in Dresden from their compatriots in Leipzig that the Swedes had resumed negotiations with von Arnim. But while no one in the

CoCs was privy to those discussions, no one thought any longer that the Swedes were simply seeking von Arnim's surrender. They were almost sure that Oxenstierna was trying to hire von Arnim himself—not to fight the Poles, but to serve the Swedish chancellor as another repressive force inside the USE. He couldn't rely on the USE army still besieging Poznań to serve that purpose. In fact, everyone thought that he'd insisted on continuing the war with Poland precisely for the purpose of keeping the USE's army *out* of the country. He'd use mercenaries in the pay of Sweden instead. He already had Banér and his fifteen thousand men marching into Saxony. If Oxenstierna could add von Arnim and the ten thousand men he had in Leipzig, he probably figured he could overawe or if need be crush any opposition in Saxony.

"Interesting times," Eric murmured, thinking of the Chinese curse Jeff had once mentioned to him.

"Is that a 'yes'?" Tata asked.

He made a face. "I guess."

He started moving around the tower, which was built like a large turret, with Tata trailing in his wake. When he got to the other side, he leaned over the railing and began studying the walls that protected Dresden on the south. Most of the city was on the southern bank of the Elbe.

"We're not going to be able to protect all of it," he said. "Have to let the northern part go. Even then, it's going to be a lot of work to build up those walls."

"And you said you didn't know anything about sieges," Tata said. She wasn't arguing the point, just doing her usual best to squash any further protests on his part.

"Just common sense," he grumbled. "I'm *still* not an engineer."

She came close and slid an arm around his waist. "You'll do," she said.

That statement had a very expansive flavor to it. Eric felt full of good cheer again.

Eddie Junker studied the boulevard to the south. Then he swiveled and studied it to the north.

Boulevard, he told himself firmly. That sounded so much less suicidal.

An uncharitable soul might have called the thoroughfare a "street." A particularly surly specimen might have added "crooked" to the bargain.

In truth, the thoroughfare wasn't really crooked. It just...jiggled around a bit.

Standing next to him, Denise Beasley stretched out her hand and made a slow, swooping motion. "You oughta be able to pull it off, Eddie. It's a pretty straight street. Ah, avenue."

"The lack of straightness by itself isn't the problem." He stretched out his arms, pointing simultaneously to the buildings on either side of the street. "What would you say the width is?"

Denise looked back and forth. Her friend Minnie Hugelmair, always given to direct methods, walked over to the building on the left side of the street. Then she paced off the distance.

"Thirty-five feet," she announced.

Eddie nodded. "About what I figured." He gave Denise a fish-eyed look. "And what is the wingspan of the plane?"

Denise waggled her head. "I'm not sure. Twenty-five feet?"

"Ha. Thirty-two feet. Leaving me three feet of

clearance in the street—the very-not-straight street—if I have to come down into it."

"But you're not planning to," protested Denise. "Exactly."

"'Exactly,'" Eddie mimicked. "No, I would simply be following it toward the square while—not quite—coming below the surface of the roofs. That would—hopefully—allow me to come into the landing area with a lower altitude than if I had to hop over the big buildings surrounding it. But if anything goes wrong . . ."

He looked down and scuffed his boot across the surface of the road. "Then there's this little problem. You *did* notice these are cobblestones?"

She looked down. "Um. Yeah."

"And exactly how many cobblestoned airstrips have you ever seen?"

"Um. None."

"There's a reason for that." He lifted his own, much thicker hand, and shook it up and down sharply. "Cobblestones are contraindicated for landing gear."

The two CoC craftsmen standing next to them looked at each other. Their expressions were dubious.

"Hard to pull up all these cobblestones and lay new ones," said the taller of the two.

"And then they wouldn't be as solidly set," added his companion.

Eddie had already figured that much out for himself. "How about paving it?"

The two craftsmen looked at each other again.

"We don't have enough asphalt," said the one on the left. His name was Wilbart Voss.

"Not nearly enough," said his partner, Dolph Knebel.

Eddie shook his head. "I don't really need a regular landing strip. The cobblestones would made a solid foundation if we could just fill it in with gravel to even out the surface. Then, level it with a roller."

The craftsmen exchanged glances again. That seemed to be a necessary ritual before their brains engaged.

"How wide?" asked Voss.

Eddie started walking slowly toward the big square to the north. "I'd want a minimum of forty feet. I'd be a lot happier with sixty."

Knebel made a face. "That's . . . about three hundred tons of gravel."

His partner was more sanguine, however. "Not so bad," said Wilbart. "There's plenty of gravel in the area and with everyone coming into the city for shelter from Banér we've got a lot of wagons and manpower. A strong wind might blow some of it away, though."

Eddie had already considered that problem. "If need be, I figured we can coat it with pine tar. But I don't think it'll be necessary. Between building the strip and repairing the plane, there's no chance we'd be able to use it until January or February. By then, there'll be snow holding the gravel in place. Just have to pack down the snow. Really well."

Denise chimed in. "Hey, I just thought of something, Eddie. You could land and take off on skis instead of wheels."

Junker's jaws tightened a little. His girlfriend had a great deal of confidence in his ability to do most anything. As a rule, this was a pleasant state of affairs. There were times when it was awkward, however.

"There is no way I am using skis. I have been flying for only a few months, and I have no experience—none at all—with skis. On a plane, I mean. I know how to ski myself, of course."

"You don't have any skis for the plane anyway, do you?" asked Minnie.

"No."

"Can't be hard to make," said Denise, reluctant as always to give up one of her pet schemes.

"I am *not* using skis. If we can't do it the usual way, then we simply won't do it at all." Eddie shrugged. "Which we probably won't, anyway, if we lose the airstrip outside the city. This whole idea of flying in and out of the city's square is crazy to begin with."

Denise didn't argue the point. It'd be pretty hard for her to do so, given that her first reaction upon hearing that the CoC was thinking of building an airstrip inside the city walls was pungent, explosive, and consisted mostly of the Amideutsch variant of every four-letter Anglo-Saxon term known to man and girl.

"It might all be a moot point," said Minnie. "They probably can't fix the plane anyway."

Eddie had crashed the plane when he landed it on the jury-rigged strip outside the city a few weeks earlier. He'd blamed the condition of the soil. More precisely, he'd blamed the girls for having assured him the soil was suitable. They had their own opinion, of course.

The most serious damage had been to the propeller, which had been completely destroyed. There was no way to replace it with the tools and equipment available in Dresden, so Eddie's employer Francisco Nasi was having a new propeller shipped in from Grantville.

Smuggled in would be a better way to put it. The Swedish general Johan Banér had already announced a blockade on any goods coming into Dresden. His army was still too far away to enforce the blockade systematically, but he had a number of cavalry patrols searching for contraband. Given their relatively few numbers, the cavalrymen weren't trying to interdict all goods, just those that had military uses. Presumably, Nasi had had the propeller hidden some way or another. Still, it was taking time to get it into Dresden.

In the meantime, a number of the city's artisans had started working on repairing the damage to the plane's structure. That was slow-going, partly from lack of the right tools and supplies, but mostly because none of them had any good idea what they were doing.

Neither did Eddie, really. He was on the radio almost every night talking to Bob Kelly, the plane's designer. At the rate they were going, he didn't expect to have the plane ready to fly again until mid-winter.

By then, the way things were looking, Banér would have Dresden under siege and the airfield outside the city's walls might as well be on the moon.

So, this project had been launched to jury-rig an airstrip in the central square. It was a project that Eddie considered just barely this side of insane. The only reason he'd agreed to it—a reason he kept entirely to himself—was that if worse came to worst and Banér's army breached the walls and began sacking the city, Eddie would try to fly himself, Denise, Minnie and Noelle Murphy out of Dresden. If they crashed and died, as they most likely would, the women would still be better off than they would in the hands of the Swedish general's mercenaries in the midst of a rampage. At least it'd be quick.

"You're looking awfully solemn," Denise said, in a teasing tone of voice.

"He thinks we're probably all going to die," piped up Minnie, "but it's sort of okay because this way it'll be over fast. He's a pretty stoic guy."

Denise curled her lip. "I don't hold with philosophy."

"Which is itself a philosophical proposition," said Eddie mildly.

Chapter 8

Stockholm, capital of Sweden

"It's a tub," pronounced Kristina. The Swedish princess made the statement with a royal assurance that sat oddly on her slender eight-year-old shoulders.

Nine-year-old shoulders, she would have insisted herself, and never mind that her birthday was still a month away. Kristina tended to view facts with disdain, if they conflicted with her axioms.

Being fair, Prince Ulrik was pretty sure he'd had the same attitude toward facts when he'd been eight years old. Or nine, for that matter.

"I know the *Union of Kalmar* is unpleasant to travel on," he said patiently. "But it's the only ship that can get us across the Baltic without fear of being intercepted."

"If it gets across the Baltic at all," she countered. Triumphantly, she added, "You said yourself the thing was not really suited for the open sea! I heard you! And that wasn't more than four months ago!"

So, he had. Not for the first time, Ulrik reminded himself to be careful what he said in front of Kristina.

The girl had a phenomenal memory to go with her ferocious intelligence. He could only hope that she would not prove to be a grudge-holder as she aged, or their marriage would be a tense one.

But that possible problem was still a considerable number of years in the future. Right now, he had to squelch the girl's developing tantrum over the issue at hand.

"Risks are relative," he said. "No, the *Union of Kalmar* is not the best vessel in which to venture on the open sea. It's a shallow draft ironclad, designed for bombarding shoreside fortifications and destroying ships in sheltered waters. On the other hand, it is—by far—the best vessel to be in should we encounter a Swedish warship on our way across the Baltic. By now, Chancellor Oxenstierna may well have drawn the right conclusions from your silence, and have sent vessels to prevent our passage across the Baltic."

"I'm mad at him, anyway!" Kristina had a furious expression on her face, most of which Ulrik thought was play-acting. "He was *rude* in the last two letters!"

The pretense of fury vanished, replaced by another triumphant look. "So *that's* the reason I haven't answered his letters. Well, it's not really the reason, of course. We had already agreed that it would be smarter to say nothing. But he might *think* that. So he wouldn't send ships out."

Baldur Norddahl chuckled. "The key word is 'might,' girl." The burly Norwegian sat up straighter in his chair, glanced at the salon's window, and looked back at her. "But he might *not* think that, either. In which case there we are, in the middle of the Baltic, in our comfortable staterooms on a proper seagoing vessel—and fat lot of good it does us, with our plump merchantman under the guns of a Swedish warship. The captain wouldn't even think of putting up a fight. Certainly not against a Swedish ship going about the chancellor's business."

"Whereas the captain of the *Union of Kalmar* is a Dane," Ulrik added quickly, "and will certainly do whatever we tell him. Especially since his ship can destroy any warship in the Baltic—"

"Except one of the other ironclads!"

"Yes, that's true. But the other two ironclads are under the command of Admiral Simpson in Luebeck. Who is an American, not a Swede."

Kristina started to say something but Ulrik drove over her. "Yes, I know that he's formally under the authority of Prime Minister Wettin, who is doing Oxenstierna's bidding nowadays and might well order us intercepted as well. But whether Simpson would actually obey such a command is doubtful, in my opinion."

"Why? You told me yourself once he was given to formalities. So why wouldn't he do what his lawful superior ordered him to do?"

Keep—his—mouth—shut. Speak only of recipes in front of the girl.

He made that vow, knowing full well he wouldn't be able to keep it. The problem was that Kristina was both too smart and too important to his developing plans. There was no way he could manage this situation without her cooperation, and she was quite capable of withholding that cooperation if he didn't involve her fully in the project.

"Yes, I know I said that, Kristina. But . . ."

How to explain?

"Most people are complicated," he said. "Simpson certainly is. Under most circumstances, I am sure he would be the very Platonic ideal of a politically neutral military officer obeying lawful orders. But the thing is..."

"He's also very intelligent," said Baldur. "And politically sophisticated. Simpson will know full well that if he's ordered by Wettin to take into custody the lawful heir of three crowns—only one of which answers to Oxenstierna and only one of which answers to Wettin—"

"*Might* answer to Wettin," interjected Ulrik. "It's actually not at all clear if the prime minister has the right to act as regent for the crown in the event the monarch is incapacitated and his successor is not of age." He waved his hand. "The whole area is completely gray, in legal terms."

Thankfully, that piqued Kristina's interest. "Really? I thought..."

Ulrik shook his head. "The prime minister of the USE isn't equivalent to the Swedish chancellor. Perhaps more to the point, when it comes to dynastic issues the USE's Parliament is not equivalent to Oxenstierna's council. Swedish law is fairly clear that the council has the right to appoint a regent for the crown under these circumstances. There is no such clarity in the USE's constitution."

Baldur chuckled. "And Stearns, bless the man's crafty soul, insisted on a formal constitution. So the lawyers can't just do a quick shuffle of the rules. They'll need to get an official legal ruling by the supreme court. Which is not known for the celerity of its deliberations."

Ulrik spoke. "That means, in effect, that the whole

issue will be Simpson's to decide, at least for two months or so. And that's probably all the time we need."

Kristina made a last, valiant stand. "You don't know that!"

Ulrik nodded. "No, I don't. But we can find out by tomorrow, with the radio."

The princess chewed on her lower lip for a few seconds. "Okay," she finally said. "I guess if Simpson agrees, we'll take the stupid ironclad across the sea. And hope we don't sink."

USE naval base
Luebeck

Colonel Jesse Wood hung his flight jacket on a peg near the door and then took a seat in a chair against the wall in Admiral Simpson's office.

"So what's up, John? Why did you insist I fly out here at the crack of dawn?"

With the passage of time and some shared heart-aches, relations between Jesse Wood and John Chandler Simpson had gotten a lot more relaxed than they'd been in earlier days. The two men still weren't what you'd call friends, but there was a lot of mutual respect between them.

A lot of trust, too, which is what the admiral thought was most critical at the moment. He half-rose, leaned over his desk and handed Jesse a radio message. "This came in yesterday evening."

The air force commander cocked an eyebrow and started reading the message. It wasn't very long. By the time he got to the end, his relaxed half-slouch had vanished and he was sitting up straight on the edge of his chair.

"Jesus H. Christ." He looked up at Simpson. "I assume there's no chance this is a fake?"

The admiral shook his head. "The prince had his own codes, which he used. I can't see how anyone else could have gotten them, since I happen to know—he told me—that he was committing them to memory so there'd be no written copy anywhere except in our records. And who would want to fake such a message anyway? The only people I can think of who'd want to meddle in this would hardly be sending *that* message."

Jesse looked back down at the little sheet and then handed it back to the admiral. "True enough. But... What the hell is she playing at?"

"I think you're using the wrong pronoun, for starters. I'd be very surprised if the guiding mind behind this isn't Prince Ulrik's." Before Jesse could say anything, Simpson made a dismissive gesture with his hand. "Oh, don't get me wrong. I'm sure he's not coercing the girl in any way. He wouldn't need to. He's very persuasive and by now she's probably got a lot of faith in him."

The colonel grunted. "Not to mention that she's what they call 'spirited' herself." He ran fingers through his short hair, which was starting to thin quite a bit in front. It was getting gray, too—and would probably be a lot grayer before this was all finished. Simpson's own hair was turning white.

"What do you think he's up to, then?"

Simpson looked out the window. His office was on the third floor of the navy's headquarters building, so he had a good view of the city's port. It was not what anyone would call a scenic vista, but the harbor was always busy and there was usually something of interest to watch. For the few seconds it usually took him to get his thoughts in order, anyway.

"I spent a fair amount of time in discussions with that young man during the Congress of Copenhagen, Jesse. He plays it very close to the chest, but I'm pretty sure he's following the general line of reasoning that Scaglia's been developing in the Netherlands."

"Who?"

"Alessandro Scaglia. He's a former Savoyard diplomat who's now in Brussels working for Archduchess Isabella. He advocates a political policy he calls 'the soft landing.' His argument is that the Ring of Fire proves that some sort of democratic political system is inevitable in Europe's nations, and so fighting to preserve monarchical rule and aristocratic privilege is pointless as well as wrongheaded. At the same time, given the existing realities and what he sees as the excesses that democracy led to in our universe—he's not very fond of the Committees of Correspondence in this one, either—he thinks a transition period is necessary, during which time ruling monarchs gradually cede their power to democratic institutions of one kind or another. To put it another way, he advocates constitutional monarchy, with the emphasis shifting over time from 'monarchy' to 'constitutional.'"

"Is he really that important? I've never heard of the guy."

Simpson tried to figure out how to respond. It would be rude to point out that Colonel Wood rarely read any political treatises, and none at all written by contemporary down-timers. The admiral, on the other hand, had compiled quite an extensive library of such writings. His wife Mary was an even more assiduous student of the subject.

"Well, he keeps a low public profile. But he has the ear of the king in the Netherlands, I'm sure of that, as well as the queen. And since Maria Anna is the sister of Emperor Ferdinand III of Austria and Hungary—they're reported to be quite close, too—I'd be surprised if Scaglia isn't getting a hearing from that branch of the Habsburgs as well."

He picked up the radio message and gave it a little shake. "The point being that this request—proposal, whatever you want to call it—has all the earmarks of a maneuver in that direction. A very bold maneuver, and if Ulrik pulls it off probably a brilliant one."

Jesse frowned. "John, I'm a thick-headed flyboy. You're leaving me behind in the dust."

"Jesse, you know and I know that the USE is on the brink of a constitutional crisis."

"That's putting it mildly. The term 'civil war' comes to mind also."

The admiral grimaced. "Let's hope we can avoid that. But whether we can or not, there's no question the domestic situation is going to erupt. What then happens if Princess Kristina—who is the heir to the USE .throne, even if she is only eight years old—decides to side with the . . . what to call them? Plebeians, let's say."

The air force colonel shook his head. "I'm *still* in a cloud of dust. How does coming here to Luebeck put her on the side of the lower classes? I presume that's what you mean by 'plebeians.'"

"Oh, I doubt very much if she—or Ulrik, more to

the point—plans to *stay* in Luebeck. The city is just a way station, where they can get themselves out of reach of Chancellor Oxenstierna while they figure out their next move. Which, if I'm guessing right, would be as dramatic as you could ask for. If things blow wide open, they'll go to Magdeburg."

"*Magdeburg?* John, if things blow wide open—your phrase, I remind you—then I'd think Magdeburg would be the last place they'd go. For Christ's sake, the city is a CoC stronghold."

Simpson just gave him a level stare. After a few seconds, Jesse's face got a little pale. "Jesus," he whispered. "Do you really think Ulrik is that much of a daredevil?"

The admiral shrugged. "It's not actually as risky as it seems. First of all, because the girl is quite popular in Magdeburg. She's sided with the Magdeburg masses twice already—that's how it looked to everyone, anyway. Once during the crisis right after the battle of Wismar, and again during Operation Krystalnacht. And while she was living in the city she not only visited the Freedom Arches regularly but on at least one occasion I know about she went into the kitchen and helped with the cooking." He smiled. "Of course, I doubt the cooks themselves found her that helpful, but you couldn't ask for better symbolism."

Again, Jesse ran fingers through his hair. "Okay, I can see that. You said 'first of all.' That implies a second reason. What is it?"

"Rebecca Abrabanel. That young woman has a spine of steel, don't ever think otherwise. If Kristina and Ulrik show up in Magdeburg, Rebecca will make damn good and sure no harm comes to them. Not to mention milking the situation for all it's worth, politically."

Jesse cocked his head a little. "That sounds almost admiring, John. None of my business, but I'd have thought you'd be more inclined toward this guy Scaglia's viewpoint than Becky and Mike's."

"In some ways, I am. Back home, I was a rock-ribbed Republican, although I didn't have much use for the so-called 'values' crowd. I certainly didn't have much use for the fundamentalists."

Jesse grinned. "Being, as you are, the closest thing Americans have to a High Church Anglican."

Simpson nodded. "Episcopalian, through and through. And Mary's a Unitarian, so you can just imagine her opinion of the Bible-thumpers. Still, I'm a conservative, by temperament as well as conviction. I admit I screwed up badly when we first came here, and since then I've generally sided with Mike Stearns. But he still often makes me uncomfortable and there's a lot I agree with in Scaglia's approach. On the other hand..."

He trailed off into silence.

Jesse cocked his head still further. "Yes?"

The admiral sighed. "I don't always trust Mike to do the right thing, but I do trust him to do *something*. And in the situation we're coming into, I think that willingness on his part to act may be the most critical factor. Whereas I don't see how Scaglia's gradualism is going to be much of a guide in the days ahead."

"To put it in my crude terms, you'll side with Mike."

"Not...exactly. I think what's going to happen is that Prime Minister Wettin is going to start breaking the law—the spirit of it, for damn sure—and then Mike will toss the rules overboard himself. Depending on the circumstances, I don't know that I'd take Mike's side. What I'm sure and certain of, though"—his face got stiff—"is that I'm damned if I'll do Oxenstierna's dirty work for him. And Oxenstierna's the one who driving all this, it's not Wettin."

Jesse looked at the radio message lying on the table. "So you'll tell her to come here."

"Yes. She'll be taking the *Union of Kalmar* across, so there's no way the Swedish navy could intercept her. I'll guarantee her the protection of the USE Navy while she's in Luebeck. I've had my legal staff look into the matter, and while there are a lot of gray areas involved, the one thing that's clear enough is that Wettin has no authority over the heir apparent. And Oxenstierna's regency—I'm assuming that's just a matter of time—would only have authority over her on Swedish soil."

Jesse smiled. "It occurs to me that Luebeck is not Swedish soil."

"No, it is not."

"It also occurs to me that if the navy wants to, it can pretty much hold Luebeck against all comers. For a few months, anyway."

"My own estimate is that we could hold it for at least a year, actually. It's hard to take a well-defended port city when you don't control the sea it fronts on. Not impossible, of course, but very difficult. It would help, though..."

Again, he trailed off into silence. Jesse's smile widened.

"It would help if you had air support. If you needed it. God forbid."

The admiral nodded solemnly. "God forbid."

"Well, God doesn't actually run the air force. I do. And I agree with you that our eight-year-old princess has the right to visit her own domains-to-be whenever she wants to, without interference from busybodies."

There was silence in the room. After a while, Simpson said, "The Ring of Fire seems like a long time ago, doesn't it?"

Chapter 9

Poznań, Poland

The grand hetman of Poland and Lithuania finished studying the enemy lines beyond the city's fortifications. From his expression, Lukasz Opalinski thought he wasn't very happy with what he saw. Not so much because of the enemy's lines, but because of his own. Poznań had begun the process of renovating its walls with the modern *trace italienne* design, but had not finished it when the USE launched its invasion of Poland. As usual, funds had been short and erratic. King Wladyslaw IV was a spendthrift and the Sejm was feckless.

Stanislaw Koniecpolski turned away, shaking his head. "Lucky for us the Swedish bastards are preoccupied with their own affairs for the moment."

Lukasz decided that gave him the opening he'd been waiting for. "As it happens, I just got a letter from Jozef yesterday. He thinks—"

The grand hetman waved a massive hand. "I know what my n-nephew thinks, young Opalinski." Koniecpolski suffered from stuttering, if he wasn't careful. "My l-letter from him arrived the day b-before yesterday.

I am w-willing to wager that if we m-matched the two letters, they're word-for-word alm-most the same."

The stuttering was much worse than usual. That was partly an indication of the grand hetman's anxiety, and partly—so Lukasz liked to think, anyway—because Koniecpolski had developed a great deal of trust in his young new adjutant. He was less careful about his speech impediment in the presence of close friends, relatives and associates.

The grant hetman tightened his lips and took a slow, deep breath. That was his method for bringing the stuttering under control. It usually worked, as it did this time.

"I might even agree with Jozef," Koniecpolski continued. "But it's not my decision, something which Wojtowicz tends to overlook."

Overlook wasn't really the right word. Lukasz had had many long political discussions with Jozef Wojtowicz over the past two years. The grand hetman's bastard nephew was disgusted with the state of Poland's political affairs. Actually, he'd been fed up with them since he was fourteen years old. But his experience as the grand hetman's spy in Grantville and later as the head of Koniecpolski's espionage apparatus in the USE had brought that teenage semi-inchoate discontent into sharp focus. The reason Jozef kept urging courses of action on his powerful uncle was not because he "overlooked" the legal formalities but because he no longer cared much about them and had no confidence at all in either the king or in the Sejm.

Neither did Lukasz, for that matter. He wasn't prepared to go so far as his older brother Krzysztof, who had become an outright revolutionary and was off somewhere in the Ruthenian lands agitating for the overthrow of Poland's monarchy and aristocracy. Like Jozef Wojtowicz, Lukasz was still seeking a way to reform the government of the Polish and Lithuanian commonwealth.

But he was growing less and less sanguine about the prospects for doing so, as each month passed. He'd come to the point where he'd even prefer some sort of outright autocracy, if the autocrat was competent and decisive and would cut the Gordian knot of Polish and Lithuanian politics. He knew Jozef had come to that same conclusion months earlier.

There was only one realistic candidate for the position of Poland and Lithuania's dictator, however, and that was the man Lukasz was standing beside this very moment. Unfortunately—at least, under these circumstances—Grand Hetman Stanislaw Koniecpolski was a staunch adherent to legality. Whatever he thought of the Sejm or the king, he kept to himself. And while the grand hetman was quite willing to extend his authority as far as the legal parameters allowed, he was not willing to go an inch beyond those limits.

He never had been, and Lukasz was now certain he never would be. Poland's top military commander might have a supple mind on the battlefield or when it came to military affairs, but he was rigid when it came to Poland's laws and political traditions. Had he still been a young man, perhaps that might be subject to change. But Stanislaw Koniecpolski was now in his forties. Early forties, true, but forties nonetheless. Not many very successful men were willing, at that age, to call into question their basic political and social attitudes. The grand hetman was no exception.

Lukasz decided there wasn't any point in pursuing the matter. Koniecpolski would just get irritated. So, he let his eyes drift toward the fieldworks being put up by the army now besieging Poznań.

It was probably the best army in the world, leaving aside cavalry. The USE regular army's first and second divisions, under the command of Lennart Torstensson. The third division was somewhere in Bohemia, according to Jozef's reports. The American Mike Stearns was in command of that division.

The soldiers in those lines outside Poznań were not the polyglot mercenaries you found in the ranks of most European armies in the seventeenth century. Nor were many of them noblemen, as was true of the Polish military. The enlisted men were mostly Germans and almost all were commoners, volunteers driven more by ideological than pecuniary motives. They had the best military equipment in the world, thanks to the Americans, and the training to use it.

A sound from above drew his eyes to the sky. One of the USE's airplanes had arrived, taking advantage of the recent good weather. It would probably drop a few bombs on the city's walls, which wouldn't do any real damage except to morale. But the blasted things gave Torstensson superb reconnaissance, so long as the weather was good. Polish armies could no longer maneuver as they were accustomed to doing, using the speed of their powerful cavalry to confuse their opponents. In good weather, they were always under observation; in bad weather, slowed by the weather itself. They were reduced to fighting what amounted to an infantry war, something at which the USE army excelled and they did not.

One siege after another. A Dutch style of war, not a Polish one.

Yet, the same thing that gave the USE's army so much of its strength could also be its Achilles' heel. Those soldiers out there were heavily influenced by the radical Committees of Correspondence. Given the recent political developments in the USE, there was a very real chance that they might mutiny and turn their guns against their own rulers rather than Poland and Lithuania.

But they would be far less likely to mutiny so long as they were fighting a war. Their commander Torstensson was popular with his soldiers and could probably maintain discipline—provided the war continued and his army remained in Poland, and provided that his civilian superiors were not so reckless as to try to use his regular army divisions against the USE's own population.

That was exactly why Jozef Wojtowicz was urging his uncle to make peace with the USE. If necessary to get that peace, even give up the territory that Gustav Adolf had already seized before he was so severely wounded at Lake Bledno that his chancellor Oxenstierna was now managing Sweden's affairs. Those territories were only marginally Polish to begin with. Most of the population of most of the towns the USE had seized were German, not Polish.

So let the USE have them—and let Oxenstierna try to deal with an angry army coming back home, most of whose soldiers despised him and weren't much fonder of the USE's own prime minister. In all likelihood, the USE would dissolve into civil war.

Such a war wouldn't last forever, of course. It was possible that the victor, whoever that might be, would then want to resume the USE's aggression against Poland. But they'd have been weakened and, more important, Poland and Lithuania would have gained the time it needed to modernize its own military. The commonwealth didn't have the industrial base the USE possessed, but it wasn't backward and primitive Muscovy, either. With time, effort and determination, they could build a military capable of meeting the USE's on more or less equal terms.

But as always, the king and the Sejm were being pigheaded.

The damned Swedes had invaded—again!

To arms! To arms! No surrender, no retreat, no compromise!

And never mind that the king would continue to be a wastrel, showering money on his whores instead of his soldiers. Never mind that the Sejm would be miserly with its money and profligate with its factionalism. Never mind that the great magnates would keep their powerful private armies at home to fend off rivals instead of sending them to the front. Never mind that the szlachta would guard their petty privileges far more assiduously than they would guard the commonwealth's national interests.

Lukasz sighed, gave the plane circling overhead an angry glance, and turned away to follow the grand hetman.

Less than a mile away, Lieutenant General Lennart Torstensson lowered his eyeglasses. The up-time binoculars had been given to him by Mike Stearns after the Magdeburg Crisis that followed the battle of Wismar. Stearns had given no specific reason for the gift, but

Lennart was sure it was in appreciation for his restraint during that episode. Had he followed the advice of most of his subordinates—and just about every nobleman residing in the city at the time—there'd have been a bloodbath; which, in turn, would have precipitated a far greater political crisis. Instead, he'd kept his troops in their barracks and let Stearns and his associates settle things down with almost no violence at all.

That same conduct on his part had gotten him a far greater gift than a pair of binoculars from his monarch. Gustav Adolf had valued Lennart for his military abilities for some time already. But it wasn't until he saw how Torstensson handled the Magdeburg Crisis that the Swedish king gave him his full political confidence. Lennart's greatest military triumph had been the battle of Ahrensbök, but he never would have been leading the army that won that great victory if he hadn't already shown Gustav Adolf he could be trusted with a fully independent command.

Still, modest though they might be in some terms, he treasured the binoculars. Not so much for the ability to see so well at a distance, but because in some indefinable way they made it easier for Torstensson to accept what he saw and make decisions based on it. A down-time eyeglass left things . . . murkier.

As murky as the orders he kept getting from Prime Minister Wettin, which he suspected were really coming from the chancellor of Sweden. As he slid the binoculars into their case, Torstensson's jaw tightened. The respect and admiration he had long felt for Axel Oxenstierna was slipping away from him; as each week passed, more and more rapidly—and even more rapidly, his respect for Wilhelm Wettin.

He could accept Oxenstierna's near-fanatical devotion to aristocratic interests, and could accept Wettin's preoccupation with political tactics at the expense of strategic vision. Grudgingly, but he could accept them.

What he could not accept was their willingness to use his soldiers as pawns in their game; their willingness to throw away lives—a great number of lives—purely for the sake of advancing their factional interests. That was what was draining away his respect, and stoking his growing anger.

"No," he said, speaking aloud but only to himself. His nearest aide was standing ten feet away, not close enough to hear the softly growled word.

He was *not* going to order a mass assault on Poznań's walls. Those defenses might not be up to the standards of a completed star fort, bristling with a full complement of bastions and ravelins and hornworks and crownworks, but neither were they—to use terms from Wettin's last radio message—"hopelessly antiquated" and "medieval."

Even if they had been, such an assault would still be a bloody, bloody business. Stanislaw Koniecpolski was in personal command of Poznań's defending army and he had at least ten thousand hussars at his disposal. Polish hussars might be primarily known for their prowess as heavy cavalry, but they were tough bastards under any circumstances and in any situation.

As it was, a direct mass assault would be futile as well as bloody. It would take months before Torstensson's artillery had done enough damage to Poznań's defenses to make any such assault feasible in realistic military terms.

Wettin might or might not know that himself. He had some military experience, though nothing like the experience of his younger brother Bernhard, who was an accomplished general in his own right.

As was Oxenstierna, who most certainly *did* know the price Torstensson's army would pay for such an assault. Knew—and wanted the assault for that very reason. Oxenstierna was afraid of the USE's army, because he couldn't trust its soldiers to obey orders when he launched the counterrevolution he was so obviously preparing. So, he'd sent Stearns and his Third Division down to Bohemia and was keeping Torstensson and the other two divisions in Poland.

The orders were officially coming from Wettin, of course, since Oxenstierna had no legal authority over Lennart's forces. He was Sweden's chancellor, not the USE's. But Torstensson was quite sure that Oxenstierna's was the driving will in Berlin.

To hell with them. Lennart was fond of that up-time expression, even if some Lutheran pastors thought it perilously close to outright blasphemy. Wettin and Oxenstierna could send as many scolding messages as they wanted. They couldn't force him to do their bidding unless they relieved him from command—and that would be far too risky.

What if he refused? Indeed, what if he led his army back into the Germanies and went knocking on Berlin's gates?

Who would stop him? Torstensson's two divisions were as numerous as the Swedish mercenary forces the chancellor had at his disposal in Berlin, better trained, and far better equipped. They were veterans, too, and their morale would be splendid if Torstensson led them against Oxenstierna and Wettin.

As it happened, Lennart had no intention of doing

any such thing. Until the situation with Gustav Adolf became clarified, he would remain strictly within legal bounds. But Oxenstierna couldn't be sure of that.

Even if he were, what then? The discipline that held the First and Second Division in check was shaky already. If the chancellor removed Torstensson and replaced him with a new commander, there was a very real chance—a likelihood, in fact, in Lennart's own estimation—that the army would mutiny and march on Berlin anyway.

True, they'd be easier to defeat if their leadership was informal and hastily assembled, than if they still had Torstensson in command. But not *that* much easier. At the very least, they'd bleed Oxenstierna's forces badly—right at the moment he needed them most to deal with an increasingly restive populace.

No. Oxenstierna and Wettin would growl and scold and complain—possibly even shriek with fury, from time to time—but they wouldn't do any more than that. Torstensson's men would stay in the trenches. They'd suffer badly anyway, as soldiers always did in winter sieges. But there wouldn't be the butcher's bill that a mass assault would produce.

He glanced at the sun, which was nearing the horizon. Nothing more to be done this day. There wouldn't be much to do, beyond routine, for many days to come.

Later that night, after supper, Torstensson retired to his quarters in the tavern of a village he'd seized not far from Poznań. Before going to bed, he lit a lantern and resumed reading the book that had arrived from Amsterdam earlier that week.

Political Methods and the Laws of Nations, by Alessandro Scaglia. The book was one of a very limited edition, intended only for private circulation. Lennart had received it as a gift from the author himself, with a hand-written flowery dedication and signature on the frontispiece.

He was a little more than halfway through, and found the book quite absorbing.

Part Two

December 1635

Unequal laws unto a savage race

Chapter 10

Prague, capital of Bohemia

After he entered the huge salon that served Morris and Judith Roth for what Americans left back up-time would have called a living room on steroids, Mike Stearns spent half a minute or so examining the room. No casual inspection, either—this was a careful scrutiny that lingered on nothing but didn't miss any significant detail.

By the time he was finished, his hosts had seated themselves on a luxurious divan located toward the center of the room and the servants had withdrawn at Judith's signal, giving them some privacy.

Morris had a pained expression on his face. "Go ahead. Make the wisecracks about the *nouveau riche* so we can be done with it."

Mike took a last few seconds to finish his examination and then took a seat on an armchair across from his hosts.

"Actually, I was going to compliment you on your judgment," he said. "God help me for my sins, but I've become an expert on gauging ostentation, the proper degree thereof. I'd say"—he raised his hand and made a circular motion with his forefinger—"you've hit this just about right. Splendid enough to cement your position with the city's Jewish population and satisfy any gentile grandee who happens to pop over that you're a man to be taken seriously, but not so immodest as to stir up the animosity of those same gentiles."

Morris grunted. "The second reason's less important than the first. The only gentile grandee who pops over here on a regular basis is Pappenheim."

Judith winced. "Puh-leese don't use that expression in front of him, either one of you. The man has a sense of humor—pretty good one, in fact, if you allow for the rough edges—but it only extends so far, when it comes to himself. General Gottfried Heinrich Graf zu Pappenheim does *not* 'pop over.' He visits, with grace and style."

Morris and Mike both smiled. Then Morris added, "The point being, Pappenheim's the only important gentile figure in Bohemia who's ever been over here and most of what's in these public rooms is stuff that means nothing to him."

He pointed to a series of etchings on one of the walls. Morris and Judith were the subjects of three of them, two separately and one as a couple. Mike didn't recognize any of the other people portrayed, but from subtleties of their costume he thought they were probably other prominent figures in Prague's very large Jewish community.

"Those are all by Václav Hollar," Morris said. "He was born and raised here, but then moved to Cologne. Judith sweet-talked him into coming back with the offer of a number of commissions."

Mike shook his head. "Never heard of him."

"He became well enough known that there's a brief mention of him in my records," Judith said. She was referring to the files on her computer. Before the Ring of Fire, Judith's interest in her family's genealogy had led her to compile quite a bit of information from the internet on Prague's Jewish community during the seventeenth century. Her ancestors had come from here. One of them, in fact, had been the famous rabbi known as the Maharal, Judah Loew ben Bezalel, whom legend said invented the golem.

"But that happened years from now in our old timeline," Judith went on, "after he moved to England. In the here and now, he's too young to be famous. Which is a good part of the reason I wanted him. You're right that it can be a bit dangerous—might be more than a bit, under some circumstances—for Jews to be too ostentatious."

Morris shrugged. "What I was getting at, though, was that we could have commissioned Rubens or Rembrandt to do those portraits and Pappenheim wouldn't have known the difference."

"Rubens and Rembrandt wouldn't have come anyway," said Judith, "but if they had you can be sure that Wallenstein would have known about it—and he *does* know who they are."

"Speaking of Wallenstein..." Mike's expression had no humor left in it. "He doesn't look good. At all."

Mike had just come from a meeting with Wallenstein. This had been a private meeting, unlike the formal and well-attended affair that had been held a week earlier when the Third Division arrived in the city.

In the intervening week, Mike had been busy seeing to the needs of his soldiers. They'd set up a temporary camp just south of the horse market that would eventually become Wenceslaus Square in another universe. Still, he hadn't been *that* busy. He had an excellent staff and most of the work was routine. So he'd expected to be summoned to Wallenstein's palace within a day or two after the division's arrival and had been a little surprised by the long delay.

He'd assumed the delay was just petty maneuvering by the king of Bohemia; the same sort of *let-him-cool-his-heels-in-the-anteroom* silliness that was such a frequent part of office politics up-time. But when Mike had finally been ushered into Wallenstein's presence, he'd realized the more likely cause was the king's health. To use one of his mother's expressions, Wallenstein looked like death warmed over. They'd met in his bedroom, because the king could barely manage to sit up. His American nurse Edith Wild had him propped up on pillows in his bed and fussed over him the whole time Mike was there except for the quarter of an hour Wallenstein had shooed her away so he could discuss the most delicate matters with his visitor in private.

Those delicate matters had involved Mike's somewhat eccentric logistical requests and proposals. "Eccentric" being the discreet way of describing the creation of a string of supply depots that made very little sense for an army that was planning to take up positions near the southern Czech city of České Budějovice in order to bolster Bohemia's position against Austria. Whatever might be the state of his physical health, there was clearly nothing wrong with Wallenstein's brain. Before his self-elevation to the throne of Bohemia, the man had been one of the premier military contractors of Europe. He understood perfectly well that what Mike was setting up was the necessary supply chain in case he had to leave Bohemia in a hurry in order to take his army back into Saxony.

It hadn't taken the king long to make clear that he had no objection. Obviously, Wallenstein understood that the main reason Mike and his Third Division had been sent to Bohemia was to get him out of the USE for political reasons, not to satisfy Wallenstein's request for military support.

"Meaning no offense, Michael," the king had rasped, "but I don't need foot soldiers—nor did I ask for them. What I could use, and did ask for, was air support so I could keep an eye on Austrian troop movements."

He shifted uncomfortably in his bed. "Which I didn't get, even though I've built two of the best airfields in Europe—one right here in Prague, the other in České Budějovice. And now I don't have the use of the Jew's plane either, since his idiot pilot crashed the thing in Dresden. Your man Nasi tells me it'll be months before the plane is repaired and able to fly again."

Mike saw no point in arguing the matter of whether or not Francisco Nasi was "his man." In some ways, that description was still accurate, he supposed. His former spymaster was now operating his own independent business as what amounted to a contract espionage agency, but he'd made clear to Mike that he would be glad to provide him whatever assistance he could. Given that Francisco was now residing in Prague himself, Mike had every intention of taking him up on the offer. He'd already met with him twice, in fact, since he arrived the week before.

"I may be able to assist you there," he said. "I'm having an airfield built in Děčín"—he used the Czech pronunciation for Tetschen—"to provide air support for Colonel Higgins and his regiment, in the event Holk launches a surprise attack."

Both he and Wallenstein maintained completely straight faces. Perhaps Mike rushed the next sentence just a little bit.

"But I see no reason that whatever plane Colonel Wood can free up from the air force to come down here can't also overfly the Austrian lines."

Wallenstein had been satisfied with that, and no further mention was made of Mike's convoluted logistics. The king had wrung the little bell next to his bed and Edith had practically rushed back into the room. She'd become quite devoted to the man, by all accounts—which included gunning down the assassins who'd tried to murder Wallenstein shortly before he seized power, in addition to tending to his medical needs.

"Edith thinks he's dying, Mike," said Judith. "Wallenstein just won't listen to her medical advice."

"God-damned astrologers were bad enough," Morris growled. "Now he's got these new Kirlian aura screwballs whispering in his ear."

Mike cocked his head quizzically. "*Which* screwballs? I can't keep track of all these seventeenth-century superstitions."

"I'm afraid this one's our doing, Mike," said Judith. "It's based on Kirlian photography, which was developed up-time. Nobody in Grantville ever took seriously the idea that Kirlian images showed a person's life force—the 'aura,' to use the lingo. Unfortunately,

Dr. Gribbleflotz stumbled across some references to it in one of the Grantville libraries and..."

"The rest was a foregone conclusion," said Morris.

Herr Doctor Phillip Theophrastus Gribbleflotz—a great-grandson of Paracelsus, as he never tired of reminding people—was an alchemist who had an uncanny knack for reinterpreting up-time science in a down-time framework, and making a bundle of money in the process. He'd made his first fortune with baking soda, which he renamed Sal Aer Fixus. A little later he'd made aspirin, which he dyed blue on the grounds that blue was the color of serenity. Much to Tom Stone's disgust, Dr. Gribbleflotz's brand had outsold the straightforward stuff produced by Stone's pharmaceutical works. Eventually, when his father got distracted by something else, Ron Stone quietly ordered the chemists to start dying their own aspirin blue as well. Sales picked up right away.

"Don't tell me," Mike chuckled.

"Yep," said Morris. "Before you could say 'hogwash,' Gribbleflotz had half the nobility in the Germanies and Bohemia hooked on the notion, seems like. He charges a small fortune to show someone his so-called 'aura,' and then...well..."

He drifted into an uncomfortable silence. His wife gave him a glance and smiled. "What Morris isn't telling you is that we're making quite a bit of money from the side effects."

"How so?"

Morris made a face. "Somehow or other—I didn't do it, I swear I didn't, and neither did Tom Stone— people got the idea that once someone knew their Kirlian aura they needed to complement it with the proper costume and jewelry. So all of a sudden there's a booming demand for exotic dyes and exotic gem-cuts. Tom's dye works supplies most of the former and my jewelry makers provide most of the latter."

Mike didn't say anything. He didn't doubt for a moment that neither Morris nor Tom Stone had tried to take advantage of the new superstition. Tom's middle son Ron, though . . .

Ron Stone had become the de facto manager of the Stone chemical and pharmaceutical industries, and had turned out to have an unexpected gift for making money. That talent hadn't been hurt in the least by his recent marriage to Missy Jenkins, whose father had been one of Grantville's most successful businessmen before the Ring of Fire. Missy's own interest was in libraries, but the young woman had a practical streak about as wide as the Mississippi river. Between the two of them, they might very well have come up with the idea of piggybacking a new line of exotic dyes on the Kirlian craze, and quietly hired someone to do the necessary promotion.

If they had, Mike didn't object. Down-time noble-men could find the silliest ways imaginable to waste their money, and this one seemed reasonably harmless.

True, it wasn't doing Wallenstein any good. But that was a lost cause, anyway. The king of Bohemia had been proving for years that no matter how shrewd he was in most respects, he was a sucker for supersti-tious twaddle. That was especially true when it came to anything bearing on his health. Whatever nostrums he was getting from his new obsession with Kirlian auras, Mike figured it couldn't be any worse than the medical advice he got from his astrologers.

He said as much, and the Roths both nodded.

"Edith actually prefers the Kirlian crap," said Morris. "It mostly just leads to the king loading himself down with jewelry—which he can certainly afford—and overheating himself in bed because of the heavy robes he wears. But at least he's not bleeding himself under the light of a full moon when Sagittarius is rising in Venus."

"I think it's the other way around," said Judith.

Morris sniffed. "Who cares?"

If Wallenstein really was that ill...

"What happens if he dies?" Mike asked.

Morris and Judith looked at each other. "Well..." said Judith. "I don't think it'll be too bad."

"A year ago, things would have probably gotten pretty hairy," her husband added. "But Wallenstein's wife finally bore him a son this past February. Karl Albrecht Eusebius is his name. The kid's pretty healthy and thankfully his mother ignores Wallenstein and listens to Edith when it comes to his medical care."

Mike had known of the boy's birth, but he hadn't really considered all the political ramifications. In light of what he now knew about Wallenstein's health, he started to do so and almost immediately came to the critical issue.

"How does Pappenheim feel about the kid?"

The expressions on the faces of his host were identical: relief. Vast relief, you might almost say.

"Gottfried is devoted to Wallenstein," Morris said, "and the man really seems to have no political ambitions of his own."

"So far as we can tell, anyway," Judith cautioned.

Morris shrugged. "You never really know until the

time comes, of course. But I really do think Pappenheim will be satisfied with remaining the commander of Bohemia's army—so long as he thinks there's no danger to Wallenstein's legitimate heir."

Mike nodded. "So the task becomes making sure a stable regency gets set up right away. How will Isabella Katharina handle that? I've met the queen, but I can't say I know her at all."

"Isabella's not interested in politics herself," said Judith. "All she'll really care about is that her son is safe and his inheritance is secure. She'll be happy as the figurehead of a regency council, as long as we're getting along with Gottfried and the rest of the council is solid."

"I take it she's not an anti-Semite, then?"

Morris shook his head. "She tends to be suspicious of most people, but she's what you might call an equal-opportunity bigot. Jews aren't worth much, in her book, but then neither are goyim."

"She and I have become a bit close, actually," said Judith. "And Isabella practically worships the ground under Edith's feet—and we're about the only friends Edith has in the whole world."

Edith Wild had been friendless most of her life. The big woman was taciturn and had a harsh personality. She was one of the people in Grantville for whom the Ring of Fire had proved to be a blessing. She'd gone from being a factory worker scraping by to living in a palace as a king's nurse and one of the closest confidants of his queen.

Mike had taken off his officer's hat when he entered the Roth's mansion, and had it perched on his lap. Now he rose and placed it back on his head.

"I need to get back to the division," he said. "But I can return the day after tomorrow, if you'd like me to."

Morris rose to usher him out. "Yes, I would. And I know Gottfried would like to have a private word with you also. Can I tell him you'll come by his headquarters?"

"Yes, please do." Mike had his own reasons for wanting to stay on good terms with Bohemia's leading general. But those reasons were almost petty compared to the importance of keeping Bohemia stable and friendly to the USE.

There were enough wars already, he figured.

Chapter 11

Berlin

The applause of the crowd gathered in the assembly hall could be heard all the way across the palace. Colonel Erik Haakansson Hand paused at the entrance to the emperor's rooms in order to listen for a moment.

He couldn't quite make out the slogans being chanted by the mob, but he didn't need to. He'd heard enough—more than enough—from the noblemen and urban patricians who'd been pouring into Berlin for the past month to know their complaints, grievances and proposed remedies. Stripped of the curlicues, they were simple enough:

Restore the upper classes to their rightful place in the Germanies.

Abase the pretensions to citizenship of the low orders.

Discipline the common citizenry.

Restore religious stability. (The exact prescriptions involved varied between Lutherans and Calvinists and Catholics, but they all wanted an end to chaos.)

Above all, crush the Committees of Correspondence.

Notably absent from the list were any anti-Semitic proposals. The hammer blows delivered on organized anti-Semitism by the CoCs during Operation Krystalnacht had effectively destroyed that variety of reaction. Sooner or later it would come back, of course; if for no other reason, because of the prominence of Mike Stearns' Jewish wife in the political affairs of the United States of Europe. But for the moment, the Jew-baiters were silent.

Taking each proposition on its own merits, Hand was sympathetic to some of them. As a member of Sweden's Vasa dynasty—a bastard member, but a member nonetheless; even one in good standing—he was hardly an ally of Gretchen Richter and her cohorts. But taking the program as a whole, as Oxenstierna was driving it forward, the colonel thought it bordered on lunacy.

Whether it did or not, however, he was sure of one thing: if Gustav Adolf still had his wits about him, none of this would be happening. The king of Sweden had his differences with Mike Stearns, and even larger differences with the Committees of Correspondence. But Erik had spoken with Gustav Adolf at length in times past and knew that his cousin viewed the compromises he'd made to become emperor of the USE as necessary parts of the bargain—a bargain that had made him the most powerful ruler in Europe.

What could Oxenstierna possibly hope to gain that would be worth the cost? Even if he triumphed in the civil war he was instigating, the USE that emerged would be far weaker than the one that currently existed. If for no other reason, because his triumph would necessitate abasing the Americans as well as the

CoCs—and what did the damn fool chancellor think would happen *then*? Any American with any skills at all could get himself—herself, even—employed almost anywhere in Europe. The technical wizardry and mechanical ingenuity that had heretofore bolstered the position of the Vasa dynasty would soon become buttresses for the Habsburgs, the Bourbons, and most of the continent's lesser houses as well.

The colonel opened the door, entered the emperor's suite and passed through the outer rooms until he reached the bedroom. But Oxenstierna simply didn't care, Hand had concluded. The man was so obsessed with restoring aristocratic dominance that he ignored the inevitable consequences if he succeeded.

The same was not true, however, of Hand himself— much less the man lying on the bed before him.

Gustav Adolf raised his head and looked up when he entered. The king's blue eyes seemed perhaps a bit clearer today.

"Where is Kristina?" he asked.

Startled, Hand glanced at Erling Ljungberg. The big bodyguard shrugged. "Don't know if it means anything," he said. "But starting yesterday he began saying stuff that makes sense, now and then. Doesn't last more than a sentence or two, though."

Erik looked back down at his cousin. Gustav Adolf was still watching him.

"Why is my daughter rowing violets?" The king's brows were furrowed.

Puzzled? Angry? It was impossible to tell.

"Under a kitchen some antlers jumped," he continued. Clearly, the moment of coherence—if that's what it had been at all—was over.

"Your tailor went thatch and flung," said Gustav Adolf. Then he closed his eyes and seemed to fall asleep.

Erik placed a hand on the king's shoulder. The thick muscle was still there, at least. Physically, his cousin had largely recovered from his injuries at the battle of Lake Bledno. If only his mind . . .

He gave his head a little shake. No point in dwelling on that.

A particularly loud roar from the distant assembly hall penetrated the room. Ljungberg glanced in that direction and scowled slightly.

"Assholes," he muttered.

That was the first indication Hand had ever gotten that the king's new bodyguard wasn't entirely pleased with the new dispensation. Ljungberg was normally as taciturn as a doorpost.

He decided to risk pursuing the matter. "Your loyalty is entirely to the king, I take it?"

The bodyguard gave him a look from under lowered brows. "The Vasas always sided with the common folk," Ljungberg said. He nodded toward Gustav Adolf. "Him too, even if he did give the chancellor and his people most of what they wanted."

Gustav Adolf's father had died when he was only seventeen—too young, legally, to inherit the throne without a regent. Axel Oxenstierna, the leader of Sweden's noblemen, had supported Gustav Adolf's ascension to the throne in exchange for concessions that restored much of the nobility's power taken away by the new king's grandfather, who had founded the Vasa dynasty.

"So they did," said Hand. "And will again, if my cousin recovers."

For a moment, the two men stared at each other. Then Ljungberg looked away. "I'm the king's man. No other."

"And I as well," said Erik.

A good day's work, he thought. Best to leave things as they were, though, rather than rushing matters. Nothing could be done anyway unless Gustav Adolf regained his senses.

Linz, Austria

Janos Drugeth finished rereading the letter from Noelle Stull.

He was not a happy man. Rather, his feelings were mixed. The very evident warmth of the letter pleased him greatly, of course. But what had possessed the woman to go to Dresden?

True, this was the same woman who had once emptied her pistol by firing into the Danube, in a moment of pique. But even for Noelle, this was incredibly rash.

Janos was not privy to most of the details, of course. But one of his duties was to monitor Austria's espionage network and he received regular reports from his spymasters. So he knew that the Swedish general Johan Banér was marching into Saxony and would soon be at the gates of Dresden—and that Gretchen Richter had taken up residence in the city.

Given Richter's nature—still more, given Banér's—the result was a foregone conclusion. Dresden was about to become a city under siege, and if Banér broke into the city there would most likely be a bloodbath. The

Swedish general wasn't as purely brutish as Heinrich Holk, but he came fairly close. And, unlike Holk, Banér was a very competent commander.

Janos was no stranger to sieges, from either side of the walls. He didn't think there was much chance that amateur hotheads like Richter could hold Dresden against the likes of Banér and his mercenaries.

True, the woman had managed the defenses of Amsterdam quite well, by all accounts. But Janos was sure that a large factor involved had been the cardinal-infante's unwillingness to risk destroying Amsterdam and thereby losing its resources and skilled workers. Banér would have no such compunctions at Dresden.

What was Noelle *thinking*?

He sighed, and put aside the letter. There was another letter in the batch that had just arrived, and this one came from his monarch. By rights, he should have read it first. But he'd been in the privacy of his own chambers in the army's headquarters at Linz, so his personal concerns had momentarily overridden his duty.

When he unsealed the letter, he discovered nothing but a short message:

> *Come to Vienna at once. The Turks have taken Baghdad.*
>
> > Ferdinand

Drugeth rose and strode to the door, moving so quickly that a servant barely opened the door in time. "My horse!" he bellowed.

Noelle would have to wait. For the first time in his life, Janos Drugeth found himself in the preposterous position of hoping that a notorious malcontent like Richter was indeed a capable military commander. Such was the strange world produced by the Ring of Fire.

Bamberg, capital of the State of Thuringia-Franconia

Ed Piazza still hadn't gotten used to down-time desks. The blasted things were *tiny*—what he thought of as a lady's writing desk, not the reasonably-sized pieces of furniture that a man could use to get some work done. For about the hundredth time since he'd moved to Bamberg—no, make that the thousandth time—he found himself wishing he still had the desk from his study in Grantville.

Unfortunately, when he and Annabelle sold their house they'd sold all the furniture with it. And when Ed had inquired as to whether the down-timer who'd bought the house might be willing to let him have the desk back, the answer had been an unequivocal "no." The new owner was a young nobleman with a nice income and a firm conviction that literary greatness would soon be his—especially with the help of such a magnificently expansive desk to work on.

True enough, Ed and Annabelle had gotten a small fortune for their house. Real estate prices in Grantville were now astronomical. With a small portion of that money he could easily afford to have the sort of desk he wanted custom-made for him—and, indeed, he'd commissioned the work quite a while ago. Alas, down-time furniture makers in Bamberg were artisans. *Medieval* artisans, from what Ed could tell, for whom timely delivery of a commissioned work came a very long way second to craftsmanship. They seemed to measure time in feast days, nones and matins, not workdays, hours and minutes.

So, he suffered at his miniature desk. At least it was the modern style, by seventeenth-century values of "modern." That meant he could sit at it, instead of standing at the more traditional lectern type of desk.

A good, thing, too, given how long today's meeting had gone on. The only people Ed had ever encountered who rivaled theologians disputing fine points of doctrine were soldiers wrangling over fine points of logistics.

"The gist of it," he said, trying not to sound impatient, "is that you're confident you can supply our soldiers in the event we have to send them down to the Oberpfalz."

He almost burst into laughter, seeing the expressions on the faces of the three officers in the room. Horror combined with outrage, muted by the need to keep a civilian superior from realizing his military commanders thought he was a nincompoop. Much the sort of look he saw on the faces of his son and daughter whenever he made so bold as to advise them on matters of teenage protocol.

Naturally, as with his children, the reaction was due to the precise formulation of his statement rather than the content of the statement itself.

"I wouldn't go so far as to use the term 'confident,' sir," demurred Major Tom Simpson.

"Indeed not," concurred his immediate superior, Colonel Friedrich Engels.

The third officer present was General Heinrich

Schmidt. "We do not *lack* confidence, certainly, but I think it would be more accurate to say that we are reasonably assured of the matter," was his judicious contribution.

Theologians, soldiers and teenagers—who would have guessed they shared such a close kinship? But Ed Piazza kept the observation to himself. Taken each on his own, all three of the officers in the room had good senses of humor. But they were quite young for their ranks and in the case of two of them, Schmidt and Engels, newly promoted to boot. Like Ed's son and daughter, they would be hypersensitive to anything that sounded like criticism coming from him, especially if it sounded derisive or sarcastic.

Besides, it didn't matter. Stripped of their fussiness over terminology, it was clear that the three officers were . . . call it "relaxed," that they could keep their troops provisioned in case war with Bavaria broke out again in the Upper Palatinate.

That was really all that Ed cared about. Like many able-bodied West Virginia males of his generation, he was a Vietnam veteran. He'd seen a fair amount of combat too, since he'd been in the 1st Brigade of the 5th Mechanized Division and had taken part in the Cambodia incursion in 1970. But he'd been an enlisted man swept up by the draft, with no more interest in military affairs than he needed to stay alive and get back home. Now in his mid-fifties with the adult life experience of someone who'd worked in education, he made no pretense of being able to second-guess his commanding officers, much less be a backseat driver.

If they said they were "reasonably assured" of their preparedness, that was good enough for him.

"We may never come to it anyway," said Tom.

Engels shook his head. "That Bavarian shithead will jump on us with both boots if he sees a chance. Duke Maximilian's the worst of a bad lot—and that's saying something, when you're talking about Hochadel."

Hochadel was the German term for the upper nobility, the small elite crust—no more than a few dozen families—who lorded it over the much more numerous lower nobility, the *Niederadel*. Engels came from the fringes of that Niederadel class, but he'd adopted the radical attitudes of the CoCs, most of whose members were commoners.

How much of Engels' political viewpoint stemmed from serious consideration of the issues themselves was unclear. Tom Simpson had once told Ed that he thought his commanding officer was just tickled pink—tickled red, rather—when he discovered he had exactly the same name as the very famous close friend and associate of Karl Marx in another universe.

"That 'more revolutionary than thou' act on Fred's part is mostly for show," Tom had said. "The truth is that he's a professional soldier and doesn't really think that much about politics. He sure as hell doesn't read any political tracts. Although"—the huge American major grinned—"he was mightily pleased when I gave him a copy of his namesake's *Socialism: Utopian and Scientific* for his birthday."

"Where in God's name did you get *that* book? I didn't know any of our libraries had a copy."

"They wouldn't have sold it to me even if they had," pointed out Tom. He was still grinning. "From Melissa, who else? The book's more in the way of a pamphlet, actually, and she had a stack of them in her basement. Well, *did* have a stack. She says she gave most of them to Red Sybolt before he left for Poland."

Ed rolled his eyes. The thought of Red Sybolt—before the Ring of Fire, Marion County's most notorious labor organizer—loose in Poland with a pile of flaming socialist pamphlets was . . .

Well, rather charming, actually. By all accounts, Poland's aristocracy could stand to have its feet held to the fire.

"Don't fool yourself, Tom," said Heinrich Schmidt, after they left the SoTF president's office. "Leaving aside the great Murphy's principles, Colonel Engels has the right of it. Maximilian has not forgiven us for taking Ingolstadt from him. If a civil war breaks out in the USE, he will surely try to take it back."

Sardonic as always, Schmidt gave the two USE officers a half-jeer. "At which point, the two of you will have to hold the bastard off with your one little regiment while I"—his chest came out, in a parody of self-importance—"marshal the mighty forces of the SoTF to come to your rescue."

Unlike Simpson and Engels, in their field-gray USE uniforms, Heinrich Schmidt was wearing the blue uniform of the State of Thuringia-Franconia's National Guard. He'd transferred from the USE army a year earlier when Ed Piazza had waved a brigadier's star under his nose as an enticement.

Schmidt wasn't the National Guard's commander. That was Cliff Priest, who'd been the military administrator for Bamberg before the SoTF's capital was moved there from Grantville. There'd been a vague, lingering sentiment, given the peculiar history of the province, that the formal commander of the National Guard—it had even been named after its up-time counterparts—should continue to be an American. So Priest, whom everyone agreed was a good administrator, got the title. But it was privately understood that operational control of the soldiers and combat leadership would be provided by the top down-time officers. Those were Heinrich Schmidt and Hartman Menninger, each of whom commanded a brigade.

In the event hostilities broke out with Bavaria in the Oberpfalz again, Schmidt would march there immediately with his entire brigade. He'd be joined by one of the regiments from Menninger's 1st Brigade, the 3rd Regiment, stationed in Eichstätt. (The SoTF National Guard didn't have the USE army's custom of naming regiments.) Brigadier Menninger would stay behind in order to protect the SoTF and maintain order with his two remaining regiments.

Like all such plans, neither Heinrich nor Tom expected it to last long once contact with the enemy was made. Neither did Engels, if Tom was correctly interpreting his occasional mutterings on the dialectic.

Munich, capital of Bavaria

"We are agreed, then." The count of Nassau-Hadamar rose from his chair and extended his hand to the duke of Bavaria. Maximilian rose quite a bit more slowly and his handshake was perfunctory. He was being just short of rude.

He couldn't help it. Duke Maximilian despised Johann Ludwig. He was quite sure the count of

Nassau-Hadamar had converted to Catholicism in 1629 simply to prevent Ferdinand II from seizing his family's possessions. Prior to that time, Johann Ludwig had been a partisan for Protestant causes. As a youth, he'd been friends with Friedrick V of the Palatinate—the same man who later, as the notorious "Winter King," had triggered off the great religious war when he accepted the throne of Bohemia offered to him by heretic rebels. The count had also fought on the side of the Protestant Dutch rebels against their Spanish Catholic monarch.

A man, in short, to whom treason came as naturally as waddling to a duck—and here he was, once again engaged in treason.

To be sure, it could be argued—rightfully argued, in Maximilian's opinion—that the so-called United States of Europe was a bastard state to begin with. Stabbing it in the back could hardly be called treason; it was more akin to summarily executing a criminal. Still, the motives of the man who committed such an act had a stench to them.

The count was still standing there, as if waiting for something. What . . . ?

Ah, of course. By the nature of their own nature, traitors needed constant reassurance.

"I will invade the Oberpfalz as soon as the opportunity arises, be sure of it." He cocked his head and gave Johann Ludwig a look so stern it bordered on accusation. "And in return, tell that chancellor of yours I will expect him to keep the USE's army from coming into things."

The count smiled and held a finger alongside his

nose. "Please! No names. I am acting solely on my own recognizance."

Where in the name of all that was holy did the scoundrel come up with that absurd phrase? It was blindingly obvious he was acting as Sweden's envoy. Probably not on Wettin's behalf, from subtle shadings of Johann Ludwig's remarks; but certainly on behalf of Oxenstierna.

Maximilian reminded himself that expecting logic from heretics was foolish. Indeed, might border on heresy itself. And none of it mattered, anyway.

The count was *still* standing there, as if expecting something. What...?

The duke's jaws tightened as he restrained his anger.

No. Absolutely not. Under no condition would he personally escort the swine out of the palace. He snapped his fingers, summoning a servant.

Not even an armed retainer. A house servant. Let the man comprehend his true place in the scheme of things.

"Show the count his way out," said Bavaria's ruler. He turned away to examine one of the portraits on the wall of the audience chamber. Hearing a slight gasp of outrage behind him, he bestowed a smile upon the image of his ancestor.

The Holy Roman Emperor Frederick III, as it happened.

Take Ingolstadt from him, would they? The duke of Bavaria would have it back, and the rest of the Oberpfalz with it.

Chapter 12

Magdeburg, capital of the United States of Europe

"No," said Rebecca. "Not yet."

Gunther Achterhof wasn't quite glaring at her, but his look was far from friendly. For that matter, neither were the looks she was getting from many of the people gathered around the big conference table.

That table wasn't quite as full as it had been on some occasions in the past, because none of the people from the State of Thuringia-Franconia were present except Kathe Scheiner—and she was purely a CoC organizer, not someone with a position in the provincial government. Ed Piazza and Helene Gundelfinger had planned to attend the meeting, but had decided they had to stay in Bamberg. Tensions with both the Bavarians and General Banér were now very high.

They were high in Banér's case because the route his army had to take from the Upper Palatinate to Saxony crossed part of SoTF territory—and, one way or another, the provincial officials had managed to delay his march for at least a week. By the end, he was threatening to seize and burn Hof.

At that point, Ed Piazza had quietly instructed his subordinates to cease interfering with Banér's army. The Swedish general now had to march his troops through the Vogtland, and the delay had given Georg Kresse and his irregulars the time they needed to sabotage the roads the Swedish army would have to take through the mountains.

The sabotage had been carefully done. There was nothing that could be proved to result from human action. Suspected to be, yes; darkly and angrily suspected, in fact. But not proved. Just... bridges somehow washed out by sluggish streams; roads running by other streams mysteriously caved in; other roads blocked by rockfalls and fallen timbers.

All of the obstacles could be cleared aside and the roads repaired, of course. But a march that should have taken no more than two weeks was taking well over a month. By the time Banér's army finally entered the Saxon plain and reached Dresden, Gretchen and Tata and their Committee of Correspondence would have had the time to strengthen the city's already-impressive fortifications, store food and supplies for a siege, and consolidate their political control.

As jury-rigged operations went, this one had been extremely successful. But time was now running out.

Banér was within sight of Dresden. And the gathering of reactionaries in Berlin was now public knowledge throughout the Germanies. A major pronouncement by the new prime minister and the chancellor of Sweden was expected at any moment.

Hence today's dispute. It had been brewing for days and had now finally erupted.

"I have to say I agree with Gunther," said Matthias Strigel.

Rebecca felt a spike of anxiety. The governor of Magdeburg province was normally one of the more judicious members of the emergency council. But he was under tremendous pressure from his constituents. For all practical purposes, Magdeburg—the whole province, not just the city—was now being governed by the Committees of Correspondence and the Fourth of July Party. That being so, why not acknowledge the fact openly and toss aside the pointless pretense that Wettin's officials had any authority left?

The problem was not a new one. It had erupted before, most notably during the so-called Magdeburg Crisis that followed the battle of Wismar, when the capital city's celebration of the victory began transforming itself into an insurrection. Only the quick and shrewd action of Mike Stearns and Spartacus averted a catastrophe, when they managed—just barely—to turn the uprising into a mass rally and celebration.

Even two years ago, with Torstensson and his troops camped just outside the city, the rebels might very well have managed to seize Magdeburg itself. The whole province would surely then have followed. It was conceivable, though not likely, that Thuringia and Franconia might have followed suit.

But the rest of the Germanies would not, as Mike had known very well. Soon enough, the traditional elites would have rallied most of the populace behind them—and they'd have the full backing of the Swedish army with Gustav Adolf at their head. He would view such an insurrection as treason and a personal betrayal, and conduct himself accordingly. The end result would have been a crushed rebellion and a monstrous setback for the democratic movement.

Most of the same factors were still in play two years later, although the variables had all changed. The greatest change of all, of course, was the incapacity of Gustav Adolf. With his heir a girl still just short of nine years old and an unsettled order of succession in two out of the three realms for which Gustav Adolf had a crown, legitimacy and legal authority had murky edges and lots of gray areas.

But for that very reason, Rebecca thought, the democratic movement had to avoid anything that clearly transgressed legality. Oxenstierna was driving this conflict, with Wilhelm Wettin trailing behind. That meant that it was the Swedish chancellor who, willy-nilly, had to make the first moves that would be clearly revolutionary. It was *essential* that the blame for upsetting the established order could be clearly and squarely placed on the forces of reaction. Clearly enough and squarely enough, furthermore, that most of the USE's populace could see and understand what had happened.

The very worst mistake they could make was to launch their own offensive. As unpleasant and frustrating as it might be, they had to wait until the time was right—and if that meant giving Oxenstierna the first blows, so be it.

Her husband called it "counterpunching," and he'd told her many times that the greatest danger an inexperienced boxer faced in the ring was being unable to control himself.

"You're nervous, you're excited, the adrenaline's

pumping—dammit, you came here to *fight*, not dance around. So you haul off and throw a haymaker, and the next thing you know the referee's standing over you counting to ten. And it looks like there's at least two of him, you're so dizzy."

She wished desperately that he was here. Michael could have kept control over the situation. Whether or not she could was still an open question.

For a moment, she also wished that Ed Piazza were here. But...

Most likely, he wouldn't be able to help much. The problem was that the most hardcore CoC leaders like Gunther and many of the people around the table—Gretchen Richter too, although she wasn't present—were suspicious of Americans.

Well... "suspicious" wasn't really the right term. The CoC hardliners didn't doubt that most Americans had good intentions. But they viewed the up-timers as squeamish, hesitant, and prone to vacillation.

In a private conversation, Constantin Ableidinger had once said to her: "They led a sheltered life, Rebecca. Study their history. Once they gained their independence, they were only invaded once—and that was two centuries before the Ring of Fire, and it was really just a raid on their coast. In that same stretch of time, at least half a dozen wars and several revolutions were fought on German soil. And that's not counting everything that came earlier—the Peasant War and all the rest of it.

"They're good and decent people, by and large, I'll be the first to say it. And there's no question that their arrival in the Ring of Fire is what broke everything open. But you just can't trust them not to flinch and turn aside when the time comes to settle accounts. They're like a farm boy who gets upset by the sight of blood trying to butcher a hog. They'll make a bloody, bungled mess of it."

There was enough truth to his viewpoint to make it hard to argue with. All the more so, because in the four and a half years since the Ring of Fire the Americans had mostly been able to sidestep the problem.

In the first year and a half, to be sure, they'd had to fight off enemies who came right at them—at the Battle of the Crapper, at Jena, at Eisenach and the Wartburg, and the Croat raid on Grantville itself. But those had been simple and straightforward military clashes, with no political subtleties and complexities involved.

Thereafter, Mike Stearns had always been able to reach a compromise with the king of Sweden that kept the situation reasonably stable. But that was no longer true, and the new situation was completely unlike anything they'd faced before. Either here in the seventeenth century, or in their own world before the Ring of Fire.

How would they react, without Mike Stearns to lead them?

No one really knew.

Rebecca was surprised, therefore, when Constantin Ableidinger spoke up. Unusually for him, he'd been silent thus far in the meeting.

"I'm with Rebecca on this, Gunther." He matched Achterhof's hard look with one of his own.

"And stop glaring at me. It's not my fault you insist on being stupid today. It's not Rebecca's fault, either."

He spent a moment giving everyone at the table that same hard look.

"What is wrong with you people? This is not complicated. If we are seen to be responsible for the coming civil war, then we've probably lost it before it even starts." He jabbed a finger at Matthias Strigel. "You! You need to get out of Magdeburg sometime and travel around the country. You live in a hothouse here. Most of you do."

Now he jabbed the finger at the Mecklenburger, Charlotte Kienitz. "You too! Spend all your time when you're not here jabbering with your fellow revolutionaries in the taverns in Schwerin."

Charlotte didn't like alcohol, as it happened. But it was true enough that she habituated the capital of Mecklenburg's radical gathering places whenever she went back home.

Ableidinger now swiveled his finger around the table, as if he were a gunner bringing a cannon to bear.

"That's the whole trouble!" he boomed. "You spend too much time talking to people who already agree with you and not enough time—no time at all, in the case of some of you!—listening to people out there"—now the finger jabbed at the windows—"who don't see things the way you do."

Looked at from one angle, there was something preposterous about Constantin Ableidinger lecturing other people on talking too much and not listening enough. But Rebecca was not about to chide him for it, under the circumstances.

The Franconian leader stood up and went to one of the windows that faced to the west. "This is what will happen if you act too soon." He stared through the glass for a moment. "First, you give Wettin a lever to force the Hessians to support him—where, if we let *him* launch the attack, the landgravine will have the excuse she so clearly wants to keep Hesse-Kassel neutral."

He half-turned, to bestow something very close to a sneer on Achterhof. "You *do* understand, I hope, why we want Hesse-Kassel to remain neutral, Gunther? We have no chance at all of overthrowing the landgravine—if you don't believe me, ask her."

He pointed to Liesel Hahn, a member of Parliament from Hesse-Kassel. Hahn had been looking distinctly unhappy so far in the meeting. Now she nodded her head several times.

"The truth is, she's pretty popular," she said. "Even more than her husband Wilhelm was."

Achterhof looked like he was about to say something, but Constantin drove over him. The Franconian could out-boom just about anybody.

"The last thing we need is to have one of the most powerful provincial armies in the nation fighting on the side of Oxenstierna and Wettin. But it's not just Hesse-Kassel that's at stake! Some of the other western provinces are unsteady, and could go either way."

He stepped away from the window and held up his thumb. "Start with Brunswick, which borders on Magdeburg province. Lucky for us, Brunswick's ruler is off in Poland with Torstensson, besieging Poznań. Let's make sure he stays there, shall we? If he does what Torstensson is most likely to do—call down a plague on both houses—then Brunswick also remains neutral. That's good for us, because we have no more chance of taking power in Brunswick than we do in Hesse-Kassel."

"What are you talking about?" demanded Albert Bugenhagen. The mayor of Hamburg rose to his own feet and pointed accusingly in the direction of Berlin. "At least half the stinking noblemen—and just about all the Hochadel—from Brunswick and Westphalia are in Berlin right now, plotting with Oxenstierna."

"And there are just as many from my province and the Upper Rhine," said Anselm Keller. He was a member of Parliament from the Province of the Main.

Now, Constantin sneered openly. "Who cares? The danger doesn't come from that pack of jackals."

"Most of them can raise their own armies!" said Bugenhagen.

Ableidinger's sneer grew more expansive. "'Armies' is a bit grandiose, don't you think? Even the Hochadel among them can't raise more than a few hundred men—and you don't want to look too closely at them, either. A fair number of those 'armed retainers' are sixty years old and missing an arm or an eye. Admit it, Albert—against such as those, our stout CoC contingents will send them packing. Just as we did in Operation Krystalnacht."

That was a bit of an exaggeration, but it was close enough to the mark that Bugenhagen sat down without pursuing the argument. And while Keller's jaws were tight, he didn't contest the matter.

"The real military threat lies elsewhere," continued Constantin. "First and foremost, in the provincial armies—real armies, those are—that can be raised by the provincial rulers. Stop worrying about Freiherr Feckless and Reichsritter Holes-in-His-Boots. Start worrying about the Landgravine of Hesse-Kassel and the Duke of Brunswick and the Prince of Westphalia, instead."

"They never made that Danish bastard a prince," said Keller sullenly.

Rebecca wondered how long Constantin could keep that sneer on his face.

"*Who* didn't?" sneered Ableidinger. "They didn't

make him a prince because Gustav Adolf put his foot down. But what do you think are the odds that *Oxenstierna* won't hand him the title, if Frederick gets pissed at us and makes friendly noises toward Berlin?"

There was silence in the room. Ableidinger maintained the sneer right through it.

"Then there's the other serious threat," he went on. "Those are the town militias, especially the ones from the bigger towns. They won't fight in the countryside, but they'll keep their towns solid against us—"

"Not Hamburg!" protested its mayor.

"No, you're right. Not Hamburg. Not Luebeck or Frankfurt, either. But they'll hold Augsburg and Ulm, won't they? And probably Strassburg, too—and what's more important, they'll hold at least three-quarters of the smaller towns in every province except Magdeburg, the SoTF and Mecklenburg. All right, fine. Only two-thirds of the towns in the Oberpfalz. How parochial can you be, Albert? You think the world begins and ends in Hamburg?"

Rebecca decided to intervene before Ableidinger's abrasive manner set off a pointless eruption.

"I think we need to consider Constantin's points carefully," she said. "He's right that if there's a full-scale civil war most of the official militias will be arrayed against us—and that's especially true if they believe we are the ones who started the war. If they hold the towns against us and our CoC contingents have to face regular provincial armies in the field, we will lose. It is as simple as that."

Achterhof scowled and crossed his arms over his chest. "In effect, you're saying we've lost the war already."

"She said a *full-scale* civil war, Gunther." That came from Ulbrecht Riemann, who had been silent up until this point. He was a central figure in the Fourth of July Party in Westphalia, although he held no post in government.

"As opposed to what?" asked Keller.

Riemann shrugged. "There are lots of different kinds of wars, Anselm. So why shouldn't there be different types of civil wars? The thing some of you don't seem to grasp is that Oxenstierna has to win this conflict outright. We don't. Why? Because we're winning every day as it is, day in and day out. Week by week, month by month, our cause advances and his cause retreats. That's why he's taking this opportunity, for all the risks involved. I don't know if he realizes it consciously or not, but on some level Oxenstierna—all those reactionary swine—have to sense they're losing."

Achterhof was staring at him, practically cross-eyed. Rebecca had to stifle a smile.

Riemann was right, though, whether Achterhof understood his point or not. Her husband had said much the same thing to her, many times. He'd used different words, but the gist was the same.

The aristocracy and the city patricians *needed* formal power in order to maintain their control over the Germanies. The democratic movement didn't—although holding such power was certainly helpful. Its influence spread everywhere, every day, down a thousand channels. Schools, unions, insurance associations, all manner of cooperatives and granges. Steadily, if sometimes slowly, the strength of the reactionaries faded.

Constantin could see it also, probably because he came from Franconia. Achterhof and the other

Magdeburg militants suffered from a perhaps inevitable myopia. Say rather, tunnel vision. Everything in the nation's capital was clear, crisp, sharp. Magdeburg was a place of factories and working-class apartments. Over here were the toiling masses, who constituted the city's great majority. Over there, in the palaces, were the class enemies.

There were not many of them, either. So why not just sweep them aside?

Franconia—still more so, Thuringia—was a very different place. The USE's most populous province had many political shadings, and well-nigh innumerable layers in its populace. The Americans and their allies had been able to politically dominate it since the Ring of Fire primarily because they had provided stability and security. They had put a stop to mercenary plundering, fostered the economy, built and maintained roads, schools and hospitals.

Whether or not they agreed with the Fourth of July Party's program—and a great many of them didn't—the majority of the population of the State of Thuringia-Franconia kept voting for them, election after election. For some, out of radical conviction. But for just as many, for the opposite reason—a conservative reluctance to upset the applecart. The very full applecart.

It helped a great deal, too, that the president of the SoTF was Ed Piazza. He was not a flamboyant, exciting, romantic—and rather scary—figure like Mike Stearns. Rather, he exuded steadiness and stability. He governed his province much the same way, as a high school principal, he had governed his teaching staff and his students, with relaxed confidence and equanimity.

So, despite the many features of Thuringian and Franconian society that resisted the democratic movement, even resented it bitterly, that movement continued to broaden and deepen its influence.

"Don't give them a clear target," Michael had told her. "Let them wear themselves out for a while. They haven't got the wind for a long fight. As long as you keep them from winning by knockout, you're staying ahead on points."

Her husband was fond of boxing analogies. She decided to share one of them with the group.

"We've been discussing this for hours," she said. "I think we are ready to take a vote."

She looked around the table and was greeted by nods. From Gunther, Anselm and Albert, also. They'd been the most intransigent of her opponents.

"Very well. All in favor of Gunther's proposal to seize official power in Magdeburg, raise your hands."

The number was clearly short of a majority.

"Very well. All in favor of my approach—which, following my husband's guidance, I shall call 'rope-a-dope'—raise your hands."

The jest was perhaps unwise, since there was an immediate outcry to explain it that delayed the vote. But in the end, her viewpoint was adopted.

Afterward, Achterhof grunted and leaned back in his chair. "Easy for us to say 'rope-a-dope.' But it'll be Gretchen and her people in Dresden who have to take the punches."

Chapter 13

Dresden, capital of Saxony

Jozef Wojtowicz watched workmen laying gravel onto the cobblestones of the huge city square. *What madness possessed me,* he wondered, *to come to Dresden?*

He was still possessed by the same madness, to make things worse. He had more than enough money to have gotten out of the city any time he wanted, His employer was his uncle Stanislaw Koniecpolski, the grand hetman of Poland and Lithuania and one of the commonwealth's half-dozen richest men. He was no miser, either. Jozef had never lacked for the financial resources he needed.

Yes, here he still was. And if he didn't leave by tomorrow—the day after, at the outside—he probably wouldn't be able to leave at all. Banér's army was already setting up camp just south and west of Dresden's walls. It wouldn't take the Swedish general very long to have regular cavalry patrols surrounding the city.

Jozef might still be able to pass through, if the cavalrymen were susceptible to bribery. Mercenaries usually were. It would be risky, though. There were already reports that Banér's troops had committed atrocities in some of the villages northeast of Chemnitz, in their march through southern Saxony. Banér was known for his temper and his brutality, and commanders usually transmitted their attitudes to their soldiers. A cavalry patrol that Jozef encountered might decide to murder him and take all his money rather than settle for a bribe.

But...

He couldn't bring himself to leave. Dresden was just too interesting, too exciting, right now. When he'd lived in Grantville, Jozef had come across the up-time term "adrenaline junkie" and realized that it described him quite well. Since he was a boy he'd enjoyed dangerous sports—he was an avid rock-climber, among other things—and part of the reason he'd agreed to become his uncle's spy in the USE was because of the near-constant tension involved. Whenever he contemplated his notion of Hell it didn't involve any of the tortures depicted in Dante's *Inferno*; rather, it was to be locked in a room for eternity with nothing to do. Jozef had a very high pain threshold, but an equally low boredom threshold.

Besides, he could always justify the risk on the grounds that staying in Dresden gave him an unparalleled opportunity to study the Committees of Correspondence in action. Gretchen Richter herself was in charge here! What better opportunity could you ask for?

That very moment, as it happened, he saw her entering the square from the direction of the Residenzschloss, surrounded by a dozen or so people. She and her CoC cohorts had effectively taken over the palace of the former elector of Saxony, John George, as their own headquarters.

. You had to add that term "effectively" because Richter still maintained the pretense that the Residenzschloss was primarily being used as a hospital for wounded soldiers. She'd also been heard to point out that the province's official administrator—that was Ernst Wettin, the USE prime minister's younger brother—also had his offices and quarters in the Residenzschloss. The fanciest ones available, in fact, the chambers and rooms that had been used by John George and his family before they fled the city.

Both claims were threadbare. True enough, Richter was reportedly always polite to the provincial administrator and made sure his stay in the palace was a pleasant one. She even provided him with a security detail, since Wettin had no soldiers of his own. But that fact alone made it clear who really wielded power in the city.

As for the soldiers who'd been sent to Dresden to recuperate from their wounds, by now most of them had regained their health. They still lived in the section of the Residenzschloss that had been designated as the hospital, but that was simply because there were no barracks available and Richter had decreed that no soldiers would be billeted on the city's inhabitants. Nor had the few officers objected, although the woman had absolutely no authority to be making any decisions concerning soldiers in the USE army.

And there was another thing Jozef found interesting about the situation. All of the USE officers here were very junior. There was not so much as a single captain among them, much less any majors or colonels. They were all lieutenants—and newly minted ones, at that, for the most part.

How was that possible? How could an army division fight as many battles as the Third Division had fought during the summer and fall without any of its company commanders or field grade officers being wounded?

Had they all been killed? The odds against that happening were astronomical.

And they had to have been engaged in the fighting. No army could possibly win battles if the only officers who placed themselves in harm's way were lieutenants.

There was only one possible answer, from what Jozef could see. For whatever reason, the commanding general of the Third Division had deliberately sent only his most junior officers and his enlisted men to Dresden. Those of higher rank who'd been wounded he must have sent elsewhere.

Jena, probably. The USE had a big new hospital there, already reputed to be one of the very best in the world. General Stearns could have sent the more senior officers there on the grounds that there was only limited space in Jena so he was making a priority of giving them the best treatment available.

Whatever his thinking had been, the end result was that several hundred combat veterans—almost all of them no older than their twenties—were in a city about to undergo a siege, and they had allied themselves with Dresden's inhabitants. And this was no grudging alliance, either. Jozef had seen for himself that tactical command of the city's defenses had been taken over by the dozen or so USE army lieutenants present. The one named Krenz seemed to be in overall charge.

Could Stearns have foreseen that?

He...might. By all accounts, he was a canny bastard. And a labor organizer, in his background, not a military man. That meant he was accustomed to fluid relations of command and obedience, where a man's authority derived almost entirely from his ability to gain and retain the confidence of the men around him. To use an up-time expression, he had to have very finely honed "people skills."

It was all quite fascinating.

"I'm warning you," said a voice from behind him, "there's no point trying to seduce her."

Turning around—and feeling quite stupid; had he really been ogling the woman that openly?—he saw one of the men he'd met the night before in the Rathaus. The basement tavern of the city hall had been taken over by the CoC, for all practical purposes.

Another Pole, as it happened. Tadeusz Szklenski, a Silesian from a town near Krakow.

The only thing Jozef remembered about him from the previous evening was that the man's Amideutsch was pretty decent if heavily accented and he insisted on being called by the up-time nickname of "Ted."

The grin he had on his face was just friendly, so Jozef decided to return it with a grin of his own.

"And why would you think I'd have that in mind to begin with?"

"Three reasons. The first is that Gretchen Richter's very good-looking. The second and the third are named Ilse and Ursula."

Jozef couldn't stop himself from wincing. Ilse and Ursula were waitresses in the Rathaus tavern. He'd slept with both of them in the course of the past week. Once again, and for perhaps the hundredth time, he cautioned himself that his attraction to women was foolish for a spy.

The problem was partly that Jozef himself was very good-looking, a quality that most men might prize but was a nuisance for someone working in espionage. The other part of the problem was that he had a personality that many women seemed to find irresistibly charming—and, alas, the reverse was also true, if the women were bright and had a sense of humor.

"I hadn't realized anyone was monitoring my personal habits," he said stiffly.

Szklenski shrugged. "The fellows came to me about it. They wanted to make sure you were okay. We're both Poles, you see."

He seemed to think all of that was self-explanatory. But Jozef found it all very murky.

Who were "the fellows?" Why would they come to Szklenski? What did "okay" mean in this context? And what difference did it make that they were both Poles?

His puzzlement must have been evident. "CoC guys," Szklenski explained. "They're always looking out for spies. They figured I could sniff you out if you were, since we're both Polish." He shrugged. "I don't think that last part makes a lot of sense, myself, but that's how they felt about it."

"They thought I was a *spy?*" Jozef tried to put as much in the way of outraged innocence into the term as he could—while keeping in mind the danger of overacting given that he was, in point of fact, a spy.

"Silly notion, isn't it?—and I told them so right off. What kind of idiot spy would screw two girls in one week who both worked in the same tavern?"

An excellent question, Jozef thought grimly. Perhaps

he should start flagellating himself to drive out these evil urges. Or wear a hair shirt.

"You'd better stay out of Ursula's sight for a while, by the way. Ilse is easygoing but Ursula's not at all."

He glanced over to where Richter had stopped to talk to another group of people. Shopkeepers, from the look of them. "And you can forget about her altogether. Not even the reactionaries try to spread rumors about her. They say she dotes on that up-time husband of hers, even if he is fat and ugly. Well, plain-looking."

Jozef hadn't even been thinking about Richter in those terms. He'd admit to being stupid when it came to attractive women, but he wasn't insane. And right now, he was much more concerned about people suspecting him of being a spy. Especially CoC-type people, who were notorious for being prone to summary justice.

"Why would anyone think Poland would send a spy here? We're not really very close to where the war is going on."

Szklenski stared at him, frowning. "What's Poland got to do with anything? The guys were worried you might be a spy for the Swedes."

Jozef shook his head. The gesture was not one of negation; just an attempt to clear his head.

"And the logic of thinking a Swedish general would hire a Pole to spy on Saxons is . . . what, exactly?"

Szklenski's grin was back. "Don't ask me. I told you I thought it was silly—and I told them so as well. But just to calm them down, I said I'd talk to you. There aren't that many Polish CoCers in Dresden, so I figure we need to look out for each other."

Jozef cleared his throat. "And . . . ah . . . why, exactly, would you assume I was a member of the CoCs myself?"

Szklenski got a sly look on his face. "Don't want to talk about it, huh? That's okay—but don't think you're fooling anybody. Why else would a Pole be in Dresden right now, unless he was a lunatic?"

Another excellent question.

That evening, Jozef decided it would be wise to follow Szklenski's advice and spend his time at a different tavern. Where the now-revealed-to-be-not-entirely-good-humored Ursula did not work.

Szklenski himself escorted him there. "It's where most of us Poles go," he explained.

So it proved.

"You led me into a trap," Jozef said. Accusingly, but not angrily. He wasn't hot-tempered to begin with, and even if he had been he would have restrained himself. Being hot-tempered when you're surrounded at a corner table in a dark tavern by eight men at least two of whom were armed with knives would be even more stupid than seducing two waitresses in one week who worked at the same establishment.

Szklenski shrugged, looking a bit embarrassed. Only a bit, though.

"Sorry, but we really do have to make sure," he said. "We've got a good reputation with the USE guys here and we can't afford to let it get damaged."

Jozef looked around. "I take it all of you are in the CoCs?"

"We're asking the questions, not you," said one of them. That was Bogumil—no last name provided—whom Jozef had already pegged as the surliest of the lot. He didn't think it was an act, either.

"Give us some names," said the man to Bogumil's left. That was Waclaw, who had also failed to provide a last name. "Something."

Jozef thought about it, for a moment. Acting as if he were an innocent Pole not involved with politics who just happened to wander into Dresden right now was probably pointless. The question then became, what did he claim to be?

In for a penny, in for a pound, as the up-timers said. "Krzysztof Opalinski."

"What about him?" That came from a third man at the table, who had provided no name at all. He was quite short, but very thick-shouldered and dangerous-looking.

"Nothing about him," said Jozef, sounding bored. "I hope you're not expecting me to provide you with details of what we're doing? How do I know *you're* not spies?"

"Who would we be spying for?" said Bogumil, jeeringly.

Jozef shrugged. "I can think of at least half a dozen great magnates who might be employing spies in the Germanies. So can you, so let's stop playing."

Bogumil started to say something but Waclaw held up his hand. "He's right. But I want to make sure you really know him." He stood up and held his hand, palm down, a few inches above his own head. "He's about this tall, well-built, blond, blue eyes, and he favors a tight-cut beard?"

Jozef leaned back in his chair and smiled. "That's a pretty fair description of his younger brother Lukasz. But Krzysztof's about two inches taller, to begin with. He's got broad shoulders and he's certainly in good shape, but nothing like Lukasz, who's a hussar and bloody damn good at it. They both have blond hair and blue eyes, but Krzysztof's hair is a bit lighter and his eyes shade into green. What else do you want to know?"

He stood up himself—slowly, though, so as not to alarm anyone—lifted his shirt and pointed to a spot on his side just above the hip. "Krzysztof's got a birthmark here, shaped like a crooked hourglass. His brother—as you'd expect with a hussar—has several scars. You want to know where they are and what they look like?"

Bogumil glared up at him. "How do you know what his body looks like? You a faggot?"

"We bathe, how else? Try it sometime."

Bogumil spluttered and started to get up, but Waclaw placed a hand on his shoulder and drove him back down on the bench they shared. "You started the insults, so don't complain."

He studied Jozef for a few seconds, and then looked at his companions. "I think he's probably okay. He obviously knows Krzysztof."

The short, muscular fellow still looked a bit dubious. "Yes, but he could have known him from something else. By his accent, he's szlachta himself."

"So is one Pole in ten," said a fellow sitting in the very corner. He was thin, sharp-featured, and called himself Kazimierz. "Including two of us at this table. Means nothing."

Jozef pursed his lips. "All right. The up-timer, Red Sybolt."

Eight pairs of eyes got a bit wider. "You know *Sybolt*?" asked the short one.

Jozef shook his head. "I wouldn't say I 'know' him. We've met only twice. But that's the business I've been engaged in and that's all I'm going to say about it.

The truth is, I don't know myself where Red is right now. Or Krzysztof."

He said that with relaxed confidence, since for the most part it was perfectly true. He had no idea where either Red Sybolt or Krzysztof Opalinski was located at the moment. Or last month, or last year. Somewhere in the Ruthenian lands—which covered an area larger than France or Spain.

He was fudging with the business of having met Sybolt twice. He'd never met him at all. But he had seen two photographs of the man; good enough ones that he could describe him fairly well if necessary.

God help him, of course, if either Sybolt or Krzysztof showed up in Dresden.

"Good enough," said Waclaw, sitting back down. He glanced at Bogumil, who still looked angry, and slapped him playfully on the head. "Come on, you started it! Say hello to our new comrade."

"Hello, comrade," Bogumil said. "And fuck both of you."

Szklenski laughed. "You'll get used to him, Joe."

Jozef managed not to sigh. He'd gotten through months living in Grantville without getting saddled with one of those asinine American nicknames. One week in Dresden and he was saddled with *Joe*. And from a fellow Pole, to boot!

Probably a punishment visited on him by the patron saint of spies for sleeping with two women in the same week who both worked in the same tavern.

Who *was* the patron saint for spies, anyway? He thought it was Joshua, but he wasn't sure.

He couldn't very well ask his tablemates, under the circumstances.

Chapter 14

"We are ready, then?" Gretchen looked at Tata.

Tata looked at Eric Krenz. "Our people are ready. He'll have to answer for the soldiers."

Eric had taken off his hat when he entered the conference room and hung it on a hook by the door. Now, he wished he were still wearing it. He could pull down the brim in order to avoid Gretchen's gaze without having to look away from her entirely.

"He hates giving a straight answer to anything, Gretchen," said Tata. "You know that."

"Yes, and normally I accommodate him. But I can't this time. We need to *know*. Now." She turned her head to look at a man sitting at the far end of the long conference table. That was Wilhelm Kuefer, one of the Vogtlanders. Their leader Georg Kresse had appointed him to serve as liaison to Dresden's Committee of Correspondence.

"Tell him, Wilhelm," she said.

"Banér's cavalrymen burned three more villages yesterday. The populations of two of them ran off in time, but the people in the third one got caught sleeping. There weren't any survivors except for—we're not sure about this, but we couldn't find any such bodies—perhaps the young women."

Gretchen turned back to face Eric, who was sitting across the table from her. "That makes nine villages so far—and these three were right out in the Saxon plain, not in the mountains. There is no way this is happening without Banér's approval. Tacit approval, maybe, but he's still responsible."

She stopped and waited.

And waited.

Eric felt like screaming: *I'm just a fucking lieutenant! How am I supposed to know if we can hold the bastards off?*

But he knew what Tata's response would be. She'd point to herself with a thumb—*I'm just a tavern-keeper's daughter*—and then at Gretchen with a forefinger. *And her father ran a print shop. So stop whining.*

Gretchen was quite obviously prepared to wait all day for his answer. By mid-afternoon, though, Tata's sarcasm would become unbearable.

"Yes," he said, sighing. "I think. As best I can tell."

"Not good enough, Lieutenant Krenz." Gretchen's voice was soft but her tone was iron. "I do not ask for guarantees. That would be silly. But I need a more firm response than that. If I order the gates closed and openly forbid Banér from coming into the city, that moment I make myself and every person in Dresden an outlaw. If the Swedes break in, they'll massacre half the population."

"As it is, even if we let them in without a fight, they'll kill some people," said Tata. "Me and Gretchen, for sure, if they catch us. Any CoC member—and there'll be plenty who'll serve as informers to ferret them out. There are always toadies, anywhere you go."

Eric rose, strode to the door, plucked his hat off the hook, jammed it on, and came back to the table.

"I feel better now. Don't ask me why the hat makes a difference. It just does. Here's your answer, Gretchen. It may not be what you want but it's the only answer I can give you. I don't honestly know if we can hold off Banér. There are too many unknown variables in the equation. To name what's probably the biggest, what will von Arnim do? If he adds his ten thousand men to Banér's fifteen, we'll be very badly outnumbered."

He took a deep breath, to steel his will. "Here's what I will promise. If you can hold the city's populace firm, we'll bleed the bastards till they're white as sheets. If they do take the city, there won't be more than half of them left standing."

She nodded. "That's good enough, I think. Those are mercenaries out there. If you bleed them enough, I think they'll start deserting in droves. And we're into winter, now. Disease will start ravaging them."

"Ravage the city also," said Friedrich Nagel. His tone was dark—but then, it usually was. Eric's fellow lieutenant was possibly the most pessimistic man he'd ever met. Odd, really, that they'd become such good friends.

Gretchen made a face. It wasn't a grimace; just an expression that conveyed the stoic outlook that was such an inseparable part of the woman. Nagel called it "the Richter Lack of Rue."

"Not as badly as they'll suffer," she said. "Our patrols maintain sanitation a lot better than Banér will."

"Well, that's true," said Friedrich. One thing you could always count on with Nagel was that he was a dispassionate pessimist. It wasn't that he thought his lot in life was particularly hard. Everyone's was, including his enemies'. Eric would have assumed the attitude was that of a stark Calvinist, except that he knew Friedrich was an outright freethinker. What the up-timers called a deist. He didn't think God had any personal animus against him. He'd simply set the universe in motion and went on His way, indifferent to the details that followed. Does a miller care if an unlucky gnat gets crushed between the stones, so long as the flour gets made?

Gretchen now looked back at Kuefer. "Have you gotten an answer from Kresse?"

She didn't specify the question involved, because she didn't need to. Everyone at the table knew that she'd proposed that the Vogtlanders unite formally with Dresden instead of simply maintaining a liaison.

Wilhelm nodded. "Yes. Georg says he'll agree to it—on one condition. We're not joining the CoCs. Meaning no offense, but we don't necessarily agree with you on all issues and we reserve the right to express such disputes openly and publicly."

"Understood," said Gretchen. "We have the same arrangement with the Ram people in Franconia. So does the Fourth of July Party."

She looked around the table. The majority of people sitting there were members of the city's Committee of Correspondence. "Anybody disagree?"

She waited patiently, long enough to give anyone with doubts a chance to speak up. They would have done so, too. Richter was the dominant figure at that table, but she was not domineering. In fact, she went out of her way to make sure people felt at ease and were not afraid to express their opinions. That was a good part of the reason she was so dominant, of course. Her followers trusted her, they weren't simply cowed by her.

"All right, then. We'll need to form a new committee to take charge of the resistance against the Swedes. Politically neutral, as it were. I propose one-third of the seats will be held by the CoC, one-third will be divided between the soldiers, the militias, and the city council—however they choose to divide them—and the remaining third will be split evenly between the Vogtlanders and representatives of the towns in the plain."

That was an exceedingly generous gesture on the part of the CoC, especially toward the Vogtlanders. Of course, the generosity was more formal than real, in some ways. The militias and especially the regular soldiers were so heavily influenced by the CoC that they could be relied upon to follow its guidance. Even the city council by now was close to the CoC, since most of its former patrician members had fled the city.

Still, the formalities were significant, not just empty posturing. The fact that Richter was willing to make such a proposal indicated that she would listen to people outside the CoC also.

"We'll need a new name for it, Gretchen," said Tata.

"Yes, I know. I propose to call it the Committee of Public Safety."

Eric had to stifle a sudden, semi-hysterical laugh. Out of the corner of his eye, he saw Friedrich's lips purse.

But Nagel didn't say anything. Looking around the table, Eric realized that he and his fellow lieutenant

were the only ones there—leaving aside Gretchen
herself, he presumed—who understood the historical
allusion.

"I like it," grunted Kuefer. "It's neutral sounding
but it ought to send the right message to the Swedes."

After the meeting broke up, Eric and Friedrich
waited for Gretchen in the corridor outside the conference chamber.

"What is it?" she asked, when she emerged. "I don't
have much time right now. I need to give Wettin the
news myself. I don't want him hearing it first in the
form of rumor."

Eric cleared his throat. "Friedrich and I were
talking and...ah...that title for the committee you
proposed..."

"That I proposed and everyone agreed to, including
you. At least, you raised no objection. What about it?"

"Well...ah...some people might think we were
being provocative..." He trailed off.

"For God's sake, Gretchen," burst out Nagel, "it's
the name Robespierre and his people used!"

"Leaving aside the metaphysical issue of whether
the verb 'use' makes sense in the past tense for something that won't happen for a century and a half in
another universe, you're right. That's why I chose it."

She paused and gave both of them a cold stare.
"Since you've apparently read the history, I will point
out that this same Committee of Public Safety was
responsible for defeating every one of the royalist
nations who invaded France to restore the king. The
reactionary propagandists against Robespierre and
Danton don't like to talk much about that, do they?"

"But... Surely you don't propose to erect a guillotine in the central square?"

She frowned. "Why in the world would we do that, when we've got plenty of stout German axes at hand? We're not French sissies."

She swept off, down the corridor, headed toward the administrator's chambers.

"I... think that was a joke," ventured Friedrich.

Eric took off his hat and ran fingers through his hair. Then, jammed it back on. "With Gretchen, who knows? But we'll take that as our working hypothesis. Anyway, what's the difference? We'll probably all be dead in a couple of months anyway, between Banér and typhus."

"Don't forget the plague," said Friedrich, as they began walking in the other direction. He was more chipper already, now that he had catastrophes to dwell on. "Always a reliable guest in such affairs. And I hear there's a new disease we'll be encountering one of these days. They call it 'cholera.' It's quite fascinating. Apparently, your bowels turn to water and you shit and puke yourself to death."

After Gretchen Richter left his office, Ernst Wettin rose from his desk and went to the northern window. That provided him with his favorite view of the valley.

There were settlements over there on the north bank of the Elbe, but the big majority of the city's populace lived south of the river. He'd been told by a friend who'd gotten a look at an up-time travel guide in Grantville that someday—about half a century from now, during a period they would call "the Baroque"—the city would expand greatly over there.

But in this day and age, the walls of the city did not include those north bank settlements. They'd have no protection once a siege began.

They wouldn't be there much longer, however. One of the things Richter had told him was that she'd ordered the destruction of all buildings north of the river. Most of the inhabitants had already fled into the city, as news spread of the atrocities being committed by the oncoming Swedish army. Richter would have the ones who remained evacuated also, and then they'd burn everything to the ground.

She'd sent orders to have every village within ten miles evacuated and burned also. The inhabitants would either come into the city or find refuge with the Vogtlanders in the mountains to the south. Banér and his army would have no choice but to spend the coming winter in camps.

Technically, the orders would come from this new "Committee of Public Safety." (Odd title, that. He wondered where they'd gotten it from?) Because of the very visible and prominent place on it given to the Vogtlanders and leaders of some of the important towns in the plain, those orders would probably be obeyed, too.

She hadn't said so, but Ernst was quite sure that it had been Richter herself who saw to it that the rural folk had plenty of representation on the new Committee. She'd understood that Dresden had to have the support of the surrounding countryside—all of Saxony, not just the city itself—if it was to withstand a siege by an army the strength of Banér's. And that same support would be a constant drain on the besiegers.

Regardless of who sat on the Committee, the driving

will was Richter's. She made even the notoriously
harsh Georg Kresse seem soft, once she'd decided
on a course of action. The woman had always been
polite and pleasant in her dealings with him, but
Ernst had not fooled himself. Beneath that attractive
surface lay a granite mind; as unyielding as the Alps
and as ruthless as an avalanche.

They had no idea what they were unleashing, those
idiots in Berlin. They dreamed of another bloodbath
like the one that had drowned the rebellion during
the Peasant War, that would once again restore their
power and privileges. But even that slaughter had
only stemmed the tide for a century.

What was a century? Nothing, if a man was capable
of stepping back and measuring human affairs by a
yardstick longer than his own life—and what was a
life? Also nothing, if a man was capable of stepping
back and measuring his soul against eternity.

But . . . they listened to those parsons they chose to
listen to. The ones who assured them that the Almighty
who created the sun and the moon and the heavens
favored the wealthy and powerful—never mind what
the Christ said—and would approve of their butchery.
The God who filled oceans would gaze with favor
upon the men who filled abattoirs.

Idiots, now; greater idiots still, when they faced
judgment.

For butchery it would have to be. Richter would
not yield, and neither would her followers—who now
included hundreds of soldiers from the regular army's
Third Division. Whose commander had somehow
forgotten them.

That would be Mike Stearns. The same man whom

Ernst's brother had once described, half-angrily and half-admiringly, with the up-time expression "he's got a mind like a steel trap."

That would be his brother Wilhelm, now one of the idiots in Berlin. What had happened to him? How and when had he lost his judgment and his good sense?

What did Wilhelm think would happen when those soldiers in Dresden came under fire from a Swedish army? Did he—did that still greater idiot Oxenstierna—think Stearns would remain obediently in Bohemia?

For a time, maybe. Probably, in fact. In his own way, Stearns was every bit as ruthless as Richter. He was quite capable of biding his time while the defenders of Dresden bled Banér's army—and von Arnim's too, if he ventured out of Leipzig.

But sooner or later, he would be back. Leading the same soldiers who defeated the Poles at Zwenkau and Zielona Góra, and now had their comrades threatened by Banér. Did they think those soldiers would refuse to follow Stearns?

Were they mad?

And what did they think Torstensson would do with the rest of the USE army? At best, he would hold them in Poland, out of the fray—because if they joined that fray, they would certainly not join it on behalf of Oxenstierna.

The whole nation would dissolve into civil war. There was no way of knowing in advance who would win, but if Ernst had been a gambling man—which he most certainly was not—he would not have placed his wager on Berlin.

There was a blindness that came with power, if the man who wielded it was not careful. One got accustomed to obedience, to having one's will enforced. The idea that it could be thwarted—certainly by a wretch who'd been no more than a printer's daughter and a near-prostitute—faded into the shadows. Became unthinkable, even. The practical realities of power transmuted as if by a philosopher's stone into a self-evident law of nature.

I am mighty because I am, and therefore always will be.

He sighed, shook his head, and returned to his desk. Sitting down, he pulled some sheets of paper from a drawer and took out his pen.

No miserable quill pen, this. He only used those for public display. This was an up-time fountain pen, which he'd purchased in Grantville. The type that could be continually refilled, not the much cheaper kind that had to be thrown away after a while. He'd had it for two years now, and adored the thing. It was worth every dollar—the very many dollars—he'd spent on it.

Later, he'd write to his brother Wilhelm. That letter would be useless anyway, since Wilhelm had made it quite clear he was no longer listening. Ernst would write it purely out of a sense of family obligation.

The letter he would write first would be equally useless, of course, if you looked at it solely in terms of its immediate effect. But Ernst was not one of those idiots who confused days with months and years with centuries.

He would give no legitimacy to this madness. Come what may, to him as well as the city. He also did not confuse a life with eternity.

He did not bother with the customary salutations. Under the circumstances, flowery prose was just silly.

General Johan Banér—

I remind you that I am the administrator of Saxony. The appointment was given to me directly by Gustav II Adolf, Emperor of the United States of Europe, and has not been rescinded by him.

Dresden is in good order. There is neither cause nor justification for your army to enter the city. I therefore order you to keep a distance of fifteen miles, lest your presence provoke disturbances.

> *Ernst Wettin,*
> *Administrator of Saxony,*
> *Duke of Saxe-Weimar*

Chapter 15

*Tetschen, near the border between
Saxony and Bohemia*

The plane taxied over to the newly built hangar and
came to a stop just before the open doors. Soon
thereafter, a figure emerged out of the cockpit. When
Jeff Higgins recognized who it was, he whistled softly.

"To what do we owe the honor of a visit by Jesse
Wood himself?" he said.

Standing next to him, Thorsten Engler made no
reply. He figured they'd find out soon enough.

When Jesse came up, he shook both their hands.
"Good afternoon, Colonel Higgins. Captain Engler."

"Not that it isn't always nice to see you, Jesse, but
since when does the air force send its commander to
fly routine reconnaissance patrols?" Jeff asked.

Colonel Wood gave him an exasperated look. "Don't
play stupid, Jeff. This is hardly 'routine.' We're on
the edge of a civil war, in case you hadn't noticed. I
wanted to see how things stood for myself. I'm flying
down to Prague to meet with Mike as soon as we're
done here."

"Let's get inside," said Higgins. He gestured toward the airfield's administration building. It was a small two story edifice that officially served as:

The field's weather station—with no equipment beyond a mercury thermometer and a crude barometer.

Its control tower—with nothing to control; Wood's plane was the first one to ever land here.

Its radio tower—with no radio capable of reaching Dresden or Prague except under perfect conditions.

Its only real function so far: a place to get out of the cold and warm up over a pot of tea. There was quite a comfortable lounge on the bottom floor.

"Would you like me to have your plane rolled into the hangar, Colonel?" Thorsten gestured at a small ground crew standing in the hangar's wide doorway.

Jesse shook his head. "I won't be here that long. I need to get to Prague before nightfall, while the weather holds up."

"... burning everything north of the river, so far as I could see," Jesse concluded. He drained his tea cup and set it down on the side table next to his chair. Then, gave Higgins a look that somehow managed to combine respect and derision.

"Don't know as I'd want to be sleeping in the same bed with your wife, Jeff. You're so much crispy bacon if she ever gets really pissed at you."

Jeff grinned. "Just call her Gasoline Gretchen— except she wouldn't waste the gasoline. She knows how to use an ax. Give her husband forty whacks and then turn the bed into kindling."

He seemed quite unperturbed by the peril.

Jesse studied him for a moment, and then looked

toward the corner where the radio was perched on a bench. "Will it reach Dresden or Prague?"

"Only sometimes, and unpredictably. We're nestled in the mountains here." Thorsten glanced at Jeff. When he saw that his commanding officer's posture didn't seem to indicate any reservation about the air force colonel, he added, "But we have other ways to stay in regular touch with the people in the city."

"Midnight derring-do, eh? Ninjas slipping through the walls in the dead of night." Wood flicked his fingers, as if brushing something away. "None of my business."

Thorsten had no idea what a "ninja" was. A superb spy of some kind, he presumed.

In point of fact, although they did maintain a small cadre of military couriers who could make the journey overland to Dresden very quickly, their normal method of staying in touch with Gretchen and her people was simply to use a courier from one of the private postal services. Such men were excellent riders and quite discreet.

They couldn't be bribed or tortured successfully either, since the messages were apparently innocuous. In fact, by and large they *were* innocuous, just the communications of a husband and his wife. If and when they needed to say something else, Jeff had sent her a one-time pad. The cipher had been designed by David Bartley. It turned out the youthful financier had been fascinated with cryptography since boyhood.

"What do you plan to do, Jesse?" Jeff asked abruptly. "If—oh, let's cut the bullshit—when the civil war breaks out."

The air force commander's eyes moved to the

window. Not looking at anything in particular, just keeping an eye on the weather.

"To be honest, I'm not sure. Admiral Simpson thinks we should both stay neutral. Mind you, that would include refusing to obey any orders—even ones from the prime minister—that would get us involved. So I guess we could still be accused of mutiny."

"Neither Wettin nor Oxenstierna is that stupid," said Jeff. "They're acting as if they were right now, but they're not. They know perfectly well the most they can hope for from the USE navy and air force—not to mention the USE army—is to stay neutral. They'll be using nothing but Swedish mercenary troops and whatever they can get from the provincial armies."

"Have to be careful about that last, too," said Thorsten. "Or the SoTF will throw its army into the fight, and it's probably stronger than any of the provincial forces except possibly Hesse-Kassel's."

"No, it won't," said Jesse. "I've talked to Ed Piazza about it, not more than a week ago. He's expecting the Bavarians to attack the Oberpfalz if—when—the civil war starts. It's got no protection left except Engels' regiment, since Oxenstierna ordered Banér to march his troops into Saxony. If they do, he doesn't see where he has any choice but to commit the SoTF army against them."

Thorsten grimaced. "I hadn't thought of that possibility. It seems a bit risky for Maximilian, though."

"Not if he's been given assurances that the Swedes won't intervene," Jesse said, his tone harsh. "Assurances that he figures come from Oxenstierna, even if nothing's said openly."

"But . . . That would be—"

"Treason? What does Oxenstierna care if he loses

one USE province but gets the rest of it? None of which he had before anyway, the way he sees it."

Engler leaned back in his chair and brought his cup to his mouth. He didn't drink from it, though, and after a few seconds he set it back down again. He was a little shaken. Thorsten was not a cynical man by nature. *Still something of a country rube*, was the way he'd once put it to his betrothed, Caroline Platzer. The idea that Sweden's own chancellor would connive with an open enemy like the duke of Bavaria against his own nation . . .

Except he wouldn't see it that way. Jesse was right. Oxenstierna would always look at the world from a Swedish vantage point—and that of Sweden's aristocracy, to boot. From his perspective, the USE was an ignoble bastard. Not even that, a domestic animal run amok. Was it "treason" for a farmer to use hounds to bring down unruly livestock?

"You didn't get around to answering my question, Jesse," said Jeff.

Jesse smiled thinly. "Noticed that, did you? Well, a good part of the reason I'm flying to Prague is to talk to Mike about it. I want to know what he thinks."

"He'll tell you the same thing Simpson did," said Jeff.

The air force colonel's eyes widened. "You think so? I was kind of figuring . . ." He sat up very straight, suddenly. "Don't tell me that *you* . . ."

"Different situation, Jesse. The air force and the navy are seen by most people as up-timer services. The army isn't. Whatever Mike winds up doing won't automatically have repercussions on Americans. That's not true for you and Simpson."

Wood frowned. "That logic seems kind of twisted to me. What the hell, Mike himself is an American."

Thorsten extended his hand, waggling it back and forth. "Yes and no. American by origin, certainly. But what do they call him now? 'Prince of Germany,' no? With everything that's happened, he's transcended his origin in the eyes of most people in the Germanies. Certainly most commoners. They almost forget about it—where they are reminded any time they see an airplane or an ironclad. No, I think Colonel Higgins has the right of it here."

Jesse went back to looking out the window. After a few seconds, he said, "And what about you, Jeff? Leaving aside whatever Mike decides to do."

Higgins shrugged. "I don't expect I'll have to worry about Mike Stearns." He drained the last of his own cup. "My wife's in Dresden, Jesse. The time comes I think she's against the ropes, fuck everything else. I figure my men will come with me, too."

Thorsten didn't have any doubt about that. Jesse glanced at him and must have read his posture correctly. "You're only one regiment," he pointed out.

Jeff still seemed quite unperturbed. "An oversized regiment that goes by the name of the Hangman. But, yes, you're right. We're only one regiment."

He grinned, suddenly. "Look at it this way, Jesse—by the time Banér manages to get Gretchen against the ropes, what kind of shape do you think *he's* going to be in?"

Prague, capital of Bohemia

"Stay out of it, Jesse. Openly, at least. What Jeff said to you was right on the money."

Mike Stearns leaned over the railing of the great bridge that spanned the Vltava in the center of the city, and idly watched a barge passing below. "What the army does is one thing. The air force and navy, something else. To put it a bit crudely, the army's German and the other two services are American."

"Hell, Mike, the navy's personnel is already almost all German. Once you get past John Chandler Simpson, anyway, and a few others like Eddie Cantrell. So's the air force, except for the pilots. And even there . . ." He paused for an instant, to do a quick calculation. "Give it six months and the majority of my pilots will be down-timers too."

"Doesn't matter. It's the technology involved that makes all the difference. Especially with the air force. The navy's new generation of warships are sailing ships, where it's the down-timers who really have most of the know-how. So I expect it won't be long before people think of the navy the way they do the army. But whenever they see one of your planes in the sky, you might as well be skywriting: 'Look! American gadget!'"

The air force officer thought about it for a while. Eventually, albeit reluctantly, he nodded his head. "Okay. I guess. But you said 'openly.' That implies something."

Mike grinned at him. "You can keep me informed of all important troop movements in or around Saxony, can't you? That doesn't involve doing anything more than flying reconnaissance, which you do anyway. Got to keep an eye on the Polish border and the Austrians"—he gestured with his chin to the south—"just down there a ways."

"Sure. What else?"

"Well, it occurs to me that you overfly the fortress at Königstein every time you come down this way."

Jessed smiled thinly. "Well, not quite. But it'd be easy enough to vary the route. If the powers-that-be whine about it, I'll make noises about tailwinds and tetchy weather and such forcing me a tad off course. I take it you want regular reports about the state of the garrison there?"

Mike shook his head. "Actually, no. I want you to keep Colonel Higgins up to date. It'll be his Hangman Regiment that has to deal with Königstein."

"It's easy enough for me justify landing here, Mike, or at České Budějovice when you get the airfield down there finished. But—"

"That'll be in four days, my engineers tell me. Most of my division's already there."

"But landing in Tetschen's something else. Once or twice, sure. But I don't see how I can legitimately explain regular landings. And they're bound to find out."

"Higgins has a radio. It won't reach here or Dresden reliably, but it'll reach a plane flying right overhead, won't it?"

Jesse pursed his lips. "Yeah, it will. Have to make sure nobody's listening in, but . . . that's easy enough."

He glanced up at the imposing sight of Prague Castle, atop the Hradčany. The huge palace and the great hill it sat upon dominated the whole city. "What about Wallenstein?"

"What about him?" Mike followed Jesse's gaze, then pointed toward a palace at the foot of the hill. "He lives in his own palace down here, by the way, not up in the Hradčany. I don't think he's been up there in months, since his health . . ."

He let that sentence die a natural death. "Wallenstein's not very concerned about the inner workings of the USE, Jesse. Just as long as we back him against the Austrians and don't get in his way if he nibbles at Ruthenia."

"If you take the Third Division out of Bohemia, he might squawk."

"If I have to take the Third Division out of Bohemia, squawks coming from Prague will be the least of my concerns."

Jesse chuckled. "Well, that's true."

Mike shrugged. "He's not really that worried about the Austrians anyway, I don't think. They've been awfully quiet these past few months, and they certainly won't launch any attack on Bohemia in the middle of winter."

Vienna, capital of the Austro-Hungarian Empire

Janos Drugeth finished reading the report. For the third time, actually. It hadn't taken but a few minutes, because the report was only two pages long.

"This wasn't sent by Schmid," he said, waggling the sheets. "It's much too sketchy. It's got very little detail and no analysis at all."

The Austrian emperor frowned down on the papers in Drugeth's hand. "You think the report is a fake? A Turkish scheme of some kind?"

"No. What would be the point? I think it was sent by one of Schmid's underlings. Which would lead me to believe that he's gone into hiding. Or he's dead or in a Turkish prison somewhere."

He rose from his chair in Ferdinand's private audience chamber and began pacing about. He didn't even think of asking permission to do so. Janos and his monarch had been close friends since boyhood.

The emperor just watched him, for a minute or so. Then he said, "Come on, speak up! It won't irritate me any less if you wait another hour. Or another day."

Drugeth smiled. "So hard to keep anything from you. But I do hope you aren't being encouraged to do something rash, Ferdinand." He was one of the handful of men who could address Austria's ruler in that manner. Only when they were alone, of course.

The emperor threw up his hands. "Ah! I knew you would say that!" The hands came down and gripped the armrests. Quite fiercely. Ferdinand spent the next minute just glaring. Ten seconds, at Janos; the rest of the time, at one of the portraits on the wall. That of his great-grandmother, Anne of Bohemia—who was quite blameless in the matter. She'd been dead for almost ninety years.

"Ah!" he exclaimed again. "I *knew* you'd say that!"

"This changes nothing, Ferdinand, that I can see. If anything, it makes the possibility of a threat from the Ottoman Empire even greater. The Persians were the main thing holding them in check. Now that they've retaken Baghdad, Murad may well make peace with the Safavids."

"Who says they'll agree?"

Janos shrugged. "They did in that other universe, didn't they? When Murad took Baghdad in 1638 instead of three years earlier, as he did in this one."

He looked back down at the sheets. "And why did he move so quickly, one has to wonder?"

The emperor grunted. "He reads the history books too. Saw that he'd managed it in another time and place and figured, why wait?"

"Possibly, yes. But here's what else is possible, if Murad ponders the larger lessons of those history books. In the end, the Ottomans were not brought down by the Persians. They were brought down by Christian powers."

"Not by us!" Ferdinand said, making a face. "We were allied with them in that miserable war."

"That doesn't really matter. The Austria of that other world is not the Austria of this one. The changes have already begun. Murad would understand that, I think. And would sense that, in whatever form, it will always be Europe that truly threatens his empire. In the long run, if not now. But he's a young man and expects to rule for a long time, I imagine."

Ferdinand took a deep breath and held it for some time, then he let it out in a rush.

Again, he threw up his hands. "Fine! Fine! I accept your advice. Reluctantly. Grudgingly. I'm so aggravated, in fact, I'm not inviting you to dinner with the royal family tonight. Nor breakfast tomorrow. Lunch . . . possibly."

Drugeth nodded, looking very solemn. "Punishment, indeed."

The emperor made a snorting noise. "But don't plan for a long lunch! Since you've made such an issue of this, I want you back down in the Balkans, seeing what you can find out. Right away."

Janos decided not to tell Ferdinand he'd been about to make the same proposal. The emperor's peevish mood would just get worse.

Chapter 16

"Look! There's the admiral!" Kristina pointed excitedly to a figure standing on the dock toward which the *Union of Kalmar* was slowly moving. "He came down to meet us himself."

Prince Ulrik nodded sagely. That seemed wiser, under the circumstances, than stating openly that he'd have been astonished if the admiral *hadn't* come down to greet them in person as soon as they arrived. Merely as a matter of protocol, being the heir apparent to his own nation as well as two others, the princess outranked the admiral by a considerable margin.

Still, she was only eight years old—no, nine now, he reminded himself. Her birthday was still a few days away, on December 18, but Kristina was already referring to herself as nine years old in the same manner in which she'd say the sun and the moon were in the sky. A fact, an established truth, a philosophical and ethical axiom.

You contradicted her at your peril. In less than a week, it would be true anyway, so why not accept the inevitable? If ever there lived a prince who was the

185

diametric opposite of Don Quixote, it was Ulrik of Denmark—a land that was almost entirely flat, windy, and had plenty of windmills going about their useful business. What sort of fool would want to knock one down?

Ulrik had assumed that Simpson would greet them at the dock, but his purpose in doing so remained to be seen. From the very pleased expression on Kristina's face, it was obvious the princess simply assumed that Simpson was there to extend a welcome. Ulrik, on the other hand, would not be at all surprised if the American admiral had come down to order them to steam right back out of the harbor.

He could enforce such orders, too, if it came to that. Simpson had seen to it that his naval base in Luebeck would not suffer the same ignominious fate as the ironclads had visited on Copenhagen and Hamburg. In the year and a half that had passed since Denmark's capitulation, the admiral had overseen the creation of a ship-building and armaments industrial complex in Luebeck. It might be better to say, he'd completed what Gustav Adolf had begun during the months the emperor had stayed in Luebeck while it was being besieged by the Ostend armies.

Some of the fruits of that project were quite visible from the deck of the *Union of Kalmar*: a battery of four guns positioned behind thick fortifications that commanded the entire harbor. From a distance, their precise size couldn't be determined. At a guess, Ulrik thought they probably didn't quite match the *Union of Kalmar's* ten-inch main guns. But they didn't really need to, either. At this range, rifled eight-inch guns firing explosive shells could destroy the ironclad long before its own fire could do much damage to the harbor's fortifications. Even six-inch guns would probably manage the job.

It wouldn't come to that, of course. If Simpson ordered them to steam out of Luebeck, Ulrik would not argue the matter. He'd do it and head north for Copenhagen.

He really wanted to avoid that option, though, if at all possible. He and Kristina would certainly be safe from Oxenstierna in Copenhagen. But Ulrik was almost as anxious to stay out of his father's grasp as he was to stay out of the Swedish chancellor's.

Rather to Ulrik's surprise and certainly to his relief, King Christian IV of Denmark had kept what the Americans called a low profile since the beginning of the political crisis produced by Gustav Adolf's incapacitation. Why? The prince didn't know, he could only guess. He wouldn't have been astonished if his mercurial father had been reckless enough to announce that he was dissolving the Union of Kalmar and reasserting Denmark's complete independence.

Thankfully, he hadn't. At a guess, because Christian was a very intelligent man, beneath the grandiose ambitions and consumption of alcohol. He could even be shrewd, from time to time. Perhaps he'd calculated that the crisis was just as likely to enhance Denmark's status as diminish it—which was Ulrik's own assessment—and so it would be wiser to let things unfold for a while without meddling.

If Ulrik and Kristina had to seek refuge in Copenhagen, however, he thought his father's prudence would fly right out the window and head south for the winter. The temptation would be too great. Christian could . . .

God only knew what might come to his mind, especially when he was drunk. Declaring himself the new ruler of the Union of Kalmar would be almost certain. Gustav Adolf had had his wits addled two months ago and there was no sign of recovery.

Long enough! Long live the new High King!

A few tankards later, the blessed parent might decide his offspring should now be declared the regent of the USE on the grounds that her father's incapacity had made Kristina the rightful empress—but since she was a mere child, could not rule on her own behalf, and who was the most suitable person to become regent other than the prince to whom she was betrothed?

Unless, of course—let's say, three tankards later— the king of Denmark decided that his son Ulrik was after all a mere stripling—but twenty-four years of age; pfah! barely weaned—and so Christian himself should assume the burden of regency.

The worst of such schemes is that they would actually work...for a while. No matter who won the civil war in the USE that Oxenstierna and Wilhelm Wettin seemed determined to precipitate, both the USE and Sweden would be greatly weakened. In the case of Sweden, quite possibly weakened enough that Denmark could regain its former dominance of Scandinavia.

Scandinavians! Ulrik supposed it was inevitable that people were parochial, and found it hard to see the world except through their own lenses and prisms. Still, even allowing for that natural bias, did Scandinavian princes have to set the standard for myopic stupidity? Couldn't they at least strive for the status of mere dullards?

There were today a total of perhaps five million

people in all of the Scandinavian lands. There was nothing close to what the Americans would consider a real census, to be sure, but for these purposes the figure was accurate enough. Say, two million each in Denmark and Sweden, and a half million each in Norway and Finland.

There were already at least fifteen million Germans.

And the disparity would simply get worse, as time passed. Ulrik had taken the opportunity on one of his visits to Grantville to look up the figures for himself in one of their "almanacs." According to the latest almanac in their possession, that of the year 1999—the Ring of Fire had happened in May of 2000, by their reckoning—the population of Germany had been slightly over eighty million people. It was the most populous nation in Europe outside of gigantic Russia.

That same year, Denmark had a little more than five million people; Sweden was the largest of the Scandinavian countries with almost nine million; Norway, four and a half million; and Finland was about the same as Denmark. In other words, in less than four centuries a three-to-one population disparity would becomes four-to-one.

And that was the least of it. The German lands were rich; the Scandinavian, poor, outside of a few important resources such as iron. And petroleum, at a much later date when technology had advanced far enough to drill for oil in the sea beds.

But the one critical resource that was lacking in Scandinavia—was lacking today; would be lacking centuries from now; would *always* be lacking short of a great climatic transformation—was arable soil. The Scandinavian lands had and would always have a much smaller population than the Germanies. That was a reality dictated by nature, not by any human factor that might be subject to change.

The historical end result was inevitable. It had been inevitable in the world the Americans came from; it was just as inevitable in this one. The Germanies were the center of gravity of Europe. Not Denmark, not Sweden—not even France. Only the Russias would emerge as a true counterweight, once they were united. But Russia was too far to the east to really dominate European political affairs. It was almost as much an Asian country as a European one.

So what sort of madman would imagine that a Scandinavian ruler could maintain his control of the Germans for more than a few years?

A rhetorical question, of course. Two answers sprang immediately forward: His own father and Gustav II Adolf. If Ulrik could round up a Lapp chieftain somewhere in northern Finland, they'd make the same claim.

Well, maybe not. They had the advantage of being illiterate.

Ulrik, however, was not subject to the same insanity. And he had, by his estimate, at least a decade in which to persuade his future wife to forego it as well.

He thought he could succeed in that project. True, Kristina had an imperious temperament. But she was not engrossed with power, as such. She just liked the end results she could obtain from it. Even at the age of nine, her basic character was already evident—and Ulrik had confirmed his assessment by consulting the American history books to see how she'd turned out in that alternate universe. By now, very quietly, he'd had every single item of information Grantville possessed about Kristina stored in his private records, and had studied them to the point of having them memorized.

There was quite a bit, as it turned out. The up-timers had even once made a movie about her with someone named Greta Garbo cast as Kristina. There was no copy of it in Grantville, but that was probably just as well. When he inquired, he was told by one of the librarians that the Garbo woman had been a famous actress in her day. The librarian had some photographs of her in one of their books and had shown them to Ulrik.

The Garbo woman was quite beautiful. That had been enough, right there, to tell Ulrik that the movie had fictionalized Kristina's life to the point of absurdity. The only thing that would save the Swedish princess from being downright ugly when she grew up was that her vibrant personality would outshine her features.

Still, there had been a number of mentions of her in the various history texts. Far more than almost any other royal of the time period outside of Britain, even male ones.

Vibrant personality, indeed. Glimmers of it had lasted through four centuries and even made their way to another continent. But what people remembered was not her rule, but her discomfort with that rule. The simple truth was that Kristina had no natural aptitude or inclination to be a monarch. That was evident even now. In that other universe, her discomfort had eventually led her to abdicate the throne of Sweden, convert to Catholicism, and move to Rome.

Ulrik thought they could avoid the worst of that, in this universe. Kristina had already told him that her great ambition was to emulate someone named

Elkheart and be the first woman to fly an airplane all the way around the world. He would encourage her in that direction—smoothing away the absurd edges, of course. Circumnavigating the Earth herself was out of the question, but Kristina had an active intellect as well as an adventurous spirit. There was no reason she couldn't become this world's equivalent of Henry the Navigator, was there? Exceed him, in fact.

Ever since the Congress of Copenhagen, Ulrik had been pondering these matters. What sort of USE should they aim for? What would his role be? Kristina's?

Much remained unclear and uncertain, but Ulrik had reached some conclusions already.

First. The USE would soon—it already did, in many ways—surpass all other European lands as a center of population, industry, commerce, education and culture. It would certainly surpass the Scandinavian nations, regardless of political formalities.

Second. It would be a German nation. Not the only one, since Germans were a colonizing folk. But it would be the center of the German people.

Three. This was more in the way of a goal than a conclusion. In the universe the Americans had come from, the Germans had been politically fragmented until very late in their history. The vacuum that had created in European affairs had been disastrous. In the short run, disastrous for Germans. In the long run, disastrous for everyone.

It would not be so in this universe. Ulrik had spoken enough to Mike Stearns to know that the former prime minister was determined to avoid that at all costs. On that if nothing else, Ulrik agreed with him completely. That was one of the reasons he would oppose his father if Christian tried to pull the USE apart in Denmark's narrow immediate interest.

Europe needed a stable, powerful, secure and prosperous Germany at its center. Without that, there would always be chaos. Lurking right under the surface if not always in the open.

Four. The national sentiments of the German people, long dormant, were now rising very rapidly. The Ring of Fire had accelerated the process greatly. Something that had taken decades in the Americans' universe was happening in this one in a handful of years.

Five. Most importantly for Ulrik and Kristina's own situation, what all of this meant was that the USE's ruling dynasty would only survive if it transformed itself into a German dynasty. "German," at least, insofar as the populace accepted Kristina and Ulrik as legitimate and not foreign. Their Scandinavian roots would then be a moot point. Many European dynasties had origins outside their own countries; people took that much in stride as long as they felt the monarch was *theirs* and not the instrument of another power.

Six. This was his latest conclusion and still a bit tentative, but he was now almost certain that in order to accomplish any of his goals he—and Kristina; without her it would be impossible—had to accept that the future belonged to democracy and not monarchy. He'd read some of Scaglia's writings and agreed with him at least that far.

The Americans had had a peculiar sport, of which he'd watched videotapes. "Surfing," they called it.

Needless to say, Ulrik had no intention of half-freezing in the Baltic and risking his life on a flimsy little board. But stripped of the physical aspect and transformed into a political metaphor, "surfing" was exactly what he and Kristina would have to do for the rest of their lives. Ride the ever-growing, thundering waves of German nationalism and democracy toward the shore; understanding that they did not and could not control it. No one could, really. But they could learn to surf well. They—their children; grandchildren—could reach the shore safely. And if they did it well enough, help many other people to get there safely as well. Perhaps entire nations.

The *Union of Kalmar* had reached the dock, been tied up, and a gangway laid. Admiral Simpson started to come across.

"What did you say?" asked Kristina.

Ulrik realized he'd been muttering. "Ah..."

"He said, 'and here comes the big one.'" Baldur was grinning. He'd spent hours discussing these issues with Ulrik. "But he's quite wrong. This is just the outrider wave. The big one will be riding into Magdeburg."

"What is he talking about?" She glared up at Ulrik. "You're keeping things from me again, aren't you? And you promised you wouldn't!"

So. Once again, Baldur Norddahl demonstrated his perfidious, foul, treacherous nature. On the brighter side, once again Kristina dispelled any fears that he might have dimwitted children.

Chapter 17

"Please, have a seat." Admiral Simpson gestured toward a comfortable-looking divan with four equally comfortable-looking chairs clustered around a low table. The ensemble was located in one half of what Ulrik took to be the admiral's office. Part of his suite, rather. He could see other rooms connected to it, in one of which he spotted an up-time computer perched on a long desk.

The walls were decorated with paintings, but they were seascapes rather than the usual portraits. Three of them were representations of sailing vessels underway.

The variation from custom in the decor was a subtle reminder of the differences between the American and down-timers. At least, down-timers who could afford to commission art work in the first place. For such down-timers, the art's purpose was in large part to remind anyone who looked—perhaps themselves, first and foremost—of their lineage. To a very large degree, though not always and not entirely, it was that ancestry that explained and justified their present status.

Americans also cherished their ancestry, Ulrik had discovered, but the logic behind that esteem was often peculiar from a down-timer's standpoint. He'd been struck, for instance, by the fact that several Americans with whom he'd discussed the matter claimed—with great obvious pride—to number a "Cherokee" among their ancestors. In one case, a "Choctaw." Curious, Ulrik had looked up the references and discovered the Cherokees and Choctaws were barbarian tribes who'd been conquered by the white settlers of North America. Conquered, and then driven entirely off their land into the wilderness.

All Americans who could do so—which many couldn't, since they were the product of recent immigration—boasted of their polyglot lineage. *Father's side is mostly Polish, but with some Irish mixed in there. Mother's side is part-Italian, part-Pennsylvania Dutch—those were actually Germans, not Dutch—and part Scots-Irish.*

Something along those lines was what you generally heard, where a European nobleman would stress the narrowness of his line. Its purity, to look at it another way.

Not royal families, of course. There simply weren't enough of them to avoid constant marriages across national lines. But that simply reinforced the status of royal blood as a special category of its own.

For the up-timers, the pride they took in their lineage had very little to do with their present status. That was defined almost entirely by their occupation. Indeed, it was considered a mark of honor for a man to have achieved a high position *without* the benefit of family patronage, although such patronage was certainly common and not derided.

So, John Chandler Simpson's walls had paintings of

ships and the sea on them. As well he might, given the ships in question. Ulrik had enjoyed this second crossing of the Baltic in an ironclad even less than the first. The warships were tolerable enough in calm waters, if you could ignore their acrid stench. But any sort of rough seas—and it didn't take much, for a sea to be rough for an ironclad—made them thoroughly unpleasant. On two occasions, Ulrik had begun to worry that they might sink.

The one thing he hadn't been worried about, however, was Chancellor Oxenstierna. Had a Swedish warship crossed their path and tried to prevent the *Union of Kalmar* from taking its royal passengers to their destination . . .

But its commander never would have tried in the first place. No more would a mouse try to impede a bull crossing a pasture. The ironclads completely dominated any patch of the seas they passed through.

Simpson's ironclads—and, as the diagrams and designs on some of the walls in the anteroom showed, the same man was now creating a new line of warships. Sailing ships, these, but Ulrik didn't doubt they would overshadow any sailing ships that currently existed in any navy in the world.

Once they were seated, Simpson asked: "Would you care for any refreshments?" He looked at Caroline Platzer. "I have some real coffee, I might mention."

Platzer's hand flew to her throat, her expression one of histrionic relief and pleasure. "Oh, thank Go—gosh. Yes, Admiral, please. A bit of cream, if you have it."

"Sugar? I have some actual sugar, too, it's not the usual honey."

"Really? Then, yes, I'd appreciate some sugar also."

The admiral turned to the down-timers. "Your Highnesses? Mister...ah..."

"Baldur Norddahl," said Ulrik. "He is my...ah..."

The admiral smiled thinly. "I'm familiar with Mr. Norddahl, at least by reputation."

Baldur looked a bit alarmed. Perhaps for that reason, he asked for nothing. Ulrik and Kristina both settled on broth.

The admiral rang a small bell that had been sitting on a side table. A moment later, a servant appeared. A naval enlisted man, judging from the uniform, not a house servant.

And there was another variation in custom. Americans used servants—indeed, ones who'd been wealthy like Simpson were quite accustomed to doing so—but they used them differently. Even a man as powerful and prestigious as Simpson did not think twice about asking his guests for their preferences, as if he were a mere waiter in a restaurant. The orders taken, he would then summon a servant to do the actual work—but he would have to *summon* them. Usually, with a bell of some sort. He couldn't simply crook his finger at one of the servants already in the room. There weren't any.

This was an American custom that Ulrik had already adopted for his own, and had every intention of expanding into imperial practice once he and Kristina were married. He would gladly exchange the trivial chore of having to ring a bell for the great advantage of having some *privacy*—the one commodity that was in shortest supply for a royal family.

There were two other advantages to the custom, as well, both of them cold-bloodedly practical. The first was that it made it more difficult for enemies to spy on you. They couldn't just suborn one of the servants. The second was that it would add a bit to the patina of egalitarianism that Ulrik intended to slather all over the new dynasty.

In truth, Ulrik was not burdened with any high regard for egalitarianism. But that sentiment was already burgeoning in this new world and he knew it would only continue to swell. Establishing the new dynasty's friendliness toward the sentiment—perhaps no more than a tip of the hat, here and there, but polite formalities were important—was just part of the surfing process.

The naval enlisted man returned shortly with a tray bearing the various refreshments ordered. The admiral himself, like Platzer, had ordered coffee. Simpson waited politely until everyone else had sipped from their cups, and then took a sip from his own.

From the slight grimace, he found the coffee still too hot. He set down the cup and said, "I need to ask—my apologies, but this is an awkward position you've put me in—what your intentions are."

Ulrik had expected the question, and had given careful consideration to the right answer. He thought he'd come up with one that would be suitably vague without being transparently vacuous.

Kristina made it all a moot point, however. "We're going to Magdeburg!" she exclaimed cheerfully.

Simpson stared at her for a moment. Then, at Ulrik. Then, at Platzer. He gave Baldur no more than a glance.

That wasn't an indication of anyone's status in the admiral's eyes, just his judgment of who was immediately critical. Quite good judgment, it turned out.

"Your Highness"—this was said directly to Kristina—"with your permission, I would like to speak privately to Prince Ulrik."

She frowned. "Well..."

"Of course, Admiral," said Platzer. She rose and extended her hand to the princess. "Come on, Kristina." Seeing the girl's stubborn expression, Caroline added gently, "It's a perfectly reasonable request on the admiral's part."

Kristina was still looking stubborn.

"Now, Kristina."

The girl pouted, but rose. After giving Ulrik a sharp glance—*you'd better not try to keep any secrets from me!*—she took Caroline's hand and followed her out of the room. Baldur came right behind them.

After the door closed, Simpson smiled. "I have to say I am deeply impressed."

Ulrik shook his head. The gesture was simultaneously admiring and rueful. "No one else can do it. I certainly can't. Caroline's come to be something close to the mother Kristina never had. Well...more like a very respected governess crossed with a favorite aunt. We're quite fortunate to have found her."

"Yes, I think you are." Simpson leaned forward and picked up his cup. This time, he took a full drink from it.

"I need to know your intentions, Your Highness. Frankly, and in full. This is not a situation into which I can afford to steam blindly."

Ulrik had been thinking quickly ever since Kristina blurted out the truth. More precisely, he'd been trying to discipline his will after figuring out what to do. That much had taken no more than ten seconds, since he really had no alternatives.

Unfortunately—or not; it could be argued either way—speaking frankly and in full came as unnaturally to a prince as dancing to a bear. Not . . . impossible, as it would have been for a fish. Just difficult to do, much less to do well.

Where to start?

"I'd like to avert a civil war, if possible."

Simpson shook his head. "So would I—but I think that time has passed."

Yes, difficult to do well. Ulrik had exactly the same opinion as the admiral, so why had he wasted their time with pious platitudes?

"Well, yes, I agree. I should have said that I hope to limit the damages produced by the coming civil war."

"Limit them, how? I'm sorry, Your Highness—"

"I think you'd better call me Ulrik," the prince interrupted brusquely. Informality came no easier than speaking frankly or fully. But under these circumstances, he needed to adopt—accept, at least—another up-time custom.

Simpson paused, then nodded. "Probably a good idea, given what we face. And please call me John."

"Not 'John Chandler'?"

The admiral smiled—quite widely, this time. "Not unless you're announcing me to a crowd of rich people whom my wife is planning to fleece for one of her charities. Or you're my mother about to give me a scolding."

Ulrik laughed. So the fearsome admiral had a sense of humor? Who would have guessed? He'd sooner expected to see a dancing fish.

"To be honest, John, I'm feeling my way here. Operating by instinct, as I once heard an American say. If that's too vague for you, my apologies. But it's the simple truth."

"I can accept that. I've done the same myself, at times. Still, you must have a sense of the parameters within which your instincts are operating."

"Oh, yes. There are three such parameters, I think. The first is that Oxenstierna's goal, regardless of its intrinsic merits—I'm simply not interested in that issue any longer—is impossible. For good or ill, monarchical rule and aristocratic privilege is crumbling. 'Privilege,' at least, insofar as it pertains to wielding political influence."

The admiral nodded. "That's the critical issue. We still had plenty of noblemen in the world I came from, and a high percentage of them were still wealthy. But you were far more likely to find them gambling in the casinos in Monaco than playing for stakes on the fields of power. Go on."

"The second parameter is military. Neither side has a clear advantage there. The provincial armies are fairly evenly matched. I think that of the SoTF is probably better than any of the others, even the highly-regarded forces of Hesse-Kassel. But the provinces that will naturally lean toward Oxenstierna and Wettin can place more soldiers on the field."

"Agreed."

"So it will come down to the Swedish mercenaries against whatever forces the democratic movement can muster."

"You're overlooking the city and town militias," said Simpson. "They'll mostly side with Oxenstierna. Well,

Wettin—they're no fans of the chancellor. But Wettin is giving the Swedes the needed cover."

"That...depends a great deal on how the Fourth of July Party and the CoCs conduct themselves, John. If they're belligerent and provocative, then yes, certainly. By and large the town militias are instruments of the patricianate, who are even less fond of the CoCs than they are of the Swedes. But if Oxenstierna is seen as the aggressor, then I think you might be surprised at how many militias will choose to stand aside. There's a great deal of resentment toward the Swedes, although the dynasty itself is rather popular."

"All right. What's the third parameter, as you see it?"

"Legitimacy. Here again, both sides are about equally matched. It might be more accurate to say, equally mismatched."

The admiral grunted softly. "Both bastards, you're saying? On one side, a bunch of scruffy lowborn radicals. On the other, a bunch of arrogant noblemen, at least some of whom are Swedish puppets."

"Yes, precisely. That is the reason, of course, that if Gustav Adolf still had his wits about him, none of this would be happening. He *does* have legitimacy, and it's recognized by everyone. Not even the CoCs have ever challenged the dynasty; not openly, at any rate, however much they may mutter in their cups of an evening."

Again, there was a pause. Simpson left off his scrutiny of the prince to look out one of the windows.

"She's only nine years old, Ulrik," the admiral said softly.

"I understand that. But she's all the nation has left, John, unless the emperor recovers. And after two months, my hopes for that happening are fading."

Simpson sighed. "Yes, mine too. Strokes are things people usually recover from quickly or they never recover at all. I'm not as familiar with this sort of brain injury, but I think it's not too different."

His eyes came back to Ulrik. "Even if you go to Magdeburg—even if you proclaim Kristina the new empress from the steps of the royal palace—you won't be able to stop the war. There's too much momentum behind it now. Oxenstierna is too committed, for one thing. For another—I don't know if you've heard yet—Banér has reached Dresden and his troops have been committing atrocities since they entered Saxony. The city has closed its gates to him. Gretchen Richter is now ruling Dresden—and she's taken off all the gloves and stripped away whatever fig leaves she still had on. I don't know if this will mean anything to you, but she's calling the city's new governing council the Committee of Public Safety."

Ulrik scowled. "Does that woman *always* have to sow the earth with salt?"

"In this case, I have to say I think she's doing the right thing. Banér has made it crystal clear that he'll be following no rules except those of the blade. And Oxenstierna is obviously making no effort to restrain him. Under those circumstances, what do you expect Richter to do, Ulrik? Try to play nice? That would not only be pointless, it'd sap the morale of her own people. The way it is, she's matching an ax to the Swedish sword." His lips twisted a little. "Or a guillotine, soon enough."

Ulrik pursed his lips, as if he'd bitten into a lemon. "I suppose. But to get back to where we were, I don't expect to stop the civil war, John. As I said earlier, I hope to limit the damages. And there is only one way I can see to do that. With this civil war, at any rate."

"How?"

"End it as quickly as possible, by helping one or the other side to win. But do so in a way that precludes—limits, at least—any wreaking of vengeance in the aftermath."

Slowly, Simpson picked up his cup again and drained it. Just as slowly, he set it down. "You're a nobleman, yourself. As highly ranked as it gets, in fact." He said that in a flat, even tone. Neutral, as it were; simply a statement of fact.

Ulrik shrugged, irritably. "Yes, I know. And I won't claim that the course of action I propose to takes is one I find very comfortable. But reality is what it is, John, whether I like or not. Whether that imbecile Oxenstierna likes it or not."

The admiral chuckled. "Not often you hear those two words put together. 'Oxenstierna' and 'imbecile.' The chancellor's actually a very intelligent man."

"There's no evidence of it right now. Just the instinctive behavior of an aristocrat, as brainless as a bull in rutting season." Ulrik waved his hand, in another irritable gesture. "In the long run, the victor in this contest is inevitable—and Oxenstierna should be able to see that for himself. All he will accomplish is to prolong the process, at the cost of great agony—and the risk of producing a Germany as distorted as the one in the universe you came from. Which is the last thing anyone needs."

The prince looked down at his own cup. He'd barely touched the broth, and found he had no more desire to do so now. Nothing wrong with it; the beverage was quite tasty. But when Ulrik was on edge, he lost all his appetite. It was hard to explain what he was groping for, exactly.

"What I hope, John—it's a gamble, I'll be the first to agree, and probably one at long odds—is that the legitimacy Kristina can give the democratic movement if she moves to Magdeburg will tip the scale in the civil war. And because of the way she tipped it, will restrain the victors from inflicting excessive punishment on the losers." He grimaced. "Whereas you can be sure that if *they* win, Oxenstierna and that pack of curs following him will drown the nation in a bloodbath even worse than the one which closed the Peasant War."

"Not in the SoTF, they won't," Simpson said, in a steely tone. "Make no mistake about this, Ulrik. I am trying to obey the law. So is Jesse Wood. So is Mike Stearns, for that matter. But if Oxenstierna starts massacring Americans, all bets are off."

The prince shook his head. "He won't do that. And if someone else starts, he'll put a stop to it. If for no other reason, no one wants to lose the Americans' skills. He doesn't need to destroy you Americans, John. He simply needs to hamstring your political influence. If he crushes the Committees of Correspondence and drives the Fourth of July Party under—to the fringes of power, at least—he will have accomplished that."

Simpson stared at him. "You're right, you know." He waved his hand also. "Not about the massacring business, about all of it. Americans have no magic powers. We simply... How to put it? Ignited something that would have erupted on its own anyway. You could put every American in a box and it wouldn't matter, in the long run."

"Not...exactly." Ulrik paused, while he tried to sort out his thoughts. "I think what Mike Stearns has been aiming for all along—from things he let drop in conversations; mostly from watching him—is to produce a Europe much less maimed and distorted than the one that came to be in your world. If so, with respect to his goal if not necessarily his methods, I have no dispute with him. Indeed, I'd be glad to lend a hand. And in that process, I think it's actually rather important that as many Americans as possible be kept out of boxes."

He and the admiral suddenly grinned at each other.

"Well!" said Simpson, rubbing his hands. "On *that*, we see eye-to-eye."

He leaned back in his chair and looked at the window again, for a few seconds. "All right, Ulrik. I will provide you and the princess with a refuge here. If Oxenstierna snarls at me, I will simply snarl back, point out that the laws involved are completely murky—and that if he pushes me too far, I can make his life a lot more miserable still."

Ulrik nodded. "Thank you. I take it you're trying to keep the navy as neutral as possible in the conflict?"

"Yes. Colonel Wood has agreed to do the same with the air force."

"Quite wise, I think. In any event, you won't be in this awkward position for more than a few days. Just long enough for us to make suitable arrangements to get to Magdeburg."

"Ah...Ulrik, I'd make a suggestion."

"Yes?"

"Stay here for a while. A few weeks, possibly even a month or two."

The prince's eyes widened. "Why?"

"Hard to explain. Now, *I'm* the one operating on instinct—and in a situation that doesn't come naturally to me, to make things worse." Simpson rose and went over to the window. "Back home, I was very far removed from a radical firebrand. Although I do think the charges of being a hidebound dinosaur leveled at me on occasion were quite unfair. Well, somewhat unfair."

For a few seconds, his hands clasped behind his back, he stared out the window. "I think you should let the situation unfold on its own, for a while. It's going to *anyway*, Ulrik. Even if you pop up in Magdeburg tomorrow, you can't stop Banér from attacking Dresden and you can't stop Richter and her people from fighting back. You can't stop Oxenstierna and Wettin from issuing whatever decrees they plan to issue from Berlin. One of which, by the way, I expect to be a decree that Berlin is henceforth the new capital."

"Yes, that's almost certain. Go on."

"Once those decrees come out, there'll be eruptions all over the Germanies—and counterattacks, in many places. The whole nation is soon going to be drowned in chaos and hubbub. Anything you and Kristina try to say will just get lost in the ruckus."

Ulrik thought about it. The admiral . . . had a point.

"In a month or so, though, the situation will be a lot clearer. At *that* point, moving to Magdeburg would have a tremendous impact. Probably not enough it itself to tip the scales. But . . ."

"But . . . what?"

Simpson scratched his chin. "There's one other variable we haven't talked about. That's Mike Stearns, sitting in Bohemia with a whole division at hand. And I happen to know—old boys' network, if you will—that he's made sure he can get back to Saxony very quickly, if and when the time comes."

Ulrik felt his face grow a bit pale. A bit paler, rather. He was a Danish prince whom no one would ever mistake for an Italian.

"Dear Lord," he whispered. "That would..."

He shook his head abruptly. "But do you think he'd do it?"

"Mike?" Simpson's tone was steely again. "Of all the stupid things Oxenstierna is doing, that's the stupidest. He'd do better to ask Lennart Torstensson instead of listening to his cronies."

Ulrik didn't understand the reference to Torstensson. His puzzlement must have shown.

"Sorry, you weren't there. I was standing next to Torstensson when the Magdeburg Crisis blew up. Me, Lennart and Mike Stearns. I've forgotten Mike's exact words, but they were something like this." His voice got that slight singsong that people slide into when they recite something from memory. "'I'll compromise, if possible, but don't make the mistake of thinking I don't know whose side I'm on.'

"He then pointed to a man standing nearby, in the crowd watching us. I don't know if the name will mean anything to you, but the man he pointed to was Gunther Achterhof."

Ulrik shook his head. "No, I'm afraid it doesn't."

"Gunther Achterhof is one of the central leaders of the CoC in Magdeburg, which is without a doubt the most radically inclined CoC in the Germanies. And even in *that* crowd, he's considered implacable."

"Ah."

"Lennart believed him. Then, and I imagine still now. I'm pretty sure, in fact, that's why he's been content to stay in Poznań, rather than intervene in what's taking place in Berlin. For somewhat different reasons, he's probably just as concerned as I am to keep the armed forces neutral and out of the direct fighting. Because he knows that sooner or later, a demon prince is going to come boiling out of Bohemia."

"Uh...when, would you think?"

The admiral's smile was now almost seraphic. "Oh, don't ever mistake Mike Stearns for a hothead. That man knows how to bide his time with the best of them."

"Ah. I see." After a while, the smile that came to Ulrik's face could almost be described as seraphic itself.

Part Three

January 1636

A rugged people

Chapter 18

Dresden

The first thing Eric Krenz sensed of the dawn was Tata's snoring. It wasn't a loud sound, just a soft and quite feminine snuffling. He found it rather attractive, actually. Granted, his viewpoint was heavily biased by his second sensation, which was the feel of her nude body plastered to his own under the heavy blankets.

Oh, what a splendid night had just passed! He opened his eyes and gave the ceiling no more than a glance. The window, likewise. The sun was starting to rise. He'd seen a lot of sunrises. Nothing of any great interest there. Not when...

He muzzled the back of Tata's neck. His hands began exploring. More precisely, returned to places already explored. Quite thoroughly, in fact.

Tata began stirring in response. Oh, what a splendid morning had just begun!

The sound of cannon fire erupted in the distance.

Tata sat up, as abruptly as a jack-in-the-box popping out. "It's started!"

She turned and gave Eric a shove. "Up! Up! You have to get out there!"

Eric groaned.

"Now!" Alas, Tata was in full dominatrix mode. The Tavern Keeper's Daughter Rampant.

Or the Barmaid On Steroids, as Friedrich Nagel liked to call her. He'd had to explain the up-time reference to Krenz. As it turned out, the lieutenant was planning to become a pharmacist after the war. He'd had to explain that term to Eric, as well. There was no such thing as a "pharmacist" in the year 1635, outside of a handful of Americans. A lot of apothecaries, to be sure, but apothecaries were usually hostile to the new methods and concepts emanating from Grantville.

"Get up, Eric! This is no time for dawdling! The Swedes are attacking!"

"They're just starting a barrage," he grumbled. His hands clutched the bedding in a last-ditch effort to stay in paradise. "This'll go on for weeks. *Weeks,* Tata."

"Up! Up! Up!" She swiveled in the bed, planted her feet on Eric's back and buttocks, and thrust mightily. Tata was short, but quite strong. Eric flew out of the bed onto the floor.

Paradise lost.

He was in a cheerier mood a few minutes later, though. As she bustled him out the door, Tata said, "You may as well move your things in here as soon as you get a chance. That'll give Friedrich some privacy."

She made those statements with the same assertiveness that Tata made most statements. The woman was bossy, there was no doubt about it. On the other hand, Eric didn't really mind being bossed around by Tata;

not, at least, when he considered the side benefits. She was just as assertive in bed and very affectionate.

So. If all went well and the damn Swedes didn't get overly rambunctious, tonight would be paradise regained.

Tata lived in one of the many small apartments in the Residenzschloss that had formerly been used by servants. At the end of the corridor leading from her apartment, Eric turned right as he usually did to get to the tower that gave the best view of the city. But before he could take more than two steps, Tata had him by the scruff of the neck and was dragging him the other way.

"No, you don't! No sightseeing today! You have to get out on the battlements!"

"Why?" he demanded. "I can see what's happening better from the tower."

"The troops need to see you on the battlements. It's *important*, Eric. You're one of the commanding officers."

He shrugged off her clutching hand but didn't try to alter their course. "Don't call them 'battlements,'" he said. "The term's silly. This isn't a medieval castle with arrow slits."

"Fine, fine. Fortified things. Whatever makes you happy. As long as you move faster."

She picked up the pace, forcing him to do likewise.

"The only thing the walls of a star fort have in common with ancient battlements is that they're both freezing in January," he grumbled. "Whereas the tower—which gives a commanding officer a far better view of the field—has a fireplace inside."

"Stop whining. The men have to be cold, don't they? You have to share their trials."

"Not my fault they're unambitious slackers."

"Ha!" She gave him a glance that was half-irritated and half-affectionate. Eric got a lot of those looks from her. "I don't think I've ever met a man with less ambition than you have. You just stumble into things."

That was true enough, Eric admitted to himself. He'd certainly never planned to become an officer!

He retraced the steps of his life, as they moved through the huge palace toward the entrance. He'd started as a gunsmith's apprentice after he finished his schooling, simply because that was the family trade. He'd found the work quite fascinating, though; not so much because he had any particular interest in guns but because he enjoyed the intricate craftsmanship involved.

He liked mechanical things. He'd found the same interest in the equipment he'd maintained once he joined the army. At first, anyway, when he'd been an enlisted man in the artillery. He'd had many fewer opportunities to do mechanical work once he became an officer.

And why had he done *that*? He tried to remember.

They reached the entrance and went outside. Immediately, the cold clamped down.

"January!" Eric hissed. "The ugliest word in the language."

"Stop whining."

They started slogging through the snow toward the fortifications. Well, "slogging" was mostly Eric's disgruntled mood at work. In truth, there was less than two inches of snow on the ground, hardly enough to impede their progress to any noticeable degree.

Oh, yes. As an officer, Eric had found it possible to enroll in the new college the army had set up. That had been the factor that tipped his decision to accept a commission. With his own resources, Krenz couldn't have afforded to attend a college or university.

Eventually, he'd heard from one of the college's instructors, Torstensson planned to turn it into a full-fledged military academy—the first such created in the world. Their world, at least. It would be patterned after institutions in the world the Americans came from. Places with names like West Point, Sandhurst and Saint-Cyr.

In the meantime, though, it had been a fairly modest sort of school. For one thing, it only gave two years of instruction. Jeff Higgins had told him it was the equivalent of what up-timers called a "junior" or "community" college. But it was better than any other educational option available at the time.

His course of study had been general, with no particular focus. Had *intended* to be general, it would be better to say. He'd barely finished one semester when Gustav Adolf started this new war. (What was it about Swedes, anyway? Did the milk they drank as youngsters come from a special breed of belligerent cows?) Eric still had no clear idea of what he wanted to do with the rest of his life, assuming he survived the war. Something involving mechanics, most likely. But beyond that, he had no idea.

Blessedly, Tata did not press him on the matter. She was odd, that way. Most young women of a bossy temperament never stopped pestering their men about their goals and ambitions. But Tata never did. She seemed content with modifying Eric's daily behavior to suit her liking, and was willing to let him figure out what he'd be doing in the months and years to come.

Maybe that was because she'd been a nobleman's leman before she got involved with Eric. Tata's way of describing that relationship—quite typical of her—was to refer to Duke Eberhard as her "boyfriend," an up-time loan word that Eric found particularly grotesque. Despite the silly term, though, not even Tata had thought to inquire as to the duke of Württemberg's ambitions and goals. Perhaps she was just carrying the habit over to her relationship with Krenz.

Eric felt occasional twinges of jealousy when he thought of that former involvement, but they were only twinges and they only came once in a while. For a start, the man was dead. Hard to feel much venom toward a corpse, after all. What possible further ill could you wish upon the fellow? But leaving that aside, Krenz was not much given to jealousy anyway. Or spite, or envy. He'd admit himself that he had faults, but they were generally the faults of a cheerful man perhaps a bit too fond of his immediate pleasures.

He heard a shrill, piercing call from ahead. A shriek, almost.

He couldn't make out the word, but he didn't need to. He'd heard that same call before, more than once. *Incoming.*

Fortunately, they'd reached a corner. He lunged forward, seized Tata around the waist, and hauled her behind the shelter of a tall building.

"What are you—!" But she didn't resist. She didn't even finish the sentence. Tata was very far from dimwitted.

A moment later, they heard a loud crashing sound. No explosion, though. Either the Swedes had fired a round shot into the city or the exploding shell had been a dud. Judging from the sound—bricks shattering; a lot of them—Eric was pretty sure it was round shot. Something awfully heavy had to have done that.

"We'll have to move carefully from here on," he said. "Stay under cover as much as we can."

When they reached the fortifications, Eric saw that Gretchen Richter was already there. She was walking slowly down the line of soldiers manning the bastions and curtain wall, talking with each gun crew as she came to them. Doing what Eric was planning to do himself, and what other officers would be doing in other bastions and along other curtain walls. The words they'd be speaking were not really that important, taken by themselves. What mattered was an officer's relaxed and calm demeanor.

No officer could do that better than Gretchen, though. The woman had a knack for projecting confidence that, given her youth—she was only twenty-six years old—was uncanny. Friedrich Nagel was of the opinion that she'd either sold her soul to the devil or to Saint Jude Thaddeus, the patron saint of lost causes and desperate situations.

Whatever the source of her poise, Krenz was glad to see her. Gretchen steadied his nerves the same way she did everyone else's.

The cannon fire from the Swedish lines started picking up. This would go on for weeks, in all likelihood. The army camped outside Dresden's walls numbered about fifteen thousand men. The city itself had a population of somewhere between thirty and forty thousand, but that had been greatly expanded by refugees pouring in from the countryside over the past weeks. Dresden's defenders could put three thousand able-bodied men on the walls, with at least that many available as a reserve in case Banér ordered a major frontal assault.

To make things still more difficult for Banér, he didn't have enough soldiers to really seal off the city. Especially not in wintertime, when his men would shirk their responsibility to maintain patrols at night and loads could be moved into the city by sleigh without needing to use roads. Dresden's population would be on short rations, but they wouldn't be in any danger of starving for at least a year.

Probably longer, in fact. Gretchen Richter and the CoC had clamped down their control of Dresden. The fact that Richter used a velvet glove whenever she could didn't change the fact that the grip itself was one of iron. Whatever anyone thought of the political program and policies of the CoC, one thing was indisputable: they greatly strengthened a city under siege, if they were in charge. Rations would be evenly and fairly apportioned; sanitation and medical measures would be rigorously applied and enforced; spies and traitors would be watched for vigilantly.

Those measures directly addressed the most common reasons a city fell—hunger, disease and treachery. The risks weren't eliminated, but they were significantly reduced. At a guess, Eric thought any city run by Gretchen Richter could withstand a siege half again as long as it would otherwise. Maybe even twice as long. She was one of those rare people of great notoriety whose reputations weren't overblown at all.

Odd, really, to think that she was the wife of his good friend Jeff Higgins.

"Stop daydreaming!" scolded Tata, giving his shoulder a little nudge. "Shouldn't you be ordering the men to fire a cannon or something?"

✧　　✧　　✧

Noelle Stull tried to ignore the sound of the cannonade. The house she'd rented was large, well built, and located toward the center of the city. The odds that a cannon ball fired from one of the besiegers' guns would strike her down at her writing desk were very slight. She'd faced much greater risks any number of times in the past. Although she'd been classified as a statistician, her real duties for the State of Thuringia-Franconia's innocuously named Department of Economic Resources had been those of an undercover operative. An investigator, officially, although given the murky realities of power in which she'd moved, she'd been as much a spy as a detective. At one time or another she'd been shot at, imprisoned, shackled, bombed—usually by someone seeking to do her personal harm.

Compared to that, the chance that a haphazardly aimed cannon ball fired from a great distance would come anywhere close to her was not even worth worrying about. Yet, somehow, it was the very random, impersonal vagaries involved that made her nervous.

She tried to concentrate on the letter she was writing to Janos Drugeth. That wasn't helped any by her knowledge that sending the letter off would be almost as much a matter of chance and happenstance as the trajectory of the cannonballs coming over the walls. Normal postal service was erratic, to say the least.

Amazingly, though, it still existed. The couriers who worked for the Thurn and Taxis service were like rats and cockroaches. Impossible to eradicate and able to squeeze through the tiniest cracks.

But not even such couriers could deliver a letter to an unknown address. Noelle had no idea where Janos was at present, just as she was quite sure he had no

idea she was in Dresden. She hadn't gotten a letter
from him in months. With another man, she might
have worried that he'd lost interest and simply stopped
writing her. But with Janos, somehow, she wasn't.
That spoke well for their possible future, of course.

If they had one. A muted crash had come from
not too far away. A cannon ball had caved in a wall
somewhere.

"See?" said Denise triumphantly. She pointed to
the spot across the square where a Swedish can-
nonball had punched a large hole in the upper floor
of a building. "Give it a few weeks and there'll be a
plenty big enough runway."

Next to her, Minnie nodded. "Just have to shovel
up the wreckage. Some of it'll make good gravel, too."

Eddie examined the scene of their optimism. The
siege would have to last for several years before the
Swedish army's gunfire removed enough of the buildings fronting the square and lining the main boulevard
leading from it to allow for an airplane runway that
wasn't just an elaborate form of suicide.

He did not bother to point that out, however.
Denise's response was a foregone conclusion.

*So? A few years are nothing, in a siege! Those
Trojan guys lasted . . . what? Twenty years? They'd still
be holding out, too, if the stupid jerks hadn't fallen
for that old wooden shoe trick.*

Ernst Wettin turned away from the window. When
all was said and done, and unless you happened to
have exceptionally bad fortune and fall victim to a stray
cannon ball, watching a siege was about as boring as

watching ants at work. Not at the very end, of course, if the defense gave way. Then tedium would turn to terror. But until then . . .

He sat back down at his writing desk. Ernst was the sort of man who believed firmly that all situations provided their own advantages. Since he retained the formal trappings of authority here in Saxony but had had the real power stripped away from him by Richter, he no longer had any tasks to perform that required more than a modicum of attention, for not more than two hours a day. Yet he still had all his comforts and facilities available.

Ernst Wettin came from a very prominent noble family and was himself a very capable official and administrator. Inevitably, therefore, since he'd reached his majority, he'd had very little time to himself.

Now, he did. At last, he had the opportunity he needed to concentrate on what he believed to be his true calling. The development of a systematic and reasoned program of educational reform for the whole of the Germanies.

A faint crash came from the distance. Presumably, a lucky cannon ball had done some significant damage. But the sound barely registered on his consciousness.

What to call the essay? Tentatively, he penned a title.

*A Treatise on the Subject of the
Education of the German Peoples*

There was a knock at the entrance to his suite. "Come in!" he said loudly. He'd sent his servants off in order to have some quiet and the door was a room and a half away.

The title was . . . suitable, he supposed.

A few seconds later, at a slight coughing noise, he swiveled in his chair. To his surprise, he saw that Gretchen Richter was standing right behind him. He'd been so engrossed he hadn't heard her approach.

"Ah! I wasn't expecting you."

"I'm not planning to stay long. I just wanted to see if there was anything you needed."

He smiled crookedly. "I don't suppose you'd accept an answer of 'my power returned.'"

She smiled, just as crookedly. "No. Well . . . not now, at any rate. In the future . . . we'll see what happens."

She leaned over to look at the line he'd just written. "I take it this is that major treatise you've been talking about wanting to write?"

"Yes."

She shook her head. "The title is awful. I'd call it *A Summons to Duty*. Or if that's not militant enough for you, *Educational Reform: A Call to Arms*."

The next few minutes passed pleasantly enough, as they always did in Richter's company. Say what else you would about the young woman, she was invariably gracious in her blunt sort of way.

After she left, Ernst went back to examining the title. Finally, he crumpled the initial sheet and took out another. Again with a crooked smile on his face, he began to write.

Educational Reform: A Summons to Duty

Chapter 19

Berlin

"For pity's sake, we're about to launch our great campaign!" It was all Oxenstierna could not to snarl openly. "Your Grace," he added, in an attempt to remain polite.

A pointless attempt. "I remind you again that I'm no longer a duke," said Wilhelm Wettin stiffly. "And as for the other, I think a plot to commit treason in collusion with a hostile foreign power needs to take precedence over our domestic concerns."

The Swedish chancellor stared down at the smaller man. For a moment, he was disoriented by a clutter of disconnected thoughts. He hadn't foreseen this development.

We're dealing with a matter of internal treason, you idiot, which is far more dangerous than anything else.

Maximilian is playing over his head, anyway. We can get the Oberpfalz back soon enough, once order is established.

One of the first things we'll do once we've consolidated power is get rid of that "house of commons" nonsense. Can there be anything more absurd than a duke having to give up his title in order to rule?

How in God's name did he find out?

The answer to the last question was probably the simplest. The problem with working through men like Johann Ludwig was that they were...men like Johann Ludwig. The count of Nassau-Hadamar had none of the great virtues, so why should it be surprising that he lacked the lesser ones as well? Such as being able to keep his mouth shut and refrain from bragging.

No matter. Johann Ludwig was playing over his head too. Oxenstierna had been careful not to deal with the man directly. When the time came, and Duke Maximilian of Bavaria needed to be humbled again, the count of Nassau-Hadamar's treasonous role could be exposed and the man sent to the executioner's block.

For the moment, there was this much greater problem of Wettin to deal with. The USE's prime minister had been balking more and more at the necessary measures to be taken, as time went by. He'd become a nuisance to everyone, especially Oxenstierna.

Perhaps more to the point, he'd also by now thoroughly aggravated most of his own followers. The staunch ones, by his vacillations; those even more inclined toward compromise, such as the landgravine of Hesse-Kassel, by his accommodations.

So, perhaps not such a great problem after all.

He placed a hand on Wettin's shoulder. "There's someone you need to speak to, who is intimately familiar with the Bavarian situation. The information you've received, from whatever source that might be"—*which you've refused to tell me*, but he left that unsaid—"has grossly misrepresented the true state of affairs."

Again, the prime minister nodded stiffly. "I assure you, Chancellor, that no one would be happier to be proven wrong than myself, with regard to this matter."

"Please wait here, then, while I fetch the person. If won't take but a moment."

Wettin's head inclined toward the sound of the crowd in the nearby assembly hall. No one was orating or shouting slogans, at the moment, since they were all waiting for Oxenstierna and Wettin to appear. But that large a crowd makes a lot of noise just standing around and talking to each other.

Understanding the gesture, Oxenstierna gave the prime minister's shoulder a friendly little squeeze. "The mob can wait, Wilhelm. Reassuring you regarding this Bavarian business is more important." And with that, he left.

As he'd promised the prime minister, he returned very quickly. Within less than a minute, in fact. For weeks, the chancellor had made sure that the Swedish soldiers who served Wettin as bodyguards were completely reliable. The two he found currently on duty just outside the prime minister's quarters would do as well as any.

"I'm afraid I have to put you under arrest, Your Grace," Oxenstierna announced, quietly and coldly.

Wettin stared at the two guards approaching him. At the last minute, he tried to draw the sword scabbarded to his waist. It was a valiant if pointless gesture. The sword was a ceremonial blade; capable of killing a man, to be sure, but not really well-suited to the task. The soldiers, in contrast, were armed with halberds and pistols.

They were also quite a bit larger than the prime minister and in much better physical condition. Wettin was a fairly young man, still, not even forty years of age. But he'd spent the past few years in sedentary pursuits, where these men were in their twenties and had remained physically active. It was the work of but a few seconds to subdue him.

Wettin began shouting. Curses at Oxenstierna, at the moment, but it wouldn't be long before he began calling for help.

In all likelihood, none would come. But there was no point taking the risk.

"Gag him," Oxenstierna commanded. "Place him for the moment in my chambers. Keep him gagged and under close watch until I return."

That wouldn't be for some hours, which would be most unpleasant for Wettin. Having a cloth gag in one's mouth was a nuisance for a short time; uncomfortable, for an hour; and the cause of bleeding sores after several. But the man had made his choice, so let him live with it.

On his way to the assembly hall, Oxenstierna pondered the prime minister's—no, the former prime minister's—final disposition.

Executing him would be unwise. That would stiffen the resistance of such people as Amalie Elizabeth of Hesse-Kassel and Duke George of Brunswick, not to mention the man's two brothers still in the USE. Ernst Wettin had to be replaced in Saxony anyway, of course, since he'd also proven unreliable. But he and Albrecht would remain influential in some circles regardless of the positions they currently held.

There was no way of knowing what reaction Wilhelm's execution would elicit from his youngest brother

Bernhard. But for the moment, that was another pot that Oxenstierna would just as soon leave unstirred.

And there was no need for such drastic action, anyway. Oxenstierna was not given to killing people for the sake of it. Exiling Wettin to one of the more isolated castles in Sweden—even better, Finland— would serve the chancellor's purposes perfectly well. The former prime minister really had worn out his welcome even with his own followers. A popular pretender kept in exile always posed a potential threat. Wilhelm Wettin would not.

Oxenstierna's assessment proved quite accurate. He began the assembly by making the announcement that Wilhelm Wettin had been discovered plotting with seditious elements and been placed under arrest. Following the laws of the USE, his successor would be whatever person was chosen by the party in power, the Crown Loyalists. The Swedish chancellor elided over the fact that he had no authority in the USE to be arresting anyone and that he was planning to discard those same laws as soon as possible.

"If you will allow me to offer my advice, I would recommend that you choose Johann Wilhelm Neumair von Ramsla." He pointed to an elderly man seated in the front row.

Von Ramsla stared back at him, his mouth agape. The chancellor's proposal came as a complete surprise to the man. He'd played no part in the dealings with Bavaria, of course. Johann Wilhelm was a political theorist, full to the brim with axiomatic principles—hardly the sort of man you wanted to use for such gray purposes. However, he'd be splendid as the new prime minister. The combination of his age—he was in his mid-sixties—and his ineffectual temperament would make him a pliant tool for the eventual destruction of his own office.

There was silence in the room for a few seconds. Then, a few more seconds in which the room was filled with quiet hubbub, as people hastily consulted with each other in whispers. Then, not more than ten seconds after the Swedish chancellor stopped speaking, a man toward the back of the huge chamber climbed onto his chair and shouted:

"Hurrah for the new prime minister! I vote for Johann Wilhelm!"

That was Johann Schweikhard, Freiherr von Sickingen. As a nobleman, he had no business casting a vote for the leader of the Crown Loyalists in the House of Commons, but no one in that chamber cared very much about such legal niceties any more. At least a third of the crowd were also noblemen, after all.

Not more than two seconds later, a roar of approval erupted. If not from the entire crowd, certainly from its majority.

Given that he was ignoring all rules anyway, Oxenstierna decided he could safely accept that roar as a vote of approval by acclamation. He stepped down onto the floor of the assembly hall, took Johann Wilhelm by the arm, and hauled him onto the dais. Von Ramsla put up no resistance, even if he was not exactly active in his so-very-rapid rise to power.

Oxenstierna saw no point in giving the old man the speaker's podium, however. Von Ramsla was a fig leaf, and the sooner he learned that fig leaves were mute, the better.

"And now, my friends, let us move on to the purpose

of this assembly. The first order of business is to adopt our new Charter of Rights and Duties." He swept the crowd with his forefinger. "You've all had time to read the Charter, by now, so I will move to a vote by acclamation of each point in order."

He paused just long enough to allow everyone to take their copy of the charter in hand, if they didn't have it in hand already.

"Point One. The capital and seat of government of the United States of Europe is henceforth to be located in Berlin."

Huge roar of approval.

"Point Two. For purposes of determining citizenship—"

Colonel Erik Haakansson Hand found out about Wilhelm Wettin's arrest at the same time everyone else did, from Oxenstierna's announcement at the assembly. (The "convention," they were calling it—and never mind that the event was more in the nature of a staged political rally than anything you could reasonably call a deliberative undertaking.) He wasn't quite as surprised as most people present, because the tensions between the USE prime minister and the Swedish chancellor had become quite obvious to him. Still, Erik certainly hadn't expected the development.

Why? he wondered. Oxenstierna's terse explanation didn't make a lot of sense to him. "Plotting with seditious elements." Which elements, and what was the nature of the plot?

A thought suddenly occurred to him. He left the assembly hall and made his way hurriedly to the nearest of the city's gates. Fortunately, the sky was clear and there was still at least an hour of daylight left.

Nothing. The guards said no one of any significance had left the city within the past few days.

He then made his way to the southwestern gate, the Leipziger Thor.

Again, nothing. And the same at Cöpenicker Thor.

By now, evening had come. He was about to give up the project but decided to make one last effort at the southeastern gate, the Stralower Thor.

Finally, success. A result, at least. Whether it was significant or not was still to be determined.

"Yesterday, around this time," the guard said, nodding firmly. "I remember them because they were unpleasant. Both of them."

"Hard to pick between the two," chimed in one of the other guards. "Baron Shithead and Ritter Asshole."

Erik chuckled. "I know the type. But do you remember their actual names?"

"It'll be in the record book," said a third soldier, standing in the entrance to the guardhouse. "I'll go check."

He was back with the names in short order. Hand knew both of the men, although not particularly well. One of them was a baron, in point of fact, a Freiherr from the Province of the Main. His companion was not a nobleman at all, on the other hand. He was a guildmaster and one of the leaders of the Crown Loyalist party in Frankfurt.

The Freiherr had certainly not been close to Wettin. He'd been one of the prime minister's more vociferous critics, in fact. Erik didn't know about the guildmaster, but what he did know was that the Crown Loyalists of Frankfort were a particularly crusty bunch. That was probably a reaction to the city's very influential and prominent Committee of Correspondence.

The point being that neither man was likely to have feared repercussions if Wettin was arrested—and they'd left the city a day earlier, in any event.

Was there any connection between these two men and the prime minister's fall from power? Or was their departure simply a coincidence?

But if it was a coincidence, why did they leave Berlin *now*—literally, on the eve of their triumph? Hand would double-check with his many contacts and agents, but he was almost certain that both men had been members of the faction that had been most critical of Wettin.

Slowly, thinking as he walked, the colonel made his way back to the palace. While serving with Duke Ernst in the Oberpfalz, Erik had come to know an American officer named Jake Ebeling. The two had become something in the way of friends. When Ebeling learned that Hand could read English, he lent him a copy of what he said was one of his three favorite books. *Alice in Wonderland*, by a certain Lewis Carroll.

Colonel Hand had found the book quite charming and remembered a bit of it.

"Curiouser and curiouser," he murmured. "Curiouser and curiouser."

Chapter 20

Magdeburg

"And here comes the only concession," Rebecca continued, reading from the sheet in her hand. "It is in the last two items, on matters of religion. 'Point Eight. All provinces shall be required to designate a single established church, with the exception of the State of Thuringia-Franconia, which may designate several.'"

"All of them province-wide?" interjected Constantin Ableidinger. "Or must each provincial district choose a single church?"

He held up a stiff, admonishing forefinger. "I warn you! We Lutherans will not tolerate sloppiness in such matters!"

Rebecca bestowed the smile upon him that she always bestowed on Ableidinger's antics. The one that exuded long-suffering patience rather than serenity.

"Stop clowning around, Constantin," grumbled Gunther Achterhof. "What difference does it make? We're not going to abide by it anyway."

The little exchange had given Rebecca time for further thought, during the course of which she realized that Ableidinger's heavy-handed humor might actually contain a serious kernel—whether he realized it or not, which he probably didn't.

"Maybe we will, Gunther," she said. She raised her own forefinger in response to the look of outrage on his face. The gesture in this case was one that indicated a desire for forbearance rather than admonishment. "But let us not get ahead of ourselves. There is still one more provision in Point Eight and a final Point Nine in the Charter of Rights and Duties."

The pitch of her voice shifted back to a slight singsong as she resumed quoting from the sheet. "The remaining provision in Point Eight is that: 'These churches shall receive financial support from their respective provinces.' Finally: 'Point Nine. No church, whether established or not, shall be forbidden to exist, provided that it abides by the laws of the nation and its province.'"

She laid down the sheet. "As I said, a concession of sorts, at the very end."

"Not much of one," observed Helene Gundelfinger. "All it recognizes is the abstract right of nonestablished churches to 'exist.' That's a rather metaphysical proposition, taken by itself. The way that provision is couched, it seems to me, a province could recognize a church's 'existence' while simultaneously forbidding its members to meet, to collect funds, or to have church leaders."

She turned toward Werner von Dalberg, who was seated far enough down the long table to her right that she had to lean forward a little to see him. "Am I right, Werner?"

The FoJP leader from the Oberpfalz was the one person in the group who had extensive legal training.

He grinned. "Metaphysics has nothing on the law. That issue could be contested in the courts for years. In the event—the not-improbable event, actually—that a church so victimized should employ me as their lawyer, I would argue that the term 'to exist' *implies* all those things that were simultaneously banned, and hence the ban is null and void." His eyes got a slightly unfocused, distant look. "Interesting question, actually. I'm sure the judges would rule in my favor when it came to being able to collect funds. Without money on which to operate, any and all human institutions are vacant abstractions. And for much the same reason, I'm pretty sure they'd rule in my favor when it came to the right to meet. The designation of officers of the church, however—by whatever method—is considerably more—"

"Werner!" Rebecca interrupted him. "We can come back to this at a later time. We have more pressing issues to deal with."

He gave her a rueful, apologetic smile. "Sorry. I got a bit carried away. Lawyers, you know. Philosophers flee at our approach."

Rebecca gave the sheet on the table in front of her a last, considering look. "Actually, my objection was not to your lawyering but to the specific subject, which for the moment is somewhat trivial. Taken as a whole, I think the right strategy for us in response to this attack from Berlin is precisely 'to lawyer.'"

Predictably, Gunther Achterhof's face darkened. "Rebecca, if you think for a minute that we're going to tolerate—"

"Let. Her. Finish," said Helene.

"Yes, please," added Magdeburg province's governor, Matthias Strigel. "Rebecca, go on."

"They have made several bad errors, in my opinion. Within the great error of their purpose itself, I should say. The first and the worst was arresting Wilhelm Wettin. The second, and almost as bad, was to convene in Berlin. The two mistakes together make everything they've done legally invalid."

"What difference does it make?" demanded Achterhof. "They're not going to abide by the law, and neither are we. We're now in a state of civil war! The laws of the land are no longer binding on anyone."

"He's got a point, Rebecca," said Albert Bugenhagen. The mayor of Hamburg was sitting at the middle of the table almost directly opposite Helene. His fingers were steepled in front of his face, which, combined with his even tone of voice, made the statement one of judicial observation rather than actual agreement with the substance of Achterhof's argument.

"Yes—but it is much too broad." She leaned forward slightly, to give added emphasis to her next words. "What is a 'civil war' in the first place? Gunther uses the term as if it were a depiction of a concrete object, like a tree or a table. Something simple and discrete. But the phenomenon is actually very complex, and with no clear boundaries. There are civil wars and there are civil wars, no two of which are exactly the same and any one of which has its own peculiar characteristics."

By now, either Achterhof or Ableidinger would have started interrupting, had anyone else been talking. But even they had learned that Rebecca's trains of thoughts were worth following.

"When it comes to *this* civil war, I would qualify the term with several addenda. As follows." She began counting off her fingers. "First, it is a civil war triggered off *not* by the collapse of final authority but by its mere absence—an absence, furthermore, which may well prove temporary."

Constantin was frowning. "What does that mean?"

Von Dalberg spoke up. "What she means is that the crisis was precipitated by Gustav Adolf's injury. As opposed, for instance, to one or another side in the conflict rejecting the emperor's authority in itself. What happens, then, if he recovers?"

Rebecca nodded. "Yes, precisely. This is a critical issue because it drives the pace of Oxenstierna's actions and maneuvers. If Gustav Adolf recovers before he completes his project, it is likely the project will be discontinued. So the chancellor has no choice but to force the process, risking blunders for the sake of celerity."

She counted off another finger. "Second, it is a civil war clouded by great uncertainty when it comes to the issue of the succession. Or rather, the issue of a regency. The succession itself is clear—Princess Kristina, the emperor's only child—but she is still a minor and thus cannot take the throne herself. And the USE is not Sweden, which has clear and established rules governing the establishment of a regency. So, as with the state of Gustav Adolf's own condition, everything is murky—which, again, forces Oxenstierna to drive forward with great haste.

"Third, by convening in Berlin instead of Magdeburg, Oxenstierna and his reactionary plotters have denied themselves the possibility of a quorum. The constitution is quite clear on this point—a majority of the members of Parliament must be present or there is no quorum and Parliament cannot legitimately conduct any business."

"But..." Liesel Hahn, an MP from Hesse-Kassel, was frowning. "But they have a majority, Rebecca."

"Ha!" Constantin Ableidinger slapped the table. "Rebecca is right!"

"Yes, she is," agreed von Dalberg. He looked toward Hahn. "The fact that they have a majority doesn't matter, Liesel, unless they can get a majority actually *present* at the session of Parliament."

Hahn's frown cleared away. "Oh, of course. Silly of me. But perhaps..."

Rebecca was shaking her head. "There is no chance at all that they had a quorum in Berlin. Their majority is a slim one to begin with—fifty-two percent. No member of our party was present, of course, and probably no more than a third of the people belonging to the small parties. That means the Crown Loyalists would have had to get almost every single one of their MPs to attend the session."

"Ha!" Ableidinger boomed again. "In Berlin? In winter? Not a chance!"

"It wouldn't be hard to prove, either," said Strigel. "In fact, I'd be willing to bet they didn't even take a roll call."

"And it gets still worse," said Rebecca. She counted off her pinkie. "Fourth, when they arrested Wilhelm Wettin they also removed any legitimacy to the executive branch of the government as well."

Achterhof was now frowning, and scratching his jaw. "I'll be the first to say they're a pack of bastards, Rebecca, but I'm not following you here. Quorum or no quorum, the Crown Loyalists are still the majority party. By our constitution, that gives them the right to form a cabinet of whichever members of their party they select, including the post of prime minister. So if they choose this von Ramsla jackass, they have the right to do so."

Now Werner slapped the table in glee. "Yes, granted, Gunther—but by the same constitution, the new head of the government is actually a *recommendation* made to the head of state. Legally speaking, von Ramsla can't become the prime minister until Gustav II Adolf confirms his appointment. Which he certainly hasn't done, since he's still speaking in tongues."

Rebecca and several other people at the table winced a little at von Dalberg's indecorous description of their monarch's condition. But that was a matter of taste; the depiction itself was accurate enough.

"Yes," she said. "To sum it all up, Oxenstierna has been in such a hurry to launch his counterrevolution that he has jettisoned the legitimacy of his own government's executive and legislative branches. Which leaves, as the only surviving legitimate branch, the judiciary—who, regardless of how conservative they might be, will be aghast at these reckless procedures."

"To put it mildly," said Werner, snorting with amusement. "You can be accused of committing any crime in the books, and a judge will remain calm and even-tempered. Violate established legal protocol, and that same judge will become red-faced and indignant."

Gunther Achterhof still looked skeptical. "And what does Oxenstierna care, whether a pack of judges rules with or against him? I repeat: we're in a civil war. He'll simply have them arrested along with Wettin."

By the time he finished, however, at least half the

heads at the conference table were shaking. Even Gunther seemed to recognize he'd ventured onto thin ice, from the way his forceful tone diminished.

"And lose at least ninety percent of the militias who would otherwise support him," said Hamburg's mayor. "I can guarantee that the militia of my city would abandon his cause. They might even be upset enough to support *us.*"

"The same would be true for most of the provincial governments as well," said Strigel. "Hesse-Kassel would certainly come out in opposition, and so would Brunswick."

"Westphalia's a given, of course," added Helene Gundelfinger, "with a Danish prince as its administrator and official head of state. Even if he doesn't much like his younger brother, Frederik would hardly side with the Swedes."

"It will be true down the line," said Rebecca. "Oxenstierna has blundered badly. He has handed us on a plate the one single factor that a counterrevolution normally has working in its favor—legitimacy. You are more right than you know, Gunther. Indeed, the chancellor of Sweden and his followers *are* now the bastards in this conflict."

"And we—ha! what a charming twist!—are now the champions of the established laws," said Ableidinger.

"Our strategy and our tactics must be guided by that understanding," said Rebecca. "As Constantin says, we are the ones defending the laws, not they. So we must be patient, not hasty; considerate of established customs and practices, not dismissive of them; and, most of all, present ourselves as the guardians of order and stability."

Achterhof was back to scowling. "If by that you're saying we have to sit on our hands—"

"I said nothing of the sort, Gunther." Rebecca managed to maintain a cordial tone of voice. The man could sometimes be a real trial. "What matters is not the content of what we do, but the form. So, here in Magdeburg, we seize all the reins of power—what few we don't already possess, at any rate. But we do so in order to *defend* the laws, not to overthrow them. Oxenstierna and those outlaws in Berlin are the revolutionaries, not us."

She looked at Albert Bugenhagen. "Every province and town will have to adopt its own tactics, of course, to suit the local conditions. But the same method should apply everywhere. Thus, in Hamburg, I recommend that you summon the town militia to defend the city's rights and laws against illegal aggression coming from Berlin."

Bugenhagen grinned. "They'll squirm, you watch. But . . . in the end, they might very well do it."

"And even if they don't," said Constantin, "you can mobilize the CoC's armed units in the city on the same grounds. You're not *clashing* with the militia, you're—oh, this is truly delightful—coming out to support them in their righteous task."

Rebecca nodded. "Everywhere, we must follow that course. Defense, not offense. This is no time, in other words, for the CoCs to launch another Operation Krystalnacht. Let the reactionaries start the violence. Let everyone see that they are the instigators of mayhem, just as they are the ones who shredded the nation's constitution and laws."

She now looked at Gunther Achterhof. "We are, of

course, permitted to act in self-defense, should the outlaws make so bold as to attack us."

The head of Magdeburg's Committee of Correspondence looked mollified. Well, somewhat mollified. But Rebecca didn't think he would be a problem. As pigheaded as he often was, Gunther was not stupid. Once he saw how effective the tactics were, he'd begin applying them with his usual adroit skills as an organizer.

Liesel Hahn spoke up. "I think you should write to the landgravine of Hesse-Kassel immediately, Rebecca. She thinks quite well of you, despite her political differences. She's told me so herself. Twice, now."

"I will do better than that, Liesel. I will send her a radio message—and send the same message to the heads of state of every single one of the provinces, even those like Pomerania and the Upper Rhine, which we can assume will remain actively hostile. The centerpiece of my message, of course, will be our new motto and principal slogan."

Her serene smile finally appeared. "*Justice for Wilhelm Wettin!* We demand that the prime minister be charged in a duly constituted court of law, not some outlaw travesty of a tribunal. We demand that any charges against him be made openly, so that he may exercise his right—guaranteed under the constitution— to confront his accusers. We demand that he be given a fair trial in a USE court of law, not be victimized by foreign Swedish star chamber proceedings. Last but not least, we demand that he be released until such a trial can be convened, in order to resume his duties as the still-rightful head of the USE's government."

She stopped. Everyone stared at her.

Then Ableidinger slapped the table again. Hard enough, this time, to make it jump. "Oh, how grand—to live in such splendid times! Where up is down and down is up and everything is finally in its rightful place!"

Chapter 21

Bamberg, capital of the State
of Thuringia-Franconia

At the last moment, worried about the Bavarian threat to the Oberpfalz, Ed Piazza had decided not to attend the conference Becky had called in Magdeburg. When word came the day before the conference of the so-called "Charter of Rights and Duties" passed by the convention of reactionaries taking place in Berlin and—this came as a complete surprise—the arrest of Wilhelm Wettin, he'd regretted that decision.

Today, he was deeply thankful he'd stayed in Bamberg. The president of the State of Thuringia-Franconia was facing the worst crisis of his political career.

The Bavarians attacked Ingolstadt the evening after the news arrived from Berlin. Possibly just a coincidence, of course. The attack was certainly not unexpected.

What *was* unexpected—no, profoundly shocking—was that they'd taken the highly fortified city within a few hours. By dawn, it was all over. When the Bavarians had controlled Ingolstadt, they'd withstood a siege by Banér's army for months. So how and why had the USE's defense collapsed literally overnight?

There was only one possible answer: *treason*. And not the usual sort of treason that often afflicted cities under siege—such as the treason that had turned over Ingolstadt from the Bavarians, in fact. In such cases, after long months of siege, a small party within the city would jury-rig a scheme to open the defenses to the enemy. Typically, the besiegers would come in through a gate opened by the traitors and, over many hours, force in enough men to overwhelm the city's defenders.

From the few and limited accounts they'd gotten so far, though, what had happened in Ingolstadt this time looked far different to Piazza. The Bavarians had apparently penetrated the city simultaneously in several places, after guard detachments had been overwhelmed from within. That suggested a massive conspiracy and one that had been planned over a period of time.

An utterly ruthless conspiracy, to boot. That much was obvious from the one radio message Major Tom Simpson had managed to send before he vanished. It had been transmitted in Morse code, for reasons that were unclear. Perhaps reception hadn't been good enough for voice messages. More likely, Ed thought, they'd lost their best radios.

Bavarians overrunning Ingolstadt. Colonel Engels murdered. City cannot be held. Withdrawing what remains of regiment into countryside.

That message had come early this morning. Since then, nothing.

His secretary Anton Roeder stuck his head in the door. "General Schmidt is here, sir."

"Send him—" But Heinrich was already coming through the door. He was not standing on ceremony today.

"How soon—"

"Now," Heinrich answered. "In fact, the first of the regiments is already marching out of the camp. I expect to have the entire division on the road by evening."

"How long—"

"No way to know, Mr. President, until we see what the road conditions are like." The young general shrugged his thick, muscular shoulders. "The roads are good, but with the snowfall two days ago... Still, it shouldn't take us more than three days to reach Nürnberg. From there, we can figure another three-day march to either Ingolstadt or Regensburg, whichever you've decided is more important. That assumes the authorities in Nürnberg are cooperative. If they close the border, it will take us at least another day to march around the city."

Nürnberg was a political anomaly. For centuries it had been one of the major imperial cities in the Germanies; in most respects, a completely independent city-state. It had jealously held onto that status through the collapse of the Holy Roman Empire, the formation of the Confederated Principalities of Europe, the collapse of the CPE and its replacement by the United States of Europe. Today, it was for all practical purposes an independent miniature nation, but one that was completely surrounded by the USE. The only up-time equivalent Ed could think of was Lesotho.

The Nürnbergers were generally on good terms with their much larger neighbor (or hyper-neighbor, it might be better to say) but they could sometimes get prickly. And there was no way to know yet how they'd be reacting to the turmoil inside the USE. The city's own authorities were on the conservative side, and would thus be politically inclined toward the Crown Loyalists. On the other hand, it was the intervention of the Americans on the side of Gustav Adolf that had so quickly and decisively defeated Wallenstein's army as it moved to besiege the city. In more immediate and cruder geopolitical terms, two-thirds of the city-state's border adjoined the SoTF. Ed had always made it a point to stay on good terms with the Nürnbergers and they'd been just as punctilious returning the favor.

So, he didn't expect any problems. But these were uncertain times.

On a positive note, he finally managed to get in a complete sentence. Heinrich tended to be abrupt under pressure.

"I'm inclined to think we should accept the loss of Ingolstadt—for the moment—and concentrate on defending Regensburg."

"I agree," said General Schmidt.

"Let's settle on that, then. Take the division to Regensburg."

"What are the latest radio reports coming from the city?"

"Nothing, oddly enough. A few clashes with Bavarian skirmishers south of the Danube, but nothing worse. And there's still no sign of any attempts to cross the river. Not even probes."

"Not so odd as all that, Mr. President. Duke Maximilian still hasn't built his army back up to strength. He's gambling right now—obviously, because he thought traitors had given him a particularly strong hand." Darkly, he added, "Which, indeed, they did. But he still would have concentrated all his forces at Ingolstadt. He would not have taken the risk of launching two simultaneous attacks so widely separated. It's more than thirty miles from Ingolstadt to Regensburg—on those roads at this time of year, at least a two-day march. Separated units could not reinforce each other in case of setbacks."

"In that case, how soon—"

"At least a week, would be my estimate. He'll want to assemble a large fleet of barges before he comes down the river toward Regensburg." Heinrich smiled, in that thin and humorless way he had. "No easy task, squeezing barges out of Danube rivermen. They'll hide them in places you'd never think of—burn them, sometimes, rather than give them up."

"That should give you—"

"I'll have the division in Regensburg long before then. We'll hold the city, Mr. President, never fear. How long it will take to recover Ingolstadt, on the other hand..." He shrugged again. "I would say that mainly depends on how the political situation here in the USE resolves itself."

"Yes, you're right. If all goes well—"

"The emperor recovers, Oxenstierna hangs, Wettin hangs—ask me if I care the swine got himself arrested—every other stinking traitor in Berlin hangs, we catch the traitors who sold out Ingolstadt—disembowel those bastards, hanging's too good for them—proper order is restored, the Prince of Germany is back in power where he belongs, and Maximilian is food for stray mongrels in the streets of Munich."

Ed stared at him. Heinrich could be . . . harsh.

"That seems perhaps a bit—"

"Yes, you're right. Munich's street curs are innocent parties to the business. Unfair to poison them with such foul meat. We'll feed the duke to his pigs instead."

✧   ✧   ✧

After the general left, Ed dillydallied for a few minutes before finally accepting the need to take care of the business he most desperately did not want to take care of.

He'd have to write messages to be radioed to John Chandler Simpson in Luebeck and Mike Stearns in Bohemia. Telling the admiral that his son had vanished into the chaos of war and telling the general that his sister had done the same. Rita Simpson, née Stearns, had been living in Ingolstadt with her husband Tom. God only knew what had happened to her when the Bavarians came pouring in.

Worst of all, he'd have to tell Mary Simpson, Tom's mother. And this would be no brief, antiseptic radio message. As luck would have it, she was in Bamberg at the moment, raising money for one of her many charities or cultural projects.

The Dame of Magdeburg, they called her. But before the day's end, she'd just be one of many anguished mothers.

There was something to be said for Heinrich Schmidt's simple remedies, all things considered. A Swedish chancellor throttled, a Bavarian duke munched on by hogs.

Ed could live with that. It'd still be nice to complete more than every fourth sentence, though.

Luebeck

Princess Kristina was reading the newspaper in Ulrik's hands by leaning over his shoulder. Most likely, because she found it comforting to rest her hands on his shoulders. It certainly wasn't because they could only afford one copy of the *Hamburg Morgenpost*. The money sent by King Christian had arrived the day before. Here as elsewhere, Ulrik's father had been profligate. If he wanted to—and he was tempted sometimes—the prince could now afford to launch his own newspaper.

The temptation wasn't as great at the moment, though, as it would have been at most times. Luebeck's own newspaper was wretched, but the city got quite regular delivery of Hamburg's largest newspaper. Allowing for its Fourth of July Party bias, the *Morgenpost* was quite good; one of the three or four best in central Europe, in Ulrik's opinion. It came out regularly and reliably twice a week, on Wednesdays and Saturdays, and in time of rapid developments of great public interest—such as right now—they strove to come out daily.

"Should we go right now, Ulrik?" the princess asked anxiously. "They've even arrested the prime minister!"

Yes, and what madness possessed Oxenstierna to do that? Ulrik had pondered that question from every angle, and from none of them did the deed look any more intelligent. He'd finally concluded that Baldur's initial assessment had been correct.

"Wettin found out something—something really damaging—and Oxenstierna had to shut him up."

At the time, Ulrik had dismissed the notion as being too . . . Baldurian. Norddahlish? The Norwegian adventurer was fond of imagining dark and fiendish conspiracies in every corner.

In Ulrik's experience, that gave far too much credit to human ingenuity. Conspiracies existed, to be sure;

many of them, and many were dark indeed. But fiendish? Fiendishness required brains. Nine times out of ten, conspirators behaved like buffoons and wound up exposing themselves out of sheer, bumbling incompetence.

He shook his head. "Not yet, Kristina. The more important thing isn't the news coming out of Berlin, it's the news coming out of Magdeburg."

She frowned. "But there *isn't* much news coming out of Magdeburg."

"Yes, precisely. That means someone is keeping things quiet and orderly in that city—much against my expectations, I can tell you that. By now, I'd expected accounts of rioting mobs. Well, mobs, anyway."

Baldur was sitting at a table in the corner of the salon. "At least a hanging or two!" he exclaimed, looking quite aggrieved. "Surely some nobleman was too stupid or too drunk to get out of the city before Oxenstierna blew everything up. But . . . nothing. The place seems as boring as a chur—ah . . . ah . . ."

Ulrik tried not to laugh, as the Norwegian groped for something—anything—that he found as boring as a church. And could come up with nothing. From the little smile on her face, Kristina was equally amused. Baldur Norddahl was to pastors what oil was to water, except that oil was not sarcastic.

Kristina's expression became very intent. "Oh! I see what you mean. It's like the detective says in one of those stories you lent me. The clever up-time English ones."

Ulrik made the connection almost immediately. "Yes, you're right. The curious incident of the dog in the night who did nothing—and that was what was curious."

He set down the paper. "No, I think our initial plan is still the right one. Wait for a while, and let things develop further." Another up-time expression came to him. "Give Oxenstierna some more rope with which to hang himself."

Kassel, capital of the province of Hesse-Kassel

"Poor Wilhelm," Amalie Elizabeth murmured to herself, as she gazed through the window on the snow-covered ground. That ground would turn into a very cheery and pleasant garden, come the spring. But for now, it just looked cold and bleak.

Her own mood had been cold and bleak, ever since her husband was killed in that stupid, pointless war in Poland. Mike Stearns had been right about that war, as he was right about so many things. The fact just made the landgravine's mood bleaker, of course. Her differences with Stearns and his party still remained; extraordinarily wide in most places, if nowhere quite as deep as a chasm. Why could her own side in this great political dispute not produce a man to match him?

She'd hoped that Wilhelm Wettin would be that man, once. But for all his undoubted intelligence he'd proven too prone to shortsightedness. And now that shortsightedness had led him into a prison cell. It might yet lead him to the executioner's block.

In an odd sort of way, though, the news of Wilhelm's arrest had improved her spirits. Not cheered her up, certainly. But there was a greater ease about her now, a certain lightening of dark airs. Whatever else, Wilhelm had been a good friend for many years.

It had pained her greatly—her husband, too—to watch him sink deeper and deeper into the mire.

He was out of it now. Whatever happened, no more blame or fault could be placed upon him. She was glad for that, if nothing else.

But there was something else to be glad about, as it happened. In fact, two things.

First, that foul Swedish chancellor had finally exposed himself as a tyrant as well as an unprincipled schemer. Imprisoning the former duke of Saxe-Weimar on such vague and patently absurd charges had infuriated her—and she knew full well it would infuriate many others in her class. In the Niederadel, as well.

There was an irony there, and she was not blind to it. For all that Stearns had so often bruised—badly bruised—the sentiments and sensibilities of the German aristocracy, not once had he broken his own laws when he'd been in power. Not once had he thrown a nobleman into prison on vague and obviously trumped-up charges. The fact was, whether they liked the man or not, that German noblemen could move about the USE in greater safety and security during the time of the Stearns' regime than they could now. Amalie Elizabeth herself would be nervous, if she left Hesse-Kassel.

Well . . . unless it was to visit Brunswick. Duke George was another old friend.

A pity he was off in Poland, commanding one of the army's divisions. But the man he'd left behind to run Brunswick's affairs, Loring Schultz, was both competent and pleasant to deal with. Later today, she'd write him a letter, urging that Brunswick should join Hesse-Kassel in declaring strict neutrality in the current political conflict.

But there was another letter she needed to reply to before then. And there lay the second thing to be glad about.

She left the window, moved back to her writing desk, and picked up the letter she'd received the evening before from Rebecca Abrabanel.

Shrewd, shrewd, shrewd. Who would have thought to find such subtlety—such delicacy, even—in a young Sephardic Jewess most of whose life had been cloistered and tightly circumscribed? The sheer naked intelligence involved was almost frightening.

In no other respect were the ways of God quite so mysterious as the way He sometimes divided his favors. To think that He'd provided such a wife for such a man. It seemed grossly unfair, but no doubt He had His reasons.

Tetschen

"I wasn't expecting you, sir, to put it mildly." Jeff Higgins motioned to one of the chairs in his headquarters. "Have a seat, please."

"As long as it's not an airplane seat." Mike Stearns eased himself into the offered chair. "The truth is, Jeff—I'll admit it like a man—flying makes me nervous. Always did, even the fancy airliners we had back home, much less these ramshackle gadgets Jesse has at his disposal and I never said that, you understand. Air force guys have thin skins and tender egos, it's some kind of law of nature."

Jeff sat down in another chair and nodded solemnly. "Not a word, sir, I promise. He'll be at the field for another two hours anyway, fussing over the ramshackle gadget."

Mike smiled. "For today, let's keep it to 'Jeff' and 'Mike.'"

Jeff pursed his lips. "Why does that make me nervous?"

"Most times, it probably should. But not today. The reason I twisted Jesse's arm into flying me up here—and twisted it a lot harder to get him to agree to fly me back tomorrow—is because I figured I'd better come talk to you in person." He paused for a moment, as if he were studying Jeff. "Before you got too twitchy."

"Twitchy about what, sir? Ah, Mike."

"Twitchy about the fact that there's a whole army at your wife's throat and I'm just keeping you here twiddling your thumbs and keeping myself even farther away. Twiddling my thumbs."

"Oh. That." Jeff got up and went over to a small stove in a corner. "I've got some coffee, if you'd like some. Tea, also."

"You've got *coffee*? Is it . . . ?"

"The real stuff? Sure is."

Jeff stirred up the fire, looking over his shoulder with a little grin on his face. "Fact is, Mike, the becky's become the strongest currency in the whole area. The exchange rate's terrific. So, yeah, I can afford real coffee. Not often, of course. But I figure this counts as a special occasion."

He placed a kettle on the stove and went back to his chair. "As for what you're worried about, relax. I wasn't actually getting twitchy. Well . . . a little, I guess, but I've applied it to a useful task."

"Which is?"

The young colonel's tone got noticeably harder. "Which is the moment you tell me to take the fortress at Königstein, it's toast."

"Ah. Good." Mike cocked his head a little. "But I'm a little curious. Why *aren't* you twitchy?"

"Hey, I can read." Jeff motioned toward a table against one of the walls. The table wasn't exactly piled high with newspapers, but there were a fair number of them. "Between what's happening in Berlin and what's not happening in Magdeburg and what I'm damn sure is happening in Dresden—not much news coming out of there, of course—I figure I know what we're up to."

"Keep going. I'm fascinated, watching a great detective at work."

Jeff smiled. "This ain't hardly Sherlock Holmes territory, Mike. What we're up to is that we're just biding our time, on account of we're frugal. Or maybe just lazy. You've got the smartest wife in the world and I've got the toughest one, so we're letting them soften up the opposition for a while."

Chapter 22

Mecklenburg

The first major clash outside of Saxony—and the only one, as it turned out—occurred in Mecklenburg. The nobility of that province had been chafing ever since most of them were driven out during Operation Krystalnacht. Now, emboldened by the convention in Berlin and what they saw as the new dispensation enshrined in the Charter of Rights and Duties, they formed themselves into a small army of sorts—entirely an army of officers, so far—and sallied from Berlin, calling on their retainers and supporters to join them.

A fair number did so, in fact, before they reached the Mecklenburg border. But more than half a year had passed since the change of regime in Mecklenburg. The province's Committee of Correspondence had not spent those months idly, and neither had the Fourth of July Party. The Mecklenburg CoC's initial armed contingents that they'd fielded during Operation Krystalnacht—ragged bands, more like—had been transformed into a fairly well-trained and a very well-armed militia in the intervening period.

And they sallied forth just as enthusiastically as did their betters. Class relations in Mecklenburg were more savage than in any other province in the USE. The poor soil of the region supported a poor agriculture and industrial development was still nascent and confined almost entirely to a few major towns. So, outright poverty clashed against its close cousin in the form of a hardscrabble aristocracy.

The initial skirmishes were fought in a range of sandy hills just south of Wittstock. None of the contestants realized it, then or ever, but in the universe the Americans had come from a much greater battle would be fought on that same terrain less than a year later, in October of 1636. In that battle, the Swedish army led by General Banér—the same man who was besieging Dresden in this universe—would defeat an army of Austrian Catholic imperialists and their Saxon Protestant allies. The Swedes were financed by Catholic France, proving once again that the supposed "wars of religion" were just a veneer over dynastic rivalries.

The terrain favored the reactionary forces, because of their greater strength in cavalry, but not by much. Truth be told, it was terrain that suited nobody very well—just as it hadn't (wouldn't—didn't—mightn't? the Ring of Fire played havoc with grammar) in the battle of Wittstock.

After two days of intermittent fighting, the noblemen's forces managed to push their way to the town's outskirts, but there they were stopped. As was usually true with German militias, the CoC contingents fought best on the defensive, especially when they could fight behind shelter—and by then, they'd done a fair job of fortifying Wittstock.

Another day passed during which the leadership of the reactionary army squabbled and bickered. They'd had no clearly defined leadership structure when they left Berlin, and the situation hadn't improved any since. Finally, more because a few of the leaders decided to do it and the rest just tagged along, rather than because they'd persuaded anyone, the noblemen's army headed north.

The plan, if such it could be called, was to circle around Wittstock and then strike across country toward the provincial capital of Schwerin. The logic involved was flimsy, at best. Why, after being stymied by the jury-rigged defenses of Wittstock, these leading noblemen thought they could take the larger and much better fortified city of Schwerin, was something that none of them even tried to answer. They were satisfied, it seemed, simply by the act of doing something.

Berlin

Back in Berlin, Oxenstierna was of two minds on the matter of Mecklenburg. On the one hand, he was skeptical that the aristocratic expedition had any real chance of success. On the other hand, he was glad to see someone doing something. Doing *anything*. Like the leaders of that little army, the chancellor of Sweden was getting increasingly frustrated by the defensive tactics of his opponents.

He hadn't expected that. Axel Oxenstierna was a very intelligent man, but even intelligent people are prone to being blinded by their own biases and preconceptions. The chancellor's favorite word to describe the political state of affairs brought into existence in the Germanies by Mike Stearns, the Fourth of July Party—to say nothing of Gretchen Richter and her Committees of Correspondence—was "anarchy."

He repeated the term so often that he came to believe it himself. Indeed, came to take it as a given, an axiom of political theory, the foundation of right thinking and the keystone of statesmanship.

He'd have done better to ask the Archduchess Isabella her opinion of Gretchen Richter. She'd have told him the same thing she once told her nephew Fernando, now the king in the Netherlands: "I hate to admit it, but that infuriating young woman would make a splendid queen—and if we were ever so unlucky as to live in a universe where she was an empress, we'd be calling her either 'the Great' or 'the Terrible,' depending on which side of her favor we lay."

The new king hadn't disputed the matter. He was pretty sure the canny old woman was right.

Of Mike Stearns, the chancellor would have done better to listen to the Dutch painter and diplomat Pieter Paul Rubens than to listen to himself. Rubens would have told him that he was quite sure future historians would refer to their period as the Stearns Era, or something similar, and that he could think of no more foolish error for a statesman than to underestimate Stearns.

But of all Oxenstierna's mistaken assessments of his enemies, the worst was his assessment of Rebecca Abrabanel.

He had none at all. At least, none beyond the common judgment of all heterosexually-inclined males between the ages of twelve and dead that the woman was extraordinarily attractive.

He'd met her during the course of the Congress of Copenhagen, which she'd attended. Several times, in fact. Once, he'd even been seated next to her at a formal banquet and had discovered, a bit to his surprise, that she was a charming conversationalist as well as a great beauty.

But he'd never thought much about her in any other terms, and certainly not in terms of her qualities as a political leader. Without even really thinking about the matter, he took it for granted that she was a cipher. A wife—hardly the first in history—who was able to attend affairs of state and pose as an important figure solely and simply because of the status of her husband.

Strigel, Spartacus, Achterhof—those were his enemies, now that Stearns himself had been shipped off to Bohemia. And Piazza, of course, but Piazza was tied down in Thuringia-Franconia thanks to the shrewd maneuver with the Bavarians.

Strigel was an administrator, Spartacus was a propagandist, and Achterhof was a thug. A very capable administrator, an often dazzling essayist, and a dangerous thug, to be sure—none of them were men you wanted to take lightly. Still, they moved within certain limits.

Those being, of course, the inherent limits of their anarchic rule.

So, the chancellor of Sweden was frustrated. How was it that chaos had not already spread across the Germanies, as the wild men of the CoCs erupted in fury? Chaos which would require a strong hand to suppress. How was it that entire provinces seemed to have remained perfectly calm and orderly?

Even under the pressure of the Bavarian assault, the SoTF was apparently quite stable. Hesse-Kassel had already announced it was maintaining neutrality in what the landgravine—a most aggravating woman, despite her high birth—chose to call "the current turbulence." As if the situation was the product of the weather instead of anarchy!

She was influencing Brunswick in that direction, too. That was not particularly surprising, any more than it was surprising that Prince Frederik of Denmark was keeping his province of Westphalia on the sidelines. What Oxenstierna hadn't expected, though, was to see her attitudes beginning to spread farther south. It was as if the Rhine was an infected vein carrying a female disease. Now the acting administrator of the Upper Rhine, Johann Moritz of Nassau-Siegen, was starting to coo like a dove!

Nils Brahe, the Swedish general who doubled as the administrator for the Province of the Main, was insisting that he needed to keep all his troops rather than sending some of them to Banér on the grounds that the French were behaving "suspiciously." While, at the same time, reporting that his province was orderly and undisturbed by CoC agitators.

Oxenstierna was doubtful that Brahe was telling him the truth. But what was worse was that he didn't know whether he preferred the truth in the first place. The thought that Brahe might be reporting accurately when he said the CoC was quiescent in the Main was in some ways more disturbing than if they'd been running amok.

Finally, there was the ongoing aggravation produced by General Horn in Swabia. What in the world had possessed Oxenstierna, that he'd ever agreed to let his daughter marry that wretched man? Christina's death four years earlier had had one beneficial effect:

at least her father no longer had to associate socially with his ex-son-in-law. But that wasn't any help under these circumstances, when the association was necessitated by political and—above all—military realities. Except for Banér's army at the gates of Dresden and the army Oxenstierna was keeping in reserve here in Berlin, Gustav Horn commanded the most powerful Swedish force in the USE. Being fair, Horn's claims that he needed them to counter the ever-ambitious Bernhard of Saxe-Weimar had a great deal more substance than the similar claims made by Brahe about the French. Oxenstierna was dubious that the French were behaving "suspiciously," but he didn't doubt for a moment that Bernhard was.

Horn, moreover, could also argue that he needed some of his troops to maintain order in Württemberg, which had been restive ever since the dying Duke Eberhard had bequeathed his territory to its people. Oxenstierna took a moment, again, to curse the young man's shade. Eberhard had been filled with a treasonous spirit, obviously. It was reliably reported that the duke's former concubine was now one of the leading figures among the Dresden rebels. The chancellor wondered from time to time which of them had infected the other with sedition.

Then there was the Tyrol, about which the less said, the better.

Darmstadt, Province of the Main

Upon the conclusion of the meeting, the delegation from Darmstadt's Committee of Correspondence was politely ushered to the door by the mayor, the head of the city's militia and three members of the city council. When they'd left the Rathaus, the militia's commander finally exploded.

"I hate dealing with those radical swine!"

One of the council members made a face, indicating his full agreement with the sentiment. But the expressions on the faces of the other two councilmen indicated a much more reserved attitude.

The mayor agreed with them, too. He put a friendly hand on the commander's shoulder—no feigning involved; the two men *were* good friends, and cousins to boot—and said, "Look, Gerlach, no one likes having to deal with them. But it's better than the alternative."

"I could drive them out of the city—entirely out—inside of a day." He worked his jaw for a moment. "All right, two days. Maybe three."

"And then what?" asked one of the councilmen. "Before you know it they'd be back with reinforcements from Frankfurt and we'd have an all-out war on our hands. Remember the mess after the Dreeson Incident?"

"And at what cost?" asked the other councilmen who'd been dubious. "Two or three days of fighting inside the city will leave a third of it in ruins. It's not worth it. It's not even *close* to being worth it."

The militia commander went back to working his jaw. It was a mannerism he had when he was angry but had no satisfactory way to act upon it.

"We won the election!" he exclaimed.

The mayor shook his head. "Not the way it turned out. I figured—so did you—that the duke of Saxe-Weimar would be the prime minister. Instead, he's in prison and we've got Oxenstierna in the saddle."

There was a gloomy silence for a few seconds. Then

one of the councilmen said, "I didn't like Stearns, not
one bit. But let's be honest—whatever else, he kept
the Swedes off our neck. Now here they are, back
in charge again."

Augsburg, one of the USE's seven independent imperial cities

The commander of Augsburg's militia had a very different viewpoint than his counterpart in Darmstadt. Nor
was he a cousin of Jeremias Jacob Stenglin, the head
of the city council, and they certainly weren't friends.

Augsburg didn't have a mayor, as such. Stenglin
played a somewhat similar role as head of the council, but his actual title was that of Stadtpfleger—"city
caretaker."

"Fine, then," the militia commander snarled at
Stenglin. "I'll resign and *you* can try to stand off the
Bavarians when they come."

"*If* they come," muttered one of the councilmen
at the meeting.

The militia commander shifted his glare to the muttering fellow. "We're talking about Duke Maximilian,
Herr Langenmantel, not your betrothed. He'll come,
if he takes the Oberpfalz."

That was a low blow. The councilman's intended
had failed to carry through on her vows. She'd left
the city altogether, in fact, eloping with their young
parson. It had been quite the scandal.

While the councilman was spluttering indignantly,
the head of the militia went back to glaring at the rest
of the council. "I told you and I will tell you again.

We're right on the border and Maximilian is running wild again. We can't hold the city against him without the cooperation of the CoC and its armed contingents and the support of the SoTF—which is controlled by the Fourth of July Party. Not against the Bavarian army."

Stenglin ran fingers across his scalp. Looking for the hair that was no longer there, perhaps. "I don't like those shitheads!"

The militia commander shrugged. "Who does? But the one thing about them is that they'll fight. They aren't good for much else, but they are good for that."

A tavern in Melsungen, in the province of Hesse-Kassel

"Here's to the health of our landgravine!" shouted one of the revelers, holding up his stein of beer. "Long may she reign!"

The tavern was full, as it often was on a winter's eve. Not a single stein failed to come up to join the toast.

Other provinces might suffer—would suffer, for a certainty, some of them—but not Hesse-Kassel. Not so long as Amalie Elizabeth of Hanau-Münzenberg sat in the provincial palace. The landgrave's blessed widow would keep the storm away.

A fishing boat in the Pomeranian Bay

"I wish now I'd voted for the bastard, instead of that useless Wettin." One of the two fishermen in the boat heaved at the net.

His partner frowned. "Stearns? He's too radical."

"Yes, I know. That's why I voted for the other fellow. And look what happened! When Stearns was running things, he drove all the foreign armies out of Germany. For the first time in years, we had peace. Didn't we?"

His companion made a face, but after a couple of seconds grunted his agreement.

"Right. Then we put in the duke and the first thing he does is get himself arrested and here we are, with the Swedes back on top."

He paused at their labor and stared out over the sea, gloomily. "I'll tell you this, for sure. The damn Swedes wouldn't have arrested the Prince. They wouldn't have dared."

His partner grunted agreement again. Immediately.

Mecklenburg

The noblemen's expedition never got to Schwerin. It got no farther than the southern shore of Lake Müritz. By then, CoC contingents from all over the province had gathered to meet the invaders.

They had no trouble finding them. As they had done during Operation Krystalnacht, the supposedly neutral USE Air Force had maintained reconnaissance patrols out of Wismar and provided the CoC contingents with regular reports on the location of their enemy.

Colonel Jesse Wood denied doing so, every time someone asked. But he'd kept a straight face while doing that, during Krystalnacht. Now he didn't bother to hide the grin.

The battle that followed lasted less than three hours. Once again, the Mecklenburger nobility found itself outclassed when it had to face a large force of CoC fighters coming out of the bigger cities like Schwerin and Rostock. Many of those men were not from the militias. They were former soldiers in the USE's army; some of them, veterans of the great battle at Ahrensbök.

But except for Mecklenburg—and Dresden, of course—the Germanies remained remarkably calm. There were scuffles aplenty; harsh words exchanged beyond counting; the same for threats. But rarely was any blood shed by anything more deadly than a fist or a cudgel.

Berlin

The chancellor's frustration mounted and mounted. His puzzlement, as well.

What was keeping the anarchists from anarchy?

Chapter 23

Paris, capital of France

After he finished reading Servien's précis of the latest
reports from France's agents in the United States of
Europe, Cardinal Richelieu rose from his desk and
went over to one of the window in his palace. The
Palais-Cardinal had been completed five years earlier.
It faced directly onto the Louvre and his office gave
him a marvelous view of the royal palace from which,
ultimately, derived the cardinal's own power.

Behind him, the *intendant* Servien studied his master
with considerable sympathy. It couldn't be pleasant for
him to contemplate the state of affairs in the USE.
France's chief minister was in much the same position as a tethered hawk, forced to watch squabbling
doves heedless of his presence. The tether, in his
case, being France's own very tense internal political
situation. What reliable troops the cardinal still had
in his possession needed to be kept close at hand.

Feeling the need to say something, Servien cleared
his throat. "It's a great pity, isn't it? To have to sit
here and do nothing."

The cardinal lifted his shoulders slightly, as if he'd begun a shrug and found it too much effort. "Just another reminder, Servien, if we needed it. God created the world. We did not."

Was there a trace of reproach in his tone? A suggestion that the Almighty had fallen down on the job, here and there?

Probably not. Unlike a hawk, Armand Jean du Plessis de Richelieu was philosophically inclined by nature. Not what any sane person would call a contemplative man—certainly not any one of the cardinal's many enemies. Or, if you could summon their ghosts, the even larger number of enemies he'd put in the grave. Still, he had a capacity to accept the trials and tribulations of fate in a calm and stoic manner.

He'd needed it, these past few years.

Madrid, capital of Spain

The chief minister of the Spanish crown, Gaspar de Guzmán, Count-Duke of Olivares, was far less inclined toward philosophy than Cardinal Richelieu—and his master the king of Spain less inclined still.

"You're saying we can't do *anything*?"

Olivares kept his eyes from meeting the king's gaze directly. Philip IV's tone of voice had a shrill quality that indicated his temper was badly frayed. He was normally not a bad master to serve—indeed, he could often be quite a pleasant one. But he was also a devotee of bullfighting, and in times like this was prone to act as if he was a torero in the arena himself. With, alas, one or another of his ministers designated as the bull.

"Well..."

"Nothing?" Angrily, the king slammed his palm down on the table that served him for a desk in his private audience chamber, on those occasions when he felt like dealing with affairs of state directly. Infrequent occasions, fortunately.

"Your Majesty..."

"Why am I paying for my tercios, then?"

Olivares decided this was not the time to point out that the king's payment of his soldiers was erratic. That was traditionally true for Spanish armies, but the situation had gotten even worse than usual of late.

"Answer me!"

There'd be no way to divert the king, obviously. Not today, after he'd just finished reading the latest reports on the turmoil that had enveloped the United States of Europe.

"We simply can't do anything, Your Majesty. Between the unrest in Portugal and Catalonia—"

"Why were those seditious books not banned?"

"They *were* banned, Your Majesty, but..."

It was hard to explain such things to a man who'd been born, raised and spent his entire life in the cloistered surroundings of Spanish royalty. Banning unpleasant items from the Real Alcazar was one thing; banning them from Spain, quite another. Spain was one of Europe's largest countries and more than nine-tenths of its borders were seacoast—more than three thousand miles of seacoast. Not all the tercios in the world could police it effectively, assuming Spain could afford the payroll—which it certainly couldn't.

Smuggling was even more of a national pastime for Spaniards than bullfighting. How did the king imagine that it would be possible to keep out copies of Grantville's texts on Spanish and Portuguese history, when smugglers routinely handled livestock? All the more so because there weren't that many of those texts, and most of them were just a few pages excerpted from encyclopedias.

A few pages, alas, were more than enough to encourage Portuguese and Catalan rebels to persist in their nefarious activity. In that cursed world the Americans came from, Portugal and Catalonia had rebelled in 1640—not more than five years from now. And while the Catalan revolt failed in its purpose, it had been a very close thing. As it was, Spain lost much of the province to France.

Not surprisingly, the Catalan malcontents in *this* universe were simply being encouraged to try harder.

Fortunately, the king was distracted by other thoughts. Blessedly, by angry thoughts toward someone other than his chief minister. "It's because of that fucking Borja, isn't it?"

This was not safe terrain, certainly, but it was safer than the terrain they'd been treading on. "Yes, Your Majesty, I'm afraid so. Cardinal Borja's . . . ah, papal adventure—"

"His adventure? Say better, his lunacy—no, his rampant vanity—better still, his plunge into Satanic pride!"

"Yes, Your Majesty. Well said! Whatever we call it, though, his actions have stirred up a great deal of unrest through Italy, including in our own possessions."

"Indeed." The king's glare was still ferocious, but at least it now had a different focus. "Explain to me again, Gaspar, why I can't have the bastard assassinated?"

"Ah, well . . . That would just compound the damage,

I'm afraid. As I said before, Your Majesty, Borja's precipitate action has simply left us with few options, and none of them very good. If we kill him—if *anyone* kills him—then there's little doubt that Urban will take back the papacy. And he's...ah..."

"Now bitterly hostile to us on the picayune grounds that we overthrew him and murdered several dozen of his bishops and cardinals, including his nephew Francesco."

"Well. Yes."

The king spent the next minute or so calling down a variety of divine ills and misfortunes on the person of Cardinal Gaspare de Borja y de Velasco. The tirade spilled over into outright blasphemy—not that even the boldest of Spain's inquisitors would have said a word on the subject, with the king in his current mood. It was notable also that at no time did Philip IV refer to Borja by any title other than profane and profoundly vulgar ones. He certainly never used the man's newly minted title of "pope."

When he finally wound down, most of his fury seemed to have been spent. It was replaced by a sort of sullen resignation that was not pleasant to deal with, but no longer really dangerous.

"The essence of the matter is that we have no resources to do anything significant about the heretics. The USE crumbles—the same swine who—ah! Never mind! It's too aggravating to even think about! We just have to sit here, on our hands, and do nothing."

Olivares decided to interpret that as the king's summation rather than a question. That way he could avoid, once again, having to say "Yes, we can't" where the king wanted to hear "No, we can."

Brussels, capital of the Netherlands

The king in the Netherlands—Fernando I, as he now titled himself, being the founder of his new dynasty—looked around the conference table at his closest advisers.

"We're all agreed, then? We will take no advantage of the current civil conflict in the USE. Beyond, of course, using it to apply more leverage in existing negotiations over trade matters and minor border disputes."

They'd decided on that term toward the beginning of the conference. "Civil conflict," as opposed to "civil war." There were important connotations involved.

The advisers, in turn, all looked around the table, gauging each other's expressions.

Rubens provided the summary. "Yes, Your Majesty, we're agreed. The benefits involved simply aren't worth the risks."

"Small benefits," said Alessandro Scaglia, "with very great risks."

One of the advisers wiggled his fingers. "I don't disagree with the decision, but I don't honestly think the risks are *that* great."

"No?" said Miguel de Manrique. The soldier's expression was grim. "Stearns might come back to power, you know. He's bad enough, but what's worse is that he'd only do so if Richter holds Dresden. How would you like it if *she* came back here, with a grudge to settle?"

Archduchess Isabella's hand flew to her throat. "Oh, dear God. Nephew, listen to Manrique! None of your headstrong ways, you hear? King or not, I won't have

it. I want some peace and quiet in these last few
months before I slip into the grave."

Poznań, Poland

"The king is adamant, and the Sejm still more so.
That's just the way it is, young Opalinski. They'll have
no talk of a peace settlement."

Stanislaw Koniecpolski shifted his shoulders under
the heavy bearskin coat. Even for January, the day was
cold, but the grand hetman wouldn't be seen shivering
in public. It was hard not to, though.

Lukasz Opalinski wasn't even trying. He had his
hands tucked into his armpits and was making a
veritable stage drama out of shivering.

"Dear God, it's cold!" he hissed. Then, tight-faced,
he said, "And I suppose they insisted once again that
we had to sally from the gates and smite the invaders. Applying the brilliant tactic of a hussar charge
through deep snow against rifled muskets firing from
well-built fieldworks."

Koniecpolski chuckled. "They did indeed. But there,
I'm afraid, they are trespassing onto my rightful territory, and I am not legally obliged to listen to the
silly beggars. No, rest easy, young man. There'll be no
idiotic sallies out of the gates of Poznań. We'll stay
behind these walls in comfort—using the term loosely,
I admit—while the German shits freeze out there."

He did another shift of his shoulders. A rapid succession of shifts, actually. Not an outright shiver, but
certainly a close cousin. "Besides, there's a bright side
to continuing the war."

Koniecpolski had his own hands tucked into opposing sleeves of his coat. Not wanting to expose them to the elements, he used a gesture of his head to point to the compound behind them. From their height atop one of the bastions, they had a good view of the now-largely-dismantled APC that Lukasz had captured from the enemy.

"You can be damn sure that one of Gustav Adolf's demands—he'll be inflexible about it too—will be the return of that APC. I'd much rather keep it for a while. Walenty tells me they're making great progress."

Opalinski smiled. "He's not bragging, either. I'd say he was, except every day that goes by, Ellis gets more unhappy."

Walenty Tarnowski was the young nobleman who was bound and determined to establish what he called "advanced mechanics" in the commonwealth of Poland and Lithuania. Unusually for a scholar, he was quite willing to get his hands dirty, too. Koniecpolski had given him the assignment of studying the captured war machine to see if he could duplicate it—or, since that wasn't likely, see if he could design a simpler and more primitive version of the device.

Mark Ellis was the American soldier they'd captured when they seized the APC. Under questioning, he'd claimed that he knew very little about the machine, being a civil as opposed to mechanical engineer. He'd also claimed he would refuse to talk under torture.

The latter claim was dubious, to say the least. The number of men in the world who would refuse to talk under torture was minute. The problem was rather that their talk was usually babble, and Koniecpolski saw no reason to think the up-timer would be any different. Besides, he had no desire to stir up American animosity toward Poland by mistreating one of their people. Sooner or later, after all, Poland would need to negotiate a peace treaty.

So, Tarnowski toiled on, day after day, with no help from Ellis. But he really was quite adept at this "advanced mechanics" of his. So who could say? The time might come—and much sooner than people thought—when Polish hussars would ride into battle on iron horses instead of fleshy ones.

Gloomily, Mark Ellis listened to Walenty Tarnowski's depiction of today's results. This morning's results, rather. The nobleman had all afternoon to ferret out still more knowledge.

They'd gotten in the habit of eating lunch together. Perhaps oddly, given the way they'd started, the two men had gotten to be on very cordial terms. You could even say they'd become friends, in a way.

Mark still insisted he would say nothing, nothing, nothing—subject him to what agony they would! To which Walenty replied that he was a student of advanced mechanics, not a torturer. And besides, Mark had nothing to say anyway, being a mere civil engineer. The ritual insults exchanged and mutual honor upheld, they'd then proceed to have the sort of pleasant chats that young men will have when they're in relaxed and convivial company. Walenty, being a Polish nobleman, called it "intelligent conversation." Mark, who fancied himself a West Virginia hillbilly, called it "shooting the shit."

In truth, Mark Ellis was very far from being a hillbilly, unless you chose to slap the label on any and all

West Virginians—which would certainly be objected to by at least three-fourths of the state's population. He had three years of college, just for starters, where any self-respecting hillbilly would only grudgingly admit to having graduated from high school. The one and only characteristic he shared with hillbillies was, ironically, the one he insisted to his Polish captors not to possess—he was, in fact, a very good auto mechanic.

So he knew, better than most people would, just how much progress Walenty was making. It was pretty astonishing, actually. Mark still thought there wasn't much chance the Poles could produce a functioning armored fighting vehicle of their own, not for a number of years to come. There were just too many technological obstacles to overcome—many of them ones which not even the USE could handle yet.

But that would be the only reason they couldn't, not lack of knowledge. Walenty Tarnowski already knew why an automobile or truck worked, front to back, and he'd soon be able to teach anyone with mechanical aptitude all of the basic principles involved in creating a damn *tank*.

Luckily for the USE, which had started this stupid war thanks to that idiot Gustav Adolf's medieval dynastic fetishes, the Poles simply didn't have the industrial base to make a tank, regardless of how much knowledge they had.

But how long would *that* remained true?

"So much for dumb Polacks," he muttered, after Walenty left to go back to work on the APC.

Mark got up and went to the window that gave him a view to the west. "Come on, guys. Quit screwing around and sign a damn peace treaty, will you?"

Chapter 24

USE army's siege lines, just outside of Poznań

"Some wine, Doctor?" asked George, the duke of Brunswick-Lüneburg, holding up the bottle from which he'd just poured himself a glass.

James Nichols shook his head. One of the things about the seventeenth century that he'd never gotten accustomed to was the alcohol consumption. Abstractly, he knew that the practice of drinking alcohol from the morning on was common in preindustrial societies. Melissa had told him that Americans in the early nineteenth century consumed an average of six times as much in the way of alcoholic beverages as Americans did in the late twentieth century—and they were mostly drinking whiskey, too, not beer or wine.

From a medical standpoint, it even made a certain amount of sense, in an insane sort of way. You couldn't assume the local water was potable—it very likely wasn't, in fact—and alcoholic beverages were much safer to drink in that respect.

Never mind that they also had a lot of unhealthy side effects. The thing that really drove James Nichols crazy was that one of the standard practices for drinking in the daytime was to cut the wine with water—as Duke George was doing this very moment. He'd only poured himself half a glass of wine. The rest, he was filling up from a carafe of water.

Drink wine in order to avoid microbes from infected water. Then cut it with water full of microbes. Go figure.

Something of his thoughts must have showed in his expression, because the duke smiled widely. "I assure you, Doctor!" He waved the bottle at General Torstensson, who was sitting in a comfortable chair just a few feet away—with a glass of wine cut with water in his own hand. "Lennart always insists that his orderlies have to boil the water we use for our beverages."

Torstensson chuckled and said, "And now the good doctor is wondering why we simply don't drink the water." He shrugged. "It has no taste, I'm afraid. Or tastes bad, often enough."

He used the glass to gesture at a chair positioned not far away in the chamber of his headquarters he was using for informal meetings. It was one of the rooms on the second floor of a tavern he'd seized in one of the villages not far from Poznań.

"I can have some tea made, if you'd like. I'm afraid I have no coffee."

The duke plopped his portly figure into another chair. "Tea! But it's still at least two hours short of noon!"

"That's it, make fun of the abstemious up-timer," grumbled Nichols, as he took his chair. "Thank you, General, I would appreciate a cup of tea."

He didn't ask for cream or sugar. Cream, because he wasn't willing to drink unpasteurized dairy products; sugar, because it was rarely available and he didn't much care for honey. So, he'd just learned to drink tea plain. By now, he'd even developed a taste for it.

At that, he was enjoying a luxury. Tea was even more expensive than coffee, and coffee was extremely expensive. The standard hot beverage for people at the time if they weren't drinking alcohol was a thin broth of some sort.

Torstensson wiggled a finger at the orderlies standing by the doorway and one of them left to get the tea. The other two remained in place.

And that was another seventeenth-century custom Nichols had never really gotten used to—the ubiquity of servants. By now, most Americans had adapted because they'd found they could afford servants themselves. But Melissa strongly disapproved of the practice—she was not entirely rational on the subject, in James' opinion, but it wasn't something worth arguing about—so they had no servants in their own household. Instead, they had a seemingly endless procession of cleaning ladies and cooks who didn't live on the premises and were thus not technically "servants" but who did exactly the same thing and cost about twice as much.

Go figure. It wasn't as if everything about the twentieth century had been logically coherent either.

Duke George seemed to be something of a telepath today. "And how is your estimable wife these days?"

The third general in the room was Dodo Freiherr zu Innhausen und Knyphausen. He shook his head lugubriously. "You forget the lewd American customs, George! 'Shaking up,' I believe they call it. Amazing, really, that the Lord didn't smite the lot of them for sinfulness."

"The term is actually 'shacking up,'" Nichols said mildly, "although the genteel way to depict Melissa is as my 'Significant Other.' I'm more amazed the Lord didn't smite the lot of us for mangling the language, myself. As for Melissa, she's fine. Feeling a bit ragged these days, from traveling so much. She says she's feeling her age, although she's been saying that as long as I've known her. Melissa is one of those people who feels betrayed by the march of time, as if she and the universe had an understanding that she'd always stay about twenty and the universe is welching on the deal."

George smiled. "I will not inquire as to the nature and purpose of the travel. Such a firebrand! Who would guess, beneath such a proper appearance? I swear to you, James, the first time I met her I thought she was a duchess herself."

A lot of down-timers had that reaction to Melissa Mailey, when they first met her, especially people who were members of the nobility. Nichols had always found that amusing—and been even more amused by the appalled reaction so many of them had once they discovered Melissa's radical political history and her still-radical political views.

In the case of the duke of Brunswick-Lüneburg, however, the reaction had been curiosity and interest. In the two years or so that had passed since he first encountered Melissa and James at one of Mary Simpson's soirees in Magdeburg, he and Melissa never missed a chance to discuss politics whenever they found themselves in the same city. At considerable length, too. Oddly enough, one of the highest-placed members of the Hochadel—George was Prince of Calenberg in addition to being the ruling duke of a province and the commander of an army division—had wound up becoming quite a good friend of hers.

That was the duke's temperament at work. Despite his status, George had a rare capacity to distance himself from political nostrums. He had almost a child's reaction to what Melissa called the *as-we-all-know* syndrome. He'd ask "why is that true?" where most of his class—of any class, being fair—would just take *as-we-all-know* for granted.

Brunswick-Lüneburg's own political views were quite moderate, as such things were gauged in the here and now. Like a number of highly placed people—James could see a copy of the book in Torstensson's bookcase right here and now, in fact—Duke George was being influenced by the writings of the Netherlands essayist Alessandro Scaglia.

James hadn't read *Political Methods and the Laws of Nations*, but Melissa had. The book was only being circulated privately, but when she'd asked Scaglia for a copy he'd sent it to her with his compliments.

Her depiction of the policies advocated by Scaglia had been as follows: "The gist of his argument is that the powers-that-be are going to get screwed anyway, no matter what. So they might as well relax and try to work out the best possible arrangement with the plebes. Make 'em agree to take a bath regularly and dress up for dinner, that sort of thing. He uses longer words and a lot more of them."

The orderly appeared with a tray bearing a cup of tea. He placed it on the side table next to Nichols' chair and withdrew to the back of the room. There was a moment of silence as the three generals waited politely for the doctor to take his first sip.

After he set the cup down, he said, "In answer to your unspoken question, General Torstensson, I can't

tell you anything about the emperor's condition. I was
not permitted to see him."

Torstensson grunted. "Not permitted by Chancellor
Oxenstierna?"

"I was told the orders came from him, yes. But I
didn't speak to him myself. Then or at any time in
the three days I was in Berlin."

"Told by whom?"

"Colonel Hand."

"Ah! The king's estimable cousin." That came from
Duke George. Knyphausen's contribution was to issue
one of those grunts that seemed freighted with meaning; but, alas, a meaning known only to the grunter.

"I'm interested in what else—" Torstensson started
to say, but then closed his mouth and shook his head.
"Never mind."

At a guess, Nichols thought Torstensson was going
to ask him what *else* Colonel Erik Haakansson Hand
had said to him.

If he had . . .

James wasn't sure how he'd have responded. The
colonel had asked him not to speak to anyone about
the matter they'd discussed, on the grounds that he
didn't want to raise false hopes. A bit grudgingly,
Nichols had agreed. He'd never had much use himself
for that whole "let's not raise false hopes" line of reasoning, which was rampant in the medical community.
But he'd agreed to go along. He hadn't thought much
about it, to be honest.

Now, if he was interpreting Torstensson's abrupt
silence correctly, James began to wonder if Hand
really had simply been reluctant to "raise false hopes."
What if . . .

What if what he'd *really* wanted was to keep Chancellor Oxenstierna from learning that Gustav Adolf appeared to be having flashes of coherence in his speech and his reactions to the people around him? One thing that Hand had made clear was that Oxenstierna only came to visit the stricken monarch on rare occasions now. For the past two months, understandably enough, the chancellor had been preoccupied with political affairs.

Interesting.

For the moment, though, Nichols didn't see where there was much he could do, one way or the other. So he decided to satisfy his own curiosity.

"If you don't mind my asking, General Torstensson, I'm wondering what your own intentions are." He waved his hand in a vague gesture. "About the overall political situation, I mean."

Knyphausen issued another of those meaninglessly meaningful grunts. Brunswick-Lüneburg grinned like a Cheshire cat. Which was equally meaningless, coming from him.

Torstensson pursed his lips. "To be honest, Dr. Nichols, I am not prepared to give you an answer that would be at all...how to put it?"

"Expansive," suggested Duke George.

"Yes, that's it. Expansive."

"I'll settle for terse," said Nichols.

Knyphausen grunted again.

"Not *that* terse, please."

The three generals burst into laughter. "Ah, Dodo!" exclaimed the duke. "You see? As I've told you time and again, you could drive the Oracle at Delphi mad."

Torstensson finished the wine in his glass and set it down. "Let me put it this way, Doctor. I believe—so do

George and Dodo; and, yes, of course we've discussed the matter—that nothing would be improved at all if we allowed the main forces of the USE's army to be dragged into the civil conflict. That, for any number of reasons, not the least of them being"—his own voice got stiff for a moment—"as I have now explained to the chancellor on several occasions—that it is by no means clear how the army itself would react if I did so. The enlisted men, I mean."

Knyphausen grunted again—but, finally, put some words behind the sound. "In this instance, 'enlisted men' being a euphemism for 'the fellows holding most of the guns.'"

"And know how to use them, too." That came from George; this time, without a smile. "There is a sort of unspoken, tacit agreement between ourselves—the commanding officers, I mean—and the soldiers in our army here at Poznań. They agree to obey orders—here—and we agree that we will stay here and not try to use them to enforce any sort of settlement back in the USE proper."

"That's well put," added Torstensson. "And about as much as we are prepared to say."

Nichols nodded. The truth was, they'd said everything that was critical already. He'd tell Melissa when he got back to Magdeburg, as a man will say something to the woman who shares his life and his bed. Knowing full well that she'd pass it on to Rebecca immediately.

Torstensson had to know that as well. Which meant that the tacit agreement he had with his soldiers had just gotten extended to the Fourth of July Party and the Committees of Correspondence across the entire nation. *You leave me alone and I'll leave you alone.*

Oxenstierna would have a fit, if he knew. But

James had a feeling that the chancellor was slowly but steadily losing his grip on the situation—first and foremost, his grip on his own people.

The tea was quite good, as you'd expect.

Nichols spent the next two days inspecting the sanitary and medical arrangements and facilities that the army had set up in their siege lines around Poznań. As he'd expected, they were well designed and in good order. Torstensson and his staff officers had genuinely internalized the critical role that sanitation and proper medical procedures played in fending off the diseases that typically swept through armies at war, especially armies engaged in a siege.

But what was probably even more important was that the rank and file soldiers were equally committed to those practices. So there'd be no dodging and shirking, which was often the Achilles' heel of sanitation and medical regulations. Quite the opposite, actually. The punishment a soldier who slacked off would get from his mates was likely to be a lot worse than what he'd get if an officer caught him. Even from the standpoint of its commanders, there were advantages sometimes to having an army so influenced by CoC attitudes.

On the morning of the third day, a small delegation of Polish officers came across the lines under a flag of truce. They'd come to bring Grand Hetman Koniecpolski's answer to the offer Nichols had made the day he arrived to give his advice on medical matters to the Polish army as well.

The leader of the delegation was an officer who seemed very young to be wielding as much authority

as he obviously did. But his name was Opalinski—
Lukasz Opalinski—which perhaps explained the matter.
James had a vague recollection that the Opalinskis
were one of the more prominent move-and-shaker
families in the upper crust of the Polish-Lithuanian
commonwealth's aristocracy.

Opalinski fit James' image of a hussar to a T. He
was tall, well-built, and handsome in a big-nosed sort
of way. His hair was short and blond as was his beard,
but his mustache was swept out in very dramatic
fashion. The tips of it looked as if they probably blew
in the wind as he galloped his horse toward the foe.

He was a very polite young man, as well, although
he was obviously struggling not to gape at Nichols.
In all likelihood, James was the first black man he'd
ever met in his life. Not that Germans had met very
many black people either, of course. But James and
his daughter Sharon were by now so famous in the
Germanies that most people in the USE had at least
seen a woodcut likeness of them somewhere. To Lukasz
Opalinski, James Nichols was an utterly exotic figure,
something out of the ancient tales by Herodotus about
foreign lands and their peoples. If he weren't being
polite, James was pretty sure the hussar would lift up
his shirt to see if he had another mouth or pair of
eyes on his stomach.

"I'm afraid we must refuse," Opalinski said, in heavily accented but quite good German. "Please accept
the grand hetman's regrets and his sincere thanks for
the offer. But—ah—he asked me to explain that if he
accepted, there might be trouble about it in the Sejm."

From the tinge of exasperation in the young hussar's
voice, James was pretty sure Opalinski thought there'd

be trouble in the Sejm if Koniecpolski ate porridge
for breakfast or put his boots on in the wrong order.
But this was all a diplomatic dance, in any event.
James had made the offer at Torstensson's suggestion,
but the Swedish general had told him he didn't think
there was much chance the Poles would accept.

With a polite bow, Opalinski took his leave. He
managed not to turn around and stare at James more
than twice as he and his party rode off.

"Well, you were right," he said to Torstensson.

The commander of the USE army shrugged. "Thank
heaven for the nature of Polish government. If it
weren't the way it is, I hate to think what Koniecpolski
could accomplish."

Knyphausen grunted. Duke George grinned.

One of the air force's Gustavs landed that afternoon
to take James back to Magdeburg. The pilot buzzed
the Polish lines on his way out. The Poles fired a
volley at the plane in response.

Apparently, that mutually useless display of martial
prowess seemed reasonable to both sides. James made
no objection, though. He could still remember a time,
when he'd been a young man in one of the gangs in
Chicago's south side, when he'd have thought it was
perfectly reasonable himself. Now at the age of sixty,
he'd concluded that the main difference between
gang fights and the wars of dynasties and nations was
that the gangs were a lot less pretentious about their
violence. Stripped of the long-winded folderol, from
what James could see, most formal declarations of
war came down to "the motherfuckers dissed us and
we're gonna get 'em for it."

Chapter 25

Dresden, capital of Saxony

Jozef Wojtowicz had never worked so hard in his life. Thankfully, he'd been blessed with a naturally strong and sturdy frame, so he was able to bear up under the heavy labor long enough to start getting in better condition. But all that really meant was that he was burdened with still more work.

The city's defenders maintained and even strengthened the fortifications, despite the relentless Swedish bombardment.

That was no doubt how the future history books would depict the situation he found himself involved in. His thoughts on the matter were dark, dark, dark. In the pantheon of liars, he ranked historians second only to outright swindlers—without the excuse of honest greed as a motivation.

Here was the truth behind those innocuous-sounding words, he'd come to discover.

Truth One. In a siege, able-bodied men fall into two categories—and the definition of "able-bodied" is loose to begin with. There are soldiers, who stand guard on the ramparts vigilantly watching for any sign of enemy action. That is to say, do nothing more strenuous than rub their hands to ward off the chill. And there are civilians, whom said soldiers dragoon into doing all of the work.

Truth Two. The work involved in "maintaining and even strengthening the fortifications" consists of nine parts staggering under the weight of rocks and other rubble, and one part staggering under the weight of water casks needed to keep said able-bodied civilians from collapsing while carrying out the other nine parts of the labor.

Truth Three. Rocks come in only two sizes. Too big to carry without great strain, or, if they are on the smallish side, too many to carry without great strain.

Truth four. Shovels were invented by Moloch.

Truth five. Picks were invented by Ba'alzebub.

Truth six. Wheelbarrows were invented by Belial.

Truth seven. The notion that there would someday be an end to toil and suffering was invented by Satan himself.

Truth eight. Beware of Polish compatriots—

"Hey, Joe!"

Wojtowicz was jolted out of his gloomy mental recitation of the Great Truths. Carefully, so as not to lose his balance under the weight of the basket of stones he was carrying, he turned to see who had shouted at him.

Ted Szklenski, as he'd thought. "What is it?"

Szklenski hooked a thumb over his shoulder. "They want to see you in the castle." The huge form of the Residenzschloss loomed behind him.

Jozef frowned. He did *not* like the sound of this. So

far, he'd managed to remain reasonably inconspicuous—in large part, by staying away from the Residenzschloss, which was the center of CoC activity and held their headquarters.

On the positive side, he had a legitimate excuse to put down the basket.

That took a few seconds, and would have taken longer if Szklenski hadn't lent him a hand.

"*Who* wants to see me?"

Szklenski shrugged. "Got no idea. I'm just passing along the message from Waclaw."

Waclaw—his last name had turned out to be Walczak—was the leader of the Polish CoC contingent in Dresden, insofar as the term "leader" could be applied to the group at all. Even Polish CoC members tended to have a *liberum veto* attitude toward the principles of majority rule.

Under these circumstances, though, Jozef couldn't just ignore the summons. That would draw more attention than anything else.

Besides, no one would expect him to carry rocks to the Residenzschloss. At the moment, Jozef was willing to risk outright crucifixion for that blessing.

He had to wander around the corridors for most of an hour before he finally found Walczak. In the process he got completely lost twice. He'd never been in the huge building before. Like many palaces that dated back hundreds of years, the structure was a composite; haphazard in much of its design and complex to boot. The original castle had been a Romanesque fort built around the year 1200—over four centuries ago. Toward the end of the fifteenth century, the famous master builder Arnold von Westfalen extended it considerably. A century later, a new addition was constructed, this one in the Renaissance style. At no point along the way did anyone seriously try to remove what already existed. The back-breaking labor involved would have been insane. Only idiot Poles stupid enough to come to Dresden...

He finally spotted Waclaw.

Naturally, Waclaw chided him for being late.

When Walczak ushered Jozef into the large chamber on the top floor facing the river, Wojtowicz's worst fears were realized.

Richter herself looked up from a large table where various maps were spread and studied him intently for several seconds.

"He's the one I was telling you about, Gretchen," said Waclaw.

Stabbed in the back. Ever the story of poor Poland. Who needed enemies when Poles had themselves?

"You're szlachta, yes?" That came from Richter. It was more of a statement than a question.

Jozef made one last desperate attempt to weasel out of his fate. "Yes, but so what? Two of the other Poles here in Dresden are szlachta also."

One stab in the back deserved another. He pointed at Walczak. "He's one of them."

Richter shook her head. "Yes, I know. But Waclaw doesn't have any military experience. Like most szlachta, his family has four pigs where his lowly commoner neighbors have only three. We Germans would say they're putting on airs, but what do we know?"

Waclaw was grinning. Jozef was tempted to grin

himself. Richter's sarcastic depiction of the state of affairs for most of Poland's so-called nobility was accurate enough. Where most countries had a small aristocracy—that of the Germanies was no more than five percent of the population; that of England, an even smaller three percent—no fewer than one Pole in ten counted themselves part of the szlachta. Inevitably, that formal claim fell afoul of economic reality. Most szlachta families really weren't much if any wealthier than the peasants among whom they lived.

But he resisted the temptation, easily enough. There was peril lurking here somewhere, like a leviathan beneath the waves.

"Neither does the other szlachta, Radzimierz Zawadski," Richter continued. "But he and Waclaw both think you probably do. They say you're from a better class, associated with one of the magnates."

That was always the problem with running into fellow Poles. From subtleties of dress, carriage, speech—who knew, exactly?—they could deduce things about another Pole that a foreigner would miss entirely.

There was no point trying to deny it. Jozef decided he'd skirt as close to the truth as he possibly could.

"Yes, that's true. The Koniecpolskis, as it happens. But I'm from one of the bastard offshoots of the family." He shook his head. "I'm no hussar, I can tell you that."

Richter continued to study him. Her eyes were a naturally warm color, a sort of light brown that wasn't quite hazel. But they didn't seem the least bit warm, at the moment.

Not cold, either. Just . . . dispassionate, the way a student of natural history might examine a curious-looking and possibly interesting new insect.

"I didn't expect you to be," she said. "We wouldn't have any use for a hussar anyway."

For the first time, she smiled. It was thin affair, with no more in the way of warmth than her gaze. "We're likely to have a better use for horses before winter is over than putting a hussar on top of one. And to do what, anyway? Sally out of the gates and smite the foe? All one of him against fifteen thousand? No, better to keep the horses for food, if we need them."

She went back to studying him again. "Tell me the truth," she said abruptly. "Don't exaggerate anything—but don't minimize anything, either. How much military training and experience *do* you have?"

He hesitated. Then, decided that lying to this woman was likely to be a risky proposition. "Training, quite a bit. Actual combat experience, none at all. Well, leaving aside two duels. Assuming the term 'duel' can be applied to affairs that were impromptu, unstructured, and...ah..."

"Drunken brawls where you could barely stand up and neither of you could see straight."

"Well. Yes."

"The training should be enough. Come here." She motioned him toward her with a little wave of the hand. Her eyes were already back on the maps, though, not watching to see if he'd obey. She took that for granted, in the way people will who are accustomed to command.

When Jozef came around the table and stood next to her, he saw that she was studying a map of Dresden. More in the way of a diagram, actually, that concentrated entirely on the city's fortifications.

She placed a finger on one of the bastions that

anchored the defenses along the river. "Our officers tell me that once Banér is certain the ice covering the river is solid enough, that he may attempt an assault across it. The fortifications here are not as strong as they are around the southern perimeter of the city."

Jozef studied the diagram. The military training he'd gotten had been fairly extensive, as you'd expect for a member of the Koniecpolski family. But, as was usual for men of that class, it had not concentrated much on siege warfare. Still, he'd picked up quite a bit of knowledge by osmosis, as it were. Some of his instructors had been szlachta from modest families or commoners who did have experience fighting in the infantry and artillery.

"It makes sense to me. It'll depend mostly on how much of a chance Banér is willing to take. An assault like that is likely to result in heavy casualties. It's true that the defenses along the river are weaker, but there's a reason for that. The assumption is that the river itself bolsters the defense. Which it does, even in winter when the ice makes it possible to cross." He placed his finger on the river. "There is absolutely no cover at all there, and the soldiers have to cross well over a hundred yards of ice. Which may be solid but is hardly good footing. Personally, I think he'd be foolish to take the risk."

"He may not have much choice," said Richter. "We think Oxenstierna is getting anxious, from reports we've gotten."

Jozef frowned. "Why?"

Richter's thin, humorless smile came back. "Because he expected a lot more fighting across the nation than he's getting. Which makes Dresden all the more central.

This is really the only place except Mecklenburg—and that's over by now, and not to Oxenstierna's liking—where you can use the term 'civil war' without snickering."

Jozef hadn't known that. Second only to the misery of hauling rocks every hour of daylight had been the frustration of a spy who didn't have access to any information.

Belatedly, it occurred to him that for the first time since he'd arrived in Dresden, he could actually do some real *spying*. Risky, of course, to spy on such as Richter and her cohorts.

"So . . ." Maybe he could draw her out.

"So time is not on the Swede's side. People don't like things unsettled. They start getting angry at the people they think are responsible for it, unless they can see that real progress is being made to implement whatever program is being advocated. You can't ever forget that most people don't really have very strong political convictions. They just want to get about their lives. They will be naturally drawn to leaders who project confidence and seem to be getting things accomplished, and they will be naturally repelled by leaders who seem to stir up trouble but can't get anything done."

Jozef hadn't ever thought about political conflict in those terms, but it did make sense. It was certainly true that a great deal of the confidence people felt in a leader came from the leader's own self-confidence. That was probably even more true of military leadership. Having a record of winning battles helped a great deal, of course. But the truth was that even great captains like Koniecpolski and Gustav Adolf had lost their share of battles and sieges. Yet they never lost the confidence of their followers, as much as anything because they went into each new battle as if they were certain to win.

Much the same way, he realized, that the woman standing next to him somehow exuded confidence that she would be triumphant in her struggles. As if victory were a given and all that remained to be determined was the specific manner in which it would be achieved.

"Leaders such as our blessed Swedish chancellor," she went on. "Look at what's happened. He summoned a convention of reactionaries in Berlin to launch a great counterrevolution. Well, Wettin did, officially, but everyone knew that was a formality even before Oxenstierna eliminated the pretense and threw him in prison. And, sure enough, they'd barely closed the lock on Wettin's cell when they proclaimed their so-called Charter of Rights and Duties. And..."

She grinned, now, and there was some actual humor in it. "Ha! Nothing! Within two weeks all of the moderate provincial leaders had pulled away, like proper ladies drawing up their skirts to avoid getting them muddied. The only big clash was in Mecklenburg, where they got routed again. Elsewhere, people can look around and see that the supposedly seditious rebels are keeping peace and order—in many instances, by intimidating the reactionaries who *would* like to start fighting. Except for Dresden, the only real fighting going on anywhere is in the Oberpfalz. But that's caused by a Bavarian invasion, which everyone knows—even an idiot can see this much—is entirely Oxenstierna's responsibility. Duke Maximilian wouldn't have dared to attack the Oberpfalz again if Oxenstierna hadn't started all this trouble. All of which means that it's more important than ever that the Swedes crush the Saxon rebellion. Their failure to take Dresden makes Oxenstierna look more hapless and incapable as every day goes by."

"Bavaria invaded the Oberpfalz?" That was the first Jozef had heard of that development. For a supposed spy, he felt like he was doing a good imitation of a burrowing little animal. Sees nothing, hears nothing, knows nothing. Except the dirt in front of him.

Richter was frowning at him. "Where have *you* been?"

"Hauling rocks," he said.

She shook her head. "Well, not anymore." Again, her finger came down on the bastion by the river. "I want you to organize your Poles to support the unit of soldiers we already have there. You'll be coordinating with Lieutenant Nagel, who's in charge of that stretch of the fortifications. He'll provide you with weapons, too."

No more rocks. And he could spy again. While rubbing his hands to ward off the chill, there being nothing else to do.

Chapter 26

Dresden, capital of Saxony

"Well, it's done," said Denise Beasley, looking very satisfied with herself. Amazingly so, for someone who'd actually played a very modest role in getting the airplane repaired.

But Eddie Junker saw no advantage to himself in pointing that out. Denise was often egocentric, but she was not snotty. A cheerful and self-satisfied Denise was a very friendly and affectionate Denise, a state of affairs entirely to his liking. A Denise who felt she was being unfairly criticized, on the other hand, was a sullen and belligerent Denise—and she viewed criticism as inherently unfair, when directed at herself.

This was not because the girl was more self-centered than any other seventeen-year-old. She wasn't. It is simply in the nature of seventeen-year-olds to know with a certainty usually reserved for religious fanatics that nothing is ever their fault. Eddie could remember that sublime period in his own life. Quite well, in fact, since it wasn't really all that long ago. There were times when he wondered if all of life could be

described as a long, slow slide into self-doubt and feelings of inadequacy from that all-too-brief Golden Age.

"Eddie?" Self-satisfied as she might be, Denise also
shared—albeit in smaller portion than the usual—the
seventeen-year-old need to be constantly reassured.

"Yes, it's done. All we were really waiting for was
the propeller, anyway."

The propeller had finally arrived the day before.
Smuggled in—Eddie found this quite charming—in
a load of firewood. The smugglers hadn't even had
to bribe the one cavalry patrol they'd encountered.
The mercenaries working for the Swedes had taken
one look at the load in the cart, curled their lip, and
ridden off. You might as well try to get a bribe from
a mouse as get one from a woodcutter.

Somewhat to Eddie's surprise, and certainly to his
relief, it had turned out that there was no damage to
the engine. There'd been some structural damage to
the wings and fuselage—fortunately, not much—and
the fabric of the wings had been pretty badly torn up.
But Dresden's artisans and craftsmen had the skills
and materials to repair that sort of damage. Repairing the engine would have been far more difficult, if
it was possible at all. There, the problem wasn't so
much the skills needed—seventeenth-century metal-
workers could do truly amazing work—as it was the
materials involved.

That was the great bottleneck for aviation in the
world produced by the Ring of Fire. The knowledge
was there. Not enough to have created a giant airliner
or a supersonic military aircraft, of course, but more
than enough to have filled the skies with the equivalent
of Model T automobiles. But the materials required

to make suitable internal combustion engines—or the materials required to make critical auxiliary parts like reliable and flexible fuel lines—were either not available at all or could only be produced slowly and at great expense.

In practice, that had usually meant that a heavier-than-air aircraft needed to use an existing up-time engine that had come through the Ring of Fire. True, primitive rotary engines had been developed that were good enough to get the Jupiter aloft. But there was still only one functioning Jupiter and getting more into service was proving to be difficult.

For that reason, at least for a time, aviation in the here-and-now was shifting in the direction of lighter-than-air craft. Those had enough lift that they could be powered by steam engines, which were now within the technological capability of the more advanced nations of Europe. There were even rumors that the Turks had developed some airships.

"So when do we take it up for the first test flight?" Denise asked brightly.

Eddie set his jaws. Wanting to keep Denise happy had certain inherent limits. Beginning with the demands of sanity.

"First of all, *we* aren't going to be doing any test flights. If and when—emphasis on 'if'—I decide to take this thing up for a test, I'm doing it alone. There's no point in killing two people when killing one is enough to prove you were a damn fool."

Denise pouted, but didn't try to argue. She'd have been expecting that answer, because Eddie had made it clear enough what he thought on the subject of *Denise Beasley, Intrepid Test Pilot.*

"And the first of all part probably doesn't matter anyway," Eddie continued, "because, second of all, there's no way I'm trying to take off using that so-called runway out there. That's just plain suicide."

The airstrip in the city square had finally been finished a week earlier. Perhaps oddly, completing the thing had made it clearer than ever that the whole project was absurd. There simply wasn't enough room for even a small plane such as his to get off the ground.

Well . . . not that, exactly. He'd be able to get the plane off the ground, all right, as long as he waited until he had a sufficient headwind blowing in. Just high enough to smash it into the second floor of one of the buildings surrounding the square—all of which were at least three stories tall. Theoretically, he could thread the needle required to fly the plane down the street after it left the square, long enough to lift above the level of the roof-tops. But that was pure theory, and vacant theory at that. The plane had a wingspan that was no more than a yard smaller than the width of the street—and it wasn't that straight a street to begin with. The slightest gust of wind, the slightest error on the pilot's part, and he was probably just as dead as if he'd flown into a building.

The simplest way to get around the problem would be to demolish part of the square to expand the runway. The easiest way to do that would be to widen the street by removing the buildings alongside it. But you'd need to remove a minimum of a hundred yards of existing buildings—each and every one of which was inhabited by someone and most of which doubled as places of business. Eddie was dubious, to say the least, that any such project could be carried out.

The other possibility would be to create a ramp. That . . . could be done, especially if you combined the effort with the first option. That would shorten the length of demolition required, too. You could use the rubble from tearing down fifty yards or so or street-frontage buildings as the material for the ramp. With an additional fifty yards that ended in a shallow-incline ramp . . .

Eddie thought he'd have a good chance of getting the plane into the air safely. Quite a good chance, actually.

But then what? How would he *land* the bloody thing? Taking off on a ramp was one thing, landing safely on one was something else entirely. Eddie had chewed over the problem for hours, and seen no way to solve the problem.

No way within their means, at least. If they could have built a steam catapult like the sort he'd seen in movies launching planes from the deck of an aircraft carrier . . . adapt the rear wheel of the plane to serve as a hook catching an arresting cable when he landed . . .

Blithering nonsense. By the time such devices could be built and tested in Dresden, with the resources available, the siege would be over anyway.

"Let's face it," said Minnie Hugelmair. "What we ought to do is turn this hangar"—she gestured at the structure that had been erected in the square to shelter the plane while the repair work on it was done—"into the world's first aviation museum. Because that's all this fancy airplane is anymore, a museum exhibit."

Eddie was pretty sure she was right. At least, until the civil war was over.

It didn't occur to him that the term "civil war" was

a misnomer. Everywhere else in the USE, people might
be starting to make wisecracks about the "phony civil
war." But not in Saxony. By now, Banér's army had
savaged much of the province except in the vicinity
of Leipzig where von Arnim's forces ruled the roost.
Swedish cavalry patrols never ventured into the countryside any longer except in large numbers. Georg
Kresse and his Vogtlanders had organized a large
irregular army that operated on the Saxon plain as
well as in the mountains. After the atrocities they'd
committed, God help any Swedish mercenary who
fell into their hands.

Prague, capital of Bohemia

"What an utterly charming idea," said Francisco Nasi.
He spoke softly, barely more than a murmur, because
he was talking to himself. There was no one else in
his office at the moment.

He left the radio message he'd just gotten on the
table and went to a window.

He'd established his headquarters in the Josefov, as
Prague's Jewish district was coming to be known. That
was perhaps the single most ridiculous side effect of
the Ring of Fire that Francisco had yet encountered.
In the history of Prague in the world the Americans
had come from, the Jewish district had gotten that
name in the course of the nineteenth century. The
name was in honor of the Austrian emperor Joseph
II, who'd emancipated the empire's Jews in the Tol-
eration Edict of 1781. Somehow or other—probably
through Judith Roth—that anecdote of a world that

didn't exist, and if it did was one hundred and fifty years in the future, had spread through the Jewish district. And now, more and more people were calling the district by that name.

The situation would simply be amusing, except that Francisco—and Morris Roth, he knew—were worried that Wallenstein might find out about it. The man sometimes had a volatile ego, and he might take offense that the Jews weren't naming the district after *him*. It was Wallenstein, after all, not some phantasmagorical Emperor Joseph, who had emancipated Bohemia's Jews in *this* universe.

Nasi had situated his headquarters in the Jewish district for several reasons. Those ranged from simple prudence—Wallenstein's edicts notwithstanding, no sensible Jew was yet prepared to assume that pogroms were entirely a thing of the past—to his decision that he needed to find a wife, a project that wouldn't be helped in the least if he distanced himself from the community in which he hoped to find the blessed woman. That said, he was very wealthy, so he'd obtained a building close to the river that gave him a good view of the Hradcany and the hills behind the Mala Strana. He found looking out over that very pleasant scenery helped concentrate his thoughts.

He wondered, for a moment, by what circuitous route that message had come to him. Through Rebecca Abrabanel, of course—the message itself had come directly from her. But how and from whom had she gotten it?

Given the content of the message itself, it had to have come from Luebeck. He couldn't think of any other plausible explanation.

He'd read the message enough times to have it memorized by now, and went over it again in his mind.

May soon need aircraft available for important passengers within two weeks. Military aircraft not suitable. No other civilian aircraft available in time. What are possibilities at your disposal?

He couldn't keep from grinning. "What an utterly charming idea!"

It would cost him a small fortune, though. Not even Richter would agree to demolishing entire city streets without recompensing those dislocated. There wouldn't be any immediate return, either, most likely. It would just have to be written off as a loss.

On the other hand...

Ultimately, when all was said and done, he was in the business of exchanging and facilitating favors. The actual collection of information—espionage, as such—was simply the first step in the process. Most spies and spymasters never went beyond that step, of course. That was not the least of the reasons that most spies died young and poor and most spymasters lived in garrets. The real profit was all in what you *did* with the information.

He was sure he knew what lay behind that message. So, what was it worth to have a very large favor owed to him by two people who might someday be the two most powerful people in the world? The two most influential people, at any rate, power being an increasingly elastic phenomenon.

Quite a lot, he decided. Easily worth a small fortune.

He went back to the desk and rang the little bell that sat there. A moment later, his secretary appeared.

Nasi was already writing the message. "I need to

have this sent immediately by radio. Well, by nightfall, at any rate. It's going to Dresden so we may need to wait for the evening window."

He had his own radio in his headquarters. Quite a good one, too. But radio transmission and reception was what it was, and Dresden was on the other side of the Erzgebirge.

As it turned out, conditions were suitable for immediate transmission. So, to his surprise, Jozef Wojtowicz found himself summoned back to the Residenzschloss by late afternoon, no more than a few hours after he'd left it.

When he got back to Richter's headquarters, he found her there in the company of a stocky young German. He recognized the man immediately, although they'd never actually met. He was Eddie Junker, the pilot.

"New plans," said Richter. "Let me show you."

Again, he came to stand next to her. This time, though, she had a map of the city proper in front of her. Her finger was placed on the big square and then traced a route down the large street leading south.

"We need this entire street widened. For at least fifty yards, maybe a hundred. Remove enough of the buildings to make the street"—she cocked an inquisitive gaze on Junker.

"I want at least sixty feet. That'd give me twice the wingspan of the plane. Anything less gets too risky."

She nodded. "That means widening it about thirty feet. If we're lucky, we can do that by just removing the first row of buildings on one side of the street. But if we need to, we'll level them on both sides."

Removing the first row of buildings—

Level them on both sides, maybe—

"I'm assigning you and all your Poles to the project," Richter went on. "I'll give you as many more people as I can free up. This project takes priority over everything else except defending the walls against a direct assault."

Back to hauling rocks. Did God have a grudge against Poles in general? Jozef wondered. Or was the Almighty specifically enraged at him for some reason?

Chapter 27

Magdeburg, capital of the United States of Europe

Rebecca Abrabanel tried to think of any other possibility she hadn't explored, when it came to available aircraft. The exercise was more in the way of a formality, though—the sort of final double check a careful person will do just to remind themselves to be careful—than anything she expected to produce results. There simply weren't all that many aircraft in existence in January of 1636. Most of those were military, furthermore—and Jesse Wood had made clear that he wasn't lending any of the air force's planes to this purpose.

He'd told Rebecca that himself, when he came to pass along the message from Luebeck.

"Sorry, Becky, but I talked it over with the admiral and John's adamant on the subject. I think he's probably right, and it's not something I'm going to buck him on. We've kept the navy and the air force out of this ain't-quite-a-civil-war. Formally, anyway. It's true we've bent the rules into a pretzel, but we haven't broken any. But if we did this . . ."

She hadn't argued the point. She thought Admiral Simpson was right herself.

Of the civilian aircraft, the possibilities were very limited. She didn't trust most of them—not with the lives of *these* two people. Of the ones that had demonstrated they were reliable, almost all were ruled out either by mechanical, operational or political concerns. January was not a good time to be flying in the Germanies, so most of the planes were undergoing major maintenance.

The ones based in the Netherlands would need to have at least the tacit approval of the king—for something like this, anyway—and that was a can of worms Rebecca didn't want to open. At a minimum, Fernando would insist on concessions, and he was already being a pain in the neck. He'd been careful not to cross a line when it came to taking advantage of the internal turmoil in the USE, the line being anything that might provide a clear and obvious *casus belli* at a future date when his larger neighbor was stable again. But he'd come right up to that line, every time and place he could.

Besides, in order to get his approval, she'd have no choice but to explain the purpose of using one of the Netherlands' aircraft. And that she wanted to avoid. If this secret got out . . .

She shook her head. As it was, she was more than a little amazed that it hadn't. She'd only found out herself a few days ago, when Simpson finally confided in her using the intermediary of Jesse Wood. From what Jesse had told her, it was obvious that Simpson had known for some time that Luebeck was simply a staging point for Kristina and Ulrik. Not, as Rebecca and just about everyone else had assumed, merely a safe area that the prince and princess had settled on because they didn't want to be a pawn for anybody in the conflict.

Oxenstierna had certainly made that assumption. Rebecca had been in fairly regular touch with John Chandler Simpson, either through Jesse or through the admiral's wife Mary. She knew that the Swedish chancellor had initially bombarded Kristina with messages demanding that the headstrong girl obey her Uncle Axel; bombarded Ulrik with threats of dire consequences for Denmark if he didn't stop aiding and abetting the child's monstrous willfulness; and Simpson himself for not doing what was clearly his duty and expelling the two from Luebeck. From the naval base, at least. Simpson didn't actually have any formal control over what the city's officials did. Apparently Oxenstierna assumed he could bring enough pressure to bear on Luebeck to get them to do the same.

After that initial flurry of demands and threats, though, Oxenstierna had said nothing. Rebecca suspected he'd come to the conclusion that since he couldn't force the issue right now, he'd be wiser to just let sleeping dogs lie. The way things stood, if he forced Ulrik and Kristina out of Luebeck they'd most likely go to Copenhagen—which was even worse, from his standpoint.

So, for all practical purposes, the pair of royals had been ignored for the past weeks. But Rebecca was quite sure that if Oxenstierna found out what they were *really* planning to do—had been planning all along, in fact—he would do everything possible to prevent them from carrying the project through.

And he could do quite a bit. He had no control over Magdeburg, of course. So far, in fact, he'd not even made any threatening troop movements toward the city. He'd kept that large army he had under his direct control in Berlin. But if he needed to, he could get that army moving—and there was no force in the Germanies that would be able to stop it. He couldn't take Magdeburg without a siege, and that siege would last at least as long as the siege of Dresden was lasting. But he *could* interdict the territory between Luebeck and Magdeburg. Most of it, at least.

Even if Simpson was willing to bring the ironclads back out of the Baltic and move them up the Elbe, it wouldn't do any good. The warships were immensely powerful but they had vulnerabilities also. There were too many ways an ironclad could be ambushed on a river unless it had a powerful land force running interference for it—and there was no land force at Simpson's disposal that Oxenstierna's mercenaries couldn't disperse. For that matter, the Swedes wouldn't even have to lay an ambush. They could simply wreck some of the locks that made the river passable for the big ironclads.

No, once the secret was out, the only practical way to get Kristina and Ulrik to Magdeburg was to fly them in. Given, of course, the overriding political imperatives involved.

USE naval base
Luebeck

"No, no, no, no." Ulrik matched Kristina's glare with his own. "We've been over this already."

Driven into a corner, Kristina fought back the way

any cornered child will do—with the truth instead of the folderol.

"But it'd be *fun!*"

Out of the side of his eye, Ulrik could see Baldur grinning.

"Not a word, Norddahl," he said through clenched teeth.

The Norwegian shrugged. "She's right, you know. We could have a dandy little adventure, disguising ourselves and dashing all about the land as we make our cunning way toward—"

"Shut up! You're not helping!"

Once the prince was sure that he'd silenced his servant—using the term "servant" so very, very loosely— he went back to the princess.

"Kristina, if we sneak into Magdeburg like thieves in the night, we undercut everything we're trying to accomplish. This is all about *legitimacy.* Everything! All of it! Why else have we stayed here in Luebeck for so long? Why didn't we go to Magdeburg immediately?"

Kristina wiped her nose with the back of her hand. Ulrik was relieved to see the gesture. The girl didn't have a runny nose, that was just a nervous reflex she had when she was beginning to back down from a tempestuous fight.

It was . . . unsettling, to think how well he'd gotten to know Kristina. And she'd gotten to know him, he didn't doubt. Over the centuries, royals separated by almost two decades in age had become betrothed any number of times. Nor had it been unusual if one of those royals was still a child when the betrothal was made. But normally, the formalities done—often by proxy, not even in person—the future married couple didn't see each other for years. When the time finally came to consummate the marriage, the husband and wife who climbed into the nuptial bed were almost complete strangers. Awkward, of course, in some ways. But one could still trust nature to take its course.

When the time finally came for him and Kristina, on the other hand...

It would either be hideous or very, very good. It wouldn't be anything in between, for a certainty.

He gave his head a little shake, to clear the stray thought. That problem was still a decade away. Well, eight or nine years. Seven, at the very least. Six, if you really stretched every...

He shook his head again. No little shake this time, either. "You haven't answered me."

He was careful—he was always careful—not to give her a direct command. A father could tell his daughter, "Answer me!" An older brother, even, could do the same. But he was not her father. He was her betrothed, forced to act in many ways as if he were her father or older brother, but never forgetting that he wasn't.

With a different girl, that might not have mattered. A timid, uncertain, shy—just thinking about it was enough to make one laugh. Kristina would remember each and every transgression; squirrel it away like a rodent hoarding food—no, like a commander saving ammunition—and when the time came she would bring them all forth to exact retribution.

One had to be philosophical about these things, if you were a prince in line of succession. Ulrik could—and did, and would until the day he died—console himself with the knowledge that, whatever else, life with Kristina would never, ever, be dull.

She wiped her nose. "Because—this is what *you* said—we needed to give Uncle Axel time to look foolish."

She wiped her nose again. "Well, the admiral said it, too."

Kristina had become quite attached to Simpson. In an odd sort of way, he and his wife Mary had become something like grandparents to her.

"'Foolish' isn't exactly the right word," Ulrik said. "A ruler can seem foolish to his subjects and still have legitimacy, because he had it to begin with. But the day Chancellor Oxenstierna started breaking the laws—which he did when he unilaterally moved the capital to Berlin; when he summoned a convention that had no legal authority to act; most of all, when he arrested Prime Minister Wettin—then he placed himself in a position where he had to *establish* his legitimacy."

The prince shrugged. "Not an impossible project, by any means. Every usurper in history has faced the same problem—and history is full of successful usurpers. Still, it has to be *done.* It's not something that can be allowed to drift. And that's exactly what Oxenstierna has let happen. He's drifted. Been set adrift, rather, by the shrewd tactics of his opponents. By now, many people—including many of those who followed him initially, and especially those who followed Wettin—are beginning to doubt him. That means they'll be relieved to see someone reestablish legitimacy, since the usurper apparently can't."

By now, the princess had gotten interested—always the best way, of course, to get Kristina off a tantrum. "Isn't there anything Uncle Axel can do?"

"Oh, certainly. But it would have to be something very dramatic—even more so once you arrive in Magdeburg."

"Like what?"

Ulrik didn't have to think about it. He lay awake at nights worrying—about all things, and he a prince!—that the continent's most notorious agitator would fail of her purpose.

"Dresden. He has to take Dresden, Kristina. *Has* to, now—and soon. Dresden has become the symbol of his weakness. Every day that Dresden defies him, he loses legitimacy."

The girl's expression got very intent. Eager. "Maybe we should—"

"No! We are not going to Dresden."

"But it'd be *fun!*"

Magdeburg, capital of the United States of Europe

There was never any question, Rebecca knew, where they would stay once they got here. It would have to be the royal palace. To stay anywhere else would work at cross-purposes.

That was a pity, in some ways. The palace was still not finished, for one thing. But enough of it was to serve the purpose. An entire wing already had plumbing and electricity. The bigger problem was security. The palace, as you'd expect of a structure designed for Gustav II Adolf, was immense. It had always been assumed, of course, that plenty of troops would be available to guard it. Most likely, given the Swedish king's nature, different units would be rotated through the assignment. An army base was being constructed very near the palace that would be large enough to accommodate up to an entire battalion, although it would be crowded.

Usually they'd be units from the USE army, but Rebecca was fairly sure that Gustav Adolf had planned to occasionally rotate Swedish and even Danish units into the prestigious assignment.

But none of that could be done now. There were no USE soldiers left in the city, beyond a skeleton cadre at the large training base outside the city. Using Swedish troops was out of the question, of course. Using Danish troops... might be possible, but it would be politically unwise.

Rebecca looked around at the very large foyer of her house. It was really too bad they couldn't just move Ulrik and Kristina *here*. This town house had been designed with security in mind. For all practical purposes, it was a small fortress. And she already had a superb security staff in place, the clan of former Yeoman Warders whom her husband had brought back from England.

But that would be just as politically unwise as using Danish troops for security. Two things were critical, above all.

First, everything possible had to be done to enforce the legitimacy of the pair of royals. That was the whole reason, of course, they couldn't just smuggle Kristina and Ulrik into the city. As a technical exercise, that would be extremely easy to do and almost entirely risk-free. But legitimate heirs do not skulk about. Their arrival into the capital—*their* capital—had to be public. Indeed, it had to be turned into a public spectacle.

Second, they had to appear as impartial as possible. In one sense, of course, the mere fact of their coming here would throw impartiality to the winds. They were choosing sides, quite obviously. But choosing sides was one thing; favoring factions, something else entirely.

By coming here, Kristina and Ulrik would place their stamp of legitimacy on the *existing* capital. They would be thumbing their nose at Oxenstierna's bastard capital in Berlin—and, by implication at least, everything Oxenstierna had done.

But it was still essential that they be seen by most citizens as not being the tools of the Committees of Correspondence. In the end, this peculiar civil war— this half-civil-war, as she often thought of it—would be won because large numbers of the people who'd voted for the Crown Loyalists in the election would withdraw their support. Some of them would then be willing to give their support to the Fourth of July Party.

Not all. Not even most, in her estimation. But they would be willing to give their support to the dynasty, which would appear to them to be the only thing stable that still remained. Their willingness to do so, however, would depend on the dynasty not looking as if it were anybody's puppet.

Which meant—once again she was back to squaring the circle—they couldn't be too closely associated with the Fourth of July Party, much less the Committees of Correspondence.

Who, unfortunately, were the only people in Magdeburg who could provide reliable security for Ulrik and Kristina. Certainly if they moved into that huge palace.

Her daughter Sepharad came charging in, followed

by her brother Baruch. "Mommy, Barry and I want to go to the navy yards!"

Rebecca frowned. "Why? The big ironclads are all gone. There's really not much to see there anymore."

"Not true," pronounced Baruch. Despite just having celebrated his third birthday, he spoke with the same surety—so she hoped, at any rate—with which he would someday speak on the most profound questions of metaphysics and ethics. "The Marines change the guard every day at noon. It's not noon yet."

Maria Susanna came into the room, smiling. "I can take them, Frau Abrabanel. It's very nice out today, for January. Sunny and not too cold."

Maria Susanna was one of the children whom Gretchen Richter had informally adopted in her days as an army camp follower. Once it had become clear that Gretchen was going to be stuck in Dresden for months, the children's great-grandmother had come to Rebecca.

"I'm not doing it again," Veronica Richter said firmly. "Enough! I took care of those children the last time my granddaughter went gallivanting about Europe tossing over apple carts. I'm not doing it again."

She'd then given Rebecca that stern look that no one could do as well as Veronica. "I think you should do it, this time. Because it's your fault, ultimately. Well, your husband's. But he's off gallivanting around too."

The logic involved had been circuitous at best. But Rebecca saw no reason to argue the matter. There was enough room in the town house to fit four more children into it. The three boys could share a single room, and there was a small room on the top floor that would be suitable for Maria Susanna.

None of them were so young as to require constant supervision. They ranged in ages from twelve to fifteen or so. A very rambunctious age, to be sure, but Rebecca wasn't concerned about that problem. Not with all the Yeoman Warders and their womenfolk living in the mansion, and their matriarch Patricia Hayes managing the household's daily affairs.

Then, as it turned out, Maria Susanna made an excellent companion for the younger children. Partly, an older sibling; partly a governess. She had the right temperament for the task.

"Please, Momma!" said Baruch. "I really like to watch the Marines marching around. They've got the best uniforms of anybody!"

The Marines . . .

Out of the mouths of babes, indeed.

"Yes, fine," Rebecca said, nodding. "Maria Susanna, please have them back no later than two o'clock."

As soon as the children left, she headed for the radio room upstairs.

Admiral, can we have the use of your Marines here in Magdeburg? I would need as many as possible.

She didn't need to specify the purpose. Simpson would understand. The political logic would be as clear to him as it was to her.

The navy needed to stay neutral. But the Marines . . . weren't exactly the navy. And if he were pressed, Simpson could fall back on his own traditions. In the world he'd come from, Rebecca knew, the Marines had been used for such purposes.

The answer came back almost immediately.

Yes. Will instruct Navy Yard commander to place

all Marines there at your disposal. Will send more from the units I have here in Luebeck, and the entire units from Wismar and Hamburg. And anywhere else I can scrape them up.

They'll need their dress uniforms, which many of them don't have. You'll have to bear that cost.

She thought about that for a moment. How far could she push the admiral . . . ?

It was worth a try.

I can have new uniforms designed for the purpose. Very dressy.

Again, the answer came back quickly.

Grudgingly agree. But no tricorns. Silly damn things.

Chapter 28

Magdeburg, capital of the United States of Europe

Rebecca Abrabanel was a little amused by her emotional reaction to Gunther Achterhof at the moment. *How quickly we adapt!* Her Imperial Majesty Rebecca I, annoyed by a stubborn adviser.

It really was rather amusing. It had only been a short time, after all, since she was elected the president of the recently formed executive committee that served—insofar as any group of people could be said to—as the central leadership of the revolution.

(Or perhaps it should be the counterrevolution, given that it was Oxenstierna who was trying to make major changes in the USE's political structure? But applying that term to the people who were in fact trying to overthrow the long-established state of affairs in Europe seemed just plain silly.)

It was a role Rebecca was unaccustomed to, outside of her own household. However great her prestige might have been, she'd always been a counselor, as it were. One of a number of people who proffered their opinion but made no claims to actually managing anything. And much of that prestige, being honest, stemmed from her relationship to Michael.

That had become less so, as time went on. Much less so, eventually. Still, she'd been surprised to the point of astonishment to find herself suddenly elevated to her current position.

That had been Helene Gundelfinger's doing—which meant the hand of Ed Piazza had also been at work. If there were any two political leaders in the Fourth of July Party better attuned to each other than the president and vice president of the State of Thuringia-Franconia, they'd have to have been twins joined at the hip.

Perhaps ironically, given how often they clashed, it had been Gunther Achterhof who first advanced the proposal to form an executive committee to replace the large committee that had been meeting regularly in Rebecca's town house since the crisis began. That committee had grown over time to the point where if the entire body was present, they could barely fit everyone into a single room.

"We've gotten too big to get much practical work done," Gunther had argued. "Even more importantly, most of the people sitting around this table—table? say better, indoor tennis court—should be getting back home. And as soon as possible. Things are heating up, people. We need to have our leadership out in the field leading, not sitting around here talking to each other."

He'd glared around the room, as if daring anyone to disagree with him. But no one had argued the point. Privately, most of them had already come to the same conclusion. The only one who spoke was

Werner von Dalberg, and he spoke strongly in favor of the proposal.

"I need to get back to the Oberpfalz, as fast as possible. The fight against the Bavarians is getting intense, and so is the political spill-off."

"What do you propose, then, Gunther?" Liesel Hahn asked.

"We form an executive committee with authority to make decisions in between meetings of this—this—whatever we call this body, which still has no formal existence. No more than five people, all of them people who either reside here in the capital or can move here for the duration of the crisis. And one of those people will be elected president of the executive committee, so that he can make emergency decisions whenever the executive committee can't meet."

The proposal had been discussed for a while. Eventually, it was adopted—with the proviso that it be expanded to include four members who did not reside in Magdeburg, but who could come to the city on short notice if need be.

"I don't want this executive committee to be too Magdeburg-oriented," Werner von Dalberg had explained. "I realize that it may be necessary at times for the five people in Magdeburg to make decisions before anyone else can get here. That's fine. They have a quorum. But I would like to formalize the practice of doing everything possible to bring in the viewpoints from the provinces. Most of the USE is not like Magdeburg, not even the SoTF."

"Mecklenburg's getting pretty close," said Charlotte Kienitz, smiling. "In fact—fair warning, Gunther!—I think it won't be long before Schwerin supplants

Magdeburg as the chief den of iniquity in the reactionaries' pantheon."

That occasioned a chuckle around the room. Having now twice defeated what was perhaps the USE's most detestable aristocracy in open and savage armed conflict, Mecklenburg had become a magnet for a large number of footloose young radicals, mostly but by no means entirely Germans. Poverty-stricken as it might be, the province's capital of Schwerin had grown explosively over the past year. Fortunately, enough of those newly arrived youngsters came from monied families to keep the city's economy afloat on a sort of peculiar radical tourism.

Melissa Mailey had passed through Schwerin a month earlier, on one of her speaking tours. "I swear, I got homesick," she'd told James on her return. "It was almost like being back in Haight-Ashbury again, with a hefty dose of Berkeley—except there's no university in Schwerin."

"Send a letter to Morris Roth," Nichols said. "He'd probably be willing to sponsor a university there. College, anyway. 'Course, they'd have to agree to let in women and Jews and run it on a secular basis."

"Ha! These days, I don't think you could do anything else in Schwerin. I really enjoyed the place."

Schwerin wasn't really much like Magdeburg, as Melissa's observations indicated. The USE's capital was an industrial working class city with a thin veneer of the upper crust. The population was politically radical, but its social attitudes usually remained fairly conservative. Mecklenburg's capital, on the other hand, had become a sort of radical student hotbed, allowing for the fact that the students were all taking a break from actually studying anything—formal course work, at least—in order to expound theories in the town's taverns. Those theories were just as likely, on any given evening, to deal with literary or theological issues as political ones—and questioning sexual mores was almost as ubiquitous as alcohol consumption.

It wasn't all hot air, though. A lot of those young radicals had formed volunteer detachments to fight the nobility's armed retainers. They'd acquitted themselves quite respectably on the battlefield too, most of them. Just as they'd done, in another universe, in the international brigades that fought in the Spanish civil war.

When the vote was taken, the five resident members of the executive committee were Rebecca, Gunther himself, the governor of Magdeburg province, Matthias Strigel; and Helene Gundelfinger and Anselm Keller, both of whom agreed to move to the capital for the duration of the crisis. (Or in the case of Anselm, simply stay there; he hadn't been back in the Province of the Main for almost two months.)

The four members from the provinces were the mayor of Hamburg, Albert Bugenhagen; Constantin Ableidinger; Liesel Hahn from Hesse-Kassel and Charlotte Kienitz from Mecklenburg.

Melissa Mailey would have been elected to the committee, and by a big margin, but she declined.

"First, I'm too old. The oldest person in this room except for me is Helene, and she's still on the right side of forty. The average age around this table is thirty, at most. Which is good. Revolution is a young person's game. You want a few old farts around for advice, but you don't need them getting underfoot, which they will because their bones are creaky. Second, I haven't got the temperament for it, anyway. Never did, even in my days as a twenty-year-old student radical. Third and last, let's be honest—I'm a lot more useful as a roving schoolmarm than I would be as a resident organizer."

There was a lot of truth to that, and everyone knew it. Melissa Mailey occupied a unique position in the revolutionary democratic movement. Her pre-existing reputation of being a radical intellectual, that she'd carried with her through the Ring of Fire, had become transmuted over time in the Germanies of the seventeenth century. She was viewed by members of the movement and a large number of people on its periphery as something in the way of an elder statesman and theoretician. Their Wise Old Lady, as it were. She was one of the most popular speakers the Fourth of July Party had, and was constantly in demand in the provinces.

Which, admittedly, made her protestations about creaking bones somewhat suspect. "Woman's a dyed-in-the-wool globetrotter, let's face it," was James Nichols' way of putting it.

Eventually, it was agreed that Melissa would serve as an ex officio member of the committee. She'd attend as many meetings as she could, with voice but no vote.

That settled, they moved on to electing a president.

"I nominate Rebecca," Helene said, as soon as the question was posed.

"Second the nomination," said Werner von Dalberg.

"Move the nominations be closed," said Constantin Ableidinger.

That took all of maybe five seconds. Ten, at the most. If anyone except Rebecca had been chairing the meeting, they'd probably have pushed for an immediate vote. Rebecca had been taken completely off guard, though, so she insisted on opening the floor for discussion.

There wasn't any. Not even Gunther had any alternate proposal.

And here she was, less than a month later, bridling a little because Gunther was arguing with her imperial decree. Her husband had always warned her that power was seductive.

"—still don't see why we're going through this rigmarole," Achterhof grumbled. "We could have them here in a few days, easily—and with a lot less risk than flying in a plane that just got repaired—by who, you have to wonder? that's the first aircraft anybody in Dresden ever saw, at least on the ground—and is going to be piloted by a down-time amateur. I can name three different ways to do it, right off the top of my head."

He held up a thumb. "First—"

"Oh, stop it, Gunther!" said Anselm Keller. "I can name four ways we could do it, off the top of my head. So what? The issue isn't a practical one in the first place. It's a matter of political perceptions."

Gunther shrugged. "So everyone tells me. I can't see it myself. What difference does it make how they get here? Just another damn prince and princess. The world's full of them."

He really couldn't see what was involved, Rebecca knew. That was a blind spot on Achterhof's part, although it was certainly one shared by many other people, especially in Magdeburg.

The underlying issue was central, actually. What sort of government—no, what sort of *state*—would the USE have? Achterhof, like almost everyone in the CoCs and the great majority of activists for the Fourth of July Party, was a committed republican. From his point of view, the existing situation was annoying at best. Prior to his injury, Gustav Adolf had occupied a position in the USE somewhere between that of a ruling monarch and a purely constitutional one. Analogous, roughly, to the status of the British monarchy in the up-timers' old universe during the eighteenth and part of the nineteenth centuries.

Michael Stearns was a republican, too—and Rebecca herself, for that matter. But what Michael understood was that his opinion and that of the CoCs and his own party's cadre couldn't be confused with the opinions of the millions of people who inhabited the Germanies.

"I doubt if even the majority of people who vote for us are really committed to a republic," he'd told Rebecca. "Never, ever underestimate the strength of tradition. It's not immovable, certainly. But don't think it's a feather in the wind, either. That's because 'tradition' isn't simply a state of mind, it's a *reality* rooted in people's everyday lives. That's especially true for people living close to the edge, economically, and people who've given up hostages to fortune, so to speak. Foot-loose young radicals with nothing much to lose except their own lives can be bold as all hell and willing—no, eager—to turn everything upside down. But a man in his thirties or forties who makes just enough to take care of his family—and he's got a wife and kids to take care of, not just himself—is going to be a lot more cautious. 'If it ain't broke, don't fix it.' His wife's likely to be even more skeptical of abstract theories. Having a king around makes things seem at least a little more stable. As long as the royal bugger's not doing something screwy, at least. But nobody thinks Gustav II Adolf is a screwball. Not me, not you, not anybody. The truth it, the Vasa dynasty is pretty popular with a lot of people and it's accepted by most of the others."

He hadn't changed his mind, either, because of recent events. She got letters from him fairly regularly. Actual letters—long ones—not short radio messages. However they did it, Thurn and Taxis couriers got through or around Banér's army just as easily as they crossed bridges.

And that was ultimately what was at stake here. Rebecca wasn't sure herself how critical it was for Kristina and Ulrik's arrival in Magdeburg to be done publicly and with great fanfare. Maybe she was overestimating its importance. But she didn't think so—and she thought that at least some of Gunther's resistance was because he felt, even if not entirely consciously, that if Kristina and Ulrik played a decisive role in ending the crisis, that alone would effectively seal the fate of republicanism in the USE, for at least several generations.

Which . . . it probably would.

She wished that Michael was here to make this decision. But he wasn't—and there was no point asking him by radio. He'd refuse. *You're there, I'm not. It's your call. Make it.* That would be his answer.

But, in a way, she already had his answer. Much of the content of those letters had been ruminations on the dynamic of revolutions. Michael was concerned to keep the damage as limited as possible, because a revolution that emerged from a society in ruins was likely to become distorted very quickly.

Constantin Ableidinger spoke up. As a member of Parliament from Franconia, he was present in Magdeburg at least half of the time, and regularly attended the executive committee's meetings.

"Do they know we know?" he asked. "Their highnesses, I mean. Can you use that word in the plural?"

"Who cares whether you can or not?" grunted Achterhof. "But I'd like to know the answer to the first question, myself."

"I'm not sure, actually," said Rebecca. "I was sworn to secrecy by Admiral Simpson until just three days ago, when he told me I should broach the matter—these were his words—'to those people you think are critical and no one else.' So far, that's been the people in this room. I didn't even tell Francisco Nasi why I was asking him about the availability of his aircraft."

"As if he won't figure it out!" said Helene.

"I'm sure he has," Rebecca agreed. "Still, I didn't tell him, so I didn't break my promise to the admiral. And Francisco will keep it to himself, we can be sure of that. As for the question itself..."

She thought about it, for a moment. "I simply don't know. I'd been assuming they knew Simpson had told us, but now that I consider the matter, I realize that's just an assumption on my part. Maybe they don't."

Ableidinger nodded. "That's what I figured. I think before we go any further, we need to find out the answer. And while we're at it why don't we ask *them* which way they'd rather come?" He glanced at Gunther. "I suppose we should make clear that the pilot of the aircraft will not be Jesse Wood."

"Oh, pfui!" snapped Gundelfinger. The glance she gave Achterhof was acerbic. "Anybody who knows Eddie Junker knows that he's as steady as a rock. You think *Nasi* would have hired him as his personal pilot if he didn't trust his competence? We don't have to get into that."

"I agree with Helene," said Rebecca. "We should keep the question as simple as possible."

She looked around the room, and then glanced at the window to gauge the time of day. The time of evening, now. "If there's no further discussion, I will go make the radio call right now. We can take advantage of the window if we move immediately."

She was back in less than fifteen minutes. "The answer to your question, Constantin, is: yes, they knew. In fact, it was they who asked the admiral to get in touch with me. The reason I'm back so soon is because they must have been waiting right there in the radio room at the navy base.

"And the answer is . . ."

She held up the note with the radio message. "I will read the entire thing. *Essential that our arrival in Magdeburg be done publicly, preferably with fanfare. Personal risk of travel much less important than political risk of appearing furtive. Kristina, Princess of Sweden, the United States of Europe, and the Union of Kalmar. Ulrik, Prince of Denmark.*"

Smiling, she set the message down on the table. "It's worth noting, I think, that the signature alone constitutes almost half the message."

Ableidinger chuckled. "Yes, that's a lot of what's involved, isn't it?"

It was easy to forget, sometimes, because of the

booming voice and the flamboyant personality, that the brain inside the Franconian's head was one of the most politically astute in the nation. "Let's all understand right now what we're committing ourselves to," said Constantin. "If we bring Kristina here, under these circumstances, we have as good as placed our seal of approval on the Vasa dynasty. And not just our personal seal as individuals, either. Insofar as anyone speaks officially for the democratic movement today, we do. There will be no going back from it. Not so long as she lives, anyway. And she's only nine—and I looked it up. In that other universe, even without modern medical care, Kristina lived until the year 1689. For those of you who can't count readily, that's more than a half a century from now."

Gundelfinger grinned. "And she was tough as nails throughout. You're not the only one who looked her up, Constantin. I was particularly charmed—and appalled—by the story of her celebration of the pope's birthday, after she abdicated, converted to Catholicism and moved to Rome. She threw a huge party in her villa. The party got too wild for too long, the guests ignored her orders to leave, so she had her household troops open fire on the celebrants. Eight corpses later, they did as she'd bade them. That's the girl we're inviting here, comrades—and, as Constantin says, giving our seal of approval. And if you're not familiar with Prince Ulrik, he's the young prince who personally almost sank an ironclad."

By now, Achterhof was looking alarmed. "Wait a minute! I think we need to consider this a bit more."

Rebecca nodded. "By all means. You have the floor, Gunther."

There was silence, for perhaps a minute, as Gunther tried to marshal his thoughts. Eventually, though, he threw up his hands.

"Ah! I suppose if we don't, we're just dragging out the misery. I'm not happy at the idea of being under the Vasas the rest of my life, but I *really* want Oxenstierna brought down. Um. Broken on the rack, actually, and then disemboweled and hanged. But I'll settle for brought down."

"Move to a vote," said Ableidinger immediately.

The vote was unanimous. Achterhof was probably tempted to abstain, but he didn't.

Rebecca hadn't thought he would. Gunther could be aggravating sometimes, but the one thing the man never did was dodge issues and evade responsibility.

"I'll send the message," she said.

She sent two, actually. The second one went to the radio station at the Third Division's headquarters near České Budějovice in Bohemia.

Less than an hour later, a radio message arrived from Third Division headquarters to the radio station of the Hangman Regiment in Tetschen. It was addressed to the commanding officer, Colonel Jeff Higgins, and consisted of one word:

Soon.

Chapter 29

Berlin

Wilhelm Wettin was surprised to hear the door open. Since his arrest and confinement in a small room in a corner of the palace, he'd had almost no visitors. The guards brought his meals regularly, did the same for emptying the chamber pot, provided him with wine at his request, and otherwise did not speak to him at all. The last time he'd seen anyone other than a guard had been several weeks ago, when Oxenstierna sent one of his agents to check on the prime minister's well-being. The chancellor hadn't bothered to come himself.

Still more to his surprise, the person who came through the door was Colonel Erik Haakansson Hand. The emperor's cousin was not perhaps the last person Wilhelm had expected to see, but he certainly wasn't anywhere near the top of the list. The two men barely knew each other, except by reputation.

"I haven't much time," the colonel said. He was speaking very quietly, although not in a whisper. "In the nature of things, bribes only last so long"—he pointed over his shoulder with a thumb—"and those fellows on guard out there are from the Dalana Infantry Regiment, whose former commander was none other than Oxenstierna himself. Not quite my still-close boyhood companions."

Wilhelm stared at him. Why would the king's own cousin be needing to bribe anyone?

"Something is rotten in the state of Sweden," Hand continued. "Or at least in one of my greedy cousin's three realms. I want to know what it is. Why were you arrested?"

He waved his hand abruptly. That was his left hand, the one he usually employed. His right arm couldn't be straightened due to the terrible injuries he had sustained while leading a brigade against Wallenstein a few years earlier.

"And let's skip over the twaddle about conspiring with unknown—what was Oxenstierna's phrase?—ah, yes, 'seditious elements.' Such a vague term. On his bad days, I suppose you could accuse my horse of being seditious, and he's presumably elemental." The colonel's familiar cold grin appeared. "At least, I've seen no sign that he's sprouting wings."

After a moment of silence, Hand shook his head impatiently. "Come on, come on, tell me the truth. My loyalty is entirely to my cousin, Saxe-Weimar. No one else."

Wilhelm made a quick decision. It was always possible this was a trap, but...

Not likely. Erik Haakansson Hand's personal attachment to Gustav Adolf went far back. Besides, what difference did it make, at this point? If Oxenstierna wanted him executed, he didn't have to use an elaborate subterfuge involving the emperor's own cousin.

"Maximilian of Bavaria's attack on the Oberpfalz was arranged," he said abruptly. "By that bastard Oxenstierna himself. He used the count of Nassau-Hadamar, Johann Ludwig, as his intermediary."

"How did you find out?"

"Two of the count's associates let it slip while they were drunk. I suppose they assumed I was part of the conspiracy. One of them was—"

"I know who the baron and the guildmaster were. They left Berlin the day before you were arrested. I wondered why, at the time. It makes sense now. When they sobered up and remembered the conversation, they must have started worrying what would happen if you took it to Oxenstierna. So, as rats will, they went scurrying for their holes."

The colonel tugged on his beard for a moment. "All right. I'll do what I can. Just stay here and don't do anything foolish like trying to escape." Again, the cold grin appeared. "If it will settle your nerves at all—I warn you, I know the castle involved, so it certainly wouldn't settle mine very much—our precious chancellor is not planning to have you executed. No, you're for exile in St. Olaf's Castle in Finland as soon as things settle down."

"And *are* they settling down?"

Hand sneered. "Of course not. What were you fools thinking, anyway? And then Fool One had Fool Two arrested! Talk about piling wood onto an already out of control fire! Or what's that up-time expression?"

"Pouring gasoline on the flames," said Wilhelm, his jaws tightening. He resented the insult. On the other hand . . .

Sadly, he couldn't disagree with it. In the weeks since his arrest, he'd come to much the same conclusion about himself. Although he *had* avoided terms like "fool." He thought "made some very bad mistakes" was sufficient, thank you.

The colonel turned to go, and then stopped. "And here's something else to settle your nerves—or make them worse, possibly. I'm almost certain that everything is about to explode."

"Why?"

Hand snorted. "Why do you think? You left *Stearns* with an entire division at his disposal? After you let Gretchen Richter steal Dresden from under your noses?"

A moment later, he was gone.

All of it made sense, the colonel thought, as he walked back toward the wing of the palace where his cousin was kept. At least, if you were the sort of schemer who was too clever for his own good; which, in his estimation, was a pretty fair description of Sweden's chancellor. It would be just like him not to be able to resist ladling an unnecessary scoop of treason onto the pile.

Stupid, really. To begin with, Maximilian of Bavaria probably would have invaded the Oberpfalz anyway. And while neutralizing the army of the State of Thuringia-Franconia would certainly be handy for Oxenstierna's purposes, it was not critical. So why add the risk that outright treason would be discovered?

Erik Haakansson Hand did not and never had shared in the general admiration for Axel Oxenstierna. An admiration, unfortunately, shared by his cousin the king. Such was life.

He spent a bit of time wondering if he should

protect himself in some way from the possibility that the two guards he'd bribed would report the matter to anyone. But it was not likely at all that they would. Bribees generally didn't confess their sins except under duress, after all. And even if they did, what could he do to prevent it? The only two solutions he could think of—bribe them some more or murder them—would be cures worse than the disease. His own lapse into gasoline-over-fire-pouring, as it were.

Quite a charming expression. Of course, you had to know what gasoline was—but, by now, that knowledge was quite widespread.

It didn't take him long to reach the king's quarters. Berlin's palace was a palace, yes. But it was what you'd expect in Berlin.

When he came into the room, he saw that Gustav Adolf was asleep. That was a blessing, he thought. For the past two days, his cousin had been prone to fits of anger great enough that he'd had to be restrained. But these fits, unlike the ones he'd had earlier, were more complex. There was confusion there, not just fury. In fact, Erik was pretty sure most of the anger derived from the confusion. As if the king, trying to awaken, was frustrated by his difficulty in doing so.

Before he could say anything, the king's bodyguard spoke. "He asked for you, Colonel," said Erling Ljungberg. "Twice, before he fell asleep. And the second time, what he said was: 'Where is Erik? He must see to Kristina. It's very important.'"

The colonel took a long, almost shuddering breath. Three sentences, each of which was clear and meaningful—and what he suspected was most important, all three sentences held together as a coherent, consistent and logical whole. He wished he could consult the Moor doctor, but there was no chance of that, not now. He *had* to stay in Berlin, until...

Erik realized, with a little start, that he'd never actually taken that thought to its conclusion. Until *what*? Always, he'd stopped at the edge of hoping—desperately hoping—for his cousin's recovery. But now that it seemed he might actually be recovering...

He came to one immediate decision. There was no more time for subtlety.

"My loyalties are entirely to him, Erling Ljungberg." He pointed at Gustav Adolf. "Yours?"

"Don't be an ass. You know the answer to that. What you really want to know is if I'm as dumb as the ox I look like."

Erik couldn't help laughing. A quick, nervous laugh—but a laugh it definitely was. "I'd hardly use the term 'ox'! Bull, yes. And now that you bring it up, how smart are you?"

Ljungberg heaved his massive shoulders. The gesture might have been a shrug, or it might have been a bull shifting his stance to attack, or it might be something of both. Ljungberg himself probably didn't know for sure.

"I'm not so stupid that I can't figure out the chancellor is taking advantage of my king's condition to carry through policies my king would never have agreed to himself. Nor am I so stupid that I can't figure out that the blessed chancellor is in over his head. And he's supposed to be the clever one!"

As answers went, that was the best Hand could want. "How does the rest of your unit feel about it?"

"Even Scots aren't that dumb. And they take their orders from me, anyway."

The colonel nodded. He started chewing on his lower lip again, deciding on his next steps. He'd begin with the Östergötlanders. He no longer commanded that regiment, but he had their respect, and he was on good personal terms with its current commander. After that...

"Ha!" jeered Ljungberg. "Haven't really thought about it, have you? Well, I have. You'll start with the Östergötland infantry regiment, of course. After them, go see Colonel Klas Hastfer and his Finnish regiment. He's married to my wife's half-sister, by the way. Then, I recommend you talk with Karl Hård af Segerstad."

He commanded the Västergötland infantry. Erik didn't know him very well, though.

Ljungberg grinned. His grin was as cold as Hand's own. "My cousins aren't as highly placed as yours, Colonel. But I have three of them in that regiment, one of whom is the commander's adjutant. I know what they're thinking, and it's nothing the chancellor would like to hear."

Hand spend a moment looking at the issue from all angles he could think of. On the one hand, this level of caution seemed a bit mad. No one including Oxenstierna would question Gustav Adolf's authority if he should recover. On the other hand...

Who knew, really? There was a sort of insanity lurking underneath Oxenstierna's whole enterprise. The man's resentment at the steady erosion of the aristocracy's position in the USE had obviously been much deeper than anyone realized. Hand had always assumed—so had his cousin, he was pretty sure—that

Oxenstierna would be satisfied with the still-intact position of the nobility in Sweden. But apparently the chancellor had concluded that if things continued on their present course in the Germanies it would only be a matter of time before the position of the nobility in Sweden itself was undermined.

He might even be right, for all the colonel knew. But to plunge everyone into a civil war because of it...

That was simply not sane, in Hand's opinion. Not outright madness, perhaps; but not sanity either.

So who knew what the chancellor might do, if he felt himself driven into a corner? Best to establish some safeguards ahead of time.

"I'll do as you suggest, Erling." It was the first time he'd ever used the man's given name. "In the meantime . . ."

The huge bodyguard made a dismissive gesture. "That, you needn't worry about, Erik. The bodyguard detachment is entirely reliable. I can personally vouch for that."

The colonel wasn't about to question the statement. First, because this was the first time Ljungberg had ever used his first name. Second, because the hand that made that gesture was at least half again the size of his own.

Unlike the king's chancellor, the king's cousin was not even the littlest bit insane.

Chapter 30

Baghdad

Uzun Hussein looked expectantly toward the platform that had been erected the day before. A few moments ago a brace of horsemen had appeared and fanned out around it. This suggested that the speech they had been assembled to hear was about to commence. Ordinarily, Hussein didn't have much interest in speeches, even when given by sultans. He had been a janissary long enough to see three sultans come and go before this one. He would fight whoever he was told to fight without much caring about the reason, so long as his pay came regularly.

But he would listen to the Sultan Murad. The young padishah had won him over with his courage on this campaign, as he had most of the janissaries. Besides, the rumor was that the sultan was coming to tell them they were going back to the City. That was worth listening to, whoever said it. There was no place in the world that compared to Istanbul.

Not even Baghdad, the fabled city they had just conquered. Uzun could see Baghdad from where they were assembled, just across the great river. He could see many of the towers that guarded the city from here. Not all, of course. You probably couldn't see all of those towers from any one place. He'd been told by one of the sultan's *lagimci*—military engineers, mostly miners and sappers—that there were two hundred and eleven towers on the city walls.

As impressive as they were, though, even the towers were dwarfed by the mighty walls. Twenty-five yards high, in most places, and ten yards wide at the base. Uzun had walked along a stretch of those walls after the city was taken, marveling at the cunning design. Each tower was separated from its neighbor by more than a hundred paces, with a crenel every two and a half paces. More than ten thousand embrasures in all, according to the *lagimci*.

But that very design had perhaps been the city's downfall. Baghdad should have been held by an immense army, one that could match its walls. Instead, the sultan's surprise march on Baghdad had caught the Safavid heretics off balance. There had only been a relatively small force defending the city, who couldn't keep up the defenses well enough.

Even then, it had taken several weeks to seize Baghdad. Heretics though they might be, no one claimed Persians couldn't fight.

The sultan appeared on the platform. Hussein looked up at him with approval. Murad *looked* like a sultan should look, tall and strong. And when he spoke, he got right to the point.

"My wolves, you have shown the redheads what happens when they fight the followers of the true faith!" That got him a roar of approval.

"And now, the time has come for you to turn west again, to show our people what conquerors look like!" A bigger roar.

"But do not get so caught up in the celebrations of your triumph that you fail to keep your skills sharp."

Hussein found himself a bit surprised. Murad didn't ordinarily make noises like an *odabashi* worried about an inspection.

"For in the spring we will be going to teach that German king who calls himself Austria's emperor a lesson!"

A profound silence fell. A new campaign in the spring, then. Against the Christians.

And then the roar began to build. Hussein found himself joining the roar, a roar that might have been heard in Vienna itself.

At last, a war against the true infidels. A chance for glory unparalleled in his lifetime. It seemed clear now that Sultan Murad was being led by Allah. First the success of this campaign, more complex than anything since Suleiman's day. Now a march—at long last—against the Christians.

From this day forth, Uzun Hussein would never think of the sultan as anything other than Murad *Gazi*. Perhaps he would live to see the young sultan lead them to Rome itself.

Part Four

February 1636

Among these barren crags

Chapter 31

Dresden, capital of Saxony

The take-off was even worse than Eddie had feared it would be. Partly that was because the headwind wasn't what he'd wanted. He hadn't felt he had any choice but to take off, though. The weather had been bad for a week and, this time of year, was likely to be bad again very soon. Today, the sky was clear and almost cloudless not only here in Dresden but also in Magdeburg and whatever his final destination was. So he was told over the radio, anyway. He still had no idea of the nature of his mission, other than it was apparently of supreme importance.

Whatever that final goal was, he had to get to Magdeburg first—and he almost didn't make it out of Dresden. At the very end of the impromptu runway created by the feverish demolition work of the past week, the wingtips cleared the rooftops while most of the fuselage was still inside the street once the widened part ended. If there'd been a chimney there, on either side, he'd have gone down with a wing torn off—and any unexpected gust would have done the same.

Had there been anyone sitting in the cockpit next to him, they'd have been struck by the young pilot's icy demeanor. Inside his brain, monkeys were gibbering with terror—he could hear the damn things—but there was no expression at all on his face. Nor were his hands sweaty, nor was he shivering anywhere. Eddie Junker was one of those people who somehow managed to stay completely calm in the face of danger. Noelle had once told him the French called it *sang-froid*, which she said was the only French term she knew except ones not fit for mixed company—which were the ones *he'd* have been interested in, but she'd refused to tell him.

He could only, at the end, as the wingtips emerged out of the street-canyon, thank God for giving him the courage and the tenacity and the fortitude and the pluck and the resolution and the perseverance and the valor to tell Denise *no!* and make it stick after a battle that cast any mere trifle involving huge armies into the shade.

"It's a good thing your boyfriend had big enough balls to make you stay behind," said Minnie Hugelmair, as she and Denise watched the plane fly out of Dresden, "or you'd both be dead."

"Well . . ."

"Admit it. He was right and you were wrong."

"Well . . ."

"Crash, boom, a burst of flame, they'd have to identify your body by the teeth or something."

"Well . . ."

"Maybe not, since he's barely got enough gas to make it to Magdeburg. Still, pieces of you would be scattered all over the place. Little bitty pieces."

"Well..."

"The rats would declare it a holiday. Saint Denise's Day. Well, no, just Saint Crispy's Day. It's not like they know your name. Or would care anyway."

"Well..."

The sight of the plane flying over his lines put General Johan Banér in a fouler mood than usual. And he was usually in a foul mood, these days. Who would have thought CoC riffraff could have held Dresden against him for an entire month? He'd been sure he'd break his way into the city within two or three days.

Noelle Stull hadn't watched the takeoff. She was half-sure Eddie was going to die in the attempt, and just couldn't bear the idea of watching it happen. She and Eddie were very close friends and had been through a lot together.

When the triumphant roar went up from the crowd in the square, though, she knew her fears had been groundless. Well, not *groundless*, exactly. There'd been good reason to be worried, even after Eddie stripped every spare ounce of weight out of the plane. That so-called "runway" was a travesty, even after it was lengthened by demolishing part of the street that served as the final stretch.

Almost every spare ounce, rather. He had agreed to carry out her latest letter to Janos Drugeth.

"That's silly," she'd said. "I don't even have it addressed."

"Says right here: 'Janos Drugeth, Hofburg, Vienna, Austria.'"

"As if that's going to do any good!"

Eddie shrugged. "You never know. He's the emperor's friend as well as one of his chief aides. They'd know where to find him, I think."

She'd still been dubious. "You said you needed to remove every unnecessary ounce. That letter weighs at least an ounce. Maybe two."

"I was exaggerating. Had to, on account of Denise. I should have said 'every unnecessary pound.'"

"So I can't sent him a box of chocolates, huh?"

"You've got _chocolates_?"

"I was exaggerating. On account of myself. God, I wish I could fly out of here with you."

"No."

"But I'm skinny. I only weigh—"

"No!"

"Especially now, the rations we've been on, I probably don't even weigh—"

"You and Denise both!"

Luebeck, USE naval base

"He's off," said Admiral Simpson, as soon as he entered the set of rooms in the naval base that had been transformed into a royal suite of sorts. (Emphasis on "of sorts"—the royal beds were cots. On the other hand, the plumbing was superb.) "We just got word over the radio."

Kristina and Baldur looked up from the card game they were playing at the mess bench that passed for a royal dining table. For his part, Ulrik took the time to place a bookmark in the text he was reading before doing the same. He was seated on the bench next to the princess.

"How soon will he arrive?" Kristina asked eagerly. The girl adored flying—anywhere, anytime, for any reason.

Simpson waggled his hand in a gesture indicating some uncertainty. "By late afternoon, Your Highness, assuming the weather holds. He needs to fuel up in Magdeburg first. Apparently there wasn't much petrol left in the plane. So you won't be able to make the flight back to Magdeburg until tomorrow morning."

As he had been before, Ulrik was a bit intrigued by the admiral's use of the term "petrol." The Danish prince had discovered from his research that the term was English, not American. Most up-timers would have called it "gas" or "fuel." He had not yet discovered the reason for the admiral's quirk of terminology. Was it just personal idiosyncrasy? A trace, perhaps, of the Anglophilism that Ulrik thought to detect in upper crust Americans?

Strange, really. In his day and age, England was considered an uncouth backwater. What up-timers would have called "the sticks."

Ulrik could have simply asked the admiral, of course. But where was the fun in that?

"If he makes it there in the first place," said Baldur skeptically. "By all accounts I've heard, the pilot is a novice."

"'By all accounts' would refer to me," said Simpson, "since I believe I'm the only one you've talked to on the subject. I did not say he was a 'novice.' What I said was that while Egidius Junker has not been flying for very long, he is apparently good enough that

Francisco Nasi—whom no one has ever accused of lacking anything in the brains department—was willing to make him his own personal pilot."

The admiral's tone was mild, not reproving. He sounded slightly amused, in fact.

Why? Ulrik decided to chew on that puzzle for a moment. He really did not take well to weeks of idleness. At one point, he'd made a game out of tracing the tile patterns in the floor of the communal toilet in the barracks. Alas, the game had been brief—the pattern was fully evident within two minutes.

"I don't see why they can't switch pilots in Magdeburg," Baldur grumbled. "Surely there has to be some...some..."

"Up-timer available?" Simpson seemed to be fighting down a smile.

Of course! Norddahl was made nervous by the thought of a down-time pilot—and the American was amused by the fact.

Unfortunately, now that he thought about it, Ulrik himself wasn't entirely pleased at the thought of being flown through the air by a down-timer. But he let none of his anxiety show, lest the admiral transfer that sly little not-smile onto him. Royalty had obligations as well as privileges.

Simpson shook his head. "Even if there were, you wouldn't want him. Junker's flying a Dauntless, and Nasi has the only civilian one in service. The military won't give you a pilot for the same political reasons we've talked about at length. So your choice is between a pilot who has experience with that particular plane and one who'd be coming to it cold—and would probably be another down-timer anyway."

His smile widened and became genial rather than sly. "Besides, if Germans can't fly airplanes, that would certainly come as news back where we came from. Have you ever heard of Manfred von Richtofen?"

Seeing three heads shaking, the admiral clapped his hands and rubbed them together. "Well, then! Gather 'round while I tell you the tale of the Red Baron."

Magdeburg air field

There was a small crowd waiting for Eddie when he arrived in Magdeburg. Not surprisingly, once Eddie finally discovered the nature of his mission.

No wonder they'd been willing to demolish part of Dresden!

As he listened to what mostly amounted to reassuring babble, once Rebecca Abrabanel explained the heart of the matter, Eddie pondered the political ramifications. Francesco Nasi hadn't hired Junker simply for his piloting skills. His experience working with Noelle Stull as an investigator for the SoTF's Department of Economic Resources had given him a wider and more subtle grasp of the USE's politics than most people possessed.

So it didn't take him more than a few seconds to grasp what lay at the core of this bold maneuver on the part of Kristina and Ulrik. In essence, a deal was being made. Unspoken, perhaps, but a deal nonetheless. The two royals would throw their prestige and status—which was what they possessed, given Kristina's age, rather than any recognized "legitimacy"—on the side of Fourth of July Party and the Committees of

Correspondence. In return, the FoJP and the CoCs would agree to maintain the USE as a constitutional monarchy rather than pressing for a full republic in the course of an open and full-scale civil war.

As with all bargains, everyone got something and everyone lost something at the same time. The dynasty would insure its position—but, inevitably, the actual power it wielded would diminish somewhat. Direct power, at least. The dynasty could still retain a tremendous amount of influence, depending on the personal characteristics of the specific monarch involved.

Or monarchs, in this case. Eddie wasn't sure yet, because he'd never met Prince Ulrik at all and he'd only seen Princess Kristina at a distance. But the very logic of what he was hearing led him to the tentative belief that the USE could wind up with what amounted to a dual monarchy, under the surface of a reigning queen and her prince consort. Something like the reign of Archduchess Isabella and Archduke Albert in the Netherlands, before Albert died in 1621.

After all, how likely was it that a queen who'd been relying on the advice and counsel of her husband since she was eight years old—the same man who'd protected her from assassins while being wounded himself in the deed—would treat him as a mere consort?

From the viewpoint of the FoJP and the CoCs, the bargain also had its advantages and disadvantages. On the positive side, gaining the allegiance of the dynasty would strengthen their position in the current civil war. Probably a great deal, given that it was really a semi-civil war in which a lot of people were still standing on the sidelines. Many of those people would be swayed by the actions of Kristina and Ulrik. And their actions would further undermine Oxenstierna's prestige, which had already been badly shaken by his arrest of Wettin and was being continually undermined every day that Dresden withstood the Swedish siege.

On the negative side, most members of the FoJP and just about every member of the CoCs was a committed republican. They had never been very happy with the existence of the dynasty. Not in theory, certainly. Gustav II Adolf's own character had defused that antagonism while he'd been active and in command of his wits. He was a dynamic and charismatic figure, after all, the man often called "the Lion of the North" and "the Golden King." Perhaps more importantly, the Swedish king had always been shrewd in his dealings with Mike Stearns. The fact was, for all the many times they had clashed, the two men had always managed to reach agreement when necessary. It was clear to just about anyone in the Germanies that they respected each other and quite possibly even liked each other.

Still, the nation's more radically inclined citizens chafed at the idea of being under a monarchy, and the recent developments since Gustav Adolf's injury at Lake Bledno simply drove home many of the reasons for their unhappiness with the situation. Monarchies are fine and dandy if you have a good king, but what if you have a bad one? Or, what was often even worse, faced a succession crisis?

No, best to be rid of the whole antiquated nonsense.

They wouldn't be able to do that now, though. Not once Kristina and Ulrik landed at this very same airport tomorrow morning. There'd be a huge crowd to greet them, Eddie was quite sure. Then, a huge crowd lining the road leading into Magdeburg, and another huge crowd to greet them when they arrived in Hans Richter Square. Some firm hand was guiding this odd government-in-exile, obviously, and would see to it.

(Very odd exile, given that they were located in the actual capital of the nation. But it was an odd civil war, when you got right down to it.)

Eddie wondered who that firm hand was. His own guess was Rebecca Abrabanel. But if he was right, no one except a handful would ever really know. It would be in the nature of the woman to maintain a collegial appearance at all times. Despite her striking physical appearance, she was in many ways the opposite of her husband.

Mike Stearns, like his monarch, was one of those people who strode about the stage of history. Very dramatic, very visible to all. The Prince of Germany to match the Golden King.

Rebecca Abrabanel? She would have no nicknames, carry no monicker. Or if she did, it would be something referring to her beauty rather than her brains and political skill. Yet in her own way, Eddie was coming to think, she was as important a player as almost any on that stage. More important than most, for a certainty.

The refueling was done. The plane was ready to fly again. Eddie clambered back into the cockpit.

As he settled into his seat, he caught sight of Gunther Achterhof. The leader of the capital city's Committee of Correspondence was one of a handful of people still standing near the plane.

He had what almost looked like a scowl on his

face. Moved by a sudden impulse, Eddie leaned out of the still-open window.

"Cheer up, Gunther! Look at this way. If I crash and burn, you get a republic after all."

He followed that with a thumbs up and went back to checking his gauges.

Time to go. The weather was still superb.

He gave Achterhof a last glance. The man now had a peculiar sort of vulpine smile on his face. And he returned Eddie's gesture with a thumbs-up of his own.

That gesture could be interpreted in two different ways, of course. *Good luck* or *I hope you crash and burn, you fucking jackass.*

Either way, Eddie was cheered up. He took off with a grin on his face.

Chapter 32

Dresden, capital of Saxony

Eric Krenz woke to the sound of gunfire. He didn't need Tata, this time, to roll him out of bed. Before she'd fully awakened herself, he was already half-dressed.

Those weren't simply the sounds of cannon fire. There was also the unmistakably distinctive sound of volley guns being fired. That could only mean one thing.

"What's happening?" Tata asked, her voice still a bit fuzzy from sleep.

"They're coming across the ice! I didn't think even Banér was that fucking crazy!"

He finished jerking on his boots and practically flew out of the door. "If a man insists on being an idiot, he could at least try to be intelligent about it!"

As soon as Eric reached the street, he realized why Banér had launched the attack. There was a heavy overcast, enough to make it impossible to see more than thirty yards in any direction, even with a half-moon. The Swedes would have been able to get most of the way across the Elbe before being spotted.

Not that it would do them much good now. As he hurried toward the fortifications along the river, he could see rockets firing. These weren't artillery rounds. General Stearns—his staff, rather—had never been fond of the temperamental devices and didn't use them as weapons. So, none of the soldiers from the Third Division who'd been sent to Dresden to recuperate from injuries had any experience with the heavy rockets used by some units as artillery.

The Third Division did, on the other hand, use rockets as flares and signaling devices. Krenz and his fellow officers had ordered a number made by the city's artisans, for precisely the purpose they were being put to now—illuminating the area in the event of a night assault.

They were some real advantages, Eric had discovered, to fighting a siege when you were the ones inside the walls. At least, if they were the walls of a major city like Dresden, with its many workshops and manufactories, and hundreds of skilled craftsmen. The volley guns he could hear rattling away in the distance had been made here also. Dozens of them, in just a few weeks.

By the time he got to the bastion guarding the western end of the river wall, the battle was raging. The sound of grenades had now been added to the mix, which meant the enemy had gotten all the way up to the walls along the river bank. Some of those grenades were being thrown by the Swedes, trying to clear an area wide enough to get infantry over the walls on ladders. He could tell the difference from the sounds of the explosions.

Friedrich Nagel was already there when Eric got atop the bastion. "I think they're mostly coming at the east end!" he shouted, pointing in that direction.

"Can you handle everything here?"

Nagel nodded. "It's not so bad, really. The volley guns make a lot of difference. I don't think they were expecting them."

Eric turned and went back down the stairs. He had to force himself to move a little slowly. The snow covering the steps made them slippery.

He'd thought the volley guns would help. They were easy to make, once you understood the trick of the things. Most of these weren't rifled, the way the division's own volley guns were. But for the purposes of these guns, that didn't matter so much. They were intended for the close range work of repelling assaults, not firing on an open battlefield. The key was the firing mechanism itself, the use of a single breech-loading firing strip that enabled the gun crew to fire a volley of twenty-five rounds five or six times a minute—even seven times a minute, if the crew was good enough.

These Dresden-made guns couldn't match that rate of fire, of course, because they weren't using percussion caps. No one in the city was set up to make such firing devices. Instead, these volley guns used a more primitive powder train. That cut the rate of fire in half.

Still, most of the volley gun crews along the walls could manage three volleys a minute—quite a bit better rate of fire than three-pounders loaded with canister, and far better than that of larger cannons. In fact, they could almost keep up with infantrymen firing muzzle-loading muskets.

The volley guns were quicker and cheaper to make than cannons, too, since they didn't require the specialized equipment and skills needed to make large cannon barrels. Dresden had plenty of gunsmiths able to make the simple two-foot-long musket barrels, even if only one of the gun shops was set up to rifle the bores. The same was true for the carriages. A number of artisans in the city were able to manufacture them, where making the massive carriages for a cannon would have been difficult.

Another advantage of the volley guns was that they didn't require a big crew—three men, where most cannons required at least twice than many. The ordnance was lighter and easier to handle, as well. That had made it possible to train a large number of the militiamen in their use, far more than they could have done with larger artillery.

Eric was sure that Nagel was right. The Swedish mercenaries coming across the river wouldn't have expected to run into that heavy a fire. One or two bad volleys, certainly—canister fired out of cannons. Probably only one volley, with the limited visibility caused by the darkness and the overcast. Instead, once they'd been spotted, they'd been under continuous fire.

And once the battle had started, the visibility factors would be working against them. The same darkness and overcast would make crossing the frozen river—already bad footing—more difficult still. Whereas the defenders didn't really have to worry about any of that. They weren't firing at specific individual targets anyway. No one did, in a battle, not even with rifled weapons.

❖   ❖   ❖

Eric's own footing wasn't that good, for that matter— as he was forcibly reminded twice along the way, when he slipped and fell. Luckily, he didn't suffer anything worse than a bruise. Maybe not even that. Several inches of snow isn't much of a shock absorber, of course, but the slipperiness meant that any fall except a perpendicular one tended to have much of its energy transferred into a skid instead of a direct impact.

He wouldn't know for sure until he could remove his clothes and examine the places he thought might be bruised. Better still, have Tata examine them and do her healing wonders while he sipped hot broth in front of a fire. As he *ought* to be doing this very moment, if the general in command of the Swedes hadn't been a madman.

"War sucks," he muttered. But, never faltered on his way. Krenz was one of those people who always did their duty. The grousing that went along with it was just a necessary lubricant.

Ernst Wettin spent the first fifteen minutes of the battle simply watching it from one of the windows in his bedroom in the Residenzschloss. Then, spent the next fifteen minutes pondering his own duty.

The decision, in the end, came down to a simple inability to do nothing at all—which was his only course, if he opted to stay out of the fray. He couldn't very well go back to working on his manuscript. Not even Ernst's devotion to educational reform was enough to keep him scribbling at a desk when the fate of an entire city was in the balance.

He tried his best not to let personal preferences shape his choice. It was hard, though. He detested

Johan Banér, from the months he'd been forced to work with the brute in the Upper Palatinate. And, on the flip side, had grown rather fond of the young people who'd taken charge of defending the city against the Swede. Gretchen Richter, Tata, the troll-ugly but surprisingly genial Joachim Kappel—certainly the dozen or so stalwart lieutenants from the Third Division—all of them were people whom he thought would fare rather well, when their time finally came to face the Almighty.

And should that time be now? Ernst Wettin thought not.

So, he left his little suite and made his way to the great chamber at the center of the palace where Richter had set up a command center. Surely he could be of some use, whatever it might be.

Not sure whether she should be amused, bemused, anxious or appalled, Noelle Stull watched her two young companions as they set about barricading the entrance to their town house.

Between the energy with which they set to the work and the simple fact that there was only so much that could be done anyway, they were finished within a few minutes. Then, brandishing pistols—Denise Beasley, the trusty .45 with which her father Buster had gone down to everlasting fame and glory during the Dreeson Incident; Minnie Hugelmair, an expensive-looking cap-and-ball revolver that she'd sweet-talked her employer Nasi into buying for her—the two teenage girls stood stalwart guard, ready to slaughter whatever Swedish hordes might force their way in. Minnie had a nasty-looking dagger in her left hand, too.

Noelle cleared her throat. "You know, girls, if they can't hold the walls, I really think we'd do better to try to find a hiding place in the root cellar."

Uncertainly, torn between romance and reason, the girls looked back and forth from the door leading outside to the considerably smaller and less ornate door that led to the root cellar.

"It's nasty down there," said Denise.

After a moment, Minnie shrugged. "Not so nasty as it'd be up here, when they break in. Which they will, if they get into the city. We just can't hold off all of them. Come on, let's see what we can do." She headed for the root cellar.

Denise, always the more rambunctious of the two, was still scowling. "There's probably rats down there."

Minnie unlatched the door. "Probably. On the other hand, not once in the history of the world have women been gang-raped by rats. It's always important to keep a perspective on these things."

She had a point, and not even Denise was that stubborn. On their way down the steep stairs—more like a heavy ladder, really—she consoled herself by saying: "Well, I guess we can always have our last shoot-out down here too."

Noelle was bound and determined to see it didn't come to that. She started moving sacks of onions and turnips, wondering if there were enough to pile over them.

"Hey, look at this," said Minnie. She was crouched in a corner of the small basement, holding up the lantern Noelle had brought down.

The two other women went over. When they got next to her, they saw that Minnie had scraped aside some straw and exposed what looked like a small trapdoor. Denise reached down, seized the little loop of rope that seemed to serve as a latch, and lifted the door.

It came up fairly easily, given that it was obvious no one had moved the thing for years. Minnie held the lamp over it. Looking down, they saw a very small empty room below. More in the way of an alcove, really. The walls weren't dirt, though. They'd been lined with wood, as had the floor. It was like a small, rather well-built closet that you entered from the top instead of the side.

Denise frowned. "What...?"

Minnie chuckled. "Whoever built this house was a pessimist, obviously. We don't have to create a hideout, Noelle—there's one already here."

Noelle had reached the same conclusion herself. The safe room was superb, actually. Once the trapdoor was lowered on whoever hid inside, it could be covered with straw, some dirt—plenty of that, in a root cellar—and piled high with sacks of vegetables. Not quite enough to prevent the people inside from eventually forcing the door back open, but enough to discourage any searchers. Mercenaries looking for loot and women wouldn't spend much time down here anyway. Especially if they were drunk, which they almost certainly would be. The biggest danger was that they'd set the whole house on fire. Arson was often a feature of a city being sacked.

Still, it was safer than anything else.

Denise peered more closely into the hideout. "I'm not sure we can all fit in there."

Noelle had already come to that conclusion also. It didn't really matter, though. The trapdoor wasn't that well-concealed on its own. Minnie had spotted it easily, once she looked in this corner. Someone else could do the same. To make the hideout work, someone had to stay above and cover the trapdoor after it was closed.

"Give me your guns," she said, extending her hands.

The two teenagers stared at her. "You've already got one," said Minnie.

"And you can't shoot anyway," added Denise.

"I'm not going to argue about this, girls. A formality it might be, most of the time, but the fact is that you're minors under my care. You won't need those guns if you have to squeeze yourself down into that hole, and I need to stay up here to cover the trapdoor so it won't be spotted."

Noelle shrugged. "And my marksmanship is a moot point. If I have to use the guns—all three of them, and don't think I won't be blasting away like a maniac—it'll be at point blank range anyway." She looked around, squinting in the dim light. "I figure I'll make Stull's Last Stand down here, not upstairs. Less chance they could take me alive—and, either way, there'd be enough gore and stuff that they won't stick around down here afterward to look for anybody else."

Denise's eyes were wide. So was Minnie's one good eye.

Noelle shook her head. "I am not going to argue about this," she repeated. "Give. Me. Your. Guns. Now."

In the end, they settled on a compromise. Denise and Minnie would keep the guns until and unless it became clear that the walls had been breached, the city was being sacked, and all was lost. Then—only then—would the girls do as they were told.

As compromises went, Noelle figured it wasn't a bad one. Given those two.

Then, they went back upstairs. Minnie and Denise settled down for a card game in the kitchen. Noelle went upstairs to watch the street from a window.

"She's pretty cool," observed Denise, as she dealt out the first hand.

"We already knew that," said Minnie. "But it's nice to see these things confirmed."

Jozef Wojtowicz tried to cheer himself up. At least they wouldn't be hauling any rocks for a while.

And there was this, too—he was learning how to use one of these fascinating volley guns in actual combat, always the best way to really become familiar with a weapon.

The design was quite interesting. Ingenious, even. Lieutenant Krenz had told him it was modeled on an ancient up-time weapon called the Billinghurst-Requa battery gun. "Ancient," of course, as up-timers reckoned these things. Apparently the Americans had had a civil war of their own, back in the dawn of time, and the gun had first seen action then.

Best of all, it was a design that was well within the capability of Poland's artisans to make. The only tricky part of the design was the percussion cap, from what Jozef could see. But you didn't need that anyway—all of the volley guns in his bastion were being fired by simple powder trains. Percussion caps would certainly improve the rate of fire, but Jozef thought it would be possible to buy them from the French. The things weren't bulky, so shipping wouldn't be a big problem.

Still, it was an awkward situation. If Jozef's history ever got exposed, how was he going to explain to Polish hussars that his only real combat experience had been fighting on behalf of the USE? His friends wouldn't care, of course, and Grand Hetman Koniecpolski was a man of broad and wide experience, who'd take the thing in stride.

Alas, the average hussar was about as broad-minded as a rooster. Jozef would never live it down. The ridicule would follow him into the grave. Which might be an early one, if any of the hussars took it in mind to be outraged and offended.

Alas, the average hussar got outraged and offended about as readily as a rooster too.

Maybe he could argue that since he'd actually been fighting on the side of the *rebels* in the affair—

But that wouldn't do him any good if the rebels won the civil war, in which case they would become the USE themselves and he was right back in the soup, as far as hussars were concerned. Yet if the rebels lost the civil war—starting right here in Dresden, this being the only place there was any serious fighting—then hussars would be the least of Jozef's problems. Outraged and offended Swedish mercenaries would have done for him already.

Outraged and offended, indeed. They were suffering horrible casualties out there on the ice. The volley guns really were quite murderous.

When Ernst reached the command center, he found Tata there, along with Joachim Kappel. But Gretchen was gone.

"She's out walking the lines," Tata explained.

The responsibility of command. Wettin would have been doing the same, had he still been in charge. So would the best kings and queens, down through the years.

It was not always enough, to be sure. Constantine XI had personally led his troops in the final battle against the Turks in the siege of Constantinople in 1453, but they'd taken the city despite him. He'd vanished in the fighting, presumably killed, his body tossed with those of others into a mass grave.

The same might happen to Gretchen Richter, this very night.

But it might not, also—and by personally visiting the soldiers on the ramparts, she improved the odds in favor of the defenders. Quite a bit, probably. The sort of close quarter combat involved in repelling assaults during a siege required a great deal of raw courage and confidence. Richter exuded those traits. They emanated from her, almost as if they took real and physical shape.

"Is there anything I can do to help?" Ernst asked.

Tata and Joachim looked at each other. Then Joachim turned and pointed toward a long table near the back wall. Half a dozen youngsters were gathered around it, arguing about something.

"Yes, if you would. Go over there and put them in order. Make sure they get their job done."

"What are they doing?"

Tata sniffed. "They're *supposed* to be organizing supplies for the wounded."

Ernst looked back over. The oldest of the group looked to be perhaps sixteen.

Pity the poor wounded. "Shouldn't be a problem," he said, heading toward them.

✧ ✧ ✧

Eric Krenz felt his spirits pick up, when he caught sight of Gretchen Richter coming onto the bastion.

His spirits had been rather high already, as it happened. He didn't have much doubt, any longer, that they'd be able to beat off the assault. Banér had gambled, Eric was pretty sure he'd lost the gamble—and there'd be a high price to pay for it on the morrow. Mercenaries were tough, up to a point. Very tough, in fact, as you'd expect from professional soldiers. But they reacted more poorly to heavy casualties in a failed assault than regular soldiers did—and regular soldiers didn't react well. It would probably be at least a fortnight before the Swedish general could marshal another major attack.

Still, he was glad to see Richter, and so were all the men on the bastion with him. That was obvious from their pleased expressions. It was like having their own angel pay a visit.

No sweet cherubim, either. This was a sword-bearing angel from the heart of God's fury.

Good-looking, blonde, and she was actually unarmed. But none of them were fooled.

"*Gott mit uns!*" one of the men suddenly shouted, in the old anti-imperialist war cry.

"*Gott mit uns!*" roared the soldiers on the bastion. In an instant, the call was picked up and racing down the curtain wall. It sailed out over the snow and the darkness and the blood-covered ice of the Elbe.

Chapter 33

Magdeburg

At the end, their pilot chose to fly all the way around the field—and right across the whole city of Magdeburg—before he brought the plane down to land. Prince Ulrik was surprised. Egidius Junker had behaved like such a stolid and unimaginative fellow up until then, from the first moment they met him. Who would have guessed such cunning lurked beneath?

After the plane was down and was taxiing toward the crowd waiting for them at the airfield's terminal building, Ulrik leaned forward. "That was well done, Herr Junker," he said, over the pilot's shoulder.

"Yes!" agreed Kristina. She was sitting in the other seat in front, next to the pilot. "It was a wonderful flight!"

Junker glanced back and smiled. There was more intelligence in that glance and that smile than the prince would have expected, too. The pilot's expression managed to convey, simultaneously, his appreciation for the compliment; his understanding that it was really a compliment on his political and not piloting skills; and his amusement—not derision, simply amusement—at the nine-year-old princess' misunderstanding.

Ulrik spent the rest of the time until they came to a stop wondering how much an airplane like this would cost. Surely it would be within the budget of a prince?

They'd need to support a pilot as well, he realized. This was only the second time Ulrik had ever been aloft in an airplane. The first time had been a brief ride during the Congress of Copenhagen, whose sole purpose had been thrill-seeking. The truth was, he hadn't particularly enjoyed it, because he'd been too nervous. Now that he'd flown a second time, as part of an actual journey with a real purpose, he had a much better sense of the business. It would be far better to have a regular pilot, especially one who was no dullard when it came to political affairs.

Junker brought the plane to a stop. Again, Ulrik leaned over his shoulder. "I am giving some thought to buying an airplane. Would you be available as a pilot?"

"Oh, that's a wonderful idea, Ulrik!" Kristina clapped her hands.

Junker gave him another smile full of subtleties. "I'm afraid not, Your Highness. I'm rather committed to my current employer."

The smile faded a bit. "And I had to leave my betrothed behind in Dresden. Now I'll need to figure out a way to get her and her friends out of there."

"Ah." Ulrik glanced out the window. The crowd of notables was still waiting. Probably for the propeller to stop spinning, he imagined. He certainly would have waited. That thing could carve a man up like a warrior out of legend. Of course, you'd have to walk right into it—but in the press of a crowd, such things could happen.

He had a few seconds left, and it never hurt for a prince to scatter favors about.

"I'll see what I can do," he said. "Write down their names for me, if you would."

Junker cocked an eyebrow. Ulrik started removing his shoulder straps. "You never know. I might have some influence, here and there."

"Thank you. I will."

The crowd was moving in, now. There was a handy up-time expression for this sort of thing, but Ulrik couldn't quite remember what it was.

"Showtime," said Junker.

Yes, that was the one.

Even before they entered the city, Ulrik was impressed. Whoever had organized this affair had done a superb job of it.

To begin with, they were in a motorcade, riding in a large up-time automobile rather than the carriage he'd expected. Two other American self-propelled vehicles were with them, one in front and one behind. As a sheer public display, it was splendid. But Ulrik also understood—all the better now, for having been the target of such an attempt—that the vehicles and their configuration would make things quite difficult for assassins seeking to do them harm. The automobiles were moving quite slowly, not much faster than a horse could trot. But if necessary, they could speed up rapidly and soon be racing down the road at a tremendous velocity.

Given the road, of course. On most roads, even in

the USE, the great speed of which up-time automobiles were capable was a moot point. But this road from the airfield into the city was obviously of up-time design, macadamized from beginning to end.

Secondly, the organizers of the event had made sure to have a large number of spectators and well-wishers even here, while they were still in the countryside. A surprisingly large number, given the weather. The sky was clear, true—indeed, it was quite a beautiful winter's day. But it was definitely a winter's day, with the temperature below freezing. Ulrik didn't envy those people standing alongside the road out there. The automobile had a heating device. The outdoors didn't.

Thirdly, he was impressed by the shrewdness of the seating arrangement. In the front seat next to the driver rode a very large bodyguard. "Riding shotgun," the up-timers called it—and in this instance, the term was quite literal. The man was carrying an automatic shotgun and the prince had no doubt at all he was proficient in its use.

Probably more important, given that the principal response to any assassination attempt would surely be to race off, not stand and fight, the man was huge. An assassin firing from the front would have to shoot around him to have a chance of hitting Kristina. (Or Ulrik, but Kristina would be the real target of any would-be killer.) Shooting around that man to hit the princess would be a bit like trying to shoot a mouse behind an ox.

A shot from the rear would be difficult, and probably impossible. Someone had covered the rear window with a decorative banner, which prevented anyone from seeing into the vehicle from behind. And while he wasn't certain, Ulrik was pretty sure there was a steel plate hidden within the banner. Even a blind shot wouldn't penetrate.

That still left the side windows, but that was a very difficult shot to make. All the more difficult because Ulrik and Kristina were sandwiched in the middle of the back seat, with a man on either side. To their left, sitting next to Kristina, was the governor of Magdeburg province, Matthias Strigel. To their right, next to Ulrik, sat a man named Albert Bugenhagen. The prince had known he was the mayor of Hamburg, although he'd never met him before.

Ulrik was quite sure the men had been selected for two reasons. First, they held formal positions of government, they weren't simply prominent figures in the Fourth of July Party or the Committees of Correspondence. Someone was being careful—thankfully—to maintain a necessary distance between the two royals and their real hosts. As much as possible, Kristina and Ulrik had to maintain a reasonably nonpartisan public stance.

The second reason was even simpler. Both men were also very big, although not as enormous as the bodyguard up front. That made the seat very cramped. On the other hand, good luck to anyone trying to hit Kristina in the middle of all that beefy flesh.

So, Ulrik was in a good mood even before they came into Magdeburg. It was always a pleasure to deal with skill and competence.

He would always remember three things afterward about their procession through the city.

The first were the banners. They seemed to be

everywhere. On every tower, on every rooftop, hanging from every window and balcony, and waved by seemingly every hand along the streets and in the square in front of the royal palace.

The flags came in all sizes, from a gigantic one draped down the side of an entire building to a multitude of small ones that could be held in one hand. But with very few exceptions, they only came in four types.

The first and most common was the official flag of the USE, with its crossed black bars on a red field. Along the two bars were golden stars representing the provinces of the nation, and at the center was the Swedish royal insignia from the lesser national coat of arms, three coronets under a royal crown. The colors throughout were the traditional German red, black and gold.

The second flag was the simple red-black-gold tricolor that had been informally adopted by the Committees of Correspondence. Sometimes the bars were horizontal, sometimes vertical. There was no official pattern since it was not an official flag to begin with. But it had become the recognized national symbol for those who advocated an outright republic.

The third flag was one Ulrik had never seen before—indeed, had never heard of before. It was the tricolor, but with the Swedish royal insignia at the center.

There were a lot of those. Not as many as the official flag but quite a few more than the common tricolor.

Finally, there was a banner. As with the tricolor, there was no set pattern, since these were quite obviously handmade. But the most common design had a red field, a black border all the way around—sometimes these were just two stripes—and a simple inscription in the center, written in gold: *Long Live Kristina!* Sometimes, *Long Live Our Kristina!*

Those were the princess' favorites, of course.

The second thing he would always remember was his first sight of the Marine guard when they drew up before the royal palace. The sight was startling enough to drive him to blasphemy.

"Good Lord! What have they got on their heads?"

"They're called 'shakos,' Your Highness," said Albert Bugenhagen. "Apparently it was a military design in the Americans' universe. Rebecca Abrabanel had images of them in a book and had a hatmaker shop produce a few dozen of the things."

The mayor of Hamburg smiled. "She says the admiral will probably have a fit when he sees them."

The things were certainly impressive, although Ulrik couldn't help but wonder how practical they'd be on a battlefield. For that matter, nothing the Marine guards were wearing looked all that practical. They were the most elaborate and heavily decorated uniforms Ulrik had ever seen, outside of hussar uniforms—and those were not the uniforms hussars actually wore into battle.

They even had the ostrich plumes, sticking up from the shakos. No leopard skins, though.

As they got out of the automobile, Ulrik gave the guards a closer inspection. He was pleased—relieved, in fact—to see that the weapons the Marines were carrying looked a lot more functional than their uniforms. Good SRG muskets, with an up-time shotgun in the hands of the corporal in charge of this particular squad. The Marines held the weapons as if they knew how to use them, too.

Thankfully, there was not a halberd in sight. After

the fracas in Stockholm, Ulrik would be perfectly happy never to see another halberd for the rest of his life.

The thought of Stockholm drew his hand to his waist, almost involuntarily. Today he was carrying the same revolver he'd used there. There was no particular use or need for the thing, but Ulrik found its presence comforting nonetheless.

There was a very large party waiting to greet them at the palace. Every notable in the city was there, it seemed. Toward the back, almost hidden behind several other people, he spotted Rebecca Abrabanel. Her own costume was designed every bit as carefully as the costumes she'd designed for the Marine honor guard—except hers was designed to make her as inconspicuous as possible.

"I am not fooled, woman," Ulrik murmured to himself. Pleased yet again to encounter skill and competence.

The same skill and competence, he didn't doubt.

At that point a band started to play, which was the third thing Ulrik would always remember. It was a catchy tune, not one he was familiar with. (Later he would find out it was the "Vasa March," newly composed by one of the city's musicians.) But what struck him the most was the energy and enthusiasm of the band members. If he'd been one of those musicians, he thought he'd have been too cold to beat a simple drum, much less play brass instruments.

How did you keep your lips from freezing to the mouthpiece?

Ulrik did not like to give speeches, and was not very good at it. Thankfully, because of the bitter cold, no one wanted to listen to a long speech anyway. A few short shouted sentences did well enough.

It didn't much matter, because the huge crowd in the square had come here to see Kristina, not him. And the princess *did* like to give speeches.

She was quite good at it, too, adjusting the term "good" to nine-year-old standards. But those standards suited the mood of the crowd perfectly. Enthusiastic, cheerful, not hard to follow—and not too long either.

Soon enough, they were done. The only complication was produced by Kristina's final words: *I'm having a party, and everybody's invited!*

From their startled expressions, Ulrik deduced that the notables hadn't planned further festivities of any kind. Much less a party to which the entire city had been invited.

He was amused to see the way so many of them looked toward Abrabanel, and began drifting in her direction. The young Sephardic woman was already issuing quiet orders to a coterie of other young women whom she seemed to have gathered around her. Calm, relaxed, confident. What was the difficulty of organizing an impromptu festival, after all, when one has already organized an impromptu overturn of the established order?

Ulrik wondered who the young women were. Most were probably commoners, but several of them were obviously noblewomen. They reminded him of the ladies-in-waiting that could be found in any royal court. At least, those courts run by very capable queens.

By mid-afternoon, the palace was close to a shambles. Not quite, because the mob that had poured

into it was in good spirits and not particularly given
to drunken revelry. Not this day, at least, when the
party was in honor of a child. Still, there was simply
no way that number of people could pass through a
palace without producing a lot of damage.

Most of the damage could be cleaned up by the
morrow, though. Even the worst of it—an entire section of balcony collapsing; fortunately, with enough
warning for the people below to escape death and
mutilation—could be repaired within a week or two.

Well worth it, Ulrik thought. Cheap at the price.

The palace had a radio room of its own, which
Rebecca had ordered closed off within two minutes
of hearing Kristina's impromptu party announcement.
There were Marine guards at the door to enforce the
orders. These Marines weren't wearing fancy uniforms
but they were carrying exactly the same fearsome
weapons.

"Send it," Rebecca ordered the operator. This message was going out in simple Morse code. She wanted
it transmitted as far and as wide as possible.

*Princess Kristina, heiress to the thrones of Swe-
den, the Union of Kalmar, and the United States of
Europe, arrived in Magdeburg today accompanied by
her betrothed, Prince Ulrik of Denmark. The entire
populace of the nation's capital was there to greet her.
Long live the Vasa dynasty!*

"Anything else?" the operator asked, when he was
finished.

"No," she said. "I think that will do."

Chapter 34

Berlin

When he read the radio message, Axel Oxenstierna burst into a rare fury. "The girl is impossible! Why doesn't she just abdicate now and save us all twenty years of grief?"

Darmstadt, Province of the Main

The radio message was reported in every newspaper in the USE. That included Darmstadt's own *Abendzeitung*.

After the mayor finished reading the short account out loud, there was silence in the council chamber. In the streets outside the Rathaus, the sounds of celebration filtered through the thick walls. The city's CoC had organized a parade.

"Well, now what!" said the militia commander. It was not even a rhetorical question. More in the way of an exasperated outburst.

One of the council members shrugged. "Face it, Gerlach. The Swede's floundering."

In times past, "the Swede" would have been a

reference to the king, Gustav II Adolf. Today, it was a reference to Chancellor Oxenstierna.

"If only the emperor would come back," pined another council member.

And so, the status of a dynasty shifted still further.

Augsburg, one of the USE's seven independent imperial cities

As usual, the commander of Augsburg's militia had a very different viewpoint from his counterpart in Darmstadt.

He'd been reading aloud too. Now finished, he set down the copy of the *Augsburger Nachrichten* and leaned back in his chair. Less given to formalities than their counterparts in Darmstadt, Augsburg's city council had been meeting in the tavern in the Rathaus basement.

"Good for her," he said. "Good for her."

Herr Langenmantel was still holding a grudge over the personal insult concerning his former betrothed. "That borders on treason, it seems to me!"

By now, though, Langenmantel was on his own. Even the head of the city council, Jeremias Jacob Stenglin, had resigned himself to the inevitable.

"Don't be stupid," he grumbled, picking up his stein of beer. "How can the throne betray itself?"

As Stenglin drowned his sorrows, another city council member spoke up. "Face it, Adelbert. The citizenship issue is a lost cause. By now, even half the guildmasters are against making any changes."

"More like two-thirds," grunted the militia commander. "Look, it's just not that important. The city was doing well enough, wasn't it?" He waved a thick hand.

"Yeah, sure, the CoC is annoying. So is my wife, a lot of the time. But she's reliable. Things could be worse."

A tavern in Melsungen, in the province of Hesse-Kassel

"Here's to the health of our landgravine!" shouted one of the revelers, holding up his stein of beer. "Long may she reign!"

The tavern was full, as it often was on a winter's eve. Not a single stein failed to come up to join the toast.

It now seemed almost certain that Hesse-Kassel would weather the storm without damage. Thanks to the landgrave's blessed widow.

Another reveler stood up, hoisting his stein. "And here's to the empress! Long may she reign!"

"She's getting an early enough start!" shouted another.

Amidst the laughter, not a single stein failed to come up to join that toast either.

A tavern on the coast of the Pomeranian Bay

"I'm glad now I voted for the Prince," said one of the fishermen at the table.

His two companions gazed at him suspiciously. "You said you'd voted for Wettin," said one.

The fisherman shrugged. "I lied. Didn't want to get in trouble, seeing as how the rest of you were so dumb."

After a moment, the third fisherman said, "Yah, I voted for him too."

The skeptic rolled his eyes. "Give it a month and

it'll have been pure magic, the way Wettin got elected. Seeing as how apparently nobody voted for him at all."

Tetschen, near the border between Saxony and Bohemia

"Message just came in from the general," said the Hangman's radio operator. He set a slip of paper in front of Jeff Higgins.

With a sense of relief, the regiment's commander put down the newspaper he'd been laboriously working his way through. There was no German-language newspaper in Tetschen so he'd been trying to make sense out of the analysis in the *Noviny*.

With no great success. Jeff's grasp of Czech was rudimentary and mostly limited to everyday phrases you'd use about town. Order a beer, buy a loaf of bread, that sort of thing—not interpret commentary about political developments in a neighboring country.

It was probably a moot point anyway. He already knew what the radio message from Magdeburg said, since it had been picked up by the regiment's own radio as soon as it was transmitted. In fact, the *Noviny* had gotten it from them in the first place. Jeff had just been hoping he might pick up some further scraps.

When he looked at the message that had just arrived, that became a moot point also. To hell with scraps. The meal had arrived.

The message was one word.

Now.

"Showtime," said Jeff, heaving himself to his feet. "Adjutant! We're moving out!"

Chapter 35

Berlin

"What is it?" asked Colonel Hand, as soon as he entered the king's chamber. Gustav Adolf was lying on his bed, asleep.

Erling Ljungberg shook his head. "It didn't last long, and then he fell asleep again. But for a while there..."

The big bodyguard took a deep, sighing breath. "He's coming back, Erik. I finally believe that he is."

"What did he say?"

"First, he looked at me, as if he were puzzled. And then he said, 'Where is Anders?' When I explained that Jönsson was dead, he seemed uncertain as to what I meant for a few seconds. Then—it was just as if a light went on in his eyes, Erik, I swear it was—his face got very sad. He said 'It was my fault, wasn't it? Was I too reckless again?'"

The colonel looked down at his sleeping cousin. Then he also took a deep, sighing breath.

"And what did you say?"

Ljungberg shrugged. "I told him the truth. 'Yes, Your Majesty, you were too reckless. But that's just

389

part of the job. All of us know it. Anders better than anyone.' Then he looked still more sad. He asked me what happened. He said he didn't remember anything after the rain started. So I told him. Then he started to cry. That's when I sent for you. But he fell asleep after a couple of minutes."

"Dear God in Heaven," murmured Hand. Some parsons might call that blasphemy, but he didn't think so himself. Blasphemy was the sin of taking the Lord's name in vain. Up until this moment, the colonel might be fairly accused of that.

But no longer. It had apparently not been in vain at all.

"What should we do?" asked Ljungberg.

"Nothing, for the moment. We need more than flashes of coherence from him. We need *him* back. Oxenstierna is in a rage. I think he's going to mobilize the army and march on Magdeburg himself."

Ljungberg's eyebrows went up. "What happened?"

"You didn't hear?" The colonel nodded toward the king. "His blessed offspring. She and that very smart Danish prince of hers showed up in Magdeburg. Giving speeches and reviewing parades, the whole lot."

The bodyguard frowned. There was nothing wrong with Ljungberg's brains, but his interests were quite narrow. The political subtleties of Kristina's actions obviously didn't register on him.

"For all intents and purposes, Erling, she's thrown the support of the dynasty behind the rebels. Or perhaps I should say, behind the legitimate parties— those people in Magdeburg being the only ones so far who haven't broken the law and have tried to keep the peace."

"Ah." Ljungberg was still frowning. "You really think so?"

"Oh, yes. That's why our blessed chancellor is doing a pretty good imitation of an Icelandic volcano."

He looked back down at Gustav Adolf. Then, out the window. Night was falling. Very early, as it did this time of year. "All we can do, still, is keep waiting."

Chapter 36

The four guards at the main gate to the fortress didn't think much when they saw the wagon approaching, except to wonder at the fortitude of the drivers. Night was falling and it was starting to snow. It was cold, too, but that was a given in February.

"Fucking Hans," muttered one of the guards. "He has got to be the greediest provisioner in Saxony."

"In Königstein, anyway," agreed one of his mates. He shifted the musket strapped over his shoulder. "Of course, he's the only military provisioner in the town."

"All the less excuse he has," said a third guard. He was the corporal in charge of the little detachment. "He's got no competition. So why is he forcing poor Heinrich out in this miserable weather?"

The fourth guard was more philosophically inclined. "It's February and we're in Saxon Switzerland. When is the weather *not* going to be miserable? At least this way, coming this late, Heinrich and his son can spend the night here. Better than that hovel they live in down in the valley."

The cart had come nearer. The first guard frowned. "That's not Heinrich's son with him. It's some fellow I don't know."

He wasn't alarmed. There could be any number of reasons the teamster was being assisted today by someone other than his son.

"That's a new cart too," said the second soldier. "Big damn thing. What's he hauling in it, do you think?"

"Turnips, what else?"

As it turned out, Heinrich's big new wagon was full of soldiers. Soldiers who were better armed than the four guards and a lot more alert.

The teamster's new assistant turned out to be a captain in the fabled Hangman Regiment of the Third Division. Who would have guessed?

There was no violence. The guards were quick to see reason. Besides, they didn't much care anyway. They worked for General von Arnim, who hadn't moved once out of Leipzig since all the trouble started. What clearer signal could one ask for?

"We're not part of this," insisted the corporal, as he handed over his musket.

"Not any longer, for sure," agreed the Hangman captain cheerfully. "Now, fellows, we'd appreciate it if you'd open the gate. And show us to the mess hall. Most of your mates will be gathered for supper now."

They had good intelligence too.

Once the gate was opened, hundreds of soldiers materialized out of the woods below the fortress, like ghosts. They were wearing peculiar white camouflage outfits. Quite superb, really, for Saxony in winter. Who could have known they were there?

The capture of most of the garrison in the mess hall went smoothly and easily. Those soldiers were even less inclined to put up a fight than the guards, since most of them were completely unarmed.

Who brings weapons to eat supper in the mess hall? Only someone expecting a surprise attack, and who would expect that?

The garrison's commander was captured in his own rooms, where he was having a private supper with the servant who doubled as his concubine.

She screeched with outrage. He put up no fight at all.

The captain in charge of the armory was a jackass and proved it once again. He did put up a fight—such as it was; a pistol against four rifled muskets, and he fumbled the wheel-lock mechanism to boot—and got shot to pieces for his efforts.

Good riddance, was the general attitude. A man like that could get you killed.

And for what? Von Arnim was late with the pay again. To make things worse, that probably wasn't even his fault. The Swedish chancellor was turning out to be every bit as unreliable a paymaster as the late and unlamented elector of Saxony.

"You want a different job?" Heinrich asked the corporal who'd been at the gate. The teamster was in a good mood now that the danger had passed with no harm done to himself or his equipment. He'd quite forgiven the soldiers of the Hangman Regiment for high-jacking his wagon and locking his son in a closet. "I think business is going to pick up. The Hangman pays with beckies. And people I know in Tetschen say they never stiff you either."

It was worth thinking about. The soldier's trade had some major drawbacks. It wasn't as dangerous as handling livestock, if you could keep from getting sick. But the erratic pay could get nerve-wracking. Besides, the corporal was getting to an age where he should start thinking about getting married. Not too many women were willing to marry a soldier, unless he was an officer, and the ones who were . . .

Tetschen, near the border between Saxony and Bohemia

"I wasn't expecting you here this soon, sir." said David Bartley.

Mike Stearns looked around the airfield. A platoon of soldiers from the Hangman was standing at attention nearby. An honor guard to escort him to the regiment's headquarters, obviously. Next to them stood a group of worried-looking civilians.

Very worried, apparently. They were up early. The sun was just above the horizon. Colonel Wood and Mike had taken off from the airfield at České Budějovice at the crack of dawn, as soon as there was enough light to fly.

"Since Jesse had come by for a visit, I figured I might as well fly up here ahead of the division." Mike turned back to look up at Colonel Wood, who hadn't gotten out of the cockpit of the Gustav. "You coming in?" He had to raise his voice to be heard over the engine, which the colonel hadn't shut off.

Jesse shook his head. "No!" he shouted back. "I don't know how long this clear weather will last!"

Mike waved a farewell and moved away from the plane, which began taxiing back onto the runway.

"Who're the civilians?" he asked.

"Merchants and tradesmen. They're fretting on account of the Hangman left town. Most of the regiment, anyway. They're worried what'll happen to business."

"For a while, it'll drop. No way around that. Afterwards, who knows?" Mike gave the quartermaster officer a grin. "We may all be dead. Well, except you and the detachment I leave behind."

Bartley looked unhappy. "About that, sir . . ."

"No, David. N. O. Under no conditions, under no circumstances, am I taking you with me." He clapped a friendly hand on the young man's slender shoulder. "You're ten times more valuable here than you'd be anywhere else. Unless your progress reports are a pack of lies, anyway."

"Uh, no, sir. They're not. But—"

"Which letter in 'n-o' is giving you the most trouble, Captain? You're the best quartermaster in the army, hands down. And I'm about to launch a campaign in the middle of winter against one of the most capable and experienced generals in the world. One of the few things I've got on my side is that I'm damn sure I'm going to be better supplied and provisioned than Banér—so long as you're handling the logistics. That means you stay here until we take Dresden. Assuming we get that far, of course."

Again, he gave Bartley that somewhat savage grin. "But I suppose I don't need to worry that my army will freeze to death before we get to Dresden, do I?"

David looked glum. "No, sir, you don't. You won't starve, either." He nodded toward the town. "I've got enough winter outfits in the warehouses for the whole division, with a couple thousand suits to spare and at least that many extra pairs of boots. There are only enough skis and snowshoes for a couple of battalions, though."

"That'll be enough. I'd just be using them as scouts in really bad weather."

"And enough food and water to keep you going for a month."

"Wagons? Sleighs?"

"Plenty of both." Bartley smiled. "The most worried-looking of those gents over there is the guy who made them. He just had the biggest boom of his life."

"Well, then, I'd better go talk to them. A happy and secure base is always a big asset."

Mike did a much better job of cheering up the merchants and tradesmen than David could have done. Bartley was handicapped by having the mind of a financier and quartermaster. Precise numbers, predictable outcomes, sure bets—those were his stock in trade. Watching one of the world's best politicians at work was simultaneously dazzling and disturbing.

When it was over, David *still* couldn't figure out how many lies Mike had told them. If he'd told them any at all. Politicians seemed to operate in an alternate universe where concepts like cause and effect, action and result, premise and conclusion, had at least eleven more dimensions than they did in the workaday world inhabited by normal human beings.

"That's what they mean by 'campaign promises,' isn't it? Uh, sir."

"Yup." The grin came back. "Think of it as a promise that you'll campaign to make it happen. Now, show me these winter outfits. I'm dying to see the things, after hearing the reports."

David was awfully proud of them, in point of fact. He was something of a military history buff. He'd designed the outfits himself—well, allowing for a whole lot of input from actual tailors—based on what he remembered of the telogreika, the padded winter jacket that the Soviet army had used in World War II. That had been one of the great advantages the Russians had had over the Nazis.

Most of the outfits were gray, but he'd had about two thousand done in white for camouflage. The Hangman Regiment had taken almost half of them for their assault on the fortress at Königstein.

The jackets all came with matching padded trousers, and there were good winter boots and plenty of wool socks. The Third Division would be one of the few—maybe the only—large military unit in this day and age that would fight a winter campaign while properly equipped for the task.

What impressed Mike the most, though, was something David hadn't even mentioned in his reports.

"You made *sleighs* for the volley guns?"

Bartley shook his head. "It's better than that, actually. Uh, sir. These are more like detachable skis that you can add onto the regular gun carriages if you need to operate on snowfields. Here, I'll show you how they work."

Mike had half-forgotten than David Bartley had gotten started as a tycoon by helping to design down-time sewing machines based on up-time models. The young man was a good artificer as well as a whiz at finance.

"The town's blacksmiths figured out most of it," David admitted. "But it was my idea to start with."

The design was downright cunning. The ski attachments didn't weigh all that much and could be fixed to the carriages ahead of time. Once the rig was in place, it wouldn't significantly impede the teams of horses that pulled the volley guns. But with a simple cranking mechanism, the skis could be lowered in less than two minutes—at which point the carriages became sleighs, for all practical purposes.

Mike scratched his jaw. "I wonder if anyone's ever tried to tried to use cannons in winter using sleighs instead of regular carriages?"

"I know of at least one instance when it was done," said David. "During the revolutionary war, Henry Knox hauled a bunch of cannons from Fort Ticonderoga to Boston in the middle of winter using sleighs. I don't think they kept them on the sleighs while they were firing them, though. They wouldn't really need to, since they were using them against fixed British positions, not on a battlefield."

"Regular field pieces might be too heavy to fire on a sleigh. Shouldn't be a problem with volley guns, though." Mike gave Bartley a smile. "We'll find out, won't we? In the meantime, see if you can mount a field piece on something like this."

That'd keep the blacksmiths happy, at least.

✧   ✧   ✧

Three days later, accompanied by the same platoon that had been waiting for him at the airfield, Mike left for the fortress at Königstein. He'd had to wait those three days because of a snowstorm that had passed through Brandenburg and Saxony and the southern fringes of which had touched northern Bohemia.

He traveled by horse-drawn sleigh. Mike's horse-manship was perfectly good enough to have enabled him to ride a horse even in such heavy snow, but David had managed to cobble together the design for a carriage suitable for a light artillery piece and the general wanted to test it.

Not *himself,* of course. He didn't weigh nearly enough to substitute for an artillery piece. Instead he rode on an accompanying sleigh that would serve an artillery company as the winter equivalent of a battery wagon.

Half of the experiment—the half that involved him directly—proved to be successful. Unfortunately, Bartley's artillery sleigh turned out to suffer from some rather serious design flaws. The damn thing either wouldn't stay on the tracks; the skis would dig in too deeply; or, finally, one of the skis broke altogether.

As Mike had pretty much expected, things were trickier than they looked. Murphy was alive and well, obviously.

He wasn't disheartened, though. He hadn't really thought the experiment would work to begin with. Episodes from American history notwithstanding, he'd been skeptical that a hastily assembled sleigh would be up to hauling such a heavy load in such heavy snow through a mountain range. Even given the advantage of traveling alongside a river, there were just too many ways for things to go wrong.

It would be nice, certainly, to be able to field light artillery pieces in a winter battle. But what Mike was really counting on was all the rest of his equipment— starting with the fact that his soldiers wouldn't be freezing their butts off the moment they broke camp. Once Banér pulled his troops out of their siege lines, on the other hand, they'd get into sorry shape very quickly, as cold as this winter was turning out to be.

One of the major drawbacks to the seventeenth century's libertarian method of paying troops was that everybody at every link in the money chain had an incentive to chisel. That was true even of the troops themselves, who were far more likely to spend their pay on wine, women and what passed for song in siege lines than they were to keep their gear up to snuff. Their officers certainly weren't going to make up the difference, with a few rare exceptions. Any supplies they bought their men usually had to come out of their own pockets.

That was not the least of the reasons that Mike, in his days as prime minister, had insisted that the USE's soldiers be paid from the national coffers directly. The money did not pass through a chain of officers except those assigned to payroll duty, who could be easily monitored. What was just as important, the army's supplies all the way down to socks and boots were "government issue." The USE army's soldiers were GIs, not independent military sub-contractors.

It wasn't impossible to chisel, of course. A black market in government-issued supplies and weapons had accompanied every army in history, and Mike didn't doubt for a moment that it accompanied his own. Still, almost every soldier who marched out into the Saxon plain a week or two from now to meet Sweden's Finest would have socks and good boots on his feet and be wearing an outfit designed to enable him to march, maneuver and fight in the cold and the snow and the ice. Which was a lot more than Banér's mercenaries would have at their disposal.

Mike's biggest worry was actually that Banér would choose to hunker down in his siege lines and not come out to meet him in the open field. The Swedish general hadn't bothered to build lines of contravallation to guard his siegeworks—the lines of circumvallation, to use the technical term—from the possibility of being attacked by an army in the field. He hadn't expected to find any such field army to face in the first place. Still, it wouldn't be that hard to adapt siege lines for the purpose, especially in winter.

But Mike didn't think that was likely. In the end, this was more of a political than a military contest. It was now obvious that Axel Oxenstierna had bitten off more than he could chew. Even before Princess Kristina showed up in Magdeburg, the Swedish chancellor had been losing the all-important so-called "war of public opinion." His opponents' shrewd tactics of avoiding open clashes and positioning themselves as the bulwarks of stability and order had put him on the defensive. (Mike was quite sure that was largely Becky's doing, although she'd said nothing about it in her radio messages.)

Now that Kristina had placed the prestige of the dynasty on the side of Oxenstierna's opponents, he would be thrown completely off balance. The ability of Dresden to defy him had been the great wound in his side from the beginning, and Kristina had now torn the wound wide open. The chancellor had no choice any longer. He-*had* to take Dresden—and quickly, so he could marshal his armies to march on Magdeburg itself. He had no options left except naked force and violence. And if that lost him still more public support, so be it. He could rule the Germanies by dictatorship, if need be.

Or so he thought, anyway. Mike had his doubts. Five years ago, yes. Oxenstierna could probably have succeeded in such a project. Today? Mike thought it was not likely at all. Not in the long run, for sure.

He didn't intend to let things get that far, though. Kristina's action had done one other thing—it had given Mike the fig leaf he needed to bring his army back into the USE. Even technically, it would now be difficult to charge him with leading a mutiny. But that really didn't matter because a civil war was never settled by lawyers. By very definition, a civil war was a state of affairs in which the rule of law had collapsed. What remained was, on one side, the field of arms; and on the other, the battle for the populace's support.

Under those conditions, Mike didn't think Banér could stay in his siege lines once Mike entered the Saxon plain and challenged him openly. He was almost certain that Oxenstierna would order him to fight in the field.

Where he might very well win, of course. On paper, at least, his army was larger than Mike's—fifteen thousand to the Third Division's nine thousand. But Mike was certain that Banér's forces had suffered a lot of attrition by now. Mercenary armies always did, especially in winter. That was disease, mostly, although desertion was always a big factor also.

The Third Division, on the other hand, hadn't suffered at all. Mike had made sure their quarters were good, with good sanitation, and he'd kept his men well fed and well supplied. They still lost soldiers, of course, but they replaced them with new recruits. In fact, the division was a little over-strength. His paymasters told him there were now almost ten thousand men on the active rolls. Some of those added men were specialists, of course; repairmen or supply troops of one kind or another. Part of the so-called tail rather than the teeth of an army. But at least a third of them were in combat units, especially heavy weapons units.

So, Mike figured the armies were relatively even, in purely numerical terms. In the end, it would come down to leadership. Banér was one of the Swedish army's handful of top generals—and going by the record, the Swedish army could lay claim to being the best army in Europe over the past half decade. Mike, on the other hand, was still largely—not quite—a neophyte general. He didn't begin to have Banér's experience and proven skill on the battlefield.

But he didn't intend to match that skill and experience, in the first place. The one lesson Mike had learned by now was that "generalship" was a vacant abstraction. There was no such thing, really, in the sense that most people meant by the term—a definable and distinctive skill set, such as one might learn in school to become a doctor or an accountant or an architect.

There were many specific skills involved in leading an army, of course. And experience mattered, as it did in any line of work. But what there really was, at the heart of the matter, was simply leadership. And leadership was never defined abstractly. A man did not "lead." No, he led *specific* people with *specific* goals and motives to accomplish *specific* tasks.

In this instance, he would be leading an army of citizen soldiers intent on defending their nation's liberties and freedoms from the depredations of a mercenary army paid for by a foreign occupier. So long as Mike committed no outright blunders, he was confident he could triumph in *that* specific task. Banér would try to match one general against another, where Mike would be matching one army against another.

Morale would decide it, in the end. Mike was sure of that—as long as he didn't just purely screw up, at any rate. His army's morale was excellent. He'd made sure it wasn't sapped by lack of food, disease, and freezing toes, and he never failed to maintain the division's regularly-published broadsheet that kept his soldiers well informed and motivated.

That was the other reason Mike had decided to travel by sleigh. He had one of his beloved portable printing presses on board. The devices were more dear to him than anything except his wife and children.

Live by the word, die by the word. The Swedes had already lost that battle. Mike figured the rest was bound to follow.

The Third Division started arriving in Tetschen two days after Mike left. It took the division a day and half to pass through the town. Not from the marching, but from the time it took to get every man outfitted with winter clothing that fit him properly.

Properly enough, anyway. Soldiers don't expect sartorial perfection and David had made sure to err on the side of getting boots and outfits that were too big rather than too small. A man could wear two pair of socks, if need be, and there were a number of ways to pad an oversize winter outfit with jury-rigged insulating material. A lot of soldiers specifically asked for oversized clothing, in fact.

By the time it was all over and the division was on its way up the road that followed the Elbe toward Königstein and Saxony, David Bartley was the most popular officer in the division. Hands down.

He was especially popular with the flying artillery units. Those men had become deeply attached to their volley guns, in the battles they'd fought starting with their great victory over the French cavalry at Ahrensbök. Now that winter was here and they knew they'd be fighting in the snow, they'd been glumly certain they'd have to leave their volley guns behind and suffer the indignities of becoming wretched infantrymen.

No longer. Not with the new auxiliary ski attachments, which they were already calling Bartley rigs.

David was tickled pink, truth be told. It almost made up for being left behind with just two companies of supply troops.

On the down side, he was the only significant officer left in Tetschen—and now, quite famous to boot. The campaign waged by the town's matrons kicked into high gear. If there was a single eligible daughter or niece to be found anywhere in the region who was not introduced to the newly promoted Major Bartley, she had to be deaf, dumb and blind.

Literally deaf, dumb and blind. Merely being hard of hearing, tongue-tied and myopic was no disqualification at all, from what David could tell.

Chapter 37

Osijek, the Balkans

"You look tired, Doctor," said Janos Drugeth.

"I am in fact very tired." Dr. Grassi wiped his face with a handkerchief. "I've been traveling almost constantly for weeks now."

He tucked away the handkerchief and slumped back in his chair. The chair lent itself well to that, being one of the two very plush armchairs in the small suite of rooms Janos had rented in the town's best tavern. Normally, he would have kept himself less conspicuous, but he hadn't had a choice. Osijek had been packed with refugees when he arrived. Not poor refugees, who couldn't have afforded to stay in taverns at all, but more prosperous people. By the time he arrived in the town, they'd already taken all of the cheaper housing.

He hadn't expected that. Why would a war against Persians fought in Mesopotamia produce refugees in the Balkans?

Dr. Grassi had explained it to him.

"Murad's campaign caught everyone by surprise, Baron."

The doctor usually called Janos by that title. It was not technically correct, but Janos saw no reason to fuss over the matter. Rankings in the Austrian empire were complex, especially when it involved Hungarian nobility—and the Drugeth family was of French origin, to make things still more complicated. Janos was one of the handful of men in the Austrian empire who were so powerful and influential in actual fact that the formalities of titles didn't overly concern them.

"Why?" he asked. "It's been a foregone conclusion ever since the Persians seized Baghdad in 1624 that sooner or later the Ottomans would try to take it back. And Murad is a young and dynamic sultan."

Grassi inclined his head. "Yes, that's true. But copies of the American texts concerning the Ottoman-Safavid war have been circulated quite widely. Even the Persians have read them by now. And in that universe—"

Janos threw up his hands. "Is everyone a Calvinist idiot? For that matter, not even Calvinists think that because something happened in such-and-such a way in the American universe that it will happen the same way in ours, and at the same time. Unless they're idiots to begin with."

The doctor smiled. "Oh, yes—and if you ask anyone who has studied the up-time texts, be that man a Christian or a Moslem or a Jew, he will assure you he understands that events in that universe are not binding on our own. And then, nine times out of ten, he will act as if they are."

Drugeth sighed. Grassi was quite right. He'd seen the same phenomenon himself—sometimes, emanating from his own emperor. Janos knew full well that a large part of the reason that Ferdinand discounted the Turk threat was because he knew that in another world, the Ottomans had not launched a major attack on Austria between Suleiman's attempt in 1529 and Mehmed IV's in 1683. And they'd been defeated on both occasions.

Unfortunately, while the history of that other world could certainly illuminate many things, it provided no guarantees of similar outcomes. The opposite was likely to happen, in fact, if a leader tried to guide himself too closely by that history.

"No one was surprised by the attack, as such," Grassi continued. "But no one—possibly not even the Turks themselves, save only the sultan—expected such a powerful assault, and such a quick one."

"They had the new weapons you expected, then?"

The doctor shook his head. "I wish I could claim such prescience, Baron. In fact, they were far better armed than I had expected. They had twice as many rifled muskets as I told you they would have last year. At least twice as many. And that was perhaps the least of it. They used massive rocket barrages also."

"Rockets?" Drugeth's eyebrows went up. Rockets had long been a weapon in the Ottoman arsenal, but the Turks hadn't used them much in several decades now. The devices were too erratic and temperamental.

"Yes, rockets. They've improved them a great deal, it seems. I was not able to find out many details, unfortunately. I did learn that they are now enclosing them in metal cases and apparently spin them in some fashion. They are said to be more powerful and more accurate."

Spinning rockets . . .

If Janos remembered correctly, the rockets the Jews used against Holk's army when he tried to cross the great bridge in Prague had spun also. The Jews hadn't designed the rockets themselves, though. They'd been provided to them by the notorious up-time revolutionist Sybolt.

Had the Turks somehow gotten their hands on such a rocket? Or the designs for it?

There was no way to know, at the moment. Whatever information existed on the rockets would have to be found in Bohemia—with which Austria was still officially at war, because Ferdinand was being pigheaded about that also. Not much chance Wallenstein would respond to any queries Janos sent him!

"What else?" he asked Grassi. It was obvious from the doctor's expression that there was more bad news coming.

"They have new artillery also. Their own volley guns."

"They've had volley guns since the last century."

Grassi waved his hand. "Yes, I know. Those great cumbersome things with nine barrels. I saw one once, in Istanbul. But these new ones are said to be quite different. Much more like the ones the USE uses."

Wonderful. Janos hadn't faced those weapons in combat himself, but they'd become rather famous over the past year and half. The USE volley guns were credited in most accounts with having broken the French cavalry charge at Ahrensbök.

"And what else?"

"They do in fact have an air force, as I told you they might."

"It needed only this," Janos muttered. "And the nature of it is . . . ?"

"Apparently they have no airplanes like those of the USE's air force. What they have instead are lighter-than-air craft."

"Ah, yes. 'Zeppelins,' I think they're called."

"Not quite, Baron. I investigated the matter and discovered that zeppelins are difficult to make. They're the best such craft, but there are many obstacles to overcome. On the simplest side is what are called 'blimps.' Those have roughly the same elongated shape but the big envelope that lifts them is like that of a balloon—without any internal structure. Just a big bag, basically, filled either with hot air or some kind of light gas."

"So these are blimps, you're saying?"

The doctor held up his hand in a staying gesture. "Give me a moment, please. Somewhere in the middle is a hybrid design. They are only partly rigid, with a much simpler structure than that of a zeppelin properly so-named. They have what amounts to a sort of keel, but most of the bag is left to its own shape. That is apparently what the Ottomans have."

He opened a pouch hanging from his shoulder and dug out some papers. "I have some diagrams here, which I got by bribing a Turk cavalryman. I wouldn't count too much on its precision, because it's just something the man drew from memory. Still, it gives you an idea of what they look like."

Janos spent a couple of minutes studying the diagrams. There was no point spending more time than that, since it was obvious from the drawings themselves that they were only approximations based on memory.

"There is no sense of scale. How big are they?"

Grassi shrugged. "Hard to say. The cavalryman claimed they were enormous, but I imagine a device like that would inevitably seem enormous to someone who'd never seen one before. When I pressed him on the weapons they carried, though, he claimed they only occasionally dropped explosive devices and those were not large ones. Mostly, it seems, the Turk used the things as flying scouts."

Which was quite bad enough. Janos had spent a lot of time over the past few years studying the campaigns and battles fought by the USE—and before it came into existence, by the little nation created by the up-timers in Thuringia, when they first arrived. The New United States, as they'd called it. One of the things that had quickly become obvious to him was how difficult it would be to fight an enemy who always knew where your own forces were because of their aircraft. Except in bad weather, at least. The Poles under Koniecpolski had been successful because they'd been able to take advantage of storms, when the airplanes were grounded.

Possessing aircraft of any type gave an army an enormous advantage, whether or not those aircraft could carry weapons. The real danger the things posed was their extraordinary expansion of an army's reconnaissance capabilities.

He leaned back in his own chair. He was now feeling weary himself, in mind if not in body.

"I'm still puzzled, though." He gestured with a thumb toward one of the windows. That window looked out over the town's main thoroughfare. The window was closed because of the cold, but the sounds of the heavy traffic outside could easily be heard.

"What produced all these refugees?"

Grassi frowned, then rose and went to the window. After studying the scene below for a few seconds, he chuckled softly.

"Those aren't precisely 'refugees,' Baron. They're

not people fleeing their homes ahead of an invading army. They're mostly merchants racing ahead of an invading army to make sure their business concerns aren't jeopardized when the army arrives. That's why they've come so soon, even though they don't expect anything to happen for some time yet. Arranging such business can be time-consuming."

"Ah." That made sense, now that it was explained. There was a fixed season for campaigning, if you were the Turk seeking to march a huge army through the Balkans. That sort of mobilization presupposed enormous numbers of livestock. You couldn't start the march, therefore, until the spring grass was coming up or your horses and oxen would starve.

In the Balkans, once an army got past Belgrade, that meant waiting until early May. So the merchants crowded in the streets out there and packed into the taverns had three months or so to do their preparations.

"I take it they don't have any doubts that the Ottomans plan to attack Vienna next year."

Grassi chuckled again. "Not any, Baron. Neither do I. After such a great victory, the Turk is flushed with pride and ambition. That new young sultan intends to become as famous as Suleiman the Magnificent. More famous, even. And to do that..."

Suleiman had conquered most of Hungary, after the Battle of Mohacs in 1526. That, perhaps more than anything, is what had cemented his reputation as the greatest sultan in the Ottoman line. If Murad IV intended to match him, much less surpass him, he would have to take most of the Austrian empire. Conquer it, not simply defeat it and extract concessions.

Janos rose and came to stand by the window next

to Grassi. In his case, not to study the crowd in the streets but the sky.

"The weather looks to be holding up," he said. "I'll need to leave early on the morrow."

Grassi cleared his throat. "Yes, I thought you would. Back to Vienna, I assume?"

"Yes. I need to speak to the emperor as soon as possible."

"Do you remember the occasion when you offered me sanctuary, should I ever need it?"

Drugeth nodded. "Yes. The time has come, I take it."

"Indeed so. Schmid has disappeared entirely. I have no idea where he is. So has the Dutchman, Haga."

Perhaps even more than Schmid, Cornelis Haga—or van Haag, as he preferred to style himself—was the epitome of an "old Ottoman hand" when it came to European ambassadors to the Sublime Porte. He'd been Holland's ambassador in Istanbul for almost a quarter of a century. If he'd gone into hiding—or been taken in custody by the Turks—then things were getting chancy indeed.

"Is Murad on a rampage?"

Grassi made a face. "Hard to say, with that man. His rages are notorious, but I think at least some of them are feigned. Don't make the mistake of under-estimating him, Baron. He's probably the most capable sultan the Turks have had in a century. He's certainly the most dangerous."

The doctor turned away from the window. "Certainly too dangerous for me, at least for a while. I think my health would be greatly improved by a stay in Vienna."

"Early tomorrow morning, then. This time of year, the weather can also be dangerous."

Chapter 38

Pirna, in southern Saxony

Mike paused the march into Saxony when the Third Division reached Pirna, the first major town north of the border with Bohemia. He'd been driving the men hard and they needed to rest and refit. There was another storm coming across northern Europe, too, and Pirna was the best place in the area for the division to wait for it to pass. In addition to the town itself, there was a large castle nearby—Schloss Sonnenstein—that could hold a number of the division's soldiers. The castle also made an excellent spot for Mike's radio operators to set up. As soon as the storm was over, he wanted to broadcast some messages that were sure to be picked up anywhere in the USE that had a functioning radio.

The time for subterfuge and deception was almost over.

They'd learned of the coming storm from radio messages sent by the military weather stations along the Baltic coast. The air force's stance of official neutrality was now threadbare. Colonel Wood was careful to maintain the needed reconnaissance patrols for Torstensson's two divisions besieging Poznań, and he scrupulously refrained from using any sort of weapons against either Oxenstierna's own forces or the various reactionary paramilitary outfits that had sprung up in many places to counter the CoCs' armed contingents. But he provided Mike with all the reconnaissance he needed and responded to every such request from the Swedish chancellor with silence.

Simpson and the navy were being more scrupulous, still. But Jesse had told Mike that Simpson was moving the two ironclads he had under his control out of Luebeck. For the duration of the crisis he'd keep the SSIM *Constitution* and the SSIM *United States* stationed in Rostock. From that port, he could interdict the Baltic and prevent Oxenstierna from bringing any more troops over from Sweden.

He'd do it, too, Jesse had assured Mike.

"Hey, look, you know John. He's a tight-ass, sure, but you can't actually sharpen pencils in his butt. If Oxenstierna pushes it too far, the admiral will take off the gloves."

How and by what arithmetic Simpson had decided to draw the line that defined "too far" as a major Swedish troop movement across the Baltic wasn't clear to Mike. There weren't all that many soldiers left in Sweden to begin with. Once you subtracted the bare minimum needed to maintain order, Mike doubted if there were more than five or six thousand available to reinforce the twenty thousand soldiers Oxenstierna already had in Berlin.

But he'd take what he could get, with no complaining. He was already heavily outnumbered, after all. Even if you subtracted ten thousand men from the armies Oxenstierna and Banér had due to illness and desertion, the Swedes still had twenty-five thousand men against his ten thousand. Then, add the ten thousand Saxon troops on the Swedish payroll under von Arnim's command in Leipzig. All told, Mike was looking at odds no better than three-to-one and probably closer to four-to-one against him.

That was the bleakest way to look at the matter, though. On the positive side were at least three major factors:

First, every indication was that von Arnim was desperately trying to keep himself out of the fight.

Second, Oxenstierna had the strongest of the three armies—and he was in Berlin, a hundred miles to the north. That was one hundred miles as the crow flies. Swedish mercenaries not being crows, they'd have to travel at least half again that distance in order to bring themselves into play. An army that size would be doing well if they could march an average of fifteen miles a day—in summertime.

And that was the third factor, of course. General Winter. Mike was counting on that most of all. His was the only army of the lot that was really equipped to fight a winter campaign. If he could keep von Arnim penned in Leipzig while he dealt with Banér, he'd then have some time to deal with whatever Oxenstierna threw at him.

The technical expression was "defeat the enemy in detail."

In theory, it sounded great. It remained to be seen how well Mike could carry it out in practice.

There were other factors, too. One of them was standing in front of him this very moment, in the chamber in Schloss Sonnenstein that Mike had set aside for his headquarters.

Georg Kresse himself, along with his chief assistant Wilhelm Kuefer and a young Slovene cavalry officer by the name of Lovrenc Bravnicar. Somehow or other, Kresse's army of irregulars had managed to acquire the services of a troop of professional cavalrymen.

The Vogtlander leader was giving Mike an odd sort of look. Odd, but one that Mike recognized. There was a certain type of German revolutionary who thought that Americans were all a bunch of weak sisters. Too delicate, too squeamish. Nice enough people, but not ones you could count on in the crunch.

Probably best to start there.

"Are you worried that I won't come through?" he asked Kresse. He jerked his thumb over his shoulder. "You think I marched ten thousand men all the way from southern Bohemia in order to make rude noises at the Swedes and then turn around and march back?"

"Ah . . ."

Mike grinned. It was that savage grin that came naturally to him and that he'd perfected in his days as a prizefighter. He'd found it a more effective way to intimidate opponents than snarling or scowling at them. *Oh, I'm going to have so much fun beating the crap out of you, punk.*

"Rest easy, Herr Kresse. There are only a handful of Americans in the Third Division. Granted, the commander is one of them and the division's toughest regiment is commanded by another. But I can assure you that neither I nor Colonel Higgins is much given to doubts and hesitations."

"Ah . . ."

"If it makes you feel any better, people back home thought I was probably a monster."

Kresse's sidekick Kuefer started laughing, then. Not loudly, but these were real laughs, not chuckles.

"Poor Georg!" He slapped Kresse on the back. "He hates having his certain notions upset."

Kresse gave him an irritated look. "Stop clowning around." To Mike he said, "All right, General. We will assume you will make good on your promises."

"I didn't make any promises, Herr Kresse. No general with half a brain makes promises, when it comes to fighting a war. What I explained to you were my *intentions*." He pointed a finger at one of the windows facing north. "I *intend* to drive Banér out of his siege lines around Dresden. I *intend* to defeat him in battle if he chooses to fight. I *intend* to prevent von Arnim from interfering in this little civil war we're having. And I *intend* to do whatever has to be done to deal with Oxenstierna, if he comes out of Berlin."

He paused, staring at Kresse. Not quite challenging him, but close. After a few seconds, he started speaking again.

"What would be helpful here would be a discussion of the various ways you might be able to assist the Third Division in carrying out these intentions."

Kresse nodded abruptly. "Very well. We can certainly provide you with a lot of intelligence. Not as quickly as what you might sometimes get from the air force people, but probably in greater detail."

"Much greater detail," said the Slovene cavalry officer, speaking for the first time since the meeting began. "The pilots can't really tell you much except raw numbers and movement. By now, we've gotten to

know Banér's army quite well. It's like most mercenary
armies. Some units are excellent, many are good, as
many are mediocre, and some aren't worth dog piss.
Those are the sorts of details we can provide you."

His German was fluent and idiomatic. He seemed
to have a slight accent, but that might be Mike's ear
missing a cue rather than anything Bravnicar was saying. Mike's own German was also fluent and idiomatic
by now, and he didn't have a particularly pronounced
accent. Still, it wasn't his native language. He couldn't
necessarily tell when something that sounded like an
accent was just a different dialect or regional speech
pattern. Seventeenth-century German was very far
from being a standardized and homogenized language.

"That would certainly help. What about cutting
the Swedish supply lines, if Banér comes out of the
trenches?"

The Slovene cavalryman waggled his hand back and
forth. "Maybe yes, maybe no. It will depend on a lot
of things. Which unit is guarding the lines and the
weather, most of all. Still, at the very least we can
make their lives a bit miserable and force the pig to
detach units for guard duty."

"The pig," Mike had discovered, was the term that
seemed to be universally used in Saxony to refer to
Johan Banér. By anyone and everyone, from Kresse's
people to street urchins.

"We can also fight in battles," said Kresse. "But
only if you are willing to make accommodations. We
do not have the training or the equipment of regular
soldiers." A bit stiffly, he added, "Nor, being honest,
do most of our men probably have the temperament.
They're not cowards, but..."

Mike nodded. Being a soldier in this day and age, that historical period of gunpowder warfare when the weapons were very powerful but not very accurate, posed some particular challenges. Mental challenges, most of all. A man had to be willing and able to stand shoulder-to-shoulder with his mates on a battlefield, exchanging volleys with an enemy at what amounted to point blank range. It required not simply courage but a sort of almost surrealistic fatalism. Mike wondered sometimes if the rise of Calvinism had been at least partly conditioned by the warfare of the era. About the only mental armor a man could take with him onto such a battlefield was a belief in predestination—and the hope, at least, that God had selected you for His favor.

Kresse's men, on the other hand, were irregulars whose informal training was quite different. They didn't lack courage, but it was a different sort of courage.

"Yes, I understand. If I use you in a battle, it'd be to hold some defensive positions. I wouldn't expect you to be able to maneuver on an open field."

The tone of the meeting warmed up considerably, after that. Mike thought he'd probably passed some sort of test.

Two days later, the storm had passed and it was time to make the transmissions. Jimmy Andersen and his little crew of radio operators had had everything ready for some time, but Mike waited until the evening. He wanted to make the broadcast during the so-called "window," when the conditions were best for radio transmissions.

So, he took a moment to compose himself. Once he made that first transmission, he'd crossed the Rubicon.

Which—he'd looked it up once—was a river so small it would have been considered a mere creek in West Virginia.

"Piss on it," he murmured. "Okay, Jimmy, let's go. The first message is a transmission to Oxenstierna."

> *To Axel Oxenstierna, chancellor of Sweden*
>
> *From Michael Stearns, major general in command of the USE Army Third Division*
>
> *Your behavior over the past three months has become intolerable. I refer specifically to the following acts:*
>
> *First, the illegal detention and imprisonment of the nation's prime minister.*
>
> *Second, the creation of a rump so-called convention that has attempted to usurp the powers of the nation's legitimate Parliament.*
>
> *Third, the sequestration of the injured emperor under conditions of inferior medical care, a deeply suspicious act that smells of treason.*
>
> *Fourth, the imposition of martial law on Saxony and ordering General Banér's assault on Dresden, a peaceful and orderly city, despite the express orders of the province's administrator personally appointed by the emperor.*

Thank you, Ernst Wettin. Mike took a moment to think kind thoughts about a small and unprepossessing nobleman whose integrity dwarfed that of most others of his class.

*Fifth, the commission of atrocities by
Swedish troops against the Saxon populace,
such atrocities including murder, rape, arson,
bodily mutilation and theft.*

Sixth . . .

The list went on for quite some time. The kitchen
sink wasn't there, but only because Mike hadn't been
able to figure out a plausible way to accuse Oxenstierna of stealing it.

He did accuse the chancellor of imperiling the
nation's sanitation measures and increasing the danger
of epidemics, though.

"It's off, General."

"The second message is a transmission to Magdeburg. The first of two, actually."

*To Princess Kristina Vasa, heir to the throne
of the United States of Europe.*

He'd considered adding her titles to the thrones
of Sweden and the High Union of Kalmar as well,
but eventually decided against it. A great deal of the
legalities involved in all this derived from the nature
of Gustav Adolf's triple monarchy. Much of the case
against Oxenstierna, in the end, came down to the
charge that he'd used his position in the Swedish
government to interfere—completely illegally and
with no authorization whatsoever—in the affairs of a
separate nation, the United States of Europe.

Mike saw no advantage to undermining his case by
dragging in two other nations himself. Officially, his

ties to Kristina as a general in the USE army were derived solely from her position in that nation and no other.

Legal folderol, it could be argued. Hadn't Mike himself said publicly that what defined a civil war was the collapse of the rule of law?

Yes, he had. But defining something was not the same as advocating it. From the beginning, his side in this civil war had positioned itself to be the champion of law and proper procedure, and had forced Oxenstierna into the position of being the one overturning the rule of law. That might not count for much in the ranks of Oxenstierna's diehard supporters—it certainly didn't count for much in the minds of diehard CoC members—but it did matter to wide swaths of the German populace. So far, with very few exceptions, the town militias had stayed out of the fight. So had the provincial armies. Mike wanted to keep it that way.

> *Rest assured that the Third Division's loyalty to the Vasa dynasty is not in question. Our quarrel is not with you or with your father. It is with the usurper Oxenstierna and his minions.*

"That's done too, sir."

"Here's the second transmission to Magdeburg."

> *The Third Division commends the prudent actions of the legal representatives of the legitimate Parliament, who have remained at their posts in the nation's legitimate capital of Magdeburg. We give those legal*

members of Parliament the same assurances
we give the crown.

There followed a laundry list of praises heaped
upon just about everybody who'd had the good sense
to stay on the sidelines—not just the Parliament members in Magdeburg but the regional heads of state,
the mayors and councils of the imperial cities, town
militias, etc., etc., etc. This list was even longer than
the denunciations of Oxenstierna.

When he was done, Jimmy flexed his fingers for
a few seconds. He was sending the transmissions in
Morse code as well as vocally. Most of the USE's
radios were still limited to Morse code.

"Okay, sir. What's next?"

"We're almost done. This is the final one. It's a
transmission to General Banér."

To Johan Banér, general in command of
the Swedish army besieging Dresden
From Michael Stearns, major general in
command of the USE Army Third Division
Your assault on Dresden is illegal, immoral,
treasonous, and ungodly.

Mike thought the "ungodly" part was a nice touch.
Being an agnostic himself, he had no idea how you'd
parse the theology involved. But the Germanies were
crawling with theologians. Within twenty-four hours of
the transmission there'd probably be at least two compet-
ing and hostile schools of doctrine. Within forty-eight
hours, charges of heresy were sure to be thrown about.

*You have forty-eight hours to remove your
troops from the siege lines around Dresden.
Seventy-two hours after that, your troops
must have departed Saxony and returned
to the Oberpfalz, where you can employ
them to fight Bavarian invaders instead of
murdering German civilians.*

*I will expect an answer within twenty-
four hours indicating your agreement to
these conditions. Failing such an answer,
I propose to move immediately upon your
works.*

The last clause was swiped from Ulysses Grant's
terms at Fort Donelson, if he remembered his history properly. Mike thought the words had a nice
ring to them.

The entire message was designed to make Banér blow
his stack. There was no chance the Swedish general
would agree to end the siege of Dresden, no matter
how Mike put the matter. So he figured he might as
well see if he could so enrage the man—Banér's temper
was notorious—that he'd make some mistakes.

There was probably some term derived from Latin
to describe the tactic in military parlance. Street kids
playing a pick-up basketball game would call it "trash
talk." Mike had used the same term in his boxing days.

You never knew. Sometimes it worked.

"Anything else, sir?" Jimmy asked.

"No," he said. "I think that will do."

Chapter 39

Swedish army siege lines, outside Dresden

"I'll kill him!" Johan Banér roared. "I'll kill him!"

The Swedish general had already torn the message to shreds. Now he picked up the stool he'd been sitting on when he was handed the message and smashed it down on the writing desk. If his adjutant hadn't been sensible enough to retreat as soon as he'd handed over the radio slip, his own skull would probably have been the stool's target.

Banér was not a particularly large man, but he was quite powerful. That blow and the ones that followed with the leg of the shattered stool that remained in his fist were enough to reduce the desk to firewood.

"I'll fucking kill him!"

Chapter 40

Dresden, capital of Saxony

Eric and Tata found Gretchen Richter standing in the tallest tower of the Residenzschloss, looking out over the city walls toward the Swedish camp fires. They'd gone in search of her to discover what preparations she wanted made, now that they knew the Third Division was coming.

Night had fallen and it was quite dark in the tower, with only one small lamp to provide light. So it took them a while before they realized that Gretchen had been crying. No longer—but the tear-tracks were still quite visible.

Krenz was dumbfounded. He'd never once imagined Richter with tears in her eyes.

Tata went to her side. Gretchen was gripping the rail with both hands. Tata placed a hand over hers and gave it a little squeeze. "It's nice when people don't disappoint you."

"I wondered," Eric heard Gretchen whisper. "For years, I wondered."

It took Krenz perhaps a minute before he figured it out. At which point he was even more dumbfounded.

She'd wondered about the *general*?

Dear God in Heaven.

One of the letters Eric had gotten from Thorsten Engler after he was wounded at Zwenkau described the execution of twenty soldiers who'd been caught committing atrocities after the Third Division took the Polish town of Świebodzin. Thorsten's volley gun battery had been given that assignment.

Till the day I die, I'll never forget seeing those men tied to a fence being torn apart by a hail of bullets, Thorsten had written him. *But that's not what I have nightmares about, Eric. It was the look on the general's face when he gave the order. A cold, pitiless rage that seemed to have no bottom at all.*

Gretchen wiped her nose with a sleeve. "Always I wondered," she whispered again.

Eric looked out over the Swedish campfires.

Banér was already dead. He just didn't know it yet.

Chapter 41

Magdeburg, central Germany
Capital of the United States of Europe

Rebecca looked at the little stack of radio messages on her desk, wondering if she should read them again.

That was silly, though. By now, she practically had them memorized. Her desire to do so was just an emotional reflex.

Sepharad came into the room, with her brother Baruch in tow.

"Barry wants to know when Daddy's coming home."

Despite the tension of the moment, Rebecca had to fight down a smile. For whatever subtle reasons lurked in a child's developing mind, Sepharad made it a point to pose as the detached and coolheaded one—quite unlike her emotional brother, full of needs and anxieties. If you didn't know any better, you'd think she was the one who'd written the *Ethics* and the *Tractatus Theologico-Politicus* in the universe her father had come from.

"Soon, I think, children. Soon."

The answer was accurate, as far as it went. Michael

would come home soon. If he came home at all. But Rebecca saw no reason to inflict three-year-old children with that caveat.

Within an hour after dawn the next morning, the town house was filled with anxious and needy politicians. Most of them, in a way, wanting the answer to the same question. Except in their case the question was *when will the boss be coming home?* Michael had been such a dominant figure in their political movement that, at least in a crisis, most of them felt a bit lost without him.

Constantin Ableidinger was one of the exceptions, thankfully. Rebecca was finding his outsized presence a great help this morning.

"Of course he decided to march on Dresden, Albert!" the Franconian was booming at Hamburg's mayor. "Did you think we could maintain this half-baked civil war forever? Everyone—on both sides; no, on all sides!—is starting to get exhausted. Let this go on for too long and the nation will wind up siding with the damn Swede by default. If you ask me, the general chose the perfect moment to make his move. Right on the heels of Kristina and Ulrik's arrival in the capital. He has the wind of legitimacy in his sails now!"

Rebecca thought that was a rather grotesque metaphor, but she agreed with Ableidinger's underlying point. The nation *was* starting to get frayed by the constant uncertainty.

And now, as he had so many times over the past few years, the Prince of Germany was taking the decisive steps to resolve the crisis. That decisiveness alone would pull millions of the nation's inhabitants toward him, regardless of what they might think of the specific merits of his political program.

In the royal palace not far away, another child was feeling anxious.

"What should we do, Ulrik?" asked Kristina. The girl was almost literally dancing up and down, with a sheaf of radio messages clutched in her little fist.

"We do nothing, Kristina." Ulrik tried to figure out the best way to explain the matter. Then, as he had done so many times before, came to the conclusion that with Kristina it was best to just give her the same explanation he'd give an adult. An intelligent adult. She wouldn't quite understand, perhaps, but she'd know she wasn't being condescended to—which invariably threw her into a fury.

"Your role as the monarch in this situation is to *be*, not to *do*." He pointed to the messages she was holding. "That's why General Stearns was careful to stipulate his loyalty to the crown."

Kristina frowned, while she thought it through. After a while, she sighed.

"I'd rather be doing something," she complained. "I'm feeling nervous. And I don't like it. It's always better if I'm doing something."

Caroline Platzer cleared her throat. Kristina's mentor/confidant/governess was sitting on a nearby divan. She and Baldur Norddahl had finally arrived in Magdeburg a few days ago, having taken much slower means of transportation from Luebeck.

Ulrik gave her a quick, appreciative glance. "In that case, Princess, I think you should visit your subjects," he said. "They'll be feeling nervous today as well."

Now, Kristina *did* start literally jumping up and down. "Oh, yes! Oh, yes! That's a wonderful idea, Ulrik! Where should we go first?"

Had it been necessary, Ulrik would have guided her to the right destination. But it wasn't. Whether due to innate Vasa political instinct or simply childish enthusiasm, Kristina settled on the correct answer within seconds.

So, off they went. And if there was anyone in Magdeburg on that cold, clear day in February of 1636 who thought it was odd to see a large contingent of Marines in very fancy uniforms escorting the nation's princess into the city's central Freedom Arches, they said nothing about it.

The Marines probably thought it was odd—especially when Kristina told them to take off their shakos ("against sanitary regulations when working in a kitchen") so they could help her with the cooking.

She even dragooned Ulrik and Baldur into helping her with the cooking. And Caroline, of course.

Platzer seemed quite at home in a kitchen, but Ulrik was well-nigh useless. He couldn't recall ever cooking a meal in his entire life, much less preparing meals for dozens of customers. (Which soon became hundreds of customers, as the word spread.)

Baldur wasn't much better. "They don't have any salted fish," he complained. Norwegians had certain definite limits.

But their skills didn't matter. Neither did Kristina's, which weren't really any better despite the girl's own delusions. Magdeburg's central Freedom Arches was the premier such establishment in the whole of the

United States of Europe. Its kitchen was huge, its cooking staff large and very experienced. They had no trouble making up for the royal errors.

The customers in the large eating rooms didn't care in the least. They weren't flocking to the place this morning to ingest food, they were flocking to ingest symbols.

Darmstadt, Province of the Main

By noon, the entire city council had gathered at the Rathaus. So had every guildmaster in the city and the leading figures of every prominent wealthy family. The tavern in the basement was packed.

The mayor read through all the radio messages again, for the benefit of the late arrivals. When he was finished, there was silence for perhaps ten seconds. Then the head of the city militia drained his stein and slammed it down on the table. Almost hard enough to break the thick glass. As it was, everyone sitting at that table jumped in their seats a little.

"Well, fuck!" he exclaimed.

One of the city councilmen sitting at the mayor's table gave him a sour look. "Oh, give it up, Gerlach. It's over."

The militia commander scowled at him. "He'll probably get beaten. He's an amateur. Banér is as good as they come."

"Banér is a Swedish pig," said the master of the coopers' guild. "Besides, what difference does it make? Listen to them out there."

Even through the thick walls of the Rathaus, the chants of the crowd marching through the streets outside were quite audible.

Prince of Germany! Prince of Germany!

"All of my apprentices are out there," continued the guildmaster. "So is every single one of my journeymen except Ehrlichmann, and the only reason he's still at home is because he's sick. Even if Stearns loses and Banér kills him, he just becomes the national martyr. Remember how many damn streets and squares they named after Hans Richter, after he got killed? How many do you think they'll name after the Prince?"

He took a pull from his own stein. "Gunther's right. It's over."

There was silence again, for a moment.

"Well, fuck," said the militia commander. But his tone was one of resignation now, not anger.

Augsburg, one of the USE's seven independent imperial cities

As ever, the commander of Augsburg's militia had a very different viewpoint from his counterpart in Darmstadt.

"The rest of you can do as you like," he said to the city council. His gaze swept around the table, his lip curled in a sneer.

"I'm going out there to join the parade." He pointed toward a window. The sounds of the celebration outside came right through, closed or not.

Prince of Germany! Prince of Germany!

"And I'm taking the whole militia with me. Me and my boys are sick of the damn Swedes."

And off he went.

After a while, one of the council members stood up. "I'm sick of them too, now that I think about it."

And off he went.

After a while longer, Jeremias Jacob Stenglin rose from his own chair. "Come on, fellows." The head of the city council headed for the door. "The way people have their tempers up, if we don't show we'll never get elected to anything again. Under any kind of franchise."

A tavern in Melsungen, in the province of Hesse-Kassel

"Here's to the health of our landgravine!" shouted one of the revelers, holding up his stein of beer. "Long may she reign!"

The tavern was full, as it often was on a winter's eve. Not a single stein failed to come up to join the toast.

Another reveler stood up, hoisting his stein. "And here's to the Prince of Germany! May he whip that Swede like a cur!"

Not a single stein failed to come up to join that toast either. Or the seven that followed it, each succeeding one wishing a worse fate still upon Johan Banér. By the eighth toast, the revelers had him flayed, drawn, quartered, fed to hogs—and the hogs were dying of poison.

A tavern on the coast of the Pomeranian Bay

The fisherman sat down at the table in the corner where his shipmates were waiting. "Believe it or not, there's someone who admits to voting against the Prince."

The fisherman's two companions gave him a skeptical

look. "Who?" asked one, as he lifted his stein. "Josias, the village idiot?"

The fisherman who'd made the claim shook his head. "No. It's old Margarete, the baker's widow."

His two companions frowned.

"The Prince shouldn't have let women have the vote," said one.

The other nodded. "Yah. I almost didn't vote for him myself, because of that."

Leipzig

General Hans Georg von Arnim read through the message again. That was just to give himself time to think, not because he had any trouble understanding it. Chancellor Oxenstierna had been brief, blunt, very clear—and quite obviously irate.

"I thought the radio was broken," he said.

The adjutant who'd brought him the message from Berlin shook his head. "No, sir. It's working properly."

"I thought the radio was broken," von Arnim repeated.

The general's adjutants were not chosen for being stupid. It didn't take Captain Pfaff more than three seconds before the head-shake became a nod.

"Why, yes, it is, General. The operator tells me it'll take days to fix."

"At least a week, I think."

"Yes, a week."

"See to it, Captain."

After Pfaff left, von Arnim moved to the fireplace. His servants had a big fire going, which was quite pleasant on such a cold day.

It made a handy incinerator, too. The message was gone in seconds.

Oxenstierna would have sent a courier, of course. No one except up-timers—and not all that many of them—relied entirely on the new radios. But it would take a courier days to make it here from Berlin, this time of year. The recent storm had left the roads filled with snow. Such as they were, in benighted Brandenburg.

Von Arnim would have no choice but to acknowledge receipt of that message. Still, mobilizing ten thousand men was not a quick process, especially in February. By the time he could get his army onto the field to join Banér's, anything might have happened.

Banér could be dead. Stearns could be dead. Both could be dead. The chancellor could be dead. The emperor could have regained his wits.

A horse might even have learned to sing.

Paris, capital of France

After he finished reading the copies of the intercepted radio messages that Servien had given him, Cardinal Richelieu rose from his desk and went over to one of the windows in his palace.

"A real pity," said Servien, echoing the sentiment he'd expressed a month earlier.

Richelieu said nothing. He didn't agree with his *intendant*, as it happened. It might be better to say, he was feeling a different sort of pity this morning.

Pity poor France. What had the great nation done to so offend God, that he inflicted Monsieur Gaston upon it?

And an even greater mystery: What had the wretched Germanies done to gain His favor, that He would bless them with such a prince?

Madrid, capital of Spain

There was no reaction to Mike Stearns' radio messages in the court of Spain.

They had no radio. They wouldn't receive the news for days yet.

Brussels, capital of the Netherlands

Fernando I looked around the conference table at his closest advisers.

"We're all agreed, then?" said the king in the Netherlands. "We will still take no advantage of the current civil conflict in the USE, even now when it's coming to a full boil?"

"With Stearns on a rampage?" said Rubens. "Risky, that."

"He's badly outnumbered," pointed out Scaglia. "Outclassed, too, in terms of experience."

Miguel de Manrique shook his head. "The numbers probably aren't as bad as they look, Alessandro. And in that sort of fight—it'll be a slugging match, fighting in the snow in February—his army will have a great advantage when it comes to morale. I agree with Pieter. It's too risky. If Stearns wins, we'll have a bear to deal with."

"And to what purpose?" chipped in Archduchess

Isabella. The old woman's expression was even more skeptical than Miguel's. "We've done quite well so far. Minor gains, all of them, yes. But they came with no real risk and they're solid. Leave it be."

The king had listened attentively, but that was simply to be courteous. He'd already made his decision the night before, while discussing the matter with his wife. Maria Anna was as bold an adviser as any he had—and even she had urged the path of caution.

"We're all agreed, then," he stated. "We'll just wait to see what happens."

Poznań, Poland

"The king is still adamant, and the Sejm even more so," said Stanislaw Koniecpolski. The grand hetman shrugged massive shoulders. "They'll have no talk of a peace settlement. There's no point in raising the issue any longer."

Lukasz Opalinski's jaws were tight.

Stupid, stupid, stupid, stupid. As every day passed, it became clearer and clearer to him that his friend Jozef Wojtowicz had been right all along. If Stearns had the two divisions of the USE army out there in the siege lines around Poznań to add to his own, he would win this civil war easily. And everyone knew—well, perhaps not every szlachta voting in the Sejm, as pig-ignorant as so many of them were—that Stearns had been opposed to the war with Poland from the start.

It could be argued, of course, that Torstensson would stand in the way. But Lukasz didn't think even Torstensson could keep his men under control, if

Stearns summoned them. The Poles had quite good intelligence on what was happening in Torstensson's army, from all the Polish civilians employed by that army. The USE troops were restive and getting more so by the day. They'd even presented a petition to Torstensson three days ago, urging him to march on Berlin and restore the rightful prime minister.

The only thing that really enabled Torstensson to keep them under control any longer was...

The Poles. The stance of King Wladyslaw IV and the Sejm of the commonwealth.

What had poor Poland done, to so offend the Almighty that he visited seven years of stupidity upon the nation? Followed by seven years of idiocy, another seven of imbecility, yet another seven of cretinism— all that coming after seven years of dull-wittedness, preceded by seven years of struggling to count toes, seven years...

He wondered what had happened to Jozef. Was he still in Dresden? If so, was he still alive? They had heard nothing from him in weeks, since the batteries in his radio died.

Chapter 42

Dresden, capitol of Saxony

As he had in his first interview with the woman, Jozef Wojtowicz was finding Gretchen Richter unsettling. You'd think eyes that were colored a sort of light brown would be warm by nature, but hers weren't. Not, at least, when she was studying you while trying to squeeze out the truth.

The scariest thing about the whole situation was that she wasn't even *suspicious*. She wasn't trying to uncover duplicity or treachery or misdoings on Jozef's part, she was just trying to ferret out the truth about his military skills. Jozef hated to think what the woman would be like if she was running an actual inquisition. She'd terrify Torquemada. Either that, or turn him green with envy.

"You still seem hesitant, Jozef," she was saying. "I do not understand why."

He raised his hands in a gesture of frustration, as if he'd been about to raise them high in despair but then managed to control himself.

"You just don't *understand*." He blew out a breath.

"Yes, I have pretty much all of the separate skills of a hussar. To start with, I'm an excellent horseman. Better than a lot of hussars, actually. Then, I am quite good with a sword—a cavalry saber, at least. Not so much with a side sword and not at all with a rapier or a schiavona because those are—"

He waved his hand irritably. Richter's face creased into a thin smile. "Because those are silly things useless in a battle. Good only for duels. And you're not a duelist, leaving aside the occasional drunken brawl."

He cleared his throat. "No, I'm not." *A fairly good assassin, though, and I'm handy with any sort of dagger . . .*

Seemed like an unwise thing to add, under the circumstances. "Contraindicated" was the up-time term, according to Ted Szklenski, who was addicted to the damn things.

"I'm also a fair hand with a lance. Either the big ones favored by hussars or the lighter styles preferred by Tatars."

"What about guns?"

A fairly good assassin, like I said. No, didn't say. Any sane assassin would rather shoot a man in the back than stab him. Which I can do with just about any kind of pistol ever made. Wheel lock, new style flintlock, any sort of up-time revolver or pistol—I can handle any of them.

Also seemed contraindicated.

"Fair enough. Especially with pistols. Cavalrymen—that's how I was trained—don't have much use for any other sort of firearms."

She nodded. "So what's the problem, then?"

"I can do all the separate parts of being a hussar,

but it's not the same thing as actually *being* one. Gretchen, that takes *practice*. Riding a horse well is one thing and using a saber well is one thing. Doing them both at the same time—especially while people are shooting at you and trying to stab you—is another thing altogether."

Again, he made that up-raised hands gesture. More with resignation this time than frustration. "Look, I was a bastard. I got the training but I never really got accepted. So I turned my hand to other things."

"What things? Now that I think about it, you've never made clear how you made a living."

"Various . . . things. Most of them involved running errands for the Koniecpolskis."

Including running their spy network. Also contra-indicated.

"Some of those errands weren't all that respectable," he added. Covering up political misdeeds with merely criminal or immoral ones was a time-honored tactic for secret agents.

Richter cocked her head. "Somehow I have a hard time picturing you as a pimp."

He tightened his jaws. *Damn the woman.* She was even a Catholic, at least in her upbringing. Why couldn't the Spanish Inquisition have recruited her and gotten her out of his hair?

Because they didn't recruit women, was one obvious answer. They didn't recruit revolutionaries either, was another. Rather the opposite, actually.

Richter straightened up from the table. "All right, I'll let it go. That's not really any of my business. Here's what it comes down to, Jozef."

She nodded toward Eric Krenz. The lieutenant

wasn't actually "in command" of the city's garrison. He was more like the first among equals of the dozen or so lieutenants from the regular USE army who acted as a command staff. Command college might almost be a better way of putting it. Nonetheless, whenever Gretchen needed to consult an individual officer, it was usually Krenz. That might partly be due to his relationship with Richter's close associate Tata, of course. But Wojtowicz allowed that the man did seem competent in his own right.

"Eric tells me that we may need to make a sortie at some point. It's now clear that Banér is going to challenge Stearns in the field. He's starting to pull his mercenaries out of the trenches."

Jozef felt alarmed. "*Now?* Gretchen, Banér is almost certain to be expecting a sortie while he carries out such an evolution."

Richter's expression became a little sarcastic. "No real military skills? Yet you seem very familiar with all this."

Jozef flushed a little. "Fine!" he snapped, "You can't spend any time at all with Koniecpolskis without picking up a lot. Those people talk tactics over breakfast, starting at the age of four. My point remains—this is *not* a time to be talking about making a sortie. Banér will be ready for it."

"Oh, relax," said Krenz. "I'm not stupid. Stupid officers don't last in the Third Division. The general is relaxed about a lot of things, but he'll shitcan an incompetent officer very quickly."

The term *shitcan* was English, blended in smoothly and perfectly with the German that made up the rest of the sentence. That was how Amideutsch worked.

"We're not planning any sorties right now," Krenz continued. "We may never even do one at all. But we want to be ready in case the general does what we think he's going to do. Try to do, anyway."

"And that is...?" Jozef was skeptical that a commanding general with as little experience as Stearns was planning *any* sort of tactic, much less a subtle one.

Krenz apparently sensed the skepticism. He smiled a bit crookedly. "You don't really understand the general. Professional soldiers usually don't—and spare me the lecture about being not-really-a-hussar, Wojtowicz. You know a lot more than any civilian would, that's obvious."

Jozef decided to ignore that. "Please enlighten me, then."

"The general knows he isn't an experienced commander, so he relies on his staff for that. What he does himself is bear down on those things he does understand and know how to do."

"Such as?"

"He's the best organizer you'll ever meet and—this is rare as hen's teeth, in your circles—he actually gives a damn about his soldiers."

Jozef started to say something and then stopped. Protesting the skills in that area of Stanislaw Koniecpolski was also contraindicated.

Still, he must have flushed, because Eric's not-quite-a-sneering-lip curled further. "And I'm not talking about the way a good noble general will respect and appreciate his soldiers' valor and morale, either. I'm talking about *socks*."

"About...what?"

Eric pointed to his feet. "Socks. And boots. All

that sort of mundane and unromantic stuff. Do you know what the disease rate is, in the Third Division?

He didn't wait for an answer—which Jozef wouldn't have been able to provide anyway.

"The Third Division has better health than any division in the USE army. And the USE army has better health than any other army in the world. Do you know how fast the Third Division can march?"

Again, he didn't wait for the answer. "Faster than any other division in the USE army. A *lot* faster, in fact. Everyone else—our own people as much as the enemy—keeps being surprised at how soon we show up somewhere. And do you know why?"

He pressed right on. Even if he'd wanted to, Jozef couldn't have squeezed in a word.

"Because the men always have good boots. *All* the men *always* have good boots, with plenty of spares. Socks, too. The horses are always shod. *All* the horses *always* get shod, whenever they need it. The wagon wheels are always in good shape, and there are plenty of spares if something breaks. A wheel breaks, it gets fixed right then and there. Same for an axle. D'you me want to go on? I could, believe me."

Finally, he slowed down enough to take a deep breath. "The point's this, Mr. Hussar-who-isn't. You have no idea what a military force is really capable of, when it's *organized*. The general won't even try to match Banér, maneuvering on a nice open field. That's why he launched his campaign in the middle of February. What general in his right mind wants to fight in the teeth of winter? I'll tell you—a general who knows his enemy has more experience but his soldiers don't have boots that are worth a shit. Whose

soldiers have a crappy morale because they're mercenaries and no mercenary in his right mind wants to
fight a winter campaign. I know the general. Right
now, he's probably praying for another snowstorm—
because that's when he'll attack Banér."

"But . . ." Jozef was half-appalled and—by now—
half-fascinated. "How will he control his troops, in
a snowstorm?"

"Never heard of radios? Of course, you have. By
now, everyone's heard of radios. Even you Poles use
them, I've heard. But you don't have that many of
them, do you? And the ones you do have, you don't
use very well, do you? Because you don't really think
that way, do you?"

The lieutenant shrugged. "But the general won't even
be counting so much on his radios. He'll be counting on the fact that if he tells his men to fight in a
snowstorm, they will damn well fight in a snowstorm—
and they'll fight to win. They'll come right at Banér's
thugs, marching in good boots and not freezing half to
death. Most of all, they won't care so much whether
they're being maneuvered properly because they're
not thinking that way in the first place. That Swedish bastard damn well needs to be put down, and
the Third Division will damn well do it. Right here,
right now. And then what happens?"

Jozef finally saw where he was going. "Banér's
men will start coming back into their lines. Whether
Banér wants them to or not." He frowned. "That'll
only happen, though, if your fellow Stearns maneuvers
at least well enough to keep them against the river."

Krenz's sneer was now open. "I said the general
didn't hold much with fancy maneuvers. I didn't say

he couldn't tell the difference between north, south, east and west. Don't worry, Wojtowicz." He pointed out one of the windows. "We've talked it over—all of us regular army lieutenants, I mean—and we're pretty sure that's what the general will try to do. He might not do it exactly that way, of course. Nobody can predict the weather, just for starters. But we're sure he'll do something like that. Which means that one way or another, sooner or later, Banér is most likely going to try to regroup by using his existing siege lines as defensive works. And *that's* when we'd do a sortie. When he's least expecting it because he's preoccupied with the Third Division, and when it'd do the most good."

Jozef thought about it, while running fingers through his hair. He couldn't deny there was a certain . . .

Well, not charm, exactly. But the young USE lieutenant's enthusiasm was infectious. All the more so because Jozef knew Krenz well enough to know that the man was not given to thoughtless martial enthusiasms. He tended to be a skeptic about the military virtues, in fact. Not derisive as such, but not entirely respectful either.

If someone like Krenz was this full of confidence—even eagerness—when it came to fighting Banér's professionals . . .

Suddenly, all of Jozef's hesitations and misgivings vanished. No doubt there was something truly absurd about the Polish grand hetman's spymaster leading a charge for USE rebels, but he no longer cared. He *had* been trained as a hussar, and apparently there was still a small hurt lurking in his heart that he'd never been allowed that honor. Koniecpolski had never treated him like a bastard in his personal dealings, but he had used Jozef that way in professional terms. Always keeping him in the shadows.

How many hussars had led a sortie to relieve a city under siege, in the middle of a pitched battle on which the fate of an entire nation pivoted?

Not too damn many. His friend Lukasz certainly hadn't done it.

"All right, fine," he said. "I'll organize your sortie, in case the opportunity comes. But—!"

He raised a stiff, admonishing finger. "We're not hussars. Bunch of damn fools, I know them well. There is no way I'm going to lead a charge of horsemen across snow, much less a frozen river—certainly not in a snowstorm! If I did make it across, I'd be the only one. No, no, no."

He gave Krenz a beaming grin. "We'll adopt the methods of your precious General Stearns. Snowshoes, that's the trick. Skis too, maybe, for those men good on them. But they'd have to be designed so they can be removed easily. You can't fight on skis. Not amidst trenches, anyway, which is where we'd be."

He turned to Gretchen. "Can you organize that? And we'll need grenades more than anything. Lots and lots and lots of grenades."

From the look on her face, he thought he was about to be inflicted with another be-damned up-time expression.

"Don't teach your grandmother how to suck eggs," she said.

Sure enough. The worst thing about the up-time saws was that they usually made no sense. Why would a grandmother suck eggs to begin with?

Can't tell the difference between a hawk and a handsaw. Oh, nonsense. A toddler could tell the difference between a bird in the sky and a hand tool.

You can't have your cake and eat it, too. Well, of course not. But what's the point? Why would anyone want a cake *except* to eat it?

A penny saved is a penny earned. Blithering nonsense. A penny saved was money already obtained whereas a penny earned came in the future. How could a people who had travelled through time not understand the difference between the past and the future?

And so it went. On and on. *The early bird gets the worm.* Idiotic. Did they think mindless worms had—what did they call those miserable devices? Ah, yes, alarm clocks. And why would they, even if they did have minds? Worms lived underground. It was *always* dark down there.

On and on. *Haste makes waste.* Did—

"Jozef?" said Gretchen. "If there a problem? You seem preoccupied."

"Ah . . . No. There is no problem. A sortie you want, a sortie you'll get."

Chapter 43

The Saxon plain, near Dresden

Jimmy Andersen had an apologetic look on his face when he handed Mike the radio slip. "More good weather, sir."

Mike nodded, took the slip and gave it a glance—sure enough: *No storm fronts in sight or reported*—and tucked it away in a pocket of his jacket. He kept his face expressionless. There were some drawbacks to being a commanding general. You couldn't crumble up such a message, hurl it to the ground and stomp on it while cursing the fates.

He wished he could.

For one thing, it was *cold*—as cloudless days with blue skies usually were in the middle of winter. A good snowfall would bring a blanket of warmth with it. Well...not "warmth," exactly, but it would blunt the edge of this icy air.

Thank God for the jackets and trousers. As far as Mike was concerned, David Bartley was worth his weight in gold. Figuratively speaking, anyway. In literal terms, the youngster was probably worth a lot more than his weight in gold.

The whole division felt the same way. Mike was monitoring the sentiments of his soldiers carefully, not just through the chain of command and what his officers told him but through a separate network that ran through Jeff Higgins and the CoC organizers that he was in touch with.

There were lots of those in the division, as there were in almost any large unit of soldiers in the USE's army. There were some in the navy and the air force, too, but not nearly as many. The army was where the political radicals were concentrated.

CoC organizers and activists in the Third Division had a peculiar relationship with Jeff Higgins. On his own, Jeff was not and had never been a prominent figure in the Committees of Correspondence. His status in that regard was almost entirely due to being Gretchen Richter's husband. That meant that he was trusted, of course, but it didn't necessarily mean his political judgment was particularly respected.

But his status with CoC people in the division was more complicated, because by now Jeff had a lot of prestige as an officer. Just about every CoC and CoC-influenced soldier considered Higgins the best regimental commander in the division, hands down, and at least half of the other soldiers agreed with them. That was partly a function of the Hangman's reputation; partly a function of the Hangman's history; partly the result of the battle of Zielona Góra, where the Hangman had borne the brunt of the fighting; and partly because of Jeff's reputation for using egalitarian command methods.

The end result was that Jeff had his own network through the CoC organizers, which he maintained at

Mike's request. That gave Mike a binocular view of the morale of his troops, something few officers ever had.

And the morale was good. Very, very good. The troops knew what his plans were, at least in broad outline. But "broad outline" was about all that Mike had himself. *Maneuver; keep away from Banér until the weather turns sour; then go right at him*—that pretty well summed it up.

They'd been at the first stage of that for three days now, since Banér pulled his troops out of the siege lines. Mike had been worried, at first, that days of marching and avoiding combat would sap his soldiers' confidence. But, it hadn't. Most of his troops were veterans and they understood how much of a toll the maneuvers would be taking on their counterparts in Banér's army. Except those sorry bastards wouldn't have good winter equipment. Some of them would literally be marching in rags, including on their feet.

In two feet of snow, temperatures that were well below freezing, and enough of a breeze every day to produce a significant wind chill.

The whole experience was weird, to Mike. Almost surrealistic. It was like waging a war in mud, or while encased in gelatin. Everything moved unbelievably slowly.

Both armies knew exactly where the other one was. Mike got regular reports from the air force, which maintained reconnaissance patrols over the area at least twice a day. He also got reports from his own scouts—most of those, ski patrols—as well as from Kresse's irregulars.

Banér had a lot of cavalrymen, including Finn light cavalry that he used for scouts. The Finns were accustomed to the cold and, in their own way, were well prepared for it. They kept a distance from Mike's troops, after a couple of clashes had proved to them that light cavalry were no match for well-disciplined infantry armed with rifled muskets. But they had no trouble getting close enough to provide Banér with regular intelligence as to the Third Division's whereabouts.

And... in a way, it didn't matter. What difference did it make if two armies knew each other's whereabouts, when neither one of them could move much faster than five miles a day?

Mike's troops had something of an advantage, in that respect, because of their superior equipment and morale. But that just meant they could move six or seven miles in a day. Equipment and morale only took you so far, faced with some crude physical realities.

Two feet of snow was two feet of snow. When your only method of transportation was leg muscles—yours or a horse's—you didn't move that fast. Not one man—and certainly not ten thousand. When temperatures were this cold, you had to move carefully and take a lot of rest. You'd damn well better eat, plenty and regularly. Armies of thousands of men with seventeenth-century equipment do not zip in and out of fast food joints. Just cooking and eating took hours, and if you skipped those tasks too often you would quickly find yourself in a world of hurt.

The supply trains were taxed even worse. They depended heavily on oxen, and oxen do not move quickly even in summertime. And while large powerful animals like oxen and horses could plow through snow more easily than men could, the corollary was that the huge critters *ate* a lot more. For every ten pounds of food hauled to the front lines, eight or nine were going to be eaten by the livestock—and you couldn't shave that very much, or your livestock started dying on you.

You could forget about "living off the countryside." Saxony had been sheltered enough from the wars of the past seventeen years that an army might be able to do that in the summer and fall. But not February.

Slow, slow, slow. *Everything* moved slowly.

Johan Banér was in a good mood today. His mood had been improving every day since they pulled away from Dresden.

So had the mood of his soldiers. Siege lines were miserable. Maneuvering in the open in the middle of winter was miserable too, of course, but it was a different sort of misery. As long as it didn't last too long, it was a pleasant relief. Well, not "pleasant," exactly. "Less unpleasant," perhaps.

At first, Banér had been worried that Stearns might retreat south to the Vogtland. That would have been his most sensible course of action. But he'd moved his army to the west, instead, circling Dresden rather than escaping from it. By now, the two armies were approaching the town of Ostra, originally founded by Sorbians.

Again, Stearns was surprising Banér. Had he been the American swine, Banér would have passed to the west of Ostra, but Stearns looked to be passing east of it. If he did, he'd have his army almost at the outskirts of Dresden.

Banér would follow him, wherever the bastard went. That would get difficult, if Stearns chose to flee into more open country. Grudgingly, after several days of maneuvering, Banér had accepted the fact that Stearns' troops could move faster than his own. Not much faster, but no one moved quickly in winter.

So far, that hadn't made a difference, because Stearns was such a novice that he'd wasted his advantage by circling Dresden. That gave Banér the advantage of interior lines since he'd begun the maneuvering just outside of the city. As Stearns had moved west, Banér had been able to keep his own forces in step, just a mile or two closer to Dresden.

That was the fumbling of a neophyte—either that, or stupid arrogance. Either way, once Banér could come to grips with him, Stearns was done.

Done as in dead. Banér had received private orders from Oxenstierna the day before, sent in code over the radio. However it was done, the chancellor wanted Stearns removed completely from the political arena. Killed in battle would be best, but "shot while trying to escape" would do well enough. If need be, Stearns could hang himself in a cell in a fit of despondency after he was captured.

The instructions had been another example of Oxenstierna's annoying habit of lecturing people on the obvious. Banér had had no intention of letting Stearns survive. Had the chancellor instructed him to do the opposite, he would have ignored the instructions. The American troublemaker had been a plague in Europe for quite long enough.

Berlin, capital of Brandenburg

Axel Oxenstierna finished pulling on his gloves. "How much longer, then?"

Colonel Reinhold Wunsch pursed his lips. "It's a bit hard to say, Chancellor. The problem is rounding up enough wagons. We've got the horses and oxen we need."

Oxenstierna nodded. "We're in Brandenburg. Miserable place. I'm not surprised there's a shortage of wagons. So how much more time will you need?"

"Another two days, at least. More likely to be three."

"That should be soon enough. We're not really in a hurry and won't be until we get word from Banér that Stearns is dealt with. The way the up-timer is evading battle, that's likely to take several more days. But at that point, Colonel—" His expression became stern. "I want the army ready to march, and no excuses. I want to be on the outskirts of Magdeburg by no later than the Ides of March."

"You're planning to take the whole army, then."

"Beyond a regiment I'll leave here to maintain order, yes. There's nothing in Magdeburg you could call a real army, and they've been negligent when it comes to fortifying the city. Still, they have a lot of industry and they'll have their backs to the wall. And they're fanatics to begin with. So I don't expect taking the city will be that easy."

The chancellor's face was stiff and cold. Wunsch didn't have any doubt what Oxenstierna planned, once he took Magdeburg. The sack that followed would put Tilly's in the shade. Wunsch wouldn't be surprised if the chancellor ordered the ground to be sown with salt.

Some of the Americans in the city would survive, if they identified themselves quickly enough. Oxenstierna had already passed orders to his commanders to avoid unnecessary killings of up-timers, if possible. But most of them wouldn't. It was simply not possible to control a sack once it began, especially if the orders came from above in the first place. The soldiery would run amok, most of them drunk.

No one else would stay alive, unless they took refuge inside the royal palace. Oxenstierna would make sure that the palace was protected, given that the headstrong girl had chosen to put herself in it. No one wanted to see the dynasty go up in smoke along with the city itself, of course.

But that only required Kristina's survival. Wunsch wasn't privy to such things, but he also wouldn't be surprised if Oxenstierna saw to it that the Danish prince died in the chaos. Ulrik had quite outworn his welcome with the Swedish chancellor. The heir to the throne was only nine years old. There was still plenty of time to find a more suitable consort.

Wismar, Germany, on the Baltic coast

"It looks like there's a storm coming, sir," said the radio operator, as soon as he entered the headquarters of Wismar's air force base. "Headquarters," in this instance, being a fancy term for a one-room officers' lounge on the ground floor of the airfield's control tower.

There was only one officer present, as usual. Wismar was a military backwater, these days. The main purpose of the air base was monitoring the weather in the Baltic and the North Sea. In Europe, as in North America, the weather basically moved from west to east. Getting a day or two's warning of a coming storm front was useful, for the military in time of war even more than civilians.

Lieutenant Gottfried Riemann levered himself out of the arm chair where he'd been reading a training manual. He was an ambitious young man, and had no intention of remaining a ground crew officer consigned to a wretched post like Wismar. He took the radio message slip from the operator, read it quickly, and then handed it back.

"Well, what are you waiting for? You know the colonel's orders. Get this off right away."

On his way back up to the radio in the control tower, Corporal Grauman pondered the same problem he'd been pondering for weeks.

Was there any way to poison a man and remain undetected?

The lieutenant was the sort of obnoxious officer who insisted that nothing be done without his approval—and then criticized his subordinates for lack of initiative. Not too uncommon a type, of course, but Riemann was an extreme version of it. So extreme that it had only taken him a month to become thoroughly detested by every airman assigned to the base.

Naturally, he was also good at brownnosing, so his superiors were oblivious to his true nature.

The problem with using arsenic or cyanide was that they were too well known. There was some deadly poison the up-timers knew about called "strychnine." If you could get your hands on some of the stuff...

He wasn't even thinking about the message when he sent it. That was old habit by now, something he could almost do in his sleep. He certainly gave no thought to the message's potential ramifications.

Maybe an accident of some kind. The problem was that the lieutenant almost never got out of that damned arm chair. "Studying," he called it. The shithead was lazy, too. The only time he exerted himself was to criticize a subordinate for not working hard enough.

The corporal's thoughts circled back to poisons. Maybe . . .

Chapter 44

Dresden, capital of Saxony

Blessedly, Denise and Minnie had found a new enthusiasm. If they'd kept hammering away in the basement, expanding and improving the hidey-hole, Noelle would have had to start thinking seriously about poisons instead of just idly fancying them. Had she been as full of boundless enthusiasm and inexhaustible energy at that age? Surely not.

However, all bad things come to an end. The day after Eddie left, they got a radio message from their employer in Prague.

Stay put. (As if they had any choice.) *Interesting developments coming. Make preparations to restore air strip as soon as possible.*

Denise immediately interpreted that as an assurance that Eddie would be back within days. How he would manage that was unclear, given that the airstrip in question—the former airstrip—was now the site of a corral where Banér's Finnish light cavalry kept their mounts. But Denise was not given to fretting over uncertainties.

Not even she and Minnie were so insouciant that they planned to start repairing the airfield with the Finns still in the area, however. They just wanted to be ready to race out there as soon as the first opportunity arose, with the "relief expedition" ready to go.

That was their term, which Noelle thought was absurd. Relieve who? Relieve what? Did they think a field that had been cleared of rocks and obstructions was groaning with pain and despair now that it was covered with horse crap?

Had she been as careless with language at that age? Surely not.

All they were planning to do was scrape off the manure and whatever other garbage the Finns had left with a modified plow. Then they'd level off the snow with a different modification to the plow, and finish by compressing the snow with rollers of some sort.

So far, they'd gotten the plow modifications ready. They were still working on the rollers.

Noelle had been taking advantage of the peace and quiet in the town house to write the report Nasi had asked for. What *she'd* found most interesting about his radio message was that he'd stressed he wanted a full and detailed report. Not something to be sent as a radio message then, but something written on paper that would have to be carried by a courier.

There hadn't been a courier in two weeks. Even the Thurn and Taxis people had stopped coming after Banér, in one of his fits of fury, had ordered that a detained courier be executed.

Of course, now that the Swedes had pulled out of the trenches and gone after Mike Stearns, couriers might start taking the risk again. Perhaps that was what Nasi was counting on.

"More," said Jozef. "Many more."

The gunmaker was looking at him almost cross-eyed. "How many grenades can a man carry?"

"You might be surprised, when he figures his life will depend on them. And we won't be carrying them on our bodies anyway, not most of them. We're having sleds made up."

The gunmaker had been a soldier once himself. His eyes now seemed on the very verge of crossing. "You're going to carry grenades on *sleds*? Nobody does that!"

Jozef gave him a cool smile. "To the contrary, Herr Teuber. It's a standard Polish tactic."

In point of fact, hussars rarely used grenades. Even the Polish infantry didn't use them much. But he was getting annoyed with the gunmaker and wanted to cut this short. Never had he met a man who quarreled so much when people offered to pay him for his work. Granted, the money was in the form of a promissory note, but he ought to know by now that if Dresden held off the Swedes, the CoC would be good for it. Sooner or later.

Unfortunately, while any gunmaker and most apothecaries knew how to make gunpowder—so did lots of other people, for that matter—this Teuber jackass was the only one in the city whose shop was set up to make it in quantity.

Thankfully, he was not making the grenades themselves. That work was being handled by a little consortium of two gunmakers and two blacksmiths. The weapons they produced were a bit crude, heavier than

Jozef would have preferred, and he wasn't entirely happy with the fuses. But they'd work well enough and he hadn't expected anything better under the circumstances. Making grenades was normally specialized work.

Eric Krenz and Friedrich Nagel weren't any happier with the sled-maker.

"More," said Eric.

"Many more," qualified Friedrich.

The sled-maker's way of expressing disbelief was spitting. The more spittle, the greater the skepticism, as nearly as Krenz could figure.

"Why don't you just have me make you a few big sleds?" he demanded crossly. "All these little ones..." He threw up his hands. "Child's toys! You are expecting to find hordes of children somewhere?"

Eric set his teeth. "Herr Meissner, as I told you before—"

"Twice, already," Nagel interjected.

"Yes, twice already. We want these sleds to carry grenades. We need to be able to move quickly and we don't know in which direction we will need to go or how many of us will be together at any one time. It will be *snowing,* as I already mentioned."

"Twice," said Nagel.

"Yes, twice. So perhaps you can see why a few big sleds will not—"

The most irritating part of it was that Meissner had not been a soldier and had spent some time making that clear. So why was he arguing the point? Based on what self-professed lack of expertise?

Gretchen Richter came into the shop. "I was told

there is a problem," she said, as soon as she came in. "What is it?"

Eric sketched the problem. Very briefly. *We want a lot of small sleds, not a few big ones, and this assho— Herr Meissner here—seems unhappy with the order.*

Gretchen pointed to Krenz with a thumb. "Do as he says, Herr Meissner. Please do exactly as he says. Or many little Herr Meissners will replace one big one."

And off she went. Alexander the Great had nothing on Gretchen Richter when it came to cutting Gordian knots.

"I don't know," said Minnie dubiously. She walked around to the other side of the roller that the wagon-maker had designed. It was rather ingenious, admittedly. Three barrels in a line on one axle with two others following on a second axle, offset in order to flatten the ridges that would be produced between the first three barrels. The whole thing was held together by a very sturdy frame—which even came with platforms on which more weight could be placed in the form of bags full of rocks.

Yes, very ingenious, assuming it didn't fall apart under the strain. But it probably wouldn't. Herr Kienzle seemed to know what he was doing. The problem that remained was . . .

Denise had spotted it too. "That's going to take a big team of horses to pull around. Oxen would be better."

Kienzle inclined his head. It was the sort of nod an august and dignified guildsman would bestow upon two ignorant, prattling, but well-meaning young girls.

"Oh, yes. No question about it. The draft animals will help compress the snow also, of course."

Denise was looking exasperated. Minnie figured she better speak up quickly. The capabilities of Denise Beasley when it came to the *aggravate-the-hell-out-of-pompous-middle-aged-men* department were extraordinary. One might even say, astronomical.

"The problem, Herr Kienzle, is that finding such draft animals—on any notice, much less short notice—is likely to be difficult."

"We're in a city under siege," Denise growled, "you—"

"Difficult, as I said," Minnie rode over her.

The wagonmaker shrugged. "Yes, no doubt. You'll just have to do your best. My job is done."

Minnie sighed. There'd be no way to hold back Denise now.

By mid-afternoon they'd drawn a blank in their negotiations with the city's stables. Unfortunately, stable-keepers were also middle-aged men and for some peculiar reason Minnie couldn't figure out, they all seemed to be afflicted with pompous-male-middleageditis. Denise aggravated all of them. By late afternoon, they'd almost given up.

Then they were approached by a couple of young hostlers from the second stable they'd visited. The lads, definitely short of middle-age and not pompous at all, offered to provide the girls with draft horses behind their employer's back. They said that he was a lazy man who paid little attention to his business and left the details to his employees.

When Denise inquired as to the price, the lads spurned money and offered a more gallant alternative form of payment.

Had Denise been in a good mood, she would have

handled the matter casually. She was truly superb in the *brush-off-boys-with-delusions-of-grandeur* department. Since she wasn't in a good mood—quite the opposite—she fell back instead to threatening to pistol-whip the dirty rotten bastards if they weren't out of her sight in five seconds. She was accomplished in that department also.

As was Minnie herself, for that matter. Before Denise had finished the first sentence, Minnie already had her pistol in hand. So did Denise, of course.

At that point, the day began improving. One of the lads raced off but his partner proved surprisingly stout and adaptable.

"Look, it was worth a try," he said, smiling and raising his hands in a pacific gesture. "No offense meant. If you'd rather pay us with money, so be it. What's your offer?"

By sundown, they had everything in place. All negotiations had been successfully concluded and all arrangements made. The only hitch was that Minnie had to unruffle Herr Kienzle's feathers first, which were still ruffled as only Denise could ruffle feathers. She made Denise wait outside the shop until she took care of that problem.

"Okay, I finally got him settled down," she said when she came out. "He'll have the roller ready as soon as we tell him the hostlers are on the way."

Denise scowled. "You *did* tell him the hostlers were as young as we are, right? We don't need that fat sorry swell-headed son-of-a-bitch to go all Yesyourmajesty on them when they show up."

"Yeah, I told him. At this point, I don't think he

cares. Not once he started figuring out what that roller was going to cost him given that you'd made it pretty clear he wasn't getting the back half of the money on account of the agreement was 'satisfactorily built' and we didn't think it was even though a judge would probably rule in his favor but the only operating judge right now is Gretchen and most of these guildsmen are leery of dealing with her."

"Gee, wonder why?"

"Gretchen would probably rule in his favor too, you know? We were maybe a little vague about exactly what we needed."

"Well, maybe. He's still a fat sorry swell-headed son-of-a-bitch."

Denise's skills in the *forgive-and-forget* department, on the other hand, were minimal. One might even say, microscopic.

Noelle had just finished her report when she heard Denise and Minnie clumping up the steps to the front entrance. She'd been using a quill pen and down-time ink, since she'd seen no reason to hurry her writing and the few up-time pens she still had left were things she was now saving for special purposes. So she had to wait a bit for the ink on the last sheet to finish drying before she stacked it with the rest of the pages.

There were twenty-three pages all told, hand-written. Francisco had asked for a full report; a full report he'd be getting. It would have to be sent by courier, for sure. The cost of sending that long a message by radio didn't bear thinking about, not even for someone with Nasi's wealth. The cost was a moot point, in any event. There was no way the CoC people running the

radio operation would have allowed that much time
to be monopolized for a private transmission.

While she waited for the page to dry, she rose
from the writing desk, stretched her arms and began
walking about. She'd been sitting nonstop for the last
three hours and was feeling stiff.

She heard a screech from outside. Denise's voice,
clearly enough, although no words could be made out.
It had just sounded like a screech of fury.

Now alarmed, Noelle raced to the stairwell, stopping
only long enough to draw her own pistol out of the
drawer of the side table where she kept it.

The screech came again. Noelle hurried down the
stairs and threw open the door, pistol in hand and
ready to fire.

Not quite. She still had the safety on but this time
she'd *remembered* it was on and was ready to flick it
off. There'd be no repeat of . . . well, any number of
embarrassing moments on the firing range. Noelle's
capabilities in the Annie Oakley department were risible.
One might even say, the laughing stock of the continent.

But there was nothing. No danger she could see,
although she couldn't see far. It was evening and there
was a very heavy overcast.

Minnie was standing right by the entrance, looking
up at the sky with a frustrated expression on her face.
Denise had moved back into the street and was also
staring up at the sky. She had her palm out-stretched.

"What's the matter?" Noelle asked.

"Look at this shit!" Denise screeched.

"It's starting to snow," Minnie said glumly. "Now
we'll have to wait at least another day. Maybe two
or three."

Chapter 45

The Saxon plain, near Dresden

Mike was tempted to order a night attack, but yielded to the advice of his advisers. All of whom were against the idea.

"Even in daylight, fighting will be hard enough, sir," said Anthony Leebrick. His expression made clear that he'd have liked to add: *And it's a really bad idea to begin with.*

"No way to control the troops," added Colonel Duerr gruffly.

Mike chewed on the problem, trying to sort out how much of the advice he was getting came from his staff's unhappiness with the whole idea of launching an attack in the middle of a snowstorm. They'd been almost aghast at the notion when he first raised it, although by now they'd reconciled themselves to the inevitable. Their commanding general usually took their advice, but not always—and there was nothing indecisive about him. If, after listening to their objections, he said he was still going to do something, then it was going to be done.

Christopher Long, the third of Mike's regular trio of staff officers, was marginally less pessimistic than his two fellows. He was usually the more aggressively inclined of the three. But even Long was dubious about fighting in a storm. He said nothing now, but his expression made it clear that he fully agreed with Leebrick and Duerr on the subject of launching a night attack.

In the end, Mike decided that his own instincts were probably not reliable in this situation and he'd do better to listen to his staff. His eagerness to start fighting was likely to be his emotional reaction to days of tension and anxiety. As a boxer, his biggest weakness had been a tendency to start swinging too quickly, too furiously, more as way of settling his nerves than anything else.

"At first light, then," he said. "And I mean at first light. We're not waiting for the sun to come up. We'll just be waiting long enough for a man to be able to see ten yards ahead of him. Is that understood?"

As soon as he finished, he regretted the statements. That was just his nerves acting up again. He sometimes thought his staff officers were a bit too inclined toward caution, but he had no reservations at all about either their courage or their willingness to obey orders. There was no reason to have piled on that unnecessary verbiage.

Was that a slight smile on Duerr's face?

Colonel Ulbrecht Duerr was fighting down a grin, as it happened. He'd added his own words of caution to those of Leebrick and Long, because he agreed with them as a pure matter of tactics. Fighting at night in the middle of a snowstorm was just piling on too many uncertainties. .

Still, he'd been pleased to see the general's combative spirit. A commander who wanted to launch an assault even in the dark was a commander who would press through an assault in daylight. And that's what this mad little scheme of Stearns' was going to require—pressing on, pressing on, pressing on. Damn the cost, fuck the Swede bastards, just keep shooting and throwing grenades and firing everything you've got and keep at them and keep at them and keep at them.

Banér's army was going to break. Ulbrecht Duerr was as sure of that as he had been of anything in his life, on the eve of a battle. There was a flow to these things, a sort of tide summoned by Mars rather than the sun or the moon.

People, including the division itself, thought of the Third Division as "inexperienced" compared to most other military units. And so they were, by the standards of mercenary soldiers. But Duerr knew those standards, and how hollow they really were. He should, after all, being a mercenary himself. Very few armies of his day fought major pitched battles in the open field. Gustav II Adolf's great victory at Breitenfeld four years earlier had been the exception, not the rule. It was quite possible for a man to spend his entire life as a soldier—even in the middle of great wars such as the one that had wracked central Europe since 1618—and never participate in a single battle.

War in the seventeenth century was a thing of marches and counter-marches and, most of all, sieges. Sieges big and small. Sieges of cities, sieges of towns. Sometimes, sieges of villages or even hamlets.

A furious assault launched across open fields? At any time, much less February in the middle of a snowstorm?

It just wasn't done. Too imprudent—and being prudent was in the nature of a mercenary. There was nothing at stake except pay, after all.

But the soldiers in the ranks of the Third Division didn't think that way, and they had a commander who didn't think that way either. Stearns' inexperience was now actually working in his favor, just as it was working in favor of his entire division.

Because they *were* veterans, by now, even if they still didn't think of themselves that way. Many of them— more than half, probably—had fought at Ahrensbök. The greatest battle on the continent since Breitenfeld.

Stearns himself hadn't been on the field that day. But even in the time since he'd taken command of the division, the Third had fought the battles of Zwenkau and Zielona Góra. And while they hadn't fought at Lake Bledno, that was only because the Poles had withdrawn from the field before they arrived. They *would* have fought—and not one man in the division doubted for a moment that they would have whipped them, too. Piss on the famous Grand Hetman Stanislaw Koniecpolski. Just another bum to be beaten senseless.

Just as, tomorrow, they were going to piss on the famous Johan Banér and beat his army senseless.

The soldiers of the Third Division were full of confidence. Confidence in themselves, confidence in their weapons and equipment, confidence in their officers; perhaps most of all, confidence in their commander. They'd been in more battles than most soldiers of the day, and they'd won every one of them. They knew everything they needed to know in order to win a battle—and hadn't been soldiers long enough to learn all of the ways an army can could fail and usually did fail.

Colonel Duerr was in a splendid mood, actually. If he survived another day—no way to be sure of that, of course—he'd be looking back on it fondly for the rest of his life. Great victories came rarely to a soldier, even one like him whose career had now spanned three decades.

After night fell, Mike spent the better part of three hours moving among his men, visiting each unit around its campfires. He had nothing particularly intelligent to say, but the soldiers didn't need a speech, much less a lecture. They just needed to see their commander, see that he knew what they would all be doing come dawn—most of all, see that he was completely confident that they could do it.

Jeff Higgins spent less than two hours at the same task. First, because he only had a regiment's worth of men to deal with. Second, because unlike Mike Stearns he wasn't comfortable striding around the stage. Any stage.

He didn't really need to do it anyway. No regiment in the division had higher morale this night than the Hangman. They were ready to go at Banér's throat. Many of the standard bearers weren't even planning to carry the regiment's colors into battle the next day. They'd made jury-rigged substitutes, straw figures supposed to be Banér hanging from a gibbet. They'd carry the gibbets themselves into the fight, with their straw Swedish generals blowing in the wind along with the snow.

❖   ❖   ❖

Thorsten Engler spent even less time at the task. No more than forty-five minutes. First, because he only had two hundred men under his command instead of a thousand. Second, because the morale of flying artillery units was a bit eccentric. The volley gun crews considered themselves an elite force. So, unlike common garden variety soldiers, they needed no artificial stimulants like silly speeches from officers to get them ready for battle. No, no, no. They were the cold-eyed killers, the deadly ones, the men who broke cavalry charges.

They needed nothing, thank you. Beyond a commander who passed through their ranks, from campfire to campfire, quietly checking to make sure no one lacked anything in the way of equipment or supplies.

A commander like Engler, in short. Detached, intellectual, reasoned. They all knew his ambition to become a psychologist after the war. Once the meaning of the term was explained to them, each and every man in the company agreed that he would make a superb psychologist.

And not one of them would consider using his professional services as such. Even by volley gun crew standards, that man was a little scary.

Berlin, capital of Brandenburg province

Colonel Erik Haakansson Hand was also contemplating the use of poison that night. In his case, though, the thought was neither idle nor fanciful. He had a real problem on his hands.

Unfortunately, after weeks of welcome slothfulness and incompetence on their part, one of Gustav

Adolf's doctors was taking a genuine interest in the case. Instead of a perfunctory few minutes breezing in and out of the king's room every other day or so, this bastard was starting to spend time there.

A full hour, yesterday. Luckily, there had been no signs from the king that he was starting to recover from his condition. He'd been asleep most of the time and when he did wake up, immediately started shouting at the doctor in fury.

Incoherent fury, too. The annoying man had fled in five minutes.

But if he kept coming around, there was bound to be bad luck sooner or later. And once any of the doctors assigned to the king began to think Gustav Adolf might be recovering, he'd be sure to tell Oxenstierna.

Or if one of them didn't, the king's chaplain would. That was the Pomeranian Jacobus Fabricius. He'd been wounded in the battle at Lake Bledno but not badly enough that he hadn't been able to start attending the king after a few weeks. But he'd resumed those duties too early and in his weakened state he'd fallen badly ill. A stroke of luck, that was, since the chaplain hadn't been present during the recent period to see Gustav Adolf's growing flashes of coherence.

Hand didn't think any of the doctors, and certainly not the chaplain, wished any ill upon his cousin. But regardless of their motives, any of them who noticed was sure to inform Oxenstierna. Nor would it matter if the chancellor had already taken the army to Magdeburg by then. He'd be taking a radio with him. Several, in fact. Just as he'd be leaving several behind in Berlin. He'd get the news within hours.

And then . . .

There was no telling what would happen. But Erik now feared the worst. Three months ago—two months ago—perhaps even one month ago, he'd have sworn that Oxenstierna would do no personal harm to Gustav Adolf. Not to his own king, and a man who'd been a good friend for many years.

But Axel Oxenstierna had been changing, and the change had sped up rapidly over the past few weeks. The course of action he'd set for himself had careened out of his control, something which was now obvious to everyone except those reactionary imbeciles who guzzled the palace's wine, gobbled food from its kitchens, and sang praises and hosannas to Oxenstierna every drunken evening.

It was certainly obvious to Oxenstierna. Most of his followers might be dull-witted but not the chancellor himself.

Nothing had gone the way he'd planned. His enemies had not reacted as he'd foreseen. There'd been none—very little, anyway—of the chaos he'd expected and had partly been depending upon. Wilhelm Wettin had dug in his heels once he stumbled across outright treachery and had had to be arrested. The princess had not knuckled under to pressure. Indeed, she and her consort-to-be had defied Oxenstierna in the most flamboyant fashion imaginable. Dresden had defied him and held out against Banér. And now Stearns had come out in open rebellion and marched his troops back into Saxony. By all reports, there would be a battle soon between his Third Division and Banér's mercenaries. Only a new storm was delaying it.

As each setback and misadventure came, the chancellor's mood darkened. No, not just his mood, his very soul. Always a hard man, Oxenstierna was now becoming a savage man, something he'd never been in the past.

So what would he do, if the final blow fell and he learned his king was returning?

Submit—knowing full well that Gustav II Adolf would not approve of his actions?

Maybe. And then...maybe not. The chancellor had men who were loyal to him, first and foremost. By now, he probably had entire regiments who were mainly loyal to him. He'd certainly have enough such men to overwhelm Hand and Erling Ljungberg and the king's Scot bodyguards.

A few blows to the head—no need, even, for outright murder—and it would be done. Those who knew the truth silenced, some absurd concoction presented to the world in public—another treason plot, the details left vague—and the king condemned to everlasting madness, his brains turned to pulp.

So. Cyanide or arsenic? Those were the only viable alternatives.

Magdeburg, capital of the United States of Europe

Restlessly, Rebecca moved through the empty rooms of the town house, looking out of the windows to watch the snow fall. She had already made two complete circuits of all the rooms on the top floor except those of her children, whom she didn't want to awaken.

She didn't go down to the lower floors. Now that the crisis was reaching its peak, there were people there at all times. Her house had become the operating command center for the Fourth of July Party. Couriers raced back and forth from here to the Freedom Arches, where the city's CoC had its center, every hour of the day and night. They were needed because the telephone lines were often overwhelmed.

The people in Magdeburg had good intelligence coming from Berlin. As always, servants were the weak link in the aristocracy's armor, when it came to espionage. You'd think they'd learn not to talk in front of their servants, but some habits were just too deeply ingrained. That was especially true of the sort of cast-iron diehards who'd gathered in Berlin.

So they knew Oxenstierna was coming, and bringing his whole army with him. And while their intelligence didn't extend so far as to know his precise intentions—Oxenstierna himself was far too shrewd to speak in front of servants—no one had any trouble guessing what they were.

Tonight, though, Rebecca wasn't concerned about her own possible fate a few weeks or months from now. Not even that of her children. Tonight the snow was falling, and she knew what that meant.

Thought she did, at least. She'd gotten no messages from Michael. He wouldn't have divulged his tactical plans to her anyway. But she knew her husband very well.

Mike Stearns was a charming man. Even his enemies would allow as much. Gracious, pleasant, courteous, rarely given to expressing a temper.

All of it was even true. But what the qualities disguised from those who didn't know him as well as she did, was that he was also utterly pugnacious. Not belligerent, as such. He did not go looking for fights.

But when a fight did come he would throw himself into it with a pure fury. Rebecca had never seen him fight with his fists, but she knew from Melissa Mailey what his record had been. All but one of his professional fights he'd won by knockout before the end of the fourth round.

So how would such a man fight as a general?

Snow was falling. Not only here but all across the Germanies. She'd checked the weather reports.

It would be falling in Saxony too. White, cold—and gentle, as snowfalls were. But tomorrow it would be bathed in blood. She could only hope Michael's blood would not be part of that gruesome, incongruous mix.

Or not too much of it, at least. She was a Jewess. Her people had learned long ago that you had to be practical about these things.

Chapter 46

The Saxon plain, near Dresden

Johan Banér was awakened by the sound of gunfire. He came awake instantly.

"Fucking bastards! I warned them!"

He began pulling on his pants, calling for his orderly and his adjutant. The orderly arrived first, piling into the little room on the upper floor of the house. He'd have been sleeping just outside, in the hallway. The hallway was small and narrow, too, as you'd expect from a village home that wasn't quite a hovel but came close.

Without speaking, the orderly helped the general put on the rest of his clothes. The adjutant arrived seconds later.

"I warned them, Sinclair! I warned the fucks! Which one of them started it?"

The Scot officer's face was pale. "Sir, I'm not—"

"If you don't know, find out! I intend to have whoever started this brawl shot dead! No, I'll—"

"Sir, I really don't—"

"—have them hanged! Hanged, you hear me? If need be, a whole fucking company!"

"Sir, I think it's the enemy!" Sinclair shouted desperately.

Banér stared at him, as if he'd gone mad.

Sinclair pointed to the window. "Listen, sir! That's too much gunfire to be coming from a brawl between companies."

Still wide-eyed with disbelief, Banér stared at the window. An instant later, he rushed over, fumbled at the latch, and threw the window open.

The sky was lightening with the sunrise but he still couldn't see very far because of the snowfall. The sound of gunfire was growing, though, and Sinclair was right. That wasn't a brawl between drunken soldiers.

But—

"No sane man launches an attack in the middle of a snowstorm!"

He and Sinclair looked at each other. Sinclair shrugged. "He's a rank amateur, sir. You know the old saying."

Banér had always thought that saying was inane, actually. *The opponent a great swordsman fears the most is the worst swordsman.* Blithering nonsense. Still . . .

Stearns might be mad, but this could get dangerous. He had to get out there. His soldiers would be muzzy with sleep and confused. They'd no more been expecting this than he had, and the snowfall would make it difficult for his officers to get the men into proper formations. Everyone would be half-blind.

So would the enemy, though—and, just as Sinclair had said, they were rank amateurs.

Choose to fight real soldiers in a snowstorm, would they? He'd show them where children's games left off and real war began.

❖   ❖   ❖

You couldn't see a thing beyond thirty yards or so
and volley gun batteries didn't blast away at nothing.
Not batteries under Thorsten Engler's command, anyway. And he wasn't nervous, either. They'd trained with
the sled arrangements, and had actually come to prefer
them over wheels, in some ways. They were easier to
bring to bear, for one thing. Their biggest drawback
was the recoil, which could be a little unpredictable,
but that wasn't a factor in the first round. And it was
usually the first round fired by volley guns that was
the decisive one.

Finally, he could see shapes ahead. Those were the
shapes of men, too, he was sure of it.

But they weren't coming forward, they seemed to
be just milling around. And now he spotted horses
among them.

They'd caught a cavalry unit off guard then. Still
trying to mount up.

Splendid. Ten more yards and they'd fire.

The sleds moved fast, too. It was just a matter of
a few seconds before the entire battery started coming around.

By now they were only fifteen yards from their
nearest enemy soldiers and they'd been spotted themselves. One of the Swedes who'd managed to get up
onto his horse fired a wheel-lock pistol at them. In
their direction, rather. Thorsten was pretty sure the
shot had sailed at least ten feet over their heads.
Confusion, surprise and a snowstorm do not combine
to make for good marksmanship.

Happily, good marksmanship didn't matter that
much to a volley gun battery.

He glanced back and forth. All the guns he could see had been brought to bear. Good enough.

"Fire!" he screeched, in that high-pitched tone he'd learned to use on a battlefield. Not even the heavy snow coming down could blanket it.

Only two guns in one of the batteries hadn't been brought in line yet, but their fire came not more than three seconds later. Twenty-five barrels to a volley gun, six guns to a battery, six batteries to a company. Subtracting a few misfires, almost nine hundred musket balls struck the enemy just a few yards away.

That was equivalent to the fire from an entire regiment—except an entire regiment couldn't fire its muskets all at once. Not on that narrow a front.

Thorsten couldn't see most of them, but the clustered units his volley gun battery had just fired upon were two of the four companies of the Östergötland Horsemen. That first murderous volley killed and wounded dozens of them, including the commanding officer Colonel Claus Dietrich Sperreuter. The rest were sent reeling backward—where they collided into the other two companies and cast them into further confusion.

"Reload!" Thorsten screeched.

As orders went, that one was superfluous to the point of being asinine. His men had already started reloading before he finished taking in his breath. What else would they be doing on a battlefield? Picking their teeth?

But it was tradition. Elite units took traditions seriously, as pointless as they might be.

The term "elite" was no empty boast, either. The

company was ready to fire again in ten seconds—a
better rate of fire than even musketmen could manage.

"*Fire!*" he screeched.

This time, all the guns went off together. There
were misfires, here and there, but not many.

Again, almost nine hundred balls hammered the
milling cavalrymen. Thorsten's men still hadn't taken
more than a couple of dozen shots fired in return and
so far as Thorsten could tell, all of them had gone wild.

Dozens more were killed and wounded. The one
company that had started to form up was shredded
again, its captain thrown out of the saddle by a ball
that struck him in the head. He survived the shot—
just a crease, he wasn't even stunned—but after he
landed on the ground his horse stepped on his head
and crushed it into the hard soil beneath the snow.
He survived that, too, although he was no longer really
conscious. Then his horse and another trampled his
ribs before they stumbled off, away from the guns.

He survived that as well. But three ribs were broken, he was now bleeding internally, and everyone
who looked at his body assumed he was dead. Engler's
soldiers did too, when they passed by.

So, a while later, he died from hypothermia. He'd
never managed to get his boots on. He died in his
socks—and both of them had holes. His had not
been a wealthy family and the Swedes had been late
with the pay.

Again.

Thorsten gauged the enemy, as much of them as he
could see. Then, decided to take the risk. Instead of

ordering another volley, he ordered the guns moved forward.

"Ten yards up!" he screeched.

Jeff Higgins heard the screech, although he couldn't make out the exact words. In the half-blindness of the snowfall, his volley gun company had gotten separated from the regiment and charged ahead. He'd been groping his way forward with the infantry battalions, trying to find them before it was too late. The volley guns were murderous but they were a lot more fragile than the gunners themselves liked to admit. If they got caught between volleys by cavalry—even well-led infantry that could move quickly—they were dead meat.

Engler was particularly oblivious to that reality, damn him. How could a man who planned to become a psychologist behave like a blasted lunatic on a battlefield? If Jeff didn't find him and reunite the volley gun company with the regiment's infantry, things were likely to get very hairy. The Hangman was light, when it came to regular artillery, so they relied a lot on the volley guns.

He heard another screech. Again, he couldn't make out the words, but it sounded closer.

The words had been: *"Come into position!"*

Thirty-six volley guns swiveled on the snow, gliding easily on their Bartley rigs.

"Come on!" Jeff shouted, raising his sword and waving it. He detested the thing almost as much as he detested horses, but it was just a fact that an officer leading a charge had to wave a stupid sword around. Waving a pistol just didn't do the trick, not even a big down-time wheel lock.

Yes, it was asinine. Nothing but a pointless tradition left over from the days when illiterate men went into battle armed with nothing but oversized swords and blue paint. But the Hangman was an elite unit and elite units take tradition seriously.

Thankfully, Jeff was a big man and had big hands even for a man his size. So he probably wouldn't lose his grip on the sword more than twice before the battle was over.

Somehow, it never occurred to him that he might be dead or maimed before the battle was over. He never thought of that, in the middle of a battle. He'd only think of it as he tried to sleep afterward, when sometimes he'd get the shakes.

He heard another screech. He might finally have been close enough to make out the words but the screech was immediately drowned by a thunderclap. Nine hundred volley gun barrels going off at once made the term "noisy" seem inadequate if you were anywhere nearby.

That third volley—again, at point blank range— destroyed the Östergötland Horsemen. Most of them survived, as men somehow do on a battlefield. Most of them weren't even injured. But as a fighting formation, they were done. On this battlefield today, at least. The survivors raced to the rear, insofar as men could race through heavy snow and insofar as they could tell where "the rear" was in the middle of a heavy snowfall.

The sun was still invisible. It would remain invisible

through that day and most of the next. But there was now enough light that a man could distinguish, approximately, between east and west. And, that done, determine which way was north—which is where they wanted to go. Back into the siege lines.

Miserable they might be, those trenches, but they weren't as miserable as being savaged by musket balls fired by an unseen enemy.

Not more than one soldier in five of the Östergötland Horsemen had caught so much as a glimpse of the men who'd been killing them. Not more than a dozen had gotten a good look at them. Of those dozen, only two were still alive.

One of them was now hiding under the carcass of his horse, trying not to scream because of a broken leg. He was playing dead in the hopes that none of the enemy soldiers passing by would spot him. They were likely to cut his throat if he couldn't offer ransom, which he couldn't. His had not been a wealthy family, either, and the Swedes had been late with the pay.

Again.

Dresden, capital of Saxony

"Where? Where?" Jozef demanded, as soon as he came onto the platform around the tower.

Eric Krenz pointed to the south. "Over there. Somewhere. It's hard to be sure, exactly."

Wojtowicz peered into the snowfall. You really couldn't see anything worth looking at. From this high up in the Residenzschloss, you couldn't even see the city's own walls.

Gretchen Richter came onto the platform, followed by Tata.

"So what is happening?" she asked.

"We're not sure," replied Friedrich Nagel. He was standing next to Krenz. Both lieutenants had their uniforms on, but neither one had finished buttoning up their outer jackets. Like Jozef himself, they must have scrambled out of bed in response to the distant gunfire.

Suddenly, Jozef saw a flash. A dim one, but it was definitely a flash. Followed, a moment later, by a muffled boom.

"That was an artillery piece," he said. "Pretty big one, too. Probably a twelve-pounder."

He looked at Eric and Friedrich. "Does the Third Division have any field ordnance that size?"

They both shook their heads. "Biggest we've got— unless something got added after Zwenkau—are six-pounders."

So. Banér's forces. And from the flash, not more than a mile from the trenches the Swedes had dug.

Jozef came to a decision. "Now," he said. "We should sortie now."

Krenz and Nagel looked at each other. "Are you sure?" asked Eric.

"No, of course I'm not sure. I wasn't expecting a battle to start in the middle of a fucking storm. That must have been your general's doing. He's insane, by the way. But now that he's gone and done it, we should take advantage of the opportunity."

He leaned over the railing, pointing to the south— his arm angled downward. He was actually pointing at the enemy's siege lines, which couldn't be seen because of the snowfall.

"We should seize their own lines now, before they can retreat back into them."

"*If* they retreat back into them," said Friedrich, a bit dubiously. "I thought the idea was to wait until we knew they were coming back."

"Yes, it was." Jozef was suddenly sure of himself. "But they will, they will. If your blessed general was mad enough to attack them in the middle of a storm, he's mad enough to drive them back into their lines. So let's be there to deny it to them, shall we?"

Krenz and Friedrich looked at each other again.

"He's got a point," said Eric.

"He's right about Mike Stearns, too," said Gretchen. "I won't tell you what to do. I'm not a soldier and don't pretend to be one. But I think Wojtowicz is right."

"Okay, then," said Nagel. "Let's be about the mad business."

If nothing else, the noisy labors of Denise and Minnie had expanded the hiding place in the root cellar enough for all three of them to fit into it.

Barely.

There would have been room to spare, though—that racket had gone on for days—if a third of the space hadn't been taken up with barrels.

"What . . . ?"

Minnie pointed to the one Noelle's arm was lying across. "That's got food in it. The two you're crammed against on the other side are water barrels. And these two"—she patted the two barrels stacked on her left—"and the two over there by Denise—"

Her friend brought up a . . . fuse?

"These are the gunpowder barrels," Denise said

cheerfully. "If those fucks find us and want some excitement in their lives, they'll get it for sure. Pussy kaboom."

Noelle made a face. "That is *so* gross."

"Not as gross as the alternative," Minnie said phlegmatically.

"Well. No." She stuck out her hand. "But I keep the fuse. The two of you are too—too—too—"

The teenagers were grinning at her now.

"Too too-ish," Noelle finished lamely.

Chapter 47

The Saxon plain, near Dresden

Jeff finally caught up with the volley gun company just after they fired their fourth volley. By now, so far as he could tell—which was not much—they were mostly shooting at shadows. Whatever enemy they'd been facing seemed to be on the run.

"Next time, *wait*," he growled at Thorsten.

Engler gave him a cold smile. "Yes, sir. It's difficult, though, as slowly as the infantry moves."

"Very witty, Captain. My better half is amused. My other half, though—that's the one in charge right now—is not. If I have to get official and make it an order, I'll do it. Next. Time. Wait. How's that?"

Engler nodded. "Not a problem, sir. Honestly, we had no intention of getting separated. By the time we realized it..."

Jeff waved his hand. "Yeah, I know. By then, you'd come upon the foe and, being volley gun maniacs, he was yours for the taking. Also for the official record, my congratulations. Whoever you were fighting, you obviously pounded them into dog food. Now let's see about moving forward. Do you have any idea where the rest of the division is, by the way?"

Not until Jeff spoke the last sentence did it occur to him that he might fairly be accused of the same fault for which he'd just criticized Engler. Just as the volley gun battery had done with its regiment, so the Hangman had gotten separated from the other regiments and...

Done what, exactly? Where the hell were they? Ahead of the division? Behind it? Off to the side? If so, which side? They couldn't very well be to the east of the division, because they'd been over by the left flank when the attack began.

He started chewing on his lip.

"If you'll permit me the indiscretion, sir..."

Jeff gave Engler a sour look. "The formality'll kill me, just from shock. Spit it out, Thorsten."

"I really don't think there's much chance we're anywhere except in front of the rest of the division, sir."

Jeff had been coming to the same conclusion.

Fine. Now what?

Mike Stearns had been doing the same thing as Jeff—except he was searching for a whole regiment, not just a volley gun battery.

Jeff's regiment, damn his irresponsible geek heart. What had possessed him, to race ahead like that?

The radios were turning out to be almost useless. Mike could get in touch with his regiments, yes. But what good did that do when nobody knew where they were to begin with?

Christopher Long rode up. "That way, I think, sir." He was pointing a bit to the right, in the directions where Mike thought Dresden probably was.

What idiot had thought launching an attack in the middle of a snowstorm was a good idea?

By now, even Johan Banér had run out of curses. He could still manage one every two minutes or so, but the pleasure had entirely vanished from the exercise.

This was turning into a nightmare. He was still quite confident he could rout the rebels—if he could find his blasted army. More than bits and pieces of it, anyway.

The problem, insofar as Banér could reconstruct what had happened, was that one or another unit of the Third Division had punched a big hole in the middle of his line. "Line," at least, if you could dignify a string of camps set up to ride out the storm by the name.

The Östergötland Horsemen had been at the center of that hole. Somehow they'd been routed, and in their confused retreat had precipitated panic among their neighboring units. That, in turn, had led to the whole center starting to unravel.

Whatever else, Banér had to put a stop to that. If he could stabilize the center, he was sure he'd win this bastard of a battle. By now, Stearns' soldiers had to be even more disorganized than his own.

They probably were, in point of fact, on the level of the division itself. But it didn't matter because all of the regiments had stayed intact, even if none of them were really quite sure where the rest of the army was.

So, it devolved into a brawl, a pure melee in the snow, USE army regiments matched against whatever

Swedish units they stumbled across. It took a while, half an hour to an hour of savage struggle with heavy casualties on both sides, before the mercenaries began to yield.

But yield they did. They simply didn't have the stomach for this sort of fight. Drifting at first, and then moving faster and faster, they headed back toward the lines around Dresden.

In the middle of all this, Mike Stearns and his staff stumbled around trying to make sense out of senselessness.

They never succeeded. They never even came close.

Somehow, though, none of them died.

Quite.

Early on, Anthony Leebrick was struck in the leg by a stray bullet, just above the ankle. Although he didn't know it, then or ever, the ball had been fired by one of his division's own infantrymen and had struck him by sheer mischance. A lot of men were killed or wounded in that battle from friendly fire. Most of them were mercenaries working for the Swedes, since they were more confused and directionless than the oncoming USE troops, but by no means all of them.

It was a nasty wound, in the way that such wounds so often were, when gun battles were fought with muskets. The balls were slow but heavy, and shattered bones if they struck them full on—as this ball did.

Stearns ordered him taken to the rear by two of the adjutants who accompanied the staff officers. Leebrick lost his foot in a surgeon's tent, but he survived. Men usually did if the amputation was of a lower extremity, so long as they didn't get infected—and the Third

Division's sanitation practices were just as good among the surgeons as anywhere else.

Christopher Long was struck twice, again by stray bullets—although these were both fired by the enemy. The first ball caused a minor flesh wound on his left shoulder, which he had bound up and then ignored. The second wound, however, he couldn't ignore. That one struck him in the ribs. A glancing hit, it didn't penetrate the heavy buff coat he was wearing in lieu of armor. But it must have been a canister ball, twice the weight of a musket ball, because it broke at least two of his ribs. He tried to keep going but the pain was excruciating. Within minutes, over the young colonel's protest, Stearns had him taken to the rear as well.

That almost killed him. The two adjutants guiding him completely lost their way. The three men wandered for hours in the snowfall, with no idea where they were. None of them being sailors, none of them had thought to bring a compass. What soldier needs a compass?

Eventually, they came across a village. It had been deserted for weeks, and was not much more than ruins. But they were able to find some shelter in a house that had been only half-burned and one of the adjutants had some food on him.

There was no shortage of water. The snow drifts came as high as six feet in places.

Ulbrecht Duerr's injury came from a saber. A cavalryman from the unit of Courland cuirassiers came out of nowhere, shouting and swinging his blade. Duerr brought up his pistol but only had time to use it as a shield of sorts. Fortunately, it was a great heavy down-time saddle-holstered wheel lock, not a dinky little up-time pistol. So the only damage he suffered was a broken finger that got caught in the trigger guard before the pistol was flung into the snow.

That hurt like the devil, of course, but the immediate problem was that Duerr was right-handed—and he'd just lost the use of his right hand. So, forced by necessity, he drew his own sword and fought left-handed.

And won. Blind luck, really. The cuirassier got overly rash and swung a great blow that missed and dragged him half out of the saddle. Seeing his chance, Duerr drove the point of his sword into the man's exposed throat.

Tried to, rather. His strike missed also but came much closer—and he wasn't off balance. So, at the end, he was able to turn the missed stab into a slash with the part of his blade just above the handguard.

Which was like a razor, because although Duerr was slapdash when it came to keeping his blades sharp, that portion of a sword's edge almost never gets used. The man's carotid was severed as neatly as you could ask for. Off the saddle he went entirely, and bled to death in a snowbank.

Thereafter, Duerr withstood the pain of his broken finger rather cheerfully. At his age, besting an opponent left-handed! He'd be able to brag about that until his dying day.

Which might be today, of course. Still, bragging rights were bragging rights.

Mike Stearns got his own bragging rights that day. He had two horses shot out from under him.

Not one. Two.

Both times, by stray shots coming from nowhere. It was that sort of battle.

Neither shot struck him, and he was able to leap clear the first time a horse went down. But the second horse went down abruptly and his left leg got caught under its body. Luckily, none of the tack or weaponry came between his leg and the horse, just the horse itself. That big an animal put a hefty bruise on his leg, but nothing worse.

He might not have gotten up on the third horse an adjutant found for him, except that he found walking hurt too much.

What moron had thought fighting a battle in a snowstorm was a good idea?

Right around the time Mike was painfully dragging his leg from under that second horse, Johan Banér finally found his missing center. Not the Östergötlanders—they were long gone. But most of John Ruthven's infantry regiment had been rallied by its commander and was getting into formation.

"Good work, John!" Banér shouted, as he rode up. "Now let's—"

Jeff finally had everything in place—and a good thing, too. Some more Swedish soldiers were looming up out of the snowfall, and these looked to be much better organized than any of the others they'd run across.

The volley gun company was where it was supposed to be—a bit in front, for a clear line of fire, but not so far that the Hangman infantry couldn't protect them.

✦   ✦   ✦

Thorsten spotted a small knot of horsemen off to the left. Cavalry were always a volley gun unit's main target. His response was almost an automatic reflex—as was the response of his gun crews.

"*Aim left!*" he screeched. But most of the gun crews were already doing so.

"*Fire!*"

Banér's head came off. No fewer than three balls struck his neck, passing just below his chin.

His left arm came off also, which would have killed him from blood loss anyway. Three more bullets did for that. And four more struck his chest, two of which penetrated the chest wall.

John Ruthven's wounds were even worse. So were those of his adjutant.

One of Banér's adjutants was also mangled but the other, oddly enough, was completely untouched. Battles were freakish that way. He hadn't lagged or been off to one side, either. He'd been right in the middle of the little group, not much more than an arm's length from the general.

His horse, on the other hand, was worse hit than any human. The poor beast went down as if he'd been in a slaughterhouse. Still unhurt but trapped beneath his mount, that adjutant would surrender a few minutes later when the Hangman Regiment took the field.

He was the one who would identify Banér later that day. He had intended to keep silent, lest the enemy's morale be boosted. But then he saw that USE troops had stacked the general's body onto a mass of others, in preparation for an eventual mass grave, with his severed head tossed onto the pile afterward. They obviously had no idea who he was. So, finally, the adjutant spoke up. That so great a man should suffer such an indignity... The thought was just unbearable.

Jozef and his men reached the siege lines just as the first retreating Swedes began entering them from the other side. The two hours that followed were as savage as combat ever gets. It was all knives and grenades—and helmets used as clubs, sometimes.

Jozef was wounded twice, both flesh wounds, one on his thigh and the other a gash on his ribs. Neither was too serious once he staunched the blood loss. One or the other might get infected, of course, but he'd worry about that afterward. If he had an afterward.

Not all of his Poles were so lucky. Szklenski and Bogumil were both killed in the fighting. He'd miss Ted, for all the man's occasional annoying traits. Bogumil, he wouldn't miss at all. He didn't like the man any more the day he died than he had the day he met him.

Kazimierz would lose a leg by late afternoon, and lose his life by noon of the following day. Waclaw lost an arm, but survived.

Eric Krenz survived also, but his peculiar friend Friedrich Nagel did not. The same grenade that left a rather dashing little scar on Krenz's cheek tore his fellow lieutenant's throat apart.

Within two hours, most of the fighting was over. The battle in the trenches had become a stalemate, with the men from Dresden holding the inner lines and the Swedes holding the outer ones. Trying to push further, in either direction, was now tantamount to suicide.

Then the Hangman Regiment showed up, in superbly good order. How they managed that in a snowstorm was anyone's guess.

The colonel in command of the regiment had his volley guns brought into position where they could fire right down the line of trenches. "Enfilade," the French called it, if Jozef remembered correctly.

Two volleys of that and the Swedish mercenaries began surrendering wholesale. Especially once other regiments from the Third Division started appearing out of the snowfall.

By early afternoon, it was all over. Toward the end, a big man appeared on a horse and the troops started cheering him wildly. He seemed more puzzled by the applause than anything else.

Eventually, Jozef realized he was looking at Mike Stearns.

Gretchen Richter came out of Dresden shortly thereafter, overriding the protests of her assistants.

They were worried about her safety. She was worried about her husband.

She walked right by him, as Jeff stood talking to his officers about handling the huge numbers of captured enemy soldiers. Didn't give him more than a glance.

Some big, confident, obviously martial sort of fellow. No one she knew.

It was only when she heard his startled exclamation of her own name that she turned around. And even then, took a second or two to recognize him.

Thereafter, things went splendidly. The two of

them, in their embrace, got a round of applause from the troops that matched the one Stearns had gotten.

"Okay," said Denise. "I'm bored stiff. And my leg's getting cramped."

"The shooting seems to have stopped," Minnie ventured.

Noelle was still inclined toward caution. "I think we should wait another hour."

Chapter 48

Dresden, capital of Saxony

Aside from mail couriers and smugglers, the one other class of people who were willing to risk penetrating siege lines were news reporters. Such men had existed for at least a century, but the Ring of Fire had expanded their number considerably. With the romanticism of up-time examples to lean on, the none-too-reputable trade of news reporter gained a certain cachet. That was especially true if a man could claim the title of "war correspondent."

(Female reporters had a certain equivalent if they could pose as "gossip columnists." Gossip, of course, had existed for millennia. But not until the Ring of Fire did it occur to anyone that you might actually be able to make a living from the business.)

By the time of the battle, there were a handful of such men residing in Dresden. They were all out of the city and moving through the trenches before the shooting even stopped. One of them was wounded, in fact, by a fragment from a grenade. Not badly, though, and in the years to come the scar he picked up on his forehead added greatly to his prestige and even probably expanded his purse a bit.

By mid-afternoon, they'd collected the essential bits of information and had all raced back into Dresden. There, they clamored for radio time.

The CoC guards protecting the radio room refused to let them in. Tempers became frayed. A nasty incident might have ensued except that Tata showed up.

"Are you mad?" she said crossly to the guards. "Let them all in. Now."

To the reporters, she said, "Decide in what order you'll get to the radio. Then you each get three minutes."

This was akin to telling cats to decide the order in which they'd eat. Immediately, the reporters started quarreling. After two minutes of that, Tata threw up her hands.

"Idiots! Fine. We will have one report, written by all of you. Sign it in whatever order you choose."

Herding cats, again. Immediately, they fell to quarreling over the order in which their names would appear.

Tata let that go on for no more than thirty seconds.

"Shut up! Fine. None of you will sign it, then. Come up with a pseudonym or something for all of you together."

Again, quarreling.

"Shut up! Fine. Since you all have the sense of a goose, I will come up with the name."

A stray memory came to her of something she'd run across in an up-time text.

So was born the Associated Press.

The reporters quarreled all through the process of writing the news account. But eventually they managed to get it written. They would even admit—not to each other, of course, and certainly not in public—that the end product was much better than any one of them would have come up with on their own. Their trade was at a stage of development where sensationalism came a long way ahead of substance. As a result, none of them had stayed out in the field any longer than they needed to in order to grasp the sensational essence of the event. But once all their accounts were added together, a great deal of factual content wound up being included.

There was even an unexpected bonus. By the time they were finally ready to transmit the report, a breathless CoC courier piled into the radio room.

"They killed Banér! They killed Banér!"

The reporters stared at him. "How can you be sure?" asked one, moved by an unusual impulse toward accuracy.

"I saw his head myself." The young courier made a face. The grimace combined horror, fascination and glee. "It'd come right off his body. Ripped off by bullets, looked like. Some of the Prince's soldiers brought it to him in a sack. They wanted to put it on a pikehead—just like that Swede shithead said he was going to do to us!—but the Prince wouldn't let them."

He was clearly aggrieved by that last decision; but, under the circumstances, he was willing to forgive the Prince his lapse of judgment.

The reporters looked at each other.

Tata took charge again. "You'd better go make sure before you send the radio message. This is not something you want to be wrong about."

The reporters hesitated.

"Fine. Let me put it this way. You don't get to use the radio until you make sure. If you try"—she waggled a finger at the two CoC guards, putting them on alert—"I will have you shot."

Off they went.

They were back in less than an hour.

"It's Banér, all right. I did a report on him last month and got to interview him for a few minutes. Grouchy bastard."

Another reported chimed in. "I've met him too. He looks a bit the worse for wear"—that got a round of chuckles—"but it's definitely him."

It was the work of less than a minute to modify the report. Then they started quarreling over which one of them got to read the report.

"Shut up!" said Tata. "Fine. Give it to me. I'll read the blasted thing."

By then, though, it was already late afternoon and Tata decided to wait until the evening window. She'd had some time to think the matter through and realized that she wanted to make sure the transmission reached as far as possible and as many people as possible.

The reporters put up an argument, naturally, but not much of one and not for very long. Tata was a ferocious bully and had a short way with annoying men.

Finally, the time came and the report went out.

Chapter 49

Magdeburg, capital of the United States of Europe

After Rebecca got the report, she took her children and sat with them by a window, looking out into the night. The snow had finally stopped falling and there was enough of a moon to see the city. For once, its industrial filth covered in white, Magdeburg was not ugly.

Kathleen was in her lap. Sepharad sat to her left, Baruch to her right.

"Daddy will be home soon," she said, smiling.

"Is he all right?" asked Baruch anxiously.

"Oh, yes." She imagined he must have some bruises, assuming the report that he'd had two horses shot out from under him was accurate and not just a reporter's fabrication. But he was definitely alive and in fairly good health. That was clear in the report and presented in several different ways, ending with his refusal to allow Banér's head to be hoisted on a pike.

That sounded like Michael. He would have fought savagely, but with the battle now won he'd already be looking toward a peace settlement. Rubbing salt into wounds was just not his way.

She so loved that man. She envied Gretchen, then. She had survived—the report was explicit on that issue—and so had her husband. Colonel Higgins was played up in the report, in fact. Apparently it had been his regiment that was responsible for killing Banér, although Rebecca had serious doubts that Jeff had led a final charge on horseback. The man hated to ride at the best of times. In a snowstorm? Not likely.

Gretchen's children came into the room, entering slowly and hesitantly. Rebecca waved them toward her.

"Your mother is fine," she said. "So is your father."

After that, they looked out of the window in silence. There seemed nothing much more to say.

Kristina came to stand by Ulrik, as he looked out of a window in the royal palace. He, too, was struck by Magdeburg's unusual looks that night. The snow covering everything gleamed in the moonlight. If you didn't know how much soot and grime lay underneath, you might think you were in some enchanted elven city.

"What do we do now?" she asked.

"Nothing, still." He put a hand on her skinny shoulder and gave it a squeeze.

There was a great deal of affection in that squeeze, not simply reassurance. He'd become very fond of the girl in the time they'd spent together since they left for Stockholm back in . . .

Dear God. Had it only been eight months ago? It seemed more like eight years.

Impossible, of course. If it had really been eight years, Kristina would now be old enough to get married.

He thought about that for a while. And realized that for the first time since he'd become betrothed to the Swedish princess, he was looking forward to the marriage. Sometime, somewhere, somehow, it had ceased being purely a political matter.

"You're sure?" she asked.

"Oh, yes," he replied.

Brussels, capital of the Netherlands

Pieter Paul Rubens left the meeting early. Once the report was digested and the basic response settled upon—*no, obviously we're not going to try to take advantage of the situation; not with Stearns alive and so obviously well; we're not mad*—he saw no need to spend the next few hours assuring the king and queen and their advisers that they'd made the right decisions all along. Archduchess Isabella would handle that just fine.

Instead, moved by a sudden impulse—a rare impulse, lately—he wanted to start a painting.

He didn't normally do battlefield portraits. Portraits of combat, yes—he'd done many of those. But they focused on such things as Achilles' slaying of Hector or a lion hunt or the battle of the Amazons. He wasn't particularly fond of the sort of set-piece depictions of enormous battlefields, which usually portrayed the victor in the foreground. He'd done close cousins of that sort of painting on commission, like his *Triumph of Henry IV*. But he'd never before been moved to do one simply because he found the subject fascinating.

This time, though, he couldn't resist. First, because he'd already done a portrait of the subject which he'd had to keep hidden because the political content was dubious for someone in his position. In the course of that work, though, he felt he'd come to know the man and wanted the chance to portray him again—this time, in a painting that could see the light of day.

And then, there was the central image! As arresting as Judith slaying Holofernes. The conquering general, presented with the head of his defeated enemy—and spurning it. Not from horror but from majesty, as befitted a prince.

Paris, capital of France

"Your judgment was quite sound, Your Grace," said Servien, once Richelieu had finished reading the news report that had come in over the radio in the palace. "It was wise not to do anything."

The cardinal set the report aside and shrugged. "Most likely, yes. It would have been easier to deal with Oxenstierna, but I'm afraid he's in a bad place now. He should have left well enough alone."

Coming from Richelieu, that statement was perhaps dubious. There were many in France—some of them not even his enemies—who thought the accusation *couldn't leave well enough alone* belonged on his own doorstep.

Madrid, capital of Spain

There was no reaction to the news report in the court of Spain.

They had no radio. They wouldn't receive the news for days yet.

Poznań, Poland

"They claim some Poles were involved," said Lukasz Opalinski, as he scanned through the report. After reading a couple of more lines, he hissed. "I don't believe it! The fellow who was apparently their leader claims some connection to the Koniecpolskis! Some bastards will say anything."

"His name?" asked Stanislaw Koniecpolski.

Lukasz shook his head. "They don't provide it. But it's an obvious lie. The only Pole we know in Dresden is Jozef and he certainly wouldn't..."

His voice trailed off. Startled, he looked up at the grand hetman. "You don't think... Surely..."

Koniecpolski started to laugh.

Berlin, capital of Brandenburg

Keeping well off to the side of the assembly chamber, almost but not quite in the shadows, Erik Haakansson Hand listened cynically to Oxenstierna's speech. The chancellor was taking the time to rally the spirits of his followers, even as he prepared to march his army out of Berlin.

Everything is fine, lads.

He wouldn't be marching on Magdeburg, though. There'd been a last minute change of plans. He'd have to march on Dresden instead, and hope to succeed where Banér had failed.

Victory will soon be ours.

He needed to move quickly, too, before Stearns' division recuperated.

I march on the rebels tomorrow!

Great cheers rang the chamber. The colonel felt a hand tug at his elbow. Turning, he saw it was James Wallace, one of the Scot bodyguards in Ljungberg's unit.

"Erling says you have to come now. Quickly."

Gustav Adolf was sitting up in his bed when Erik entered the room. His blue eyes seemed bright and clear.

"What is happening, Cousin?" the king asked. Only the slight drawl indicated the lurking anger. He hooked a thumb at Ljungberg.

"He won't tell me anything. Me, his own king."

"That's because . . ."

Where to begin?

The king solved that problem himself. "Is my daughter . . . ?"

"She's quite well, Your Majesty," Erik said hurriedly. "In good health. Even in good spirits. Just yesterday, I listened—well . . ."

"What? *Damn you, Erik, what's happening?*"

Ah, that familiar temper. A good solid kingly sort of temper. Not a wild and unfocused rage.

Also a far more dangerous temper, of course.

"Yesterday I listened to a speech she gave over the radio. Quite a good one, too, allowing for her age. Very enthusiastic."

Gustav Adolf frowned. "Why is my daughter giving speeches? Over the *radio*, you said?"

"It's a long story, Sire."

"Then sit."

Chapter 50

The United States of Europe

All of the major newspapers in the country and many of the smaller ones came out with the story the next morning. It didn't matter what day of the week they normally published. It didn't matter whether they were morning papers or evening papers. Even if the edition was just a two-page special edition, nothing more than a broadsheet printed on both sides, they all published something.

The headlines varied from city to city and province to province, but the gist of them was essentially the same:

GREAT BATTLE AT DRESDEN

TERRIBLE CASUALTIES

THE PRINCE TRIUMPHANT

SWEDISH ARMY ROUTED

GENERAL BANÉR KILLED IN THE FIGHTING

SIEGE OF DRESDEN LIFTED

The emphasis varied from one newspaper to another. Some stressed the drama and pathos of the terrible struggle in the middle of a snowstorm. Others focused more on the tactical details, still others on the political ramifications.

None of them were restrained. Purple prose was alive, well, thriving—you might even call it the kudzu of contemporary journalese—and most writers laid it on as thickly as they could.

Fussy and slavish devotion to the facts was the poorest of cousins. The claims made in the newspapers that day would by and large become fixed in the nation's mythology. These in particular:

The Prince of Germany had waged a tactical masterpiece of a battle, anticipating his hapless Swedish opponent's every move and thwarting him at every turn.

Colonel Higgins led his Hangman Regiment in the decisive charge that routed the Swedes. On horseback, waving his sword—and a fair number of accounts had that sword responsible for sweeping off the head of Johan Banér.

Gretchen Richter personally led the sortie that took the Swedish siege lines. Some of the accounts had her bare-breasted in the doing. In February, in a snowstorm.

And the silliest of them all:

Every soldier in the Prince's army was a stout-hearted German. Every soldier in Banér's, a brutal and rapacious Swede.

The last fabrication was perhaps a necessity, for the nation that exploded that morning. For eighteen years, the great war had washed back and forth across German soil. Every nation, it seemed, had either plundered the land and brutalized the populace or (in the case of the French) paid others to do it.

(The one nation that could legitimately claim to be quite blameless in the matter was Poland—which the USE had repaid by invading. Once again illustrating the adage that no good deed goes unpunished.)

The Germanies had been helpless in the face of the catastrophe. And yet—

Almost every army that had wreaked havoc for all those years had been heavily or even largely German in its composition. The rulers who commanded the brutal deeds might have been foreigners and so might the generals. But most of the soldiers had come from the same people who were being savaged.

That had been just as true in the snowfields southwest of Dresden on February 26, 1636, as it had been on almost every battlefield of the war. Johan Banér himself was a Swede, and so were many of his officers. But at least two-thirds of his mercenaries had been Germans and at least half the officers who commanded them as well. The truth was, there were probably more Scottish officers and soldiers in Banér's army that day than there were Swedes.

The Prince of Germany didn't simply defeat an enemy that day, he erased a national humiliation. For the first time in years, an army that everyone considered a German army had decisively defeated a foreign army—in defense of a German city.

Mike Stearns would always be the Prince after that day. To almost any German, regardless of their political affiliations—regardless of whether they would have voted for him or not for political office, which many of them wouldn't, then or ever. A title that had begun as a nickname bestowed upon him by radicals had now become an accepted national verity.

His views didn't matter. His origins didn't matter. Indeed, there were plenty of Germans who thought God had sent him across the Ring of Fire for this specific purpose. Germans reacted to his victory much the same way Americans in another universe had reacted when Joe Louis defeated Max Schmeling— magnified ten-fold. Most of the people who'd cheered for Louis had had no respect for his race, wouldn't have voted for him if he ran for office, and would have had a fit if he'd come courting their daughters.

It didn't matter. On that day, in that ring, he was the national champion—against a political cause that Americans by and large detested. (Which was quite unfair to Schmeling himself, who was very far from a Nazi. But historical verdicts are often unfair to persons.)

So it was again. Almost every city and town in the United States of Europe exploded that morning, except the few who didn't get the news until the afternoon—and then exploded.

For the most part, exploded with excitement and joy, which they expressed with impromptu parades and half-organized festivities. Flags were flown, many of them handmade on that same day. Speeches were given, almost all of them cobbled together on that day. At least half of the male children born that day were given the name of Michael—a name which had previously been uncommon in the Germanies but henceforth became rather popular.

The tavern in every Rathaus did a land office business—or would have, except the town councils

often (and in some cases very wisely) offered the
beer for free.

The militias in at least three-fourths of the towns
held a march celebrating the victory. The militias in the
other fourth argued about it. In the months to come,
it was noteworthy that the militias that had refused
to march had a hard time recruiting new members.

Almost all apprentices celebrated that day; at least
four out of five journeymen; and well over half of all
guildmasters.

Here and there, the explosions came in darker colors.
The city council of Heidelberg had been dominated
by extreme reactionaries who had carried out harsh
measures against any opposition. But they'd made the
mistake of falling between two stools. They'd been more
than harsh enough to infuriate a large part of the population but not harsh enough to destroy all resistance. The
backlash on February 27 would destroy them instead.

Four of the council members got out of the city
alive. The rest all died, several of them quite horribly—
and in the case of one, with his entire family. All were
burned alive in their home.

Even more savage was an incident in Mecklenburg,
just outside of Rostock. A party of Swedish merchants
was caught by a mob and torn to pieces. The hapless
merchants were utterly bewildered. What did they
have to do with the wars of dynasties?

Those were the two worst incidents. There were
many instances of beatings and vandalism, but nowhere
else did anyone lose their lives.

Except by accident. There were quite a few accidental
deaths. Mostly due to the combination of liquor and
livestock, or liquor and heights. In what was perhaps

the most flamboyant such death, a totally inebriated apprentice fell off the famous tower of the Ulm Minster, the Lutheran church that boasted a steeple one hundred meters tall. He was trying to affix a tricolor flag to the very top. He was within four yards of the top when he fell, holding onto the flag all the way down.

The parade in Magdeburg was the largest in the nation. For all intents and purposes, the whole city turned out.

Ulrik opted for caution. Overriding Kristina's vehement protests, he insisted that they avoid any formal participation in the rally that culminated in Hans Richter Square at the end of the march. Instead, he had Kristina standing on the steps of the royal palace as the march went by, waving at the crowd—and then hustled her off to the kitchens of the Freedom Arches.

Enough to please the mob, not so much as to burn all bridges with the Swedes.

That course of action might have posed a problem, except that there was a most suitable substitute for Kristina on this occasion to serve as the official centerpiece of the rally.

Rebecca Abrabanel, the Prince's wife, who was appalled and aghast when her role was explained to her.

By everyone on the committee. She had no allies at all. Not one.

"I don't give speeches!"

She did that day. Five of them. By the time she got to the fifth one, everyone agreed it was pretty good.

The parade in Hamburg was huge as well. So was the one in Augsburg.

In Hamburg, the Battle of Ostra—as it came to be called—shifted the balance of political power still further in favor of the Fourth of July Party and the Committee of Correspondence. But that shift had been happening anyway. Hamburg's economy had been expanding rapidly, which had drawn into the city people from classes that were naturally inclined in that direction.

The political change in Augsburg was more significant, because it was much less predictable. The central figure was the militia commander, Ruprecht Amsel. The combination of Kristina and Ulrik's actions and his anxieties about the Bavarians had already inclined him toward the Fourth of July Party more than he normally would have been. Mike Stearns' victory at Ostra was the catalyst. On February 27, he announced publicly at the rally held in that city that he was switching his party allegiance. Most of his militiamen followed suit.

Thereafter, Augsburg joined most of the imperial cities as FoJP bastions. Not to the degree that Magdeburg or Luebeck were, to be sure. But certainly as much as Hamburg or Frankfurt.

A still greater political shift took place in Hesse-Kassel. Amalie Elizabeth instructed her officials and military commanders to place no obstacles in the way of anyone wanting to celebrate the events in Dresden. Indeed, she instructed them to provide quiet assistance, if they were asked for it.

Then, as a march took place that would culminate in a rally that afternoon, she spent the rest of the morning just thinking. And by noon, had decided that caution now required boldness.

She went to the radio room her husband had set up in the palace the year before and spent a bit of time there. Then, to everyone's surprise starting with her closest advisers and top officials, she made her way to the rally and politely asked the organizers to give her the platform.

They were just as surprised as anyone, but naturally they agreed at once.

Her speech was short and consisted simply of reading the message that she'd had transmitted an hour before to the entire nation. Leaving aside the flowery preface, the gist of it was simple:

General Stearns was quite correct. Chancellor Oxenstierna's actions were completely illegal. The legitimate prime minister, Wilhelm Wettin, should be released from prison and returned to office.

The applause went on and on and on. Liesel Hahn, who was on the platform herself, was simultaneously delighted and downcast. Delighted, because she thought Amalie Elizabeth's actions were entirely correct. Downcast, because the prospects for the Fourth of July Party itself in Hesse-Kassel would remain dim for some time.

Probably for the lifespan of the landgravine, in fact.

Kristina would always hold a bit of a grudge against Ulrik for keeping her from the rally. But not much of one. The truth was, he'd probably threaded the needle as well as anyone could. People in Magdeburg simply remembered her in the kitchens of the Freedom Arches that day. Within a few months, if they'd been asked, most of them would swear that Kristina had given a speech at the rally. A good one, too, allowing for her age.

Mostly, the little grudge was because she'd burned her finger on a skillet. Somehow that was Ulrik's fault.

He put up only a token protest, figuring that it was worth the price to exchange what might become a big political grudge for a petty personal one. Once again showing great skill at threading needles.

The only major cities in the USE that did not celebrate on February 27 were Dresden and Berlin.

Dresden did not celebrate because the city was mostly just relieved to have been spared what might have been a truly hideous fate—and had immediately pressing problems to deal with. First, thousands of wounded men to treat. Second—a much thornier problem—thousands of surrendered soldiers to deal with.

Georg Kresse and his Vogtlanders were inclined toward a simple solution: kill them all. But Mike Stearns refused and made it quite clear he wasn't going to tolerate any impromptu lynchings either.

That still left the problem of what to do with them. In the end, Mike opted for the traditional solution. He offered those willing to volunteer a place in the ranks of the Third Division. The ones who refused would be placed in hard labor clearing away the rubble that weeks of siege had left in Dresden.

About two-thirds of the captured soldiers volunteered. That meant Mike now had the problem of absorbing more than four thousand new men into his regiments.

That task would have been extraordinarily difficult except that the regiments accepted the challenge with confidence and even good humor. Perhaps ironically, they were the one large group of men in the Germanies who *weren't* nursing a grudge against all things Swede.

Why should they be? They'd just thrashed the Swedes senseless. As they'd known they would.

If you looked at it the right way, the willingness of Banér's mercenaries to switch allegiances was simply a reaffirmation of the Third Division's august status. Even dumb Swedes knew which end was up. (And never mind that there were only two hundred and eighty-six actual Swedes among the new volunteers, and seventy-three Finns.)

Berlin did not celebrate because Chancellor Oxenstierna had twenty thousand troops in or near the city on the Swedish payroll, and was in a fury.

A cold fury, to make things worse. He was now in a desperate situation, he knew it—and he knew he only had one option left. Sheer, stark violence.

Chapter 51

Dresden, capital of Saxony

Before dawn of the morning after the battle, the two young hostlers had the draft horses out of the stable and hooked up to the first of the plows. After paying them the first installment owed, Denise and Minnie headed out of the city. Others could celebrate the victory, tend to wounded, fuss over prisoners—but they had important work to do. By sunrise they were on the airfield and started to clear away the trash and debris.

It was slow going. The plow worked fine, but neither Denise nor Minnie had any real experience at this sort of work. Both of them were good horsewomen, but that wasn't the same skill set as that required here.

Within an hour, despite the cold, they were both sweating—and hadn't gotten much of the field cleared.

"We need a damn farmer," Denise groused.

The next best thing arrived—the two hostlers, with more draft horses hooked up to the roller sledge. After a short negotiation, they agreed to do the work as well. Fortunately for all concerned, the stable-master had taken the day off in order to join the city's festivities.

With capable hands now guiding the work, the field was cleared by mid-afternoon. By sundown, Denise and Minnie were back at the town house.

They found Noelle in the kitchen, sitting at the table and listening to the radio. With Nasi's purse to draw on, they could afford their own. It was purely a receiver, though, with no transmitting capability.

"Hey, Noelle, it's done!" Denise said cheerfully. "We even have time to get to the radio station for the evening window. Eddie could be here by tomorrow."

Noelle stared at them. Then, back at the radio. Somebody was jabbering something about Berlin.

"What's up?" asked Minnie. "Anything important?"

Noelle stared at them. Then, back at the radio. They were still jabbering something about Berlin.

"Well," she said. "Yes."

Chapter 52

A tavern on the outskirts of Berlin

Axel Oxenstierna frowned. There was some sort of racket coming from just outside the village inn where he'd set up his temporary command post. It sounded like the movement of a large body of troops. A battalion, at least.

Why would a battalion be moving here? True enough, he'd been ordering a lot of troop movements. Pulling an army of twenty thousand men out of their barracks and into marching order wasn't something you did in a couple of hours. But no large body of troops should be assembling *here*.

He caught the eye of one of his aides and nodded toward the front entrance. "Go see what's happening out there."

The aide headed toward the door, but before he got there it burst open. Erling Ljungberg came in, followed by three of his Scots and—

Oxenstierna froze. "Your Majesty . . ."

Gustav Adolf pushed past Ljungberg and stepped forward two paces. His face, always pale, was almost as white as a sheet.

✧   ✧   ✧

Colonel Erik Haakansson Hand was the seventh person through the door. He almost had to fight his way past the gaggle of Scots. Oversized Scots.

He was now very anxious. This was moving too quickly. Gustav Adolf was not following the plan they'd agreed on and Erik was sure he knew the reason why. The king had a ferocious temper. He didn't lose it that often, but when he did the results tended to be volcanic.

To get past the Scots he had to move around to the right. When he got past the last Scot, he could see his cousin's face in profile. The instant he saw that ghostly visage, he knew they were in trouble.

The king started with "You—" The next several words were utterly foul. They were blasphemous, too, which really frightened Erik. The king of Sweden was a devout Lutheran and almost never lapsed into blasphemy. Profanity, yes. This day and age was not the least bit Victorian. But pious men took the third commandment seriously.

The chancellor raised his hand, half in protest and half simply as an unconscious shielding gesture. His own face was extremely pale.

Gustav Adolf moved on to accusations that had some content, but they were still laced with profanity and blasphemy.

"—knew perfectly fucking well I never would have allowed—you God-damned bastard! My own daughter had to hide from you! Were you going to see her murdered too, you stinking son-of-a-bitch? This was fucking treason, simple as that—and don't think I won't find out what really happened with that God-damned asshole in Bavaria! You think—"

It was all spinning out of control. They'd discussed this at length and had agreed that the best way to handle it was a stiff but dignified order to arrest the chancellor. Instead, the king's fury—

And then Erik's worst fears materialized. Gustav Adolf's eyes rolled up and he collapsed to the floor.

The American doctor Nichols had warned him this might happen, months ago. He'd also described the possible symptoms.

"There are half a dozen types of what we call generalized seizures," he said. "The one that's best known because it's the most dramatic is the so-called 'grand mal' seizure. Well, you probably don't use the French term yet. It's a major convulsion which usually starts with the patient losing consciousness and collapsing. That's followed by what we call the 'tonic' phase, where there's a stiffening of the body that lasts for up to a minute. Then the 'clonic' phase starts, which lasts another minute or so and where the patient has violent convulsions. You've got to be careful, then. He may bite his tongue or injure himself some other way. After that, he'll fall into a deep sleep."

"For how long?" Hand asked.

Nichols shrugged. "There's no way to know. A few minutes, a few hours—in some instances, even a few days."

This was a disaster. The big room in the tavern was a frozen tableau, for the moment. The king on the floor and the chancellor staring down at him. Ljungberg and his half dozen Scots were doing the same. So were the eight officers on Oxenstierna's staff who'd been in the room when the king burst in.

But Oxenstierna's paralysis wouldn't last. The man was smart, he was ruthless when necessary—and the king's paralysis gave him the opening.

They'd all come in armed except the king, but they'd agreed they wouldn't have weapons in hand. Erik had made certain, though, that his pistol would come out of its holster easily.

So it did. It was a good flintlock with two rifled barrels. He strode forward three paces. He'd trained himself to shoot left-handed since the battlefield injury that had half-crippled his right arm, and he'd regained much of his former marksmanship. But he was taking no chances.

The gun came up, on target.

"Traitor!" he said. Not quite shouting.

He fired the first barrel; an instant later, the second.

Both rounds struck the chancellor squarely in the chest. Oxenstierna was wearing no armor and in the heat produced by the fire in the tavern's main room, he'd had his buff coat unbuttoned and open. The heavy .62 caliber bullets punched into his heart and knocked him off his feet.

He might not be dead yet. But that was now a meaningless technicality. He would be within a minute or two, and there was no doctor in the world, not even the Moor, who could have kept him alive.

The tableau remained frozen—though now with everyone's eyes fixed on the body of the chancellor.

Then one of Oxenstierna's staff officers muttered

a curse and drew his own pistol. Two of his fellows
began following suit.

The colonel who'd drawn first was bringing his pistol
to bear on Erik when Erling Ljungberg's automatic
began firing. Three shots took him down; two shots
each did for his would-be partners.

The shots were fired so rapidly they almost sounded
like a single noise. A sort of tearing thunder, in the
confines of the tavern room.

The three staff officers joined the chancellor on
the floor. All three were just as obviously dead as
their master.

Again, the tableau was frozen. Then all the Scots
drew their pistols. For their part, the remaining staff
officers held up their hands—part in protest; part in
surrender—and stumbled back a pace or two.

"Hold!" Erik shouted. "All hold!"

Again, a frozen tableau. Now, everyone was staring at Hand.

He pointed to the door. "Captain Stewart, go outside
and see to it that the Västergötlanders have the area
under control. Then ask Karl Hård af Segerstad to
come in here. Then check to see the dispositions of
Colonel Hastfer and his Finnish regiment."

The Scot officer holstered his pistol and left.

The rest of the Scots began holstering their own
pistols. It was obvious there would be no further
gunfire. Not now, after Ljungberg had ejected the clip
and slapped in another one. He was *not* holstering
his gun. He had it pointed squarely at the surviving
staff officers and was bestowing a grin upon them
that Erik thought would probably give some of them
nightmares later. Erling Ljungberg held his post as the

king's chief bodyguard because, just as Anders Jönsson had been before him, the man was utterly murderous.

The immediate crisis over, Erik hurried to Gustav Adolf's side. Not knowing what else to use—he'd make it a point to be prepared for this, in the future—he snatched off his hat and rolled up the brim.

Just in time. As the doctor had foreseen, the king was going into convulsions. Erik managed to shove the rolled-up hat brim into his cousin's mouth before he could damage himself.

Then, he waited out the convulsions, restraining the king as best he could. Within seconds, two of the Scots were assisting him.

After the king relaxed and fell asleep, Erik rose to his feet.

"And now what?" asked Ljungberg.

Excellent question. Erik groped for an answer.

It came to him within seconds. "Go get the prime minister and bring him here, Major Graham. Gordon, you go with him."

Wilhelm Wettin arrived an hour and a half later. Quite puzzled, obviously. Erik realized he hadn't instructed Graham and Gordon to tell him anything, just to bring him here. Scots tended to favor literal interpretations.

By then, the bodies of the chancellor and the three staff officers slain by Ljungberg had been carried into a side room. Gustav Adolf was resting on a narrow bed that had been brought into the tavern's main room by servants. In the absence of any advice from Nichols—he wasn't about to trust any of the doctors Oxenstierna had assigned to the king—Erik hadn't been willing to risk moving his cousin any farther than necessary.

Wettin stared at Gustav Adolf. "Is he . . . ?"

"Yes, he's back. But—as you can see—he's still subject to ills."

Wettin shook his head. It wasn't clear if the gesture was one of negation, denial, or simply to clear the man's brain. He probably didn't know himself.

"Where is Chancellor Oxenstierna?" he asked.

"The traitor is dead," Colonel Hand said in a flat, cold tone of voice. "At the king's command."

That was stretching the truth. You could even argue it was mangling the truth beyond all recognition. But for the moment, Erik didn't care—and who was there to dispute his claim? The surviving staff officers had been placed under arrest and taken away. The tavern keeper and his servants were so petrified they could barely speak.

"You can go look at his body yourself, if you don't believe me," he added, jerking his head toward the far door. "He's in a room just beyond."

Wettin shook his head again. "No, no. But . . . what do you want me to do?"

Erik shrugged. "How should I know? I'm just the king's cousin. *You're* the prime minister of the nation. It's on your head now."

Luckily, Gustav Adolf recovered consciousness within an hour. After he was told of what had transpired, a sad look came to his face.

"So, my fault again. First Anders, now Axel."

"It was *not* your fault, Cousin. For one thing, I'm the one who decided to shoot him."

The king's thick shoulders shifted on the cot, in what passed for a shrugging motion. "What else could you do? But if I hadn't lost control, Axel would still be alive."

Erik was tempted to ask: *For how long?* Gustav Adolf had made clear in their earlier discussions that he was inclined to simply have Oxenstierna stripped of his posts and sentenced to internal exile for the rest of his life. What Americans called "house arrest"— except the house in question was one of the finest mansions in Sweden.

But whatever the king's personal preferences might be, he'd also ordered Erik to launch a thorough investigation of what had transpired with Maximilian of Bavaria. If that investigation turned up proof that the chancellor had been involved in the treasonous plot—and Erik didn't have much doubt it would—then Gustav Adolf would really have no choice. He'd have to order Oxenstierna's execution.

Now that it was over, Erik decided it had all worked out for the best. His cousin's guilt for having lost control was a pale shadow of the anguish he would have felt, had he been forced to order his chancellor executed himself. He and Axel Oxenstierna had been good friends for many years.

Erik, on the other hand, had never liked the bastard anyway.

Wettin floundered. But the king was back, and took charge himself.

"First—there is a radio station here, yes?—the news must be broadcast to the entire nation. Along with the following..."

✧   ✧ - ✧

That and what followed was the jabbering from Berlin that Noelle had been listening to when Denise and Minnie returned from the airfield.

"Oh, wow," said Denise, after Noelle filled them in.

"Interesting times," said Minnie.

Denise shook her head. "No, that's a curse. Doesn't apply at all. God, I hate to think what my life would have been like without the Ring of Fire. Can we say 'boooooorrrrrring?' "

Noelle stared at her. Much the way she might have stared at a Martian. Or a mutant.

Chapter 53

The United States of Europe

All of the major newspapers in the country and many of the smaller ones came out with the story the next morning. It didn't matter what day of the week they normally published. It didn't matter whether they were morning papers or evening papers. Even if the edition was just a two-page special edition, nothing more than a broadsheet printed on both sides, they all published something.

The headlines varied from city to city and province to province, but the gist of them was essentially the same:

THE EMPEROR RECOVERS

**CHANCELLOR OXENSTIERNA
EXECUTED FOR TREASON**

HUNDREDS IN BERLIN ARRESTED

**PRIME MINISTER WETTIN FREED
AND RETURNED TO POWER**

THE EMPEROR ORDERS A
HALT TO ALL CONFLICT

THE EMPEROR OFFERS A TRUCE
TO KING WLADYSLAW

THE EMPEROR TO RETURN
TO MAGDEBURG

The festivities and the parades died down, although they didn't die out entirely. People of whatever political persuasion understood that the coming days were going to be a time of hard bargaining. Most of them figured they'd wait until they saw the end result before they started celebrating again.

Or started crying in their beer.

Part Five

March 1636

The thunder and the sunshine

Chapter 54

Magdeburg, capital of the United States of Europe

Gustav Adolf arrived in Magdeburg five days after Oxenstierna's killing. His advisers—that mostly meant his cousin Erik, right now—had had to talk him out of flying to the capital. Why take the (admittedly not great) risk, when there was no point to it? There would be no way to start any serious negotiations until Mike Stearns arrived in the capital, after all. Given the situation in Dresden and his responsibilities there, it would take him most of a week before he could leave for Magdeburg.

Besides, Gustav II Adolf—the full and formal name was needed here—could spend a useful two days or so dealing with the men who'd been arrested in the palace. Oxenstierna's minions, as Colonel Hand was wont to call them.

Deal with them he did. The emperor was sorely tempted to have the ringleaders summarily executed. But Wilhelm Wettin talked him out of that. The prime minister pointed out that given the chancellor's free-wheeling abuse of power, it would probably make a nice counterexample if the emperor displayed a great deal of restraint at the moment.

Gustav Adolf was a bit dubious of the logic, but since Erik weighed in on Wilhelm's side, he decided to accept their advice. He was still shaken by the results of his temper tantrum and not as inclined as he normally would be to trust his own instincts.

Having ruled out summary executions, however, he saw no problems with summary punishments short of removing heads. No way would he accept timid restrictions!

He started by stripping von Ramsla and anyone else whom Oxenstierna had given any sort of official position of all of his noble titles. Then, of all his lands, if he possessed any.

As a strictly legal proposition, his right to do any such thing was eminently disputable—and there was no shortage of lawyers in the USE ready and willing to argue the case. The problem was that Gustav Adolf did not extend the punishment to the *heirs* of the punishee—but made it very clear that he would do so the moment any of them tried to challenge him.

That made the whole thing a very risky proposition. A man could bow his head, accept the penalties, and slink back home—where, at least for most of them, their families would maintain them in more-or-less the same comfort they'd been accustomed to. Or, he could challenge the emperor in court. If he lost, though, he risked being out in the cold with his entire family.

Most of them accepted the punishments. Only three indicated an intention to file a legal challenge. In all three cases, because their families detested them and would be pitching them into the cold anyway.

That done, the emperor ordered any of Oxenstierna's minions who might conceivably—remotely, at the far edges, barely, tangentially, it didn't matter—have been involved in the plot with the Bavarians to be kept under arrest until such time as Erik Haakansson Hand got around to interrogating them and deciding they were innocent.

At which point, of course, any *other* penalties would kick in.

That done, the emperor levied heavy fines on anyone who had participated in what he chose to call the "outlaw convention." If the person in question had been a member of Parliament, the fine was doubled and the emperor unilaterally decreed that their election was null and void because they had violated their oath of office by participating in said outlaw convention.

This ruling was *very* questionable, there being no provision in the constitution that gave the emperor any such power. And, in the end, Gustav Adolf would rescind it two weeks later. The electoral disqualification, that is, not the fines. He did so not because he feared the courts but because Mike Stearns insisted on it and the emperor decided it was not an issue he was prepared to fight over tooth and nail.

That done...

He decided to rest from his labors. He'd already stripped large pieces of hide from just about everyone who'd been arrested, after all. In fact, the only exceptions were two servants who'd been rounded up by mistake.

And by then, the barge was ready to take him to Magdeburg. The very luxurious barge, with the world's best doctor on it and ready to tend to his needs. James Nichols had come up from Magdeburg at the emperor's request.

Dresden, capital of Saxony

Eddie finally arrived in Dresden just about the same time Gustav Adolf stepped aboard the barge that would take him to Magdeburg. By the time he got there, Denise and Minnie had two more accomplishments to their names. First, they'd produced one of the best-manicured airfields in Europe, certainly in wintertime. Secondly, they'd learned how to use a plow.

"A skill," Minnie pointed out, "that for girls like us is probably as useful as knowing how to grow those little miniature trees—what do they call them? Something Japanese."

"Banzai trees," said Denise.

Minnie frowned. "Are you sure?"

"Oh, yeah. Japanese people get fanatical about stuff."

They'd had plenty of advance warning, so all three of the women working for Nasi who'd gotten stranded in Dresden were waiting in the little hangar at the airfield with their luggage packed. Noelle had paid off the rent owing on the town house so they were ready to go.

The bolder of the two young hostlers waited with them. He'd continued to help them all the way through, because Minnie had relented and decided he was okay after all, on the cute side, and unlike Denise she had no boyfriend. (Steady boyfriend, anyway. Whenever she was in the mood, Minnie never lacked for male company. One-eyed or not.)

The hostler was sorry to see Minnie go. For that matter, Minnie would miss him herself. It had been a very pleasant few days.

On the other hand, once they left Dresden she'd get over the loss in about fifteen minutes and he'd get over it in twenty. Theirs had been a friendly relationship, but one driven far more by hormones than by hearts.

It didn't occur to any of the women to ask Eddie where they were going until Noelle realized they were flying south.

"Prague," he said. "The boss has a new assignment for us."

"What is it?" asked Minnie from the back of the plane. She and Noelle were crammed into a seat that was really designed for one person. They'd agreed to let Denise have the copilot's seat so she could be close to Eddie.

"How should I know? Since when did Francisco Nasi become a blabbermouth?"

"For Chrissake," Denise complained, *"we're* the ones who'll be doing the assignment. How can we do it if we don't know what it is?"

"Oh, I'm sure he'll tell you once we get there."

An upsetting thought occurred to her. "Aren't you coming with us?"

"Oh, yes."

"Then why didn't he tell *you?*"

"So I couldn't tell you, of course. Denise, you've really got to brush up on your operational security."

Vienna, capital of the Austro-Hungarian Empire

Emperor Ferdinand III gave Janos Drugeth a suspicious look from under lowered brows. "This is not simply an elaborate ploy on your part to see your American woman again, I hope?"

Janos wouldn't normally roll his eyes in response to an imperial comment—that would border on *lèse majesté*—but he did on this occasion. "Don't be absurd! And how could I have done it anyway? You think the sultan conspires with me?"

Ferdinand kept peering at him from under lowered brows.

Now, Janos threw up his hands with exasperation. "The Americans have a word for this, you know. 'Paranoia.'"

"Yes, I know. Demonstrating once again their tenuous hold on reality. Apparently they think people have no enemies." He sniffed. "It's like having a word for a fear of heights. Completely useless. Of course people are afraid of heights."

Janos decide to wait out the imperial fit. It was true enough that emperors had lots of enemies.

After a few seconds, Ferdinand sighed and slumped back in his chair. "You're certain?"

"Yes, Your Majesty. I am." Janos thought formality would help here. "As certain as I've ever been of anything in my life."

He leaned forward in his own chair, his hands extended in what was almost a pleading gesture. "Ferdinand, look at it this way. We're in the beginning of March. If I'm right, Murad will have begun his troop movements. By the end of the month—no later than sometime in April—the first detachments will have begun arriving in Belgrade. Once that happens, you know perfectly well the invasion will be underway."

After a moment, Ferdinand nodded. Like any Austrian ruler, even a young one, he knew the military realities. That great a mobilization of troops was simply too expensive for an empire—any empire, even one with the resources of the Ottomans—to use as a feint or diversion. If large numbers of soldiers started appearing in Belgrade in the spring, the Turks would be at the Austrian border by midsummer at the latest.

And Austria had lots of spies in Belgrade.

"Go on," he said.

Janos leaned back. "So let's use the intervening weeks to establish private communications with the USE. Which we can do using Nasi in Prague as the intermediary."

The emperor made a little snorting sound. "Who will no doubt use as his own intermediary a certain young woman who already has an Austro-Hungarian connection."

"Well . . . yes, I imagine he will. It would make sense, after all."

Ferdinand went back to gazing at him from under lowered brows.

"Oh, very well," he said. "Set the process in motion."

Solemnly, Janos inclined his head. He saw no need to burden the emperor with the knowledge that he'd already begun that process a week before, as soon as he returned to Vienna. What else were royal advisers for than to anticipate the decisions of their sovereign?

Magdeburg, capital of the United States of Europe

Since Mike Stearns hadn't arrived yet, Gustav Adolf spent the first two days after his return to the capital mostly with his daughter. They had not seen each other for almost a year—a year in which a great many things had happened, including an assassination attempt on the girl that came very close to succeeding and the murder of her mother that very same day. Not to mention the near-death of her father and his subsequent mental collapse.

She had held up surprisingly well. No, extraordinarily well. He was very pleased with her.

No, immensely pleased.

Most of that pleasure was personal, nothing more than the sentiments any father would feel when one of his offspring demonstrated good qualities under pressure. Some of it, though, was dynastic and quite cold-blooded. It was a simple fact that the Vasa dynasty had come out of a crisis that might easily have turned into a disaster in better shape than ever. Its position in the United States of Europe was now extremely secure, even if its direct power might have declined a bit.

That was largely thanks to Kristina. The huge, cheering crowds that had greeted Gustav Adolf when he arrived in the capital had been there as much to applaud a father as a monarch. Kristina had been riding with him in the parade, and that much was blindingly obvious.

In a much harsher way, the position of the Vasas in Sweden was stronger also. As part of his bargain with

Oxenstierna when he took the throne in 1611, Gustav Adolf had restored the Swedish aristocracy's privileges that his grandfather had stripped away from them. Now, with the chancellor's betrayal and subsequent death, the king intended to strip those privileges and powers away from them again.

Not immediately. He had many more pressing matters to attend to first. But it was now clear to him that his grandfather had been right after all. The great man who had founded their line in Sweden had understood something that Gustav Adolf himself had had to learn the hard way—a smart dynasty bases itself on the populace, not on the nobility.

There had been another change in Kristina since he'd seen her last. This one more subtle but just as unmistakable. The girl was simply more cheerful than she'd been before. More at ease in her father's presence, less anxious, less needful of being the constant center of attention. Yet no less affectionate.

Caroline Platzer deserved much of the credit for that transformation, he knew—and silently patted himself on the back for having ignored the complaints about the American woman from the princess' other ladies in waiting. She had become something in the way of a surrogate mother for the girl, in the way the world's very best governesses could manage.

But there was another influence at work also, which the emperor did not miss either.

Prince Ulrik of Denmark. A young man with depths that Gustav Adolf had only half-seen before. To name just one: the dynasty's position in the newly formed Union of Kalmar had also grown stronger. And that was well-nigh amazing. Had anyone told Gustav Adolf what was about to happen on the eve of the Battle of Lake Bledno, he would have sworn King Christian of Denmark would take advantage of the crisis to destroy the Union.

Yet, he hadn't. Gustav Adolf was quite sure that was mostly because of Ulrik. Not even so much because of his direct influence on his father but simply because of his existence. His nature, as it were. A drunk Christian IV might be, and given to grandiosity, but he was also exceedingly intelligent. On some level he must have realized that any actions he took against the Union of Kalmar would only damage his son's prospects—which were far greater than his own.

Even royal fathers are sometimes capable of putting their children's welfare first.

As Gustav Adolf would now have to do himself. He'd had another seizure on the barge, halfway through his voyage here—and this one had not been triggered off by any rage. It had come completely as a surprise to everyone, even Dr. Nichols. The lesson from the experience, which the American medician had drummed home at tedious length, was that the emperor had to accept the fact that he was now forced to operate within certain understood constraints. For how long? Quite possibly the rest of his life.

That meant he needed to develop surrogates. Men he trusted—but they also had to be men with enormous talents.

A rare combination, that. He'd thought he'd found it once before with Axel Oxenstierna. Being fair—to himself as well as his former chancellor—that productive relationship has lasted for a quarter of a century and might well have lasted for another, had Gustav Adolf not been struck down at Lake Bledno. Oxenstierna was hardly the first man to succumb to great temptation. Had the temptation never arisen, he probably would have remained faithful to his dying day.

Now, the emperor needed to find a replacement for Oxenstierna. And by great good fortune, he thought he'd found three: a son, a cousin and a brother of sorts. Perhaps the Lutheran pastors were correct and God did favor Sweden. It was tempting to think so, certainly. But temptation was ever Satan's favored tool.

Gustav Adolf had already had one long private talk with Ulrik since his arrival in Magdeburg. Two things had come out of it: one specific, one general.

The specific result had been that he'd decided to accept Ulrik's judgment that there had been something hidden in the murder of his wife. Some dark scheme that lay behind it, quite different from the conclusions one might draw from the superficial evidence. So, he'd put Ulrik in charge of ferreting out the truth.

Or rather, overseeing the ferret—that Norwegian of his, whose mechanical talents were but a veneer over more ancient and grimmer skills.

The general result had been the first step in a long journey they would take together. A king needed an heir, and an emperor needed one even more. A male heir, if at all possible. Women *could* rule, and sometimes even effectively—witness the great English queen of the past century. But in the nature of things their position was always a bit tenuous. Far better if their reign could be buttressed by a consort who could double as a king-in-all-but-name.

So, as time passed, a son-in-law would eventually become a son. As close to it as possible, at any rate.

As for the cousin, Gustav Adolf's trust and confidence in Erik Haakansson Hand had proven to be fully justified.

That left the brother of sorts. In the long and often bloody history of monarchy, nothing posed so great a threat to a king as his brothers—yet, at times, could be his greatest strength.

The first outcome was by far the most likely, of course. The Ottomans had made a veritable heathen cult of imperial fratricide. But you didn't need to venture into exotic lands to find the same phenomenon. Next door in France, Monsieur Gaston had been plotting ceaselessly for years against his brother Louis XIII, the rightful king. And while the plots of the newly crowned Fernando I in the Netherlands against his brother Philip III of Spain were not—yet, at least—of such deadly intent, they had still ripped Philip's realm in half.

Still, it wasn't always so. In his long struggle to retain his throne during the English civil wars of the fifteenth century, Edward IV's staunchest supporter had been his brother Richard, the duke of Gloucester. (His other brother George, however, betrayed him as royal brothers more commonly did.) It was true that after Edward's death his brother Richard was accused of having murdered the two legitimate heirs in order to take the throne himself. But Gustav Adolf was skeptical of that claim, given that it was advanced by the usurper who had overthrown Richard himself.

Even if the tale were true, however, it simply reinforced the lesson. More than anything, a crippled king needed men close to the throne he could rely upon—but not so close that they could succeed to the throne themselves. Princes, as it were, forever barred from becoming kings in their own name.

One other thing was obvious. Gustav Adolf and Mike Stearns would no doubt clash until one or the other fell into his grave. But there were very few men in the world he now trusted as much. His daughter might very well owe her life to the man. She certainly owed him her inheritance. Without Stearns, there would be no United States of Europe. And when the crisis came, he had placed its survival above any ambitions of his own.

Few kings in history had had more faithful brothers. Precious few.

By their nature, of course, princes worthy of the name had goals and demands of their own. It was just silly to think otherwise. But so long as they could be trusted, acceptable solutions could always be found.

So. Once more, it was time to negotiate. The Golden King would struggle again with the Prince of Germany. With him, certainly, but . . . not exactly against him. It would almost be like a family reunion. In a manner of speaking.

Chapter 55

The United States of Europe

All of the major newspapers in the country and many of the smaller ones came out with the story the next morning. It didn't matter what day of the week they normally published. It didn't matter whether they were morning papers or evening papers. Even if the edition was just a one-page special edition, nothing more than a glorified leaflet, they all published something.

The headline varied from city to city and province to province, but the gist was essentially the same:

THE PRINCE ARRIVES IN MAGDEBURG
SUMMONED TO THE PALACE
BY THE EMPEROR

Darmstadt, Province of the Main

After everyone on the city council finished reading the news report, the major cleared his throat.

"We'll just have to wait and see what happens."

The militia commander shook his head. "We're fucked is what's going to happen."

One of the city council members made a face. "You can't say that for sure, Gerlach."

"You watch," said the militia commander. "The emperor will be putty in the Prince's hands. He'll cave in across the board."

Nobody said anything. In their heart of hearts, they were pretty sure he was right.

Augsburg, one of the USE's seven independent imperial cities

The commander of Augsburg's militia, Ruprecht Amsel, was in a good mood. He'd reached the point where he didn't much care any longer how the citizenship question got resolved. If he'd had his own preferences, the requirements would be fairly stringent. A man would have to own at least a reasonable amount of property—and women wouldn't have the vote at all.

But he'd come to appreciate something far more than he had before. He'd never heard of Dr. Johnson and never would, but his thought processes over the past few months had been a perfect illustration of Johnson's quip that the prospect of being hanged concentrates the mind wonderfully.

Apprentices with uppity attitudes were annoying. So were indigents who thought they should have the same rights as solid men.

Maximilian of Bavaria, on the other hand, was not annoying. He was downright awful.

A tavern in Melsungen, in the province of Hesse-Kassel

"Here's to the health of our landgravine!" shouted one of the revelers, holding up his stein of beer. "Long may she reign!"

The tavern was full, as it often was on a winter's eve. Not a single stein failed to come up to join the toast.

Another reveler stood up, hoisting his stein. "And here's to the emperor! May he drive a hard bargain!"

Not a single stein came up to join that toast. Confused, the reveler looked around. Then, realizing his error, hoisted his stein again.

"But not too hard!"

Now the steins came up to join him.

A tavern on the coast of the Pomeranian Bay

The fisherman squinted at the newssheet. "D'you think they'll be able to reach an agreement?"

"Is the sea wet?" asked one of his companions.

"Is the sea salty?" asked the other.

Paris, capital of France

After he finished reading the copies of the intercepted radio messages that Servien had given him, Richelieu rose from his desk and went over to one of the window in his palace.

"What do you think will come out of it, Your Grace?" asked Servien.

"Nothing good for France," was the cardinal's reply.

Madrid, capital of Spain

There was no reaction to the upcoming meeting in the court of Spain.

They had no radio. They wouldn't receive the news for days yet.

Brussels, capital of the Netherlands

Fernando I looked around the conference table at his closest advisers.

"We're all agreed, then?" said the king in the Netherlands. "We will make no further effort to improve our position?"

"Not with the Swede and Stearns about to reach an agreement," said Rubens. "We'd just be wasting our time."

"Can we be so sure of that?" wondered Scaglia. "They haven't reached an agreement yet. Maybe they won't be able to."

Archduchess Isabella sniffed. "And maybe horses will learn to sing. But I'm still not wasting my time by going to the stables and sitting around in the hopes it might happen."

Poznań, Poland

"The king refuses to accept the Swede's offer of a truce," said Stanislaw Koniecpolski. "As I expected."

Lukasz Opalinski's had expected exactly the same thing. Wladyslaw IV was as predictable as the Sejm. Given a choice between two options, you could always rely on them to choose the wrong one.

"Still no word from Jozef?"

Lukasz shook his head. "He must not have found any new batteries yet."

Dresden, capital of Saxony

Actually, Jozef had found new batteries. When Eddie Junker had returned, he'd flown in some emergency supplies. They'd all been high-value and low-weight, of course. Among them had been some batteries.

Unfortunately, Gretchen Richter had placed them under lock and key and Jozef had no legitimate reason he could simply ask for some. So he'd been trying to figure out how he might steal a few.

Reluctantly. He felt like a dwarf of legend trying to figure out how to steal part of a dragon's treasure. A blonde and good-looking dragon. But still a dragon.

True, the dragon had been preoccupied of late with her husband. People had been making jokes about it.

But that was not particularly comforting. Not when the husband commanded a regiment called the Hangman and was said to have cut off a general's head with his own volley gun company.

Chapter 56

Magdeburg, capital of the United States of Europe

After the servant ushered Mike into Gustav Adolf's chamber, he left, closing the door behind him. Mike watched him go, with a slight smile on his smile.

"Yes, yes," said Gustav Adolf. "As you can see, I am adopting an up-time custom. We will actually have a private meeting."

The emperor was sitting in a very large and very comfortable-looking armchair. Another one, equally large and comfortable-looking, was positioned a few feet away, angled toward his own. A low table sat between them, with a pot and two cups on it. There was also a bowl of sugar and a small pitcher of cream.

"Your preference is coffee, if I recall correctly. Black, no cream or sugar."

"Yes, Your Majesty. Thank you."

Gustav Adolf lifted the pot and poured them both a cup. As he did so, he waved his hand. "Please, Michael. I think we would do better to keep this informal. Call me Gustav, if you would."

Mike nodded and sat down. This was . . . interesting.

Also unexpected. His relations with the king of Sweden had always been cordial, except in the heat of negotiations, but never what you'd call intimate. They'd been friendly but not friends. Was Gustav Adolf seeking to change that?

If so, Mike was certainly willing—provided the change didn't come at too high a price. The emperor would want something in return, of course. Mike didn't fault him for that. It was a given that an emperor wants something, unless he's incompetent.

He decided the best tactic was to cut right to the chase.

"Why don't we begin by you telling me the thing you want most from me that you think I'm most likely to object to, Gustav." He picked up his cup and took a sip. The coffee was superb, as you'd expect.

The emperor smiled, as he stirred some sugar into his own cup and added some cream. "Very well. We're going to need a new election soon, obviously. The existing Parliament has lost all credibility with the nation." His pleasant expression darkened for a moment. "It has certainly lost it with me."

"Until he loses a vote of confidence, Wilhelm is under no legal obligation to call for new elections," Mike pointed out. "And he can stall holding a new session of Parliament for some time, given the current...ah, chaos."

His own expression darkened a little. "If for no other reason, he can argue that your disqualification of dozens of Crown Loyalist MPs requires that special elections be held in those districts to elect new representatives before any full session of Parliament can be called. And I'd have to say I'd agree with him.

Before we go any further, by the way, I'm giving you notice that I plan to contest that issue with you very strenuously. Privately, I'll agree that those people are worthless bums and had it coming. But I can't agree to allowing the emperor the right to unilaterally declare any MP to be disqualified from office. That power needs to be reserved for the Parliament alone."

Before the emperor could respond, Mike raised his hand. "I don't ask that you do it immediately. That would make it seem as if you were caving in to pressure coming from me. By all means, wait a week or two. Wait a month, if need be. But I want those disqualifications rescinded."

In times past that would probably have led to one of their frequent clashes. A bit to Mike's surprise, after an initial stiffening of his back, Gustav Adolf visibly made himself relax. He even took another sip of coffee before replying.

"Let us leave that aside for the moment. In terms of what we were discussing, it's not relevant. I've already spoken to Wilhelm—just two days ago, in this very room—and he assured me he plans to call for new elections before the month is over."

Mike took a sip from his own coffee, while he thought that over. No one in the Fourth of July Party had known that Wettin planned such early elections. Mike knew that for a certainty because he had come here from his own house, which doubled as FoJP headquarters, after spending the first two hours of the morning discussing the political situation with his wife and several other leading figures in the party.

Interesting. Among other things, it indicated that Wilhelm Wettin was going to take the high road, so to speak, rather than engage in maneuvers that might be tactically effective in the short run but would be deleterious in the long run. Perhaps he'd learned something from the whole experience.

"Very well. What do you want from me, then?"

"I want you to step down as leader of your party. I do not want you to seek the position of prime minister again. Let someone else take your place. I want you to stay in the army."

Mike hesitated. It was so tempting...

But, no. He'd be making that same mistake. Undoubtedly the oldest mistake in the political book and probably the most destructive. You always needed to think in the long term. Stabilizing and strengthening the new relationship that Gustav Adolf was seeking with him was more important than gaining a temporary advantage in negotiations.

"Ask for something else, Gustav. That one's a freebie. Ah, 'freebie' means—"

"I know what it means." The emperor cocked his head quizzically. "But I'm not sure I understand the term in this context."

"I was not planning to run for office anyway. I made that decision before I even got here. Since I arrived, I've spent several hours discussing it with my wife and several other close political associates. We're all agreed it would be best if I didn't run again."

Clearly, the emperor had not anticipated that answer. He took a moment to finish his coffee.

"I am surprised," he said, after setting down the cup. "You could win, you know. Quite easily, I think. Your popularity is at an all-time high in the nation." He chuckled. "It's that 'Prince of Germany' business."

Mike shrugged. "Yes, I know—but that's also the problem. I've become too...what's the word? 'Princely,' I guess. I make too many people nervous, on the one hand. And on the other—which I think may be worse—I make too many other people too ambitious."

"'Too ambitious'? What do you mean?"

He gave Gustav Adolf a level stare. "You know perfectly well what I mean. A prime minister has a clearly delineated position within the law. Powerful, but limited. A prince...has no clear limits. He might be capable of anything. What produces fear in some quarters can produce delusions of grandeur in another. Well, not that, exactly. I'd have to be the one with delusions of grandeur, and while I have my faults, that's just not one of them. But some of my supporters would get too...enthusiastic, let's say."

Neither one of them said anything for perhaps half a minute. Then Gustav Adolf sighed softly and slumped a bit in his chair.

"Thank you for that, Michael. Yes, that is exactly where my fears lay." He took a slow, deep breath and let it out. "Who would you choose, then, assuming your party won the election?"

"We haven't decided yet. Either Strigel or Piazza. But since Ed isn't here yet, we can't make any final decision."

The emperor smiled a bit crookedly. "My own preference would be your wife, actually. But I suppose that's impractical."

Mike's smile was not crooked at all. "Leaving aside the fact that the Germanies are not ready for a Jewess as prime minister, Becky would have a fit if anyone proposed it. She doesn't like being in the limelight."

He finished his own coffee. "And it wouldn't be a good idea anyway—although I agree with you that she'd be superb in the office. The problem is that prince business again. Too many people—both those overly fearful as well as those overly rambunctious—would assume that she was simply my surrogate."

He shook his head. "No, it's got to be either Matthias or Ed."

"Of the two, my own recommendation would be Piazza."

"Privately, I agree. I'm curious though, Gustav. What's your reasoning?"

"Two factors are critical, I think. The first is that I believe the nation would find it a bit reassuring to have an up-timer in the position of prime minister. In a peculiar sort of way, you provide the same sort of . . . call it 'distance,' that a royal family provides. You came from so far away that people think—not entirely foolishly, either—that you are a bit removed from the petty factionalism of everyday politics."

Mike thought about it. "There's possibly some truth to that. I agree that people tend to react to us that way. At least a bit. And your second reason?"

"Strigel is from Magdeburg province, Piazza from Thuringia-Franconia. The second is the one that more closely reflects the nation as a whole. I think he'd bring a wider experience to the position than Strigel would. Between the two of us, I also think he's more capable. But that speaks more to Piazza's strengths than to any real weakness on Strigel's part. I'd certainly be comfortable enough with Strigel as prime minister."

Mike's private assessment was the same, but he saw no purpose in stating it aloud.

"To go back to the beginning, Gustav, ask me for something else."

"A compromise, then. Something—it has to be of real substance, Michael—that your party will be willing to cede to the Crown Loyalists. Or whoever winds up being your principal opponent in the election. I suspect the Crown Loyalists are on the verge of collapse as a single and unitary party."

"They were never really that to begin with. Yes, I think you're right. I think Amalie Elizabeth will now be the most influential figure in a new conservative movement. She won't seek to be prime minister herself, of course. First, because she's not about to relinquish her title; and second, because she's a woman. The nation wouldn't be much more willing to accept a gentile female prime minister than a Jewess, I think. Wilhelm will probably run for office again, more or less on her behalf."

He considered the emperor's request. Not for long, though. This didn't really come as a big surprise.

"I am not willing to compromise on the citizenship issue, Gustav. I'd rather lose the election than retreat from our basic principles there. I would be willing, though—and I believe I can persuade the FoJP to agree—to compromise on the question of the established church."

"The nature of the compromise being...?"

"Each province can decide for itself whether it wants an established church. But I would insist that the legal options would have to include complete separation of church and state. Without that, the Committees of Correspondence would dig in their heels."

Gustav picked up the pot. "More coffee?"

"Please." Mike extended his cup.

They used the brief time needed to prepare the beverages to ponder the matter silently. Or rather, the emperor did.

After he took his first sip, he set down the cup and said, "Agreed. With your permission, I will privately let the key parties on the other side know where you are prepared to compromise, and where you are not."

Mike had lifted his cup to his lips but paused just before taking a sip. "Satisfy my own curiosity, if you would. Who are these 'key parties,' as you see it?"

"Wilhelm and the landgravine, of course. Also Duke George of Brunswick. Just because he's in the siege lines around Poznań doesn't mean he's not a central figure in the nation's political life. No one of any importance in Brunswick will do anything without George's approval."

"Who else?"

The emperor named half a dozen prominent figures. All of them were in what could be called the moderate wing of the Crown Loyalist party—and not one of them had come to Berlin in response to Oxenstierna's summons.

"Finally . . ." Gustav Adolf hesitated. "I think also Ernst Wettin."

Mike's eyebrows raised. "He considers himself an administrator, you know. Not a politician."

The emperor chuckled. "Yes, I know. It is time he expanded his horizons, I think."

The next two hours went smoothly, almost effortlessly. By the end, Gustav Adolf assured Mike that he would rescind his disqualification of the Crown Loyalist MPs in a week or so.

That done, Mike stood up. "And now that we've agreed I won't seek the prime minister's post and I'll stay in the army, what *do* you want me to do?"

The emperor's nostrils flared. "You need to ask?" He pointed to the south. "I have had *enough* of Duke Maximilian! Since the Poles are being pigheaded, I have to leave Lennart and his two divisions at Poznań. So I'd appreciate it if you would take your Third Division down there and crush him like a bug."

Mike stared down at him, for a moment. "Just like that?"

"Just like that."

"You don't have any doubts—"

"Michael, please!" The emperor stood up himself. "Will you allow that I know whereof I speak, when it comes to military affairs?"

"Yes, of course."

"Then here is the truth, whether you understand or accept it. You have now won three major battles. One of them included taking a well-fortified town, another resulted in the complete destruction of the enemy army. By the end, your forces were *larger* than they were when you started. Larger in numbers—and better equipped. And you managed to do all this without generating hatred among the populace as a whole. Indeed, I'm told civilians are more likely to regret seeing your soldiers leave than they are to welcome the sight.

"These are signal accomplishments, whether you realize it or not." He raised his hand dramatically, as if to hold back the tides. "By all means, deny it! Continue to insist to any who will listen that you are a novice, a witless bumbler, and are only kept from total disaster by the desperate efforts of your staff. But please spare me the silliness. You are already one of the best generals in the continent. Still crude in some ways, but not in what really matters—you are willing to fight and you fight to win. So, as I said. Crush the Bavarian bastard for me, would you?"

There didn't seem to be anything Mike could say to that. So, off he went.

On the way back to his town house, he wondered if perhaps he should put together a brass band for the Third Division. For the endless series of triumphal parades the emperor seemed certain were in his future.

When he raised it with Becky that evening, her reply was: "Of course you should."

He raised it again several hours later, just to be sure that hadn't been her hormones at work. By then, the hormones—his too—had been given a thorough workout.

She stirred, half-asleep, and nuzzled him. "Of course you should," she said.

The next morning, at breakfast, his daughter Sepharad weighed in.

"Barry thinks you need a brass band, Daddy."

He gave Becky an accusing glance.

"I said nothing to them," she insisted. "It's obvious to all."

He looked at Baruch. The three-year-old philosopher-to-be gazed back at him solemnly.

"It's just in the nature of things, Daddy," he explained.

"I knew it!" exclaimed his wife.

It was a little unsettling, in fact. Mike steeled his

resolve again. As soon as possible, that kid needed to get a Harley-Davidson patch for his jacket.

Jeff Higgins swore he had one, buried somewhere in his old junk. He thought he might have a Cat cap too.

His wife was now giving him a suspicious look. "Hillbillies!" she accused.

"Hey, hon, I was just thinking about how many instruments I should get," he protested.

"You have no respect!"

Cast of Characters

Ableidinger, Constantin	Member of USE Parliament; leader of the Ram movement.
Abrabanel, Rebecca	Leader of the Fourth of July Party; wife of Mike Stearns.
Achterhof, Gunther	Leader of the Committees of Correspondence.
Banér, Johan Gustafsson	Swedish general.
Bartley, David	Supply officer in Third Division; also a financier.
Beasley, Denise	Teenage girl employed as an agent by Francisco Nasi; informally betrothed to Eddie Junker.
Bugenhagen, Albert	Mayor of Hamburg; leader of the Fourth of July Party.
Christian IV	King of Denmark.

Dalberg, Werner von — Leader of the Fourth of July Party in the Oberpfalz.

Donner, Agathe "Tata" — Daughter of Reichard Donner, leader of the Mainz CoC; now a CoC organizer in Dresden.

Drugeth, Janos — Hungarian nobleman; friend and adviser of Ferdinand III.

Duerr, Ulbrecht — Officer, USE Army; aide to Mike Stearns.

Engler, Thorsten — Captain in USE Army; fiancé of Caroline Platzer; also the Imperial Count of Narnia.

Ferdinand III — Emperor of Austria.

George, Brunswick-Lüneburg, duke of — Major general in command of the 1st Division, USE Army.

Gundelfinger, Helene — Vice president of the State of Thuringia-Franconia; leader of the Fourth of July Party.

Hahn, Liesel — Member of Parliament from Hesse-Kassel.

Hans Georg, von Arnim — Commanding general of the Saxon army in Leipzig.

Hesse-Kassel, Amalie Elizabeth, Landgravine of — Ruler of Hesse-Kassel, widow of Wilhelm V.

Higgins, Jeffrey "Jeff"

Lieutenant Colonel, USE Army; husband of Gretchen Richter.

Hugelmair, Minnie

Teenage girl employed as an agent by Francisco Nasi; friend of Denise Beasley; adopted daughter of Benny Pierce.

Junker, Egidius "Eddie"

Former agent of the SoTF government, now employed as an agent and pilot by Francisco Nasi; informally betrothed to Denise Beasley.

Keller, Anselm

Member of Parliament from the Province of the Main.

Kienitz, Charlotte

Leader of the Fourth of July Party in Mecklenburg.

Knyphausen, Dodo

Major general in command of the 2nd Division, USE Army.

Koniecpolski, Stanislaw

Grand Hetman of the Polish-Lithuanian Commonwealth.

Krenz, Eric

Lieutenant, USE Army.

Kresse, Georg

Leader of guerrilla movement in the Vogtland.

Kuefer, Wilhelm

Guerrilla fighter in the Vogtland; Kresse's assistant.

Leebrick, Anthony

Officer, USE Army; aide to Mike Stearns.

Long, Christopher   Officer, USE Army; aide to
Mike Stearns.

Mailey, Melissa   Adviser to Mike Stearns; leader
of the Fourth of July Party.

Nagel, Friedrich   Lieutenant, USE Army.

Nasi, Francisco   Former head of intelligence
for Mike Stearns; now operates
a private intelligence agency.

Norddahl, Baldur   Norwegian adventurer and engineer in Danish service; friend
and assistant of Prince Ulrik.

Opalinski, Lukasz   Polish hussar.

Oxenstierna, Axel   Swedish chancellor, chief advi-
sor of Gustav II Adolf.

Piazza, Edward "Ed"   President of the State of
Thuringia-Franconia; leader of
the Fourth of July Party.

Platzer, Caroline Ann   Social worker in Magdeburg;
companion for Princess Kristina;
betrothed to Thorsten Engler.

Richelieu, Armand
Jean du Plessis de   Cardinal; first minister of
Louis XIII; the effective head
of the French government.

Richter, Maria
Margaretha
"Gretchen"   Leader of the Committees of
Correspondence; wife of Jeff
Higgins.

Saxe-Weimar, Ernst, duke of	Brother of Wilhelm Wettin; administrator for Gustav Adolf of Saxony.
Saxe-Weimar, Wilhelm IV, duke of	See: Wilhelm Wettin.
Stearns, Michael "Mike"	Former prime minister of the United States of Europe; now a major general in command of the 3rd Division, USE Army; husband of Rebecca Abrabanel.
Strigel, Matthias	Governor of Magdeburg province; leader of the Fourth of July Party.
Stull, Noelle	Former agent for the SoTF government, now employed by Francisco Nasi; is being courted by Janos Drugeth.
Szklenski, Tadeusz "Ted"	Polish CoC member in Dresden.
Thierbach, Joachim von "Spartacus"	Leader of the Committees of Correspondence.
Torstensson, Lennart	Commanding general of the USE army.
Ulrik	Prince of Denmark; youngest son of Christian IV in the line of succession; betrothed to Princess Kristina of Sweden.

Vasa, Gustav II Adolf   King of Sweden; Emperor of the United States of Europe; High King of the Union of Kalmar; also known as Gustavus Adolphus.

Vasa, Kristina   Daughter and heir of Gustav II Adolf.

Vasa, Wladyslaw IV   King of the Polish-Lithuanian Commonwealth.

Walczak, Waclaw   Leader of the Polish CoC contingent in Dresden.

Wettin, Wilhelm   Prime Minister of the USE; leader of the Crown Loyalist Party (formerly Saxe-Weimar, Wilhelm IV, Duke of).

Wojtowicz, Jozef   Nephew of Grand Hetman Koniecpolski; head of Polish intelligence in the USE.

Afterword

The 1632 series, also sometimes called the Ring of Fire series, is now up to nine novels and nine anthologies of short fiction. That's what has been produced in paper editions. There is also a bi-monthly electronic magazine devoted to the series, the *Grantville Gazette*. As of the month this novel comes out, the magazine will have published thirty-four issues. If you measure things by word count, which is how authors tend to think, almost three million words have so far been published in paper editions—1,674,000 words in the novels and 1,312,000 in the anthologies. A little over two million words have also been published in purely electronic format in *Gazette* stories and articles, not counting the stories and articles that were reissued in paper editions.

About five million words, all told. To make things still more complicated, the story line of the series is very far from linear. The 1632 series isn't so much "a" story as it is a complex of stories. (See below for my suggestion for the order in which to read the various volumes.) Any given character is likely to weave in and out of both novels and short fiction, in stories that are often written by several different authors or collaborations of authors.

To give an example of a character who appears in this novel:

Denise Beasley's best friend Minnie Hugelmair was first introduced into the series in Virginia DeMarce's story in the first *Grantville Gazette* paper edition, "The Rudolstadt Colloquy." Thereafter, she reappears in Virginia's "Mule 'Round the World" (*Grantville Gazette #7*, electronic edition); Gorg Huff and Paula Goodlett's "Trommler Records" (in the same electronic issue of the *Gazette*); my story "The Austro-Hungarian Connection" in *Ring of Fire II*; Wood Hughes' "Turn Your Radio On, Episode Three" (*GG #21*, electronic edition); Virginia DeMarce's "Franconia! Parts II and III" (*GG #25*, electronic edition); my story "Steady Girl" in *Grantville Gazette V* (paper edition); Eric Flint and Virginia DeMarce's *1635: The Dreeson Incident*; Virginia DeMarce's "Or the Horse May Learn to Sing" (*GG #28*, electronic edition); and my *1635: The Eastern Front*. In some of these stories she is simply mentioned, but even so her appearance is a matter of record.

People ask me rather frequently: "How do you keep track of all that?"

The answer is: I don't.

I couldn't possibly keep track of it. The 1632 series began with the publication of my novel *1632* in February of 2000. But years ago it became transformed into a collective enterprise. I remain the major author in the series, of course. All of the novels are either written or co-authored by me, and I have stories in all but one of the anthologies. (The one exception is

1635: The Tangled Web. The stories in that anthology are all written by Virginia DeMarce.) And I have the final say-so over anything that gets published as an editor, or as the publisher, in the case of the electronic magazine.

The analogy I tend to think of is that I'm the old-style conductor of a piano concerto, where I'm both the pianist and the conductor.

Still, there is no way I could possibly keep track of everything. I rely heavily on a group of people who consist of the editorial board of the *Gazette*—that's the editor herself, Paula Goodlett, along with Karen Bergstralh, Laura Runkle and Rick Boatright—and many of the authors who have been published frequently in the series. Those include Virginia DeMarce, Iver Cooper, Kerryn Offord, Walt Boyes, Gorg Huff, David Carrico, Kim Mackey and Chuck Gannon.

I need to take the time here to thank all of them once again.

In addition, at any given time, many other people have helped me with specific issues. For this volume and the one which preceded it, *1635: The Eastern Front*, I need to extend special thanks to two people:

Danita Ewing provided me with a great deal of help with the medical issues involved with Gustav Adolf's head injury and the resulting symptoms.

Panteleimon Roberts has been a big help with Ottoman history, which is particularly thorny and difficult for authors of historical fiction. He also wrote the first draft of what became Chapter 30 of this novel. I rewrote that draft and expanded it, but most of Panteleimon's prose remains in the text as he originally wrote it.

✧　　✧　　✧

Whenever someone asks me "what's the right order?" for reading the 1632 series, I'm always tempted to respond: "I have no idea. What's the right order for studying the Thirty Years' War? If you find it, apply that same method to the 1632 series."

However, that would be a bit churlish—and when it comes down to it, authors depend upon the goodwill of their readers. So, as best I can, here goes.

The first book in the series, obviously, is *1632*. That is the foundation novel for the entire series and the only one whose place in the sequence is definitely fixed.

Thereafter, you should read either the anthology titled *Ring of Fire* or the novel *1633*, which I co-authored with David Weber. It really doesn't matter that much which of these two volumes you read first, so long as you read them both before proceeding onward. That said, if I'm pinned against the wall and threatened with bodily harm, I'd recommend that you read *Ring of Fire* before you read *1633*.

That's because *1633* has a sequel which is so closely tied to it that the two volumes almost constitute one single huge novel. So, I suppose you'd do well to read them back to back.

That sequel is *1634: The Baltic War*, which I also co-authored with David Weber. *1632, 1633, 1634: The Baltic War, 1635: The Eastern Front* and this novel constitutes what can be considered the "main line" or even the spinal cord of the entire series. Why? First, because it's in these five novels that I depict the major political and military developments that have a tremendous impact on the entire complex of stories. Secondly, because these "main line" volumes focus on certain key characters in the series—Mike

Stearns and Rebecca Abrabanel, first and foremost, as well as Gretchen Richter and Jeff Higgins.

Once you've read *1632*, *Ring of Fire*, *1633* and *1634: The Baltic War*, you will have a firm grasp of the basic framework of the series. From there, you can go in one of two directions: either read *1634: The Ram Rebellion* or *1634: The Galileo Affair*.

There are advantages and disadvantages either way. *1634: The Ram Rebellion* is an oddball volume, which has some of the characteristics of an anthology and some of the characteristics of a novel. It's perhaps a more challenging book to read than the Galileo volume, but it also has the virtue of being more closely tied to the main line books. *Ram Rebellion* is the first of several volumes which basically run parallel with the main line volumes but on what you might call a lower level of narrative. A more positive way of putting that is that these volumes depict the changes produced by the major developments in the main line novels, as those changes are seen by people who are much closer to the ground than the statesmen and generals who figure so prominently in books like *1632*, *1633*, and *1634: The Baltic War*.

Of course, the distinction is only approximate. There are plenty of characters in the main line novels—Thorsten Engler and Eric Krenz spring immediately to mind—who are every bit as "close to the ground" as any of the characters in *1634: The Ram Rebellion*.

Whichever book you read first, I do recommend that you read both of them before you move on to *1634: The Bavarian Crisis*. In a way, that's too bad, because *Bavarian Crisis* is something of a direct sequel to *1634: The Baltic War*. The problem with going immediately from

Baltic War to *Bavarian Crisis*, however, is that there is a major political development portrayed at length and in great detail in *1634: The Galileo Affair* which antedates the events portrayed in the Bavarian story.

Still, you could read any one of those three volumes— to remind you, these are *1634: The Ram Rebellion*, *1634: The Galileo Affair* and *1634: The Bavarian Crisis*—in any order you choose. Just keep in mind that if you read the Bavarian book before the other two, you will be getting at least one major development out of chronological sequence.

After those three books are read . . .

Again, it's something of a toss-up between three more volumes: the second *Ring of Fire* anthology and the two novels, *1635: The Cannon Law* and *1635: The Dreeson Incident*. On balance, though, I'd recommend reading them in this order because you'll get more in the way of a chronological sequence:

> *Ring of Fire II*
> *1635: The Cannon Law*
> *1635: The Dreeson Incident*

The time frame involved here is by no means rigidly sequential, and there are plenty of complexities involved. To name just one, my story in the second *Ring of Fire* anthology, the short novel "The Austro-Hungarian Connection," is simultaneously a sequel to Virginia's story in the same anthology, several stories in various issues of the *Gazette*—as well as my short novel in the first *Ring of Fire* anthology, "The Wallenstein Gambit."

What can I say? It's a messy world—as is the real one. Still and all, I think the reading order recommended above is certainly as good as any and probably the best.

We come now to Virginia DeMarce's *1635: The Tangled Web*. This collection of inter-related stories runs parallel to many of the episodes in *1635: The Dreeson Incident* and lays some of the basis for the stories that will be appearing in the anthology, *1635: The Wars on the Rhine* (forthcoming, no date yet). *The Tangled Web* is also where the character of Tata, who figures in *Eastern Front* and *Saxon Uprising*, is first introduced in the series.

You can then go back to the "main line" of the series and read *1635: The Eastern Front* and the volume you hold in your hand, *1636: The Saxon Uprising*. (Yes, I realize how silly it is to tell someone to read a novel who presumably just got finished doing so. But you never know. There are people in the world—I'm one of them, as it happens—who read afterwords before they read the book they're in.)

That leaves the various issues of the *Gazette*, which are *really* hard to fit into any precise sequence. The truth is, you can read them pretty much any time you choose.

It would be well-nigh impossible for me to provide any usable framework for the thirty-four electronic issues of the magazine, so I will restrict myself simply to the five volumes of the *Gazette* that have appeared in paper editions. With the caveat that there is plenty of latitude, I'd suggest reading them as follows:

Read *Gazette I* after you've read *1632* and alongside *Ring of Fire*. Read *Gazettes II* and *III* alongside *1633* and *1634: The Baltic War*, whenever you're in the mood for short fiction. Do the same for *Gazette IV*, alongside the next three books in the sequence, *1634: The Ram Rebellion*, *1634: The Galileo Affair* and *1634: The*

Bavarian Crisis. Then read *Gazette V* after you've read *Ring of Fire II,* since my story in *Gazette V* is something of a direct sequel to my story in the *Ring of Fire* volume. You can read *Gazette V* alongside *1635: The Cannon Law* and *1635: The Dreeson Incident* whenever you're in the mood for short fiction.

And...that's it, as of now. There are a lot more volumes coming. The next volume of the 1632 series that will be appearing in print is *Ring of Fire III,* in July of this year. My story in that volume is directly connected to this novel and will lay some of the basis for its sequel. The discerning (that's a polite way of saying fussbudget) reader will have noticed and perhaps been disturbed by the fact that the Bavarian invasion of the Overpfalz vanished from this novel almost as soon as it was reported in Chapter 21.

That's because if I'd included that episode in this book it would have loaded it down with a large and unwieldy—and unresolved—sub-plot. So, instead, I will tell that story in *Ring of Fire III.*

The next novel in the series, coming out in June of this year, will be *1636: The Kremlin Games.* I'm co-authoring that book with Gorg Huff and Paula Goodlett, the editor of the *Grantville Gazette.* This is an unusual novel in the series in terms of its time span. It covers a period of five years, where all other novels in the series thus far have never covered a greater time span than a year and a half and most take place over a period of only a few months. But we have a lot of ground to cover. If you've been following the series and have ever wondered *and what's been happening in Russia, meanwhile?*—this is your chance to find out.

I'm not sure yet the order in which I will write my next two solo novels in the series. The direct sequel to this book will pick up from the end of my story in *Ring of Fire III* and cover Mike Stearns' handling of the assignment that Gustav Adolf gave him in the last chapter of this novel—crush Maximilian of Bavaria. New developments involving mumble mumble will also require Mike to mumble mumble in the course of which he winds up mumble mumbling. The working title of that novel is *1636: Tum te Tum te Tum.*

Or I might decide instead to finish a novel I began a while ago and set aside when I realized I was getting ahead of myself. The title of that novel is *1636: The Anaconda Project.* That book will serve as a sequel to my short novel "The Wallenstein Gambit," which was published in the first of the *Ring of Fire* anthologies, and will tell the story of how Wallenstein—working mostly through Morris Roth—begins the expansion of his new kingdom to the east, by encroaching on the Ruthenian territory under Polish-Lithuanian rule. It will also serve as a companion volume to this novel, by recounting some of the developments in the Polish-Lithuanian Commonwealth that were left offstage here. The attentive reader of this volume will recall that it was mentioned that the hussar Lukasz Opalinski's older brother Krzysztof and the notorious up-time radical Red Sybolt were off somewhere in Ruthenia stirring up trouble for the Polish powers-that-be. That tale will be told in *1636: The Anaconda Project.*

(If you're wondering about the distinction, "attentive" readers are the readers who pay attention to the things an author wants them to notice. "Discerning" readers are the damn nuisances who insist on fussing over loose ends that the author thought he'd swept far enough under the rug to be out of sight.)

A number of other novels are in the works that deal with other story lines in the series. I will mention in particular:

Andrew Dennis and I have started working on *1635: A Parcel of Rogues*. That novel will pick up the story of the group left behind in England after the escape from the Tower of London depicted in *1634: The Baltic War*. The characters involved will include Julie Sims, Alex Mackay, Oliver Cromwell, Gayle Mason and Stephen Hamilton.

Chuck Gannon and I are writing *1635: The Papal Stakes*. That novel is the direct sequel to *1635: The Cannon Law*, which I co-authored with Andrew Dennis. It will focus on Harry Lefferts' attempt to rescue Frank Stone and his wife Giovanna from Spanish captivity and lay some of the basis for the continuing tale of Sharon Nichols, Ruy Sanchez and the now-exiled Pope Urban VIII.

Walter Hunt and I are writing a novel set in North America. Since the working title of that novel has already been announced publicly in *Locus* magazine, I suppose there's no point in me trying to keep it buried. It's *1636: Drums Along the Mohawk*, which was supposed to have been a private joke. That will not be the title under which it actually gets published.

Yes, the Iroquois will figure in the story. Beyond that, I will say nothing.

David Carrico and I are working on a novel titled *1636: Symphony for the Devil*. This is a mystery novel which takes place in Magdeburg simultaneously with many of the events depicted in *1636: The Saxon Uprising*.

Iver Cooper is putting together an anthology of his own writing, similar in format to Virginia DeMarce's *1635: The Tangled Web*. These interwoven stories focus mostly on the New World, especially the Japanese decision to colonize the west coast of North America.

Other planned volumes include:

With Mercedes Lackey, a comic novel (sub-titled *Stoned Souls*) that continues the adventures of Tom Stone and others.

With Gorg Huff and Paula Goodlett, a romantic comedy sub-titled *The Viennese Waltz*, which will run parallel to one of my later main line novels and serve also as a sequel to a number of the stories they've written about the Barbie Consortium in various issues of the *Gazette*.

(If you're wondering why I'm only providing subtitles, it's because I still don't know exactly which year they'll fall under. Either 1635 or 1636, depending on this and that and the other.)

And there it stands. For the moment.

For those of you who dote on lists, here it is. But do keep in mind, when you examine this neatly ordered sequence, that the map is not the territory.

1632
Ring of Fire
1633
1634: The Baltic War

(Somewhere along the way, after you've finished *1632*, read the stories and articles in the first three paper edition volumes of the *Gazette*.)

1634: The Ram Rebellion
1634: The Galileo Affair
1634: The Bavarian Crisis

(Somewhere along the way, read the stories and articles in the fourth paper edition volume of the *Gazette*.)

Ring of Fire II
1635: The Cannon Law
1635: The Dreeson Incident
1635: The Tangled Web

(Somewhere along the way, read the stories in *Gazette V*.)

1635: The Eastern Front
1636: The Saxon Uprising

Eric Flint
January 2011

The following is an excerpt from:

NO GOING BACK

MARK L. VAN NAME

Available from Baen Books
May 2012
hardcover

CHAPTER 1

Center of the Great Southeastern Desert
Planet Studio

"JON, THIS IS a very bad plan."

"I'm a little busy here." The wind blasted my face as I fought with the sail on the sandsurfer. The high-powered electric fan slammed more air into my back as it inflated the sail and pushed me across the black sand only moments ahead of the twilight that followed me like a cloaked assassin. The rush of speed filled me with both joy and adrenaline, but I couldn't afford to surrender to either without risking falling off the meter-wide board.

"I repeat," Lobo said, his voice clear and loud in my ear through the comm, "this is a very bad plan."

"If you have a better one, let me know. Otherwise, we're going with this one."

"Here's an idea," he said. "You turn off that stupid machine, I fly down and pick you up, and we go do something that doesn't involve you dying."

"I don't plan to die."

"You never do, but that doesn't mean it can't happen.

These are seriously powerful men, men way out of your league. You attack them, and they'll either kill you now or hunt you down later."

He was pissing me off, but I wasn't going to let him know. Lobo may be the most intelligent machine in the universe, a super-powerful brain composed of nanocomputers distributed through all the molecules of a deadly predator-class assault vehicle, but when he finds a way to needle you, he's as unrelenting as a three-year-old on a "why?" binge.

"Look on the bright side," I said. "If I die, you're free."

That did the trick. "First," he said, "I'm free now." Annoyance dripped from every single word. "I don't have to stay here. I don't need a human owner to function. I stay with you because we're in it together." He paused. "As you bloody well know." Another pause. "Besides, having a human does make it easier to move around. The gate authorities generally won't authorize unpiloted machines to jump between planets."

"So let's make sure I don't die."

"You're two minutes from the shutdown point," Lobo said. "From then on, if I come for you fast, they'll hear me. That means our risk goes up, at least as long as you won't let me kill everyone on the ground. Let me pick you up now."

The offer tempted me a little, because I wasn't thrilled at the makeshift plan we'd had to concoct earlier today. Then I remembered the expression on the face of Lydia Chang, the woman who'd asked me to find her missing Tasson, her missing son. No, no way was I going to let those men get away with what they were planning. They'd come to the planet

Studio for a very sick private party, and I was going to crash it.

I stared at the horizon ahead of me. The two small moons of Studio gleamed a faint white in the dying light. The air possessed that perfect clarity you see only on new worlds or those so inhospitable that only the crazy and the outcast bothered to colonize them. Studio was the latter. The jump gate aperture to it had opened over a hundred and twenty years ago, and as we always do, humans had flooded in. After finding a planet composed of large, arid land masses and small, acidic seas, the vast majority of those earlier settlers had fled almost as quickly. The few people who stayed fought the good survival fight in small enclaves near the toxic seas. Most of the planet remained empty to this day. The only planetary government Studio had was a tourism council, a group of savvy entrepreneurs who realized that artists, advertisers, and entertainment creators sometimes wanted to work on really big canvases. Really big. Like a hundred-mile-wide acid lake, or a chunk of a desert the size of a large city.

Some of those artists loved Studio, because for a modest fee they could do anything they wanted to a huge area, no questions asked. They'd sell exhibition tickets to anyone with enough money and spare time to make the trek. When sales faded, some took down their constructions and moved on. Others left their works to erode slowly in the heat and the dust, a way to achieve not immortality but a far longer life than other planets generally would give such art.

Studio's support for these artists had brought it a little money and a lot of notoriety. The same ask-no-questions culture had made it attractive to other types of events and to those who wanted to conduct business in a completely undisturbed and unregulated environment. As long as they paid their site fees and didn't commit any crimes so obvious they made the news waves, Studio's government left them alone.

"One minute to the shutdown point," Lobo said. "You can still safely stop."

"You know I'm not going to do that," I said, "so stop wasting energy and distracting me."

He sighed.

Before I'd bought Lobo, my experience with machines sighing was limited to dumb, theatrical appliances. Their sighs were always a bit excessive, like bad actors trying to make too much of small roles. Lobo's was spot on, a perfectly human expression.

"So we *are* going to do this," he said. It wasn't a question.

"Yes, we are."

"Two dozen bidders, half again as many catering and security staff, and none of them willing to tolerate uninvited visitors. You're going to take on all of them to save ten kids."

"No," I said. "*We're* going to take them on."

"Hardly," he said. "I can't help until after you deal with the people inside. You know that. You're on your own once I get you in the door."

"I understand, but that's how it has to be—or we let these jerks auction ten boys and girls to rich creeps who will abuse and discard them as if they were no more than disposable towels." I recalled the videos of Tasson, a thin boy with coppery skin, wide almost-black eyes, and a small but bright smile. "We have to save them."

"I agree," Lobo said, "that what these men are doing is wrong, nightmarishly wrong, but we haven't had enough time to set up a safe rescue. We won't do any of them any good if we fail."

"So we won't fail. We'll make it work. We promised Chang that we would find her son and bring him back. We found him, and now we're going to get him."

I remembered being on my own as a kid, scared and without parents or sister and abandoned by the government of my home planet on an island called Dump. What I'd experienced was bad, but it was as nothing compared to what these kids would suffer if I let them be sold.

The timer in my contact showed five seconds before I had to shut down and jettison the sandsurfer. We would make the plan work. We would not fail.

The timer hit zero. I turned off the surfer's fan and slid to a quiet stop. I was a kilometer from the gallery installation, close enough to see the lights of the ships on the opposite side of it but far enough away that I was still outside their security perimeter. The structure hadn't risen yet, so we'd timed my approach right.

"Is the mole on track?" I said.

"Yes," Lobo said. "It's under the external ring and moving forward."

"Are you reading its external feeds?"

Another sigh. "Yes, and before you can ask, the bursts are too quick for anyone not looking for them to notice. Trust me to do my part."

I nodded but said nothing. He was right, and we both knew it. Micromanaging him was a stupid waste of time and attention.

I stepped off the board and stretched for a moment.

"Jon," Lobo said, "you can't save all the children in trouble." His voice was as tender as I've ever heard it. "No one can. There are too many worlds and too many bad people."

"I know," I said, "but we can save these ten."

I jogged toward the lights, the twilight at my heels. "Let's go."

—end excerpt—

from *No Going Back*
available in hardcover,
May 2012, from Baen Books